Foggy Point Light

Jeff Burns

Copyright © 2016 2018 Jeff Burns

Foggy Point Light Publishing LLC

Charlotte, NC

All rights reserved.

ISBN: 978-0-9989742-0-0

For more information, go to:

www.foggypointlight.com

DEDICATION

This book is dedicated to my wife Julie, whose love and support throughout this project, as well as her tireless effort assisting in the editing and proofreading helped to make this project a reality.

I'd also like to dedicate it to lighthouse lovers everywhere whose interest and enthusiasm for these coastal beacons keep the lights burning.

CONTENTS

Prologue 3

Chapter 1   The Journey Begins 7

Chapter 2   Arriving at the Coast 18

Chapter 3   First Warnings 27

Chapter 4   Inspecting the Lighthouse 37

Chapter 5   We're Not Alone 47

Chapter 6   Police Investigation 58

Chapter 7   The Campout.. 68

Chapter 8   Uninvited Visitor 80

Chapter 9   More Questions than Answers 92

Chapter 10 Bill's Story 100

Chapter 11 Dr. Carson's Experiment.................................... 112

Chapter 12 Unexplained Events.. 121

Chapter 13 The Visitor Returns 131

Chapter 14 An Unexplained Object 142

Chapter 15 A Pleasant Surprise 157

Chapter 16 The Arrival 168

Chapter 17 The Island Mist Charter..................................... 176

Chapter 18 The Book Signing 186

Chapter 19 The Disappearance 197

Chapter 20 The Search... 209

Chapter 21 Always Consider the Impossible 219

Chapter 22 The Past Catches Up with the Future 233

Chapter 23 Final Goodbyes 246

Chapter 24 Dr. Philip Chandler.. 260

Chapter 25 Revelations of the Future 267

Chapter 26 An Urgent Request 277

Chapter 27 Executing the Plan.. 290
Chapter 28 The Lighthouse Dedication... 300

PROLOGUE
September 28, 1974

"What was that?!" Greg asked, startled from his sleep by an unknown sound in the darkness.

"What was what?!" asked Tim, "I was asleep!"

"Something woke me up." whispered Greg.

They both lay there in their sleeping bags, their senses on alert, listening for the slightest sound. The only sound that they heard now was the wind as it blew through the rafters and the crickets, tree frogs and other insects outside. Staring straight up, the skeleton of the rafters looked almost sinister as the light of the moon shone through them creating shadows along any walls that were still standing. Their eyes adjusted fairly quickly to the available light in the room, which was dimly lit by the moonlight. The moon actually was fairly bright tonight since it was waxing gibbous and only four days until it would be full. As they continued to stare into the rafters, the moonlight seemed to vary in brightness, getting dimmer then brighter as clouds alternated covering the moon then moving away. A shiver overtook both of them at about the same time, partly due to the chilliness of the night, and partly due to the creepiness of their surroundings. Greg held up his arm and pushed the button on his new LED watch to illuminate the time in bright red numbers. The lighted numbers indicated that it was two fifty seven in the morning. When they started out, they had set up their sleeping bags in the center of the room where they could look straight up and see the stars, but when a rain shower started around ten thirty the previous evening, they had been forced to move to a side of the room which still had some roof left so that they could stay dry. Now, however, it seemed that the rain had moved away and just left the wind and the chilliness of the night in its wake.

When Tim first had the idea of spending the night at the old lighthouse, it had seemed like it would be a fun adventure. In a way, it still was fun, though the moving shadows on the walls and the sound of the wind in the rafters, sometimes seeming to mimic ghostly voices, made it all seem a little spooky. And they both wondered what they would do if something happened to either of them as well. Nobody knew that they were out here. Each of them had told their parents that they were spending the night at the other's house, since they knew that the answer would most certainly be "No" if their parents actually knew what they had planned. As they continued to lay in the darkness, a sudden crash over to their right made them both simultaneously sit bolt upright, staring toward the direction of the sound. A shadow quickly skittered from the adjacent room and moved along the opposite wall causing both boys to shed their sleeping bags and stand straight up, poised to run.

"Raccoon!" they both said in unison as their eyes adjusted to the creature quickly scurrying along the wall and out an opening where the wall had caved in on the side of the house. They were frozen to the spot where they were standing now, both of their hearts beating out of their chests, each staring in the direction where the raccoon had just escaped.

"Listen!" said Greg suddenly.

As Tim strained to listen, he looked over at Greg, "Listen for what? I don't hear anything."

"That's just it. I don't hear anything either!"

"Greg, sometimes you don't make a bit of sense!"

"No, think back a second." Greg continued, "When we first woke up, we heard the sound of the wind in the rafters like we're hearing now, but we also heard the sounds of crickets, cicadas, and tree frogs. Where are those sounds now?!"

Greg was right, Tim thought. Except for the slight breeze blowing through the rafters, there was absolutely no sound at all! It was eerily quiet. They both shot each other a quick glance as if to ask, "What's going on here?" They both slowly walked over to the door at the back of the building, if you could even call it a door. It was mostly a piece of rotting wood hanging from a lone brass hinge near the top of the doorpost. Instead of being closed, it was hanging halfway open where it had been blown by the wind.

Looking out the door facing the rear of the house, the moon didn't seem quite as bright as it had been only minutes before. Its light seemed to be filtered through a thick fog. As they walked out onto the porch, they were both struck by the silence of the morning. All of the night life which had been singing in unison earlier had suddenly gone silent. As they walked down the steps and stepped onto the moist ground, they studied the fog, both of them shining their flashlights into it. Somehow it seemed different than other fogs that they had seen on the island. It was thicker for one thing, but also the wisps seemed to move in small circular eddies that twisted and turned in the night air. As they crossed the lawn and moved closer to the circular wall surrounding the lighthouse, they noticed that the area immediately around them was completely clear. The fog was only outside the wall, giving the appearance that they were standing in the middle of a large hollow cylinder. Looking straight up, they could actually see some stars where the clouds had thinned. Turning their attention back to the fog, they aimed their lights into it where both lights made solid beams through the mist.

"Why is the fog like that?" asked Greg, nervously. The events of the past several minutes were starting to get to him, and the eeriness of the fog as the moon struggled to shine through only added to his anxiety.

Both boys stopped just inside the gate, staring into the fog. Tim reached out his hand and let it go into the fog. As he moved his arm around in the fog, he noticed that the air was much warmer there than it was outside of it. From what he had remembered about the weather, that fact really didn't make any sense. He continued walking through the gate and into the fog.

"Tim, wait! Are you sure it's a good idea to go in there?"

Tim turned, "What could happen? It's just fog. And we're on an island. We can't get lost!"

As he continued to walk into the fog, Greg followed him as well.

While neither of them could place exactly what was different, the woods didn't seem quite the same as they moved their beams of light around as they walked. Their lights illuminated a large oak tree immediately in front of them.

"Isn't this where the big log fell across the path?" asked Greg.

"It must not be." answered Tim. "I don't see the log. This fog must have us turned around."

"Which way do we go to get out?" asked Greg, again nervously.

"I think we just turn around and go back the way we came." answered Tim, though he didn't sound at all confident this time.

They both turned and tried retracing their steps to get out of the fog, but the fog seemed to go on for a lot longer than it had when they had first entered it.

"Shouldn't we have been back out by now?" asked Greg.

"I thought so…" replied Tim, "but look, I think the fog's getting thinner. We should be able to see the lighthouse soon."

Tim was right; the wisps of fog weren't nearly as thick as they were before, and seemed to be getting thinner by the minute.

Back at the lighthouse, it was still eerily quiet. The last remnants of the fog faded away, and the stars came back out. The moon was shining in all its brilliance now, in the clear, cool night sky. Only silent sleeping bags lay on the floor inside the house where the boys started their camping adventure earlier in the evening. But now there was nobody here. The night was silent and still, with a lone deer and raccoon being the only witnesses to the boys' disappearance; a disappearance that would haunt the island for decades to come and change countless lives forever.

CHAPTER 1
March 11, 2016
The Journey Begins

Dan Nelson saw the road sign, "Asheville 28 Miles". He looked at the clock on the dash of his truck – 5:30. He had been driving now for a little over six hours, having left Cincinnati at around 10:15 that morning. He had stopped for lunch earlier in the day, so he wasn't particularly hungry, but as he approached Asheville, he thought of the vacations he had taken there with his family. The North Carolina Mountains, especially around Asheville, was one of their favorite vacation spots. It had only been six hours, but already he was missing them. It was probably the realization that he wouldn't be seeing them much for the next three months. Of course, he would see them occasionally. He planned to fly home some weekends when time would permit. But there was a lot that he had to take care of, so he didn't know how many weekends he'd be able to do that. Since the kids were born, he hadn't been away for more than a few days at a time, so this was going to be particularly difficult. He liked coming home every evening, always awaiting their cheerful greeting. Amy was 13 and Dan Jr., who went by Danny, was 10. Like most brothers and sisters, they had their disagreements at times, but usually they got along well enough with each other. He hoped that having each other would help them settle in when they joined him in June at Green Island. But right now, June seemed a long way off. He planned on staying busy, so he hoped the time would pass quickly. He knew that he had a lot of work to do before his family could join him, and three months seemed such a short time to have it all done.

He thought again about the sign. Another one was up ahead, "Asheville 18 Miles". It was only 5:35. He could probably drive for at least another three hours, and be that much closer for the drive tomorrow. But remembering the vacations to Asheville with his family only increased his desire to stop here for the night. They always stayed at an older hotel called the Mountain Park Inn. It had been built in the late 1800s and still retained much of the charm of that era. In early spring and fall, when the air was cool and crisp, it was relaxing just to sit out on the long porch overlooking the mountains. He could sit there for hours, reading a good book, or just taking in the view and the mountain air. And today was just one of those early spring days. The air was crisp and cool up here in the mountains, and the sky was clear. It seemed just what he needed before continuing the trip to the seashore. His mind was made up. He'd stop off at the Mountain Park Inn for the night, and continue on in the morning.

As he pulled his burgundy Ford F-150 pickup into the long circular drive leading to the main entrance, the sun was low in the sky, and casting a brilliant orange glow on the front of the inn. He could almost hear the kids squeal with delight, the way they'd always done after finally arriving from the long trip. At once, he recognized a familiar face.

"Good evening Mr. Nelson! I wasn't expecting you today. Where's the family?"

"They're not with me this time, Jerry. I'm just stopping by on my way to the coast." replied Dan.

Since he and his family had been coming here for vacations, he'd developed somewhat of a friendship with Jerry, the Bell Captain, and this was the first time that he remembered seeing Dan without his family.

"Nothing's wrong, I hope?" Jerry inquired.

"No, everything's fine. The family's well. I just have some business to attend to along the coast. I'm on my way there now. Meet me in the lounge in a bit, and I'll tell you all about it."

Jerry's full name was Gerald Hensley. He'd grown up in Asheville and began working at the inn while in high school. His school had always held their proms in the large ballroom, and from the first time that he set foot in the inn, he knew this was where he wanted to be. He'd started coming to the inn just to walk around. He really loved the atmosphere. After his junior year in high school, he'd gotten a summer job working with the maintenance crew. This consisted mostly of changing light bulbs, sweeping the floors, and any other odd jobs that needed doing, but he approached every one as if it were the most important job in the world. It was hard to find a burned out light bulb, or dirty floor anywhere in the inn when Jerry was on duty. It was HIS inn, and he intended to make it the finest in the country. During his senior year, he worked part time in maintenance, since his class load was light. He was given more responsibility, such as planning and scheduling vendors to perform routine maintenance, and supervising and signing off on their work. After graduation, he was offered the position of Maintenance Supervisor after the current maintenance supervisor, Ron, who was now in his early seventies retired. As Ron had always said, he didn't want to turn the inn over to just anyone. He preferred to "keep it in the family", so to speak, and Jerry had definitely become part of the inn's family. He and Jerry had also become good friends over the years, and he knew that Jerry would care for the inn as he always had. Jerry married his high school sweetheart, Glenda, in the Grand Ballroom, and they had their honeymoon at the inn. Now in his late fifties, after nearly forty years of service, he had worked his way up to Bell Captain, and he and his staff were one of the reasons that folks kept coming back. He had a unique ability to make every guest feel as if they were the most important guest there.

Jerry motioned with his hand, and a young porter in the familiar burgundy uniform immediately scurried over with a luggage cart.

"Take these bags to 215." he told the boy. He motioned again, and another porter came over.

"See that his truck's taken care of." he instructed. Then he and Dan walked into the spacious lobby.

The lobby of the Mountain Park Inn had always impressed Dan. The check in desk was to the left as you walked in the entrance, not blocking the view, so you were able to get the full effect of how large and spectacular the lobby really was. A marble fountain was the centerpiece of the lobby. It was surrounded by four ornate wooden columns that went from the floor to the ceiling. There was a stone fireplace at each end of the room which must have been at least two hundred feet from one end to the other. The fireplaces were tall enough that Dan could have walked into them standing straight up, if the fixtures and wood hadn't been in the way. There were round tables with chairs set up around each fireplace so that guests could dine by the fire during the winter months, and enjoy the flowers and greenery that was set up around the fireplaces the rest of the year. If you walked straight through past the fountain there were two large wooden doors with glass panes which opened onto a long porch that ran the length of the lobby. There were tables where folks could sit and dine, as well as wooden rocking chairs for the folks who just wanted to sit and admire the view. He paused out on the porch, remembering all of the good times that they had there. Thoughts of their first visit came back to him. He remembered Danny, who had only been 4 at the time trying to catch the fish in the pond at the base of the fountain, and Amy reminding him of the trouble that he'd be in if mom and dad saw what he was doing. That was the first time that they had met Jerry. He came running over to where Danny was, obviously concerned that the child might fall in. Dan and Jerry had introduced themselves then for what was to become a lifelong friendship. Jerry's voice brought him back to the reality of the moment.

"If you want to go on over to the lounge, I'll take care of your room." he told Dan.

"Fine, see you in a bit."

A few minutes later Jerry joined him in the lounge where they sat and talked for the better part of an hour.

"So, what's this business along the coast?" inquired Jerry.

"Remember on one of our visits last year that I mentioned I had put in a bid for some coastal property? Well, it came through earlier this year. I'm now the proud owner of twenty seven acres of beachfront property on a small island off the North Carolina coast. And the best part is that there's an old lighthouse on the property!"

"I do remember you mentioning something about that now." replied Jerry. "How'd you come across that exactly? Something your wife found in the paper, if I remember right?"

"That's right. She came across an article one day about how the government was selling some of the old lighthouses. She mentioned it in passing, as if it were funny that the government had gone into the junk business on a large scale. But I was more than a little intrigued by the idea. I read the article and went to the web address printed at the bottom. It seems that the government was auctioning off eight of their older, and more run down lighthouses to the highest bidder. Three were along the west coast and five were along the east coast. I was especially interested in the one on the North Carolina coast. I remembered it from my teenage years when we would vacation there. It had been featured in the issue of Coastal Magazine that was out at the time. I had also read accounts of the lighthouse in a book that I picked up on another occasion 'Mysteries of the North Carolina Coast'. The book was by a local historian, Jack Carlson, and he had researched quite a bit about the old lighthouse.

"It seems that there were quite a few unexplained events happening around it. It was built in 1866, right after the Civil War ended, but there were several accounts of a mysterious light being seen exactly at the spot of the current lighthouse. The earliest one was by Colonel Nathaniel Forrest and his men while they were stationed on the island DURING the Civil War. Colonel Forrest himself actually claimed to have seen the lighthouse up close on the night of October 14, 1862 while he and several of his men were returning to camp after their watch. As they were nearing camp, they were caught in a dense fog that came up seemingly out of nowhere. It was so thick that they couldn't see to continue. While they were stopped, Colonel Forrest saw a light up in the sky to his left. Upon investigating, they discovered that the light was shining from the top of a large brick tower. He claimed to walk up and actually touch the base of the tower, a story which the men who were with him corroborated. He later retracted this story. But one of the men with him, a young lieutenant named William White actually stuck by the story. He supposed that the Colonel may have retracted his story due to pressure from his superiors, since on subsequent visits by military officials there was no evidence of anything out of the ordinary, especially not a large brick lighthouse. But William White maintained that he was there that night, and that the original account by the Colonel was the story exactly as it happened. When it was built, the lighthouse had originally been named the Green Island Light Station. But nine years later, after the story of Colonel Forrest and his encounter had gained some notoriety, it was renamed Forrest Point Light, and the south end of the island where the lighthouse was located was renamed Forrest Point.

"There have been other stories as well through the years, of people seeing the light, even though the lighthouse had been decommissioned for several years and there was no beacon left to shine. The most notable story, however, happened in 1974, when two teenage boys, Greg Baker and Tim Henderson disappeared under unusual circumstances while spending the night in the lighthouse. It was a Friday night in late September. Each of them had told their parents that they were going to the others house to spend the night. Since they alternated spending almost every Friday night at one house or the other, there had been no reason for either boy's parents to call and check up on the story. It wasn't until neither boy came home on Saturday night that their plan had been discovered. Their parents called the island's police department, who discovered from some of their friends that they had planned to meet and stay the night at the lighthouse. When the lighthouse was searched, they did find some food, a lantern, and both boys' sleeping bags. There was no sign of a struggle, and everything seemed in order, except that neither boy could be found. A wide scale search was conducted over the entire island, which failed to turn up any evidence of the boys' whereabouts. And even to this day, they've never been found. Over the years, there have been many embellishments to the story, so it's really hard to tell fact from fiction. Anyway, since it had such an odd history, and somewhat an air of mystery, I put a bid on it, even though from the photos sent to me by the National Parks Service it didn't seem in the best condition. After about two months, I got a letter stating that I had been outbid, and giving me the option to raise my bid. I raised it, and this time, after another month had gone by, it was accepted. Several more months of finalizing the transaction, brings me to today. With the help of a friend and his son, who are supposed to meet me there in about a week, we're going to fix it up and get it back in livable condition. Probably even install a new electric beacon in the lantern house. The family will join me down there in June after school lets out for the summer. Hopefully by then it'll be close to being able to move in."

"Sounds like quite a story!" Jerry replied. "Maybe me and Glenda can come and visit, once you get it fixed up and all."

"That sounds great! From what I can tell by the pictures, you'll love the view!"

Dan was getting somewhat hungry by this point, having only had a light lunch earlier in the day. Jerry joined him in the Mountain View

Restaurant, and they talked for another hour while they ate.

After dinner, Dan decided it was about time to turn in for the night. He had a long drive ahead the next day, so he didn't want to be up too late. He rode the hotel's historic elevator up to the second floor, where Jerry had their regular room, 215 prepared for him. He went inside, flipped on the light, and saw all of his bags had been brought up and were laid out on the floor beside the bed waiting for him. Every time they visited the Mountain Park Inn, this was the room they requested. It was one of the larger rooms in the historic part of the inn, with two double beds, and a desk at the far end. They especially liked the view, which looked out over the front entrance of the hotel, across to the mountains in the distance. He opened the window, and even though it was dark, and he could only see lights from houses in the far off distance, and the street lamps near the hotel entrance, he still enjoyed the view. He sat on the edge of the bed nearest the window for a few minutes, breathing in the cool night air and pondering the day's events. He really was anticipating with great excitement the next couple of months. This actually was an adventure that he had always dreamed of. He took his cell phone out of its case and dialed his home number.

"Hi Daddy!" chimed an exuberant girl's voice on the other end.

"How's my girl?" he replied.

"Missing you! When are you coming home?"

"I've only been gone less than a day!"

"I know, but it seems longer. Danny's spending the night at Joe's, so it's just me and mom here. It's kind of lonely."

"Well, guess where I am?" asked Dan.

"How am I supposed to do that? Maybe North Carolina?"

"OK, good guess. I'm in our regular room at Mountain Park Inn!"

"No fair," squealed his daughter, "we need to be there! Mom! Daddy's at Mountain Park Inn!"

"How's mom doing?" he asked.

"She's right here. Want to talk to her?"

Kate Nelson had wandered into the den when she heard the phone. She knew it was probably Dan, and like her daughter, she had been missing him ever since he left that morning. It was somewhat of a surprise to find him at Mountain Park Inn, but not totally unexpected. They all enjoyed vacationing there.

"Hi, honey," his wife said, "how was the trip?"

"It's good so far. The mountains are really pretty this time of year. That's what made me want to stop off here tonight."

"You know your daughter's really jealous!" she said. "That's one of her favorite places. She likes the mountains, but she's not so sure about the ocean."

"She'll love it when she gets down there," he said, "with the warm salt air, and the sound of the waves."

They talked for more than an hour, then after that he decided it was finally time to get some sleep. He hung up the phone, then went around and picked up his computer bag and put it on the bed. He knew that he needed rest, since he had a long trip ahead of him the next day, but somehow, with all of the excitement of the first day of travel, and with just talking with his family, he suddenly wasn't sleepy. And since the trip had been rather long, he'd had plenty of time to think about all of the stories that he'd always heard about the lighthouse. He opened up the computer bag and reached into the top flap and pulled out a book, "Mysteries of the North Carolina Coast", by Jack Carlson. It had a green cover with a charcoal drawing of a lighthouse in the center. To the left of the lighthouse it looked like fog, and if you looked carefully, you could make out the faces of two people in the fog. Behind the lighthouse, and slightly to the right was an eighteenth century sailing ship. He stared at the cover for a minute or two, and then he opened the book to Chapter 3, "Forrest Point Lighthouse". This particular chapter told the 1862 account of Colonel Forrest's encounter with the lighthouse, as well as the 1974 disappearance of the two boys. It also included two other accounts by others that had taken place over the years. The account by Colonel Forrest was the earliest account which he had found documented anywhere. The two additional accounts happened in 1935 and 1962 respectively.

The 1935 account was an experience by Harland Wilson, who was the last keeper of the lighthouse. When he moved out a few weeks after his encounter, the lighthouse would be decommissioned and closed for good. It seems that he was working outside one evening when a dense fog came up. It was dusk, and his wife and children were inside. Barney, his Golden Retriever was chasing some rabbits over near the woods. In his account he had written about just how quickly the fog came up. It was like one minute it was clear and the next minute the fog was there. The strangest part to him was how the fog seemed to stay outside the round wall which completely circled the lighthouse. He described the experience as being inside a large tube. Barney became agitated when the fog came up and went bounding into it. Harland chased him into it, but was quickly surrounded by fog so thick that he could barely make out any of the trees and bushes around him. He could hear the dog barking at something over to his right, but he dared not venture any further in for fear of becoming lost himself. The fog seemed to close in around him. It was cold. He felt that it must be at least twenty degrees colder in the fog than it was inside the wall. He came back out of the fog and walked around the inside of the wall, peering into the fog to see if he could catch a glimpse of the dog anywhere. He was really uneasy as he gazed into the fog. The trees and bushes that he could see around the edge before the fog became too thick seemed different somehow. He couldn't quite place exactly why, but something really didn't seem right. Barney's barking seemed to be getting further away until it faded altogether. That was the last time that anyone ever saw Barney. The fog subsided a few minutes later, but no trace of the dog was ever found.

The 1962 account was just as strange, and every bit as eerie. Lighthouse Road was still open back then. A young couple, Karl and Bernice Schindler, staying at the Harbor Inn nearby, had driven out to try and get a look at the lighthouse. It was evening, just before dusk, but with still enough light to see. They had parked and were walking up to get a view of the light when a fog came up suddenly around them. They continued walking, but the fog only got thicker. As they reached the edge of the forest and looked toward the lighthouse, they saw a peculiar sight. The lighthouse had been vacant since the last keeper moved out in 1935, but on this night in 1962 the light in the lantern house was burning bright. They walked through the gate and inside the wall. This didn't look at all like the pictures that they'd seen, one of a run-down lighthouse overgrown with weeds and showing all the signs of years of neglect. This lighthouse looked to them as it would have looked back when the keepers and their families lived there. There were lights on in the house as well. Fascinated with the scene before them, Karl took a whole roll of film using his Brownie instamatic camera. Karl wanted to get closer, but Bernice was very uneasy about the whole situation and persuaded him to just take the photos from where they were standing. After taking the photos, they couldn't wait to get back and have the film developed. He and Bernice made their way back into the fog, which was starting to disperse slightly. By the time that they got back to their car, the fog had thinned out enough for them to drive out. They still couldn't see too far in front of the car, but by the time they reached the main road the fog was completely gone. They went into town, but the town's only photo shop was closed for the day. The next day they went back into town and sent their roll of film off for developing before driving back out to the lighthouse. On this day, however, the lighthouse was exactly like the photos that they'd seen, run-down and dilapidated. The lantern house was in such bad condition, that they didn't see how it possibly could have had a light the night before. They received their film back in about a week along with a note from the photo processing company explaining that the film had been completely exposed and that no photos could be made from the negatives. They felt that the film had been exposed before it got to them, but Karl didn't see how that could have happened. He had taken all of the precautions that he always did, making sure to wind the film completely onto the take up spool before opening the back of the camera. He had done this hundreds of times, and this was the first time that the film had no photos whatsoever. Sure enough, though, the negatives that they sent back had no discernible photos on them. Disappointed, they nevertheless told their story to the local newspaper on the island, which was how it came to be printed in Jack Carlson's book.

Dan hoped to do some more research once he got settled in on the island. There were sure to be other stories about the lighthouse, particularly from some of the local residents. He hoped that he could talk with some folks who had always lived on the island and had eyewitness accounts of their own that had never been documented. The one peculiar thing, however, was the fog. This in and of itself wasn't particularly surprising, as fog comes in fairly often along the coast, but its presence during most if not all of the events was quite interesting. The only account that didn't mention the fog was the story of the two boys' disappearance in 1974, but he wondered if it still might have been there. No one was there that night except the boys. The story began with the account of the disappearance the next day. There was no account from the actual night, so the fog may have been there then as well. He read through this chapter again, then finally turned off the light and went to sleep.

CHAPTER 2
March 12, 2016
Arriving at the Coast

The next day Dan was up early. He wanted to get on the road so as to arrive along the coast in plenty of time to find a good hotel for the night. He'd like to have time to relax before heading out to the island tomorrow. He had checked the distance the night before, and it looked like Asheville was about half way there, so he figured he had about another six hours to go.

He gathered up his bags and took the elevator to the first floor. As he was checking out, one of the porters came up and asked, "May I take those bags for you, Mr. Nelson? I can have your truck pulled around front as well. Jerry's not here this morning, but he asked me to personally take care of you."

"Yes, that would be fine. Tell Jerry that I look forward to him visiting soon."

By the time he had finished checking out, his truck was waiting by the front entrance. He thanked the porter, slipped him a ten dollar bill, and was on his way. He stopped off at Waffles and More on his way out of the city to get a quick breakfast, and then he merged onto Interstate 40 East for the drive to the coast.

The trip was long, and since this part was all interstate driving, there wasn't much to see, especially after he had driven out of the mountains. Just after he passed Statesville, he picked up his cell phone and pressed number 3 on the speed dial. "Mr. Duncan's office, how may I direct your call?" came a voice on the other end.

"Hi, Mary, it's Dan. Is Scotty around?"

"He's in a board meeting at the moment. I can have him return your call."

"No hurry, just tell him when he gets a moment to give me a ring."

Benjamin Scott Duncan was the Vice President for Operations at Perihelion Research, a research and development company, mainly funded by military contracts, but with other private sideline ventures as well. He had met Dan during their sophomore year at MIT, and they had become fast friends. They quickly discovered that they both had a common interest … the TV show Star Journeys. They could tell you all of the details of every episode, from all six seasons. They frequently travelled to Star Journeys conventions dressed as characters from the show. Scott usually went as Scotty Borland, captain of the Star Cruiser Perihelion. This was his favorite character from the show, and he frequently interjected many of the witty comments that Borland made into his own vocabulary. This, and the fact that his given name was already Scott, earned him the nickname Scotty.

Star Journeys revolved around the central character, Captain Borland, who was a scientist with the United Planetary Organization, and the chief designer and engineer of the Perihelion. It was equipped with all of the latest weapons, mostly of Scotty's design. When he became aware of a plot, involving many high ranking officials of the UPO, to use the Perihelion and its vast array of weaponry to conquer and control the known universe, he and a group of his most dedicated men stole the Perihelion and set off to warn the other worlds of the plot and to equip them for defense against the aggression. Pursued across the galaxy and beyond by Captain Leonard Krug using the Perihelion's sister ship the Aphelion, this group of peace loving rebels went for six seasons trying to outwit and foil the plans of Captain Krug and bring an end to the threat, while also making friends and having many fascinating adventures along the way.

During Dan and Scotty's senior year, they were able to room together, and their room looked like it came straight out of the science fiction series. Using a lot of wood, cardboard, paint, lights, and switches, they were able to transform their room into the bridge of the Perihelion, at least a part of it. The small size of the room made this a challenging feat, but when they were done it was quite impressive. They had both beds and both desks removed, and then they created private study areas and sleeping quarters from wood and cardboard. When they were done, the room actually had two levels, with their sleeping quarters on the second level above their study area. The sleeping quarters were accessible by crawling through tubes painted to look like the ones from the TV series. They even installed a buzzer on the door that sounded like the familiar hailing frequency from the series. It was during this time that they began discussing the future. They had both become such good friends that they knew they didn't want to simply graduate and go their separate ways. Whatever they accomplished, they wanted to do it together.

The years after graduation were eventful for both. Dan married his college sweetheart, Kate Miller, an attractive blonde whom he met while on a double date with Scotty during college. They moved to California so that he could take a job with a prestigious technology firm in Silicon Valley. Ultimately, his desire was to start his own technology company, but he felt that he needed a few years to get some experience and develop contacts in the field. Scotty moved back to his hometown of Strongsville, Ohio, and went to work for a small computer consulting company. While there, he worked with a young consultant, Belinda Cassidy, on several projects. They began dating, and were married a year later. Within a year, Belinda was pregnant with their only son, Gregory Scott. While Dan and Scotty would exchange emails and talk on the phone quite a bit, they didn't see each other much over the next six years. Then in 1992, things began to happen that would put the two friends back together again and allow them to finally begin to accomplish their dreams. The internet was in the beginning stages. Some of the larger companies were developing their own web pages, but most of the smaller ones weren't. Even some of the larger ones, not having expertise on the new technologies, were hiring consulting companies. HTML, the Hypertext Markup Language of the web was new, but it was limited in what it could do. From the articles and trade magazines that Dan had read on the subject, this was the future, and he now had the opportunity to get in on the ground floor. While he could have taken advantage of a lot of the expertise found out in Silicon Valley, he decided to move back to his home town of Cincinnati and start the company there. He did manage to bring with him two of the best software and hardware engineers that he knew from Silicon Valley, Ashwin Choudhry and Ron Lancaster.

After acquiring the necessary funding, Nelson Internet Technology was founded in May of 1992. The next several years were a flurry of activity, where the company grew by leaps and bounds. The internet was still new and evolving, and with the more than capable leadership of Ron and Ashwin, the company was able to become the leader in many of the new technologies. Even while shaping the blueprint for much of what the Internet was to become, they still were operating out of extremely modest office space, with virtually no room to expand. Out of the three of them, Dan was the only one with an office. The rest of the floor space was a common area with a large table in the middle for research and development. Server cabinets covered two complete walls of the common area. Along another wall were two desks for Ron and Ashwin. In the beginning, Ron and Ashwin spent their days wiring servers and developing new internet products, while Dan was mostly on sales calls. A large part of his job was to show businesses that had never had a website, or really used the internet at all, why they needed one now. It was still early in the internet life cycle, so most businesses didn't have a web presence, and didn't really understand the technology. Within a year they had more business than they could handle, and the staff had grown from just the three of them to a staff of twelve. They had outgrown their first office space within eight months, and Dan had found a warehouse on the outskirts of town that they had leased. While it had a lot more space than they needed at the moment, it would allow plenty of room to grow. Ron's job title changed to Executive Vice President of New Product Development, which meant that he was in charge of the research and development of new products for the company. Ashwin became the Executive Vice President for Operations, and he and his team kept all of the company's servers operational. It was an exciting time, and they were leading the way. In July of 1993, Dan brought Scotty on as a partner and the two of them were back together again. It was a partnership that would last. Over the next several years, the company experienced phenomenal growth. Within four years, the company had grown to over four hundred employees and had built a new operations center about ten miles out of town. Their internet products were used by almost all of the major corporations, and they did hosting and development for many of the smaller ones. In 1995, the company experienced another surge of growth by acquiring several important government and military contracts, mainly in the area of communication. A new facility was constructed, and the area started to take on a campus type look. Dan changed the name of the company from Nelson Internet Technology to just Nelson Technology to reflect their expanding product offerings. Ron moved over to the Government Research area, while Ashwin took over the entire Internet Operations. In 1999, the company's name was changed to Perihelion Research Group, named after the starship from Dan and Scotty's favorite show. In 2001, the company had grown in size to five buildings on the main campus, and a secure off-site research facility about a mile away. They now had over eight thousand employees. With the expanding role of government contracts, the decision was made to split the company into two divisions, Perihelion Research and Development, and Perihelion Internet Technology. The growth continued over the next decade with the company expanding into other markets, including internationally. By 2015, Perihelion Research Group was number eighteen in the list of the top twenty largest companies in the world.

Just the other side of Greensboro, Dan's phone rang. It was Scotty.

"Hey Scotty, glad you got my message! Board meeting not too bad I hope."

"You know how they can be, especially when you have those government guys wanting to advise on everything." Scotty replied. "How's the trip going?"

"Good," replied Dan, "I'm around Greensboro now. I should be getting into Southport around 5:00. I won't get to go out to the island tonight, but I'll catch the ferry first thing in the morning. I'm anxious to go out and see how much work we have to do."

"Greg called." Scotty said. "He should be there next Wednesday. I'll probably be a little longer. I've got a few things to finish up here before leaving it with Ron for the next few months. I should be out a week from Monday."

"Great, I'll look forward to Greg getting here. I imagine we'll have plenty to do, and he'll surely be a big help. From the pictures that they sent, it doesn't look too bad, but who knows when those pictures were taken." replied Dan. "Tomorrow's Sunday so I'll probably go out and have a look around to see what needs done. I'm hoping to find a Bed and Breakfast out on the island that's not too far from the lighthouse. That can be our home for the next few months. I called the island's utility company. They haven't been able to get out to the area to run power to it yet. The area's fenced off with a locked gate at the entrance, so I'll have to go out and unlock it for them. It may be several weeks before they actually run the power out to it. According to the map it's about a mile out to the lighthouse from the main road, and since it was closed in 1935, I don't think power ever was run out there. I'll probably get a portable generator that we can use while working there until then. I'll give you a call tomorrow after I've gone and checked it out."

"Sounds good," replied Scotty, "I'll look forward to your call." They talked a little more and finally ended for the day.

Once Dan got past Raleigh, the trip definitely got slower, and instead of 5:00, it was almost 6:45 PM when he finally made it into Southport. The first thing that he did was look for a place to stay for the night. Southport was basically a small seaside fishing town, but since it had a large tourist business in the summer, several of the major chain hotels had moved in there. There was also an abundance of local hotels as well to satisfy those tourists who wanted to experience a little more of the seaside charm. He finally settled on one not too far from the ferry port that was situated ocean side called the Sea Spray Motel. It had only two levels with a beige wood frame exterior. It looked like it had been one of the original hotels along the coastal part of the city and had weathered many storms. It was situated close to the two lane road with the parking spaces along the front of the hotel. It appeared to have been kept up well, though, so he decided to stay for the night.

He pulled his truck into a parking space next to the lobby. The motel didn't appear to be busy. There were only three cars parked in front, though he thought there may be more out back. A few people strolled down the street in front of the motel, mostly locals from the look of them. At this time of day, most of the tourists were probably either out to dinner, or down at the beach. Across the road was a white wood framed building with a green wooden sign over the porch which said "Anderson's Fish Market". It was lighted by three flood lights mounted on posts in front of the sign. Daylight savings time didn't arrive until 2:00 AM on Sunday morning, so it was beginning to get dark. The front door was propped open with a wooden chair, and he could hear a radio playing a country tune. He turned back to the motel. A lighted neon sign in the window said "Vacancy", and a crooked wooden sign on the door said "Check-In Here". He stepped inside to a small dimly lit lobby area. It only had a couple of fluorescent fixtures, both of which seemed to have several bulbs out. The one over the front desk was blinking constantly. There was a small sofa and table against the front window, with the table containing some coastal literature showing places to see and places to eat while visiting. The walls were paneled with a dark wood paneling which made the lobby seem even darker. The lime green carpeting was frayed and torn in several places. There was a small desk in the corner containing a computer, keyboard, and monitor. All appeared to be from the early nineties, not the latest equipment at all. He walked over to the front desk. There didn't appear to be anyone around. He rang the service bell on the counter and waited. Still, no one came out. "Hello?" he called. There was still no answer. He went back outside and walked around the corner of the motel. There was another building with more rooms around back, but these didn't look to be in any shape for occupancy. Most of the room's doors were missing and the windows were broken out. Some had air conditioning units, but most just had large rectangular holes where the air conditioning units should be. A large part of the roof was missing as well.

"Can I help you?" asked a voice from behind him. It had been so quiet, with only the wind rustling in the trees, that the voice startled him a bit.

"I'm looking for the front desk clerk. I'd like a room for the night." replied Dan. He turned to see a small elderly man with white hair.

"That'd be me." replied the man. "Come around front and we'll get you checked in. There's a convention in town, but I'll check and see if I might still have a room."

Dan couldn't tell if the man was joking or not. Though it wasn't a large motel, it still didn't look anywhere near being full. It looked to have about twenty rooms, ten on each level, and there were only the three cars in the lot. He supposed the rest could be out to dinner. He followed the man into the lobby and to the front desk. While the lobby had the computer, presumably for the guests to use, the front desk had no computer. The man kept track of which rooms were available using index cards. When a room was taken, he'd move its index card from the "Vacant" to the "Occupied" box. He could process credit cards, but that was done with an older manual credit card machine with the ink pad. He ran Dan's card through, then gave him the credit card receipt to sign. After he had signed it, the man gave him his room key, which was a standard brass key on a triangular blue fob with a large white "7" on it.

"Room 7's to your right. Ice and vending is in the hallway right down from the room. My name's Ben. I'll be here till about 10:00. If you need anything, just let me know. Harvey comes in at 10:00. If you do need anything, you might want to tell me before I leave. Harvey don't hear too good, so you never know what you'll get."

"Well, nice to meet you Ben. I'm sure everything will be fine."

He walked out of the lobby and over to his truck. The rooms were numbered 1 through 10 moving away from the lobby, so room 7 was a little more than halfway down. He reached into his truck and pulled out his computer bag and a small suitcase, then walked down to the room. He opened the door with the key, walked inside, and set his bags down by a chair near the door. The room was small but clean. Two double beds were against one wall to the right as you walk in the door. A nightstand with a table lamp was between the beds, and a dresser with a small TV was on the opposite wall. It was almost 7:30 and he had only stopped once during the day to get a small sandwich, so he realized that he was getting a bit hungry. He called Kate to let her know that he had made it down alright, and then stepped out to find dinner. He stopped by the front office on his way out to see if Ben knew of any good local places to eat.

"If it's good local eating you're looking for, I'd try Smitty's. It ain't too fancy, but the food's good. Smitty grew up here in town, and he's been running the place since he retired from the Navy. He was a cook in the Navy, and he makes the best food in town. You might want to try his 'Catch of the Day'. He don't open till 4:00, and he goes out fishing during the day, so the 'Catch of the Day' is whatever he caught today. His place is right down the street toward the ocean about a half mile from here. Look for the big blue fish. You can't miss it."

Dan thanked him and left. He drove down the street and found the big blue fish. He parked and went inside. Ben was right. The "Catch of the Day" was definitely the thing to get. It was two large pieces of fish served with hush puppies and a side of beans. By the time he was finished, he was more than full. He paid the check, drove back to the hotel, and turned in for the night. Though it was only a little after 9:00, he was pretty tired from the trip and he did want to get an early start the next day.

CHAPTER 3
March 13, 2016
First Warnings

Dan was up at 6:00 on Sunday morning. He wanted to catch the 7:15 ferry out to the island. He packed all of his belongings that he had brought into the room the night before, pulled on his hiking boots, and then went up to the front desk to check out. He stopped by his truck on the way to the lobby to put his suitcase in the back. Ben was there to greet him when he walked into the lobby, looking pretty much as he had the night before.

"Had a good night?" asked Ben.

"It was good," replied Dan, "just what I needed after a long trip."

"What'd you say you were here for?" inquired Ben.

"Not sure I ever said. I bought Forrest Point Lighthouse out on Green Island, along with twenty seven acres of land around it. Some friends and I are going to spend the next several months restoring it, and then I'll bring the family out in June." He noticed a strange look come over Ben's face when he mentioned the lighthouse. It seemed to be part curiosity and part fear.

"If I was you, I'd turn right back around and go back where you came from." Ben finally replied. "There's a reason that lighthouse was for sale, and it ain't good."

"I know about the things that happened at the lighthouse." replied Dan. "I've actually done quite a bit of research over the years about the disappearances. I'd like to find out more while I'm here."

"The last keeper moved out almost eighty years ago." replied Ben. "Moved out pretty quick; they all did. There's a lot more to the place than what you've read in the books. There's things people never talked about.

I'm bettin' you got the lighthouse and the land around it for a lot less than it should have been worth. Am I right?"

"Well...actually yes. I didn't expect to get it for what it went for."

"Exactly," said Ben, "and there's a reason for that. That land hasn't been able to sell for any price for pretty much as long as I've been alive. Most people around here won't even go out to that part of the island. You said you wanted to find out more while you're here, so you got a few minutes? Let's get a cup of coffee and I'll tell you all about it."

Dan was more than a little intrigued. He wanted to get out to the island and see what was there, but here was a chance to find out more about the lighthouse, and that was part of what he wanted as well. Maybe this was a chance to find out more than he'd read about. To finally hear firsthand from someone who had lived here. "Ok," said Dan, "let's get that coffee." Ben went into the kitchen and came back with two cups of coffee, along with some sugar and creamer. They both settled down on the sofa opposite the front desk.

"My great great grandfather was the first keeper of Forrest Point light. I assume you've read the story of Colonel Forrest?" said Ben.

"Yes, I've read a couple of different versions of that one." replied Dan.

"Strange story that one. Too bad they didn't have pocket cameras back then." continued Ben. "Anyway, as I was saying, my great great grandfather was the first keeper of the light. He moved his family into the keeper's house when it was first lit in 1866. It was February if I remember right. And he moved them out in April of that same year. He and his wife only had one child, a son named Sam. About a week after they moved in, Sam started having nightmares. They had to pretty much let him sleep with them in their room for the next few months. Then in early April, the fog moved in. As I remember, the night wasn't particularly right for fog according to what I've been told; clear and not too humid. The fog moved in around dusk, as the story went. He was outside at the time, and said it pretty much came on quick. He went over to take a look, and as I've heard the story over the years, he saw something in the fog. Nobody really knows what it was he saw, and I'm not sure he ever really said. But it scared him so much that he packed up and moved his family out the next day. Moved clear off the island over to Tennessee. That's where he lived till he died, and most of his family still lives there today. What could a person see that would scare him so bad that he'd move away the very next day and never come back? Anyway, the light was dark for a couple of months until they could get a replacement. Seems like every keeper after my great great grandfather had some sort of experience there. None of them ever lasted more than about six months. I think that was the longest. One of them even thought spacemen were coming to get him. Like I said, the place isn't normal. Strange things happen out there. Need more coffee?"

"No, I'm fine, go on."

"Well, my first personal encounter happened in 1974. I figure you've read the story of Greg Baker and Tim Henderson. It's one of the most often told stories around these parts. Even been the subject of several books, if I remember right. Well, I was living here when that happened. I was part of the search team that gathered together to look for them. But they weren't here. I don't believe the official story that they were washed out to sea either. That's what they finally say when they can't figure out anything else that could have happened and there's water around. The ocean's always a convenient explanation. The ocean never leaves any clues. But they never got to the ocean. That's one of the parts that never got in the paper or in any of the books. 'Washed out to sea during a riptide' was the official explanation only because that was the only explanation that made any sense. Only it didn't make any sense, not if you'd seen what we did. It had been raining quite a bit the week before the disappearance. So much so that everyone's shoes made a pretty deep print in the ground. We all thought that should make it pretty easy to find them. Just follow the footprints, and that'd lead us to them. At least that's what we thought. We found the two sets of prints made by the boys coming through the gate to go to the lighthouse, and we found their prints coming out of the lighthouse. We were able to follow them through the yard. We followed them all the way to the gate leading out through the stone wall, and that's where they ended. Not a print to be found outside the wall except for the ones going in. We even searched the entire perimeter around the wall thinking they might have climbed up on the wall and walked around that way, but nothing was found. We were searching the day after the disappearance, and the ground outside the wall was still so wet that we left plenty of prints, but none from the boys the night before. The only thing I can come up with is that they were taken. And it had to be something in the air, not on the ground, else we'd have found tracks, prints, something. That's why they're not here and were never found."

"Are you suggesting aliens? Maybe flying saucers?" inquired Dan.

"I ain't suggesting nothing. There's not any real good explanation. All I'm saying is that they were taken by something right at the fence. Just carried up into the air is the only way I can figure it. The police department even brought in dogs. The dogs followed the scent all the way from the lighthouse steps to the gate at the rock wall, then the only scent that they could pick up was the trail the boys made when they walked TO the lighthouse. They followed the trail up to the point where the boys met, then the trail split off to their houses. They even walked the dogs around the outside of the wall to see if they could pick the scent back up anywhere else, too, but no luck. The boys just weren't there anymore. Greg had a little sister, who was around 7 years old at the time I think. After his disappearance, his mother and father took his sister and all of them moved away from the island. Nobody I talked to ever knew where they went, we just sort of lost track of them after that. Tim had a younger brother, Alan. They stayed on the island, but it never was the same. We'd see them in town now and then, but they mostly kept to themselves. Never really spoke to anyone after that either. His mother disappeared about six years later. That part never got in any of the books. She just left one night and was never seen again. Her car was found over on Lighthouse Road. There was a search, but just like the boys, nothing ever turned up. Tim's father and brother still live on the island. His father still lives in the family's old home. Alan married his high school sweetheart and lives about a quarter mile away with his family. Most people on the island just don't talk about the lighthouse much. Too many bad memories and unexplained events around it. That's why I think you'd do good to turn around and go back home. Nothing good's ever come from the lighthouse, and nothing ever will."

"I'd still like to go take a look," said Dan, "after all, I came all this way."

"Well, I guess I can't stop you, but remember what I said. And don't go near the fog. It'll come back. Might not be this week or the next, but it'll come back."

Dan thanked Ben for his time, then left the hotel and went back to his truck. They had been talking for awhile, so he'd missed the first ferry. He should be able to catch the 8:00 one. He got into his truck, cranked it up, and headed down the road toward the ferry dock. Driving down Island Ferry Road, Dan passed a mixture of small seafood restaurants, small businesses that had sprung up over the years, and wood frame houses. This seemed to be the older part of town. He guessed that the ferry had been running for years, and this part of town just grew up around the road to the ferry. There were only two ferry ports out to the island, this one, called the Southport Ferry which left from Southport and docked at the north side of Green Island, and the Oak Island Ferry which was further south and docked near the center of the island. This one was the shortest trip, at only thirty five minutes out to the island. The Oak Island Ferry took about an hour.

The ferry port was only about a mile and a half from the motel, so it didn't take long to arrive. He passed the big blue fish where he had eaten the night before about a mile back. When he got to the port, it looked as if there were already around fifteen to twenty cars ahead of him. It was 10 till 8, so he should be on time. He got out of his truck and walked over to the sea wall where he had a good view of the ocean and anything approaching. He saw the 8:00 ferry off in the distance bringing cars from the island. As it drew closer, he could tell that it was pretty full. This wasn't too surprising as he figured that quite a few folks living on the island worked on the mainland. This was just part of their morning commute. Within minutes, the ferry docked and a steady stream of cars poured off and headed to their destination. After they had all unloaded, it was his turn. His lane began moving and he followed them until he was on board the ferry. An attendant was directing the traffic on the ferry and motioned for him to move to the center lane and pull all the way forward. He pulled in behind a late model green Ford, stopped, and set the emergency brake. Then he got out and walked over to the railing to enjoy the fresh air. Within about five minutes they were underway.

The morning air was crisp and fresh. The water was reasonably calm and the ferry rocked gently back and forth as it made its way across the Cape Fear River toward Green Island. A certain excitement and anticipation built up inside him as the ferry drew closer to the island. This was the day that he'd been waiting for. He had pictures in his mind of walking up to the lighthouse, stepping onto the porch and walking inside. He'd take in the musty odor of a brick and stone structure that had been vacant for the better part of the last eighty years. The thought definitely excited him, but had a certain foreboding as well. After all, he couldn't ignore its past. And what may have happened during the last eighty years when no one was around to see?

"Haven't seen you around here before." came a voice from behind him. He turned and faced an older gentleman with graying hair and a rough, weathered face. He wore a brown flannel shirt and blue cotton work pants. "Bud's the name." said the man.

"Dan," replied Dan, "Dan Nelson. And no, you wouldn't have seen me. This is my first trip out to the island in quite a few years."

"Thought so." said Bud. "I've been making this trip off and on for the past fifty or so years. I'm retired now, so I don't get out this way as often, but usually at least a couple of times a week. I still work part time at the general store on the island, and on occasion, when they're short-handed, I'll help out on one of the fishing boats that go out every morning. They leave before dawn, so I have to get here a lot earlier than this on those days. So what brings you out this way on such a fine morning?"

"Going to check out the old lighthouse on the island." replied Dan. "We used to vacation out here when I was a boy. I'd gone out there then, but this is the first time in probably thirty years that I've been out here."

"I hate to disappoint you," said Bud, "but you can't get out there anymore. About twenty years ago the government put up a gate on the old lighthouse road. It's posted 'Government Property - Keep Out'. Several times a year we'll have some vacationers come out here wanting to see the lighthouse. There've been several books and articles written about it, you know. Anyway, they're all pretty disappointed when they find that there's nowhere even to see the lighthouse from the island anymore. The only way to see it is by boat around the south end of the island, and I hear that it's so grown up around it now that it's even difficult to see from there unless you know exactly where to look. You have to be in just the right place to be able to pick it out from among the trees and brush. Hope you didn't come all this way just for the lighthouse."

"Well, actually I did," said Dan, "but I have a key to the gate. I purchased the lighthouse from the government several months ago, and this is the first time that I've gotten out here to take a look. Some friends and I are going to fix it up, and then I'll bring the family out this summer. Since there's already a gate, I'll probably still keep it locked while we work on getting it fixed up."

Bud had a really perplexed look on his face. One eyebrow arched up on one side, and the other arched down. He looked as though he was trying to find just the right words to say. After several long seconds of silence, he finally replied, "Not sure that's such a good idea. You do know the history of the lighthouse, right?"

"Yes," replied Dan, "I've read several of the books about it. I've always been fascinated with it."

"I've never had any real encounters out there," said Bud, "probably because I just never went out there, even before they put up the fence. The last time I was there was when we were searching for the boys, back in 1974. Odd one that was. Never really made any sense what could have happened to them. We never turned up anything. Not a trace. Officially the police department concluded that they must have gone swimming and washed out to sea. That story might fly with someone who had never been out here, but not with me. And not with anyone else that lived on the island either. We can't quite figure exactly what did happen, but that story just doesn't make sense, not from what we found out there. Problem is, no other story that anyone can think of makes any sense either. That's why most people on the island just stay away from there. From what we found in their backpacks, they didn't bring their swimsuits. And we never found any of their clothes along the waterfront either. Usually, when boys go swimming, they take off their clothes and leave them on the beach. But none were found. We did find some tracks in the soft mud outside the gate, probably made by the boys, but those tracks were going in. We figured those were from when they arrived. There were tracks going out, but only on the inside of the gate. The tracks going out ended right at the gate. Can't really figure that one."

Their conversation was cut short by several loud bursts from the ferry's whistle. "Better get back to our vehicles," Bud said, "but do remember what I said. Be careful out there. There's a lot we don't know about that place, and I'm not even sure it should be known. See you around!"

"Later." replied Dan, and he too went back to his truck. He saw Bud go around to a late model Dodge truck near the front of the ferry. He'd definitely have to find him again. It seemed that everyone he met out here had a story to tell, and all of them involved the old lighthouse.

The ferry docked, and within minutes he was on the island, driving down the only road that led from the ferry port to town. Green Island itself wasn't too large. It was about six miles long north to south, and about two and a half miles wide at the widest point. The town itself was near the ferry port. Pretty soon after leaving the ferry, there were houses on both sides of the roads, and side streets leading to more houses. Within about a half mile he was at the center of town. A large white two-story frame building with a long porch on the front was situated diagonally on the right. The sign above the porch read, "Bud's General Store". "Guess Bud's more than just a stock boy." he thought. Main Street apparently ran perpendicular to where he was and was lined with small shops and restaurants. This was basically a fishing and tourist town, and the tourists loved to eat at any of the variety of local restaurants. He turned left at the light and went down Main Street.

At the edge of town, he passed an attractive beige Victorian home with a sign that read, "Island Charm Bed and Breakfast". It reminded him of the bed and breakfast where he and his family had stayed when they vacationed on the island during the summer right before he went off to college. He pulled off to the side of the road and got out of his truck. He looked back at the Island Charm. Glancing at it again, he decided that it was the same bed and breakfast. It had been painted blue then and had a different name, Ocean Breeze Bed and Breakfast if he was remembering right. He'd have to check it out when he came back into town. He'd need a place to stay tonight, and he really didn't want to go back into Southport. He'd probably go ahead and reserve Scotty and Greg a room as well, since Greg would be out on Wednesday. He'd actually like to go in and take a look anyway, to see if it brought back memories. That was the last real vacation that he had taken with just his parents and brother. After that summer, he went off to college where he met Kate and Scotty during his sophomore year. Life was never the same after that. He got back into his truck and continued on.

After passing the Island Charm, the houses quickly thinned out and he was travelling down a really rural road with only the occasional road turning off. He pulled off to the side of the road again to check the map that was given to him as part of the package when he purchased the lighthouse. It contained a general map of the island, as well as a detailed survey map of his land around the lighthouse. He pulled it out of the black pouch where he had put it and opened it up. Since his truck had on-board GPS, it had been quite a while since he'd actually consulted a paper map for directions, but this was the exception. It looked like he was on the right road. At the edge of town, right after the bed and breakfast Main Street had turned into Livingston Road. There was a fork in the road in about another forth of a mile where Livingston Road went to the left and Henderson Road branched to the right and turned south. He stayed on Henderson Road for about three and a half miles until he came to Ocean View Lane where he turned left. In about a mile, Ocean View Lane ran into Sea Spray Drive which ran north to south along the Atlantic Coast of the island. There were quite a few houses and multi-story condominiums along this stretch of road, as well as two or three hotels. This area was where most of the island's vacationers stayed. There were several folks along Sea Spray Drive who were year-round residents, but mostly this had turned into rental property to give people from the mainland what they expected from an island vacation. He turned right onto Sea Spray Drive and went another mile down the coast until he came to Harbor Inn Lane on the right. About a mile down Harbor Inn Lane was an old rustic hotel which had been on the island since the early 1930s and was still a frequent destination for island tourists. He wouldn't need to go that far, though, because in about a forth mile, Lighthouse Road was on the left. According to the map, Lighthouse

Road went about another mile south, where it ended near the southern tip of the island. He turned left onto Lighthouse Road. In about another forth mile he came upon the gate that Bud was referring to. A crookedly hanging well weathered sign did say, "Government Property - Keep Out", but some of the letters were so worn with age and the elements that they were barely legible. He got out of the truck and walked over to the gate. Vines had grown up on the gate and he had to tear some away with his hand to get a good look on the other side. He was a bit disappointed at what he saw. Lighthouse Road had gradually gotten narrower as he drove toward the gate, but the road on the other side of the gate was so overgrown with weeds that you could barely make out the road. He'd probably be able to get his truck down it, but he'd definitely have to hire someone to come out and clear it. He reached into his pocket and pulled out a brass key, then found the padlock that secured the rusty hinges to the gate. He unlocked the padlock and pulled the gate open. At first, the right gate didn't want to move, but finally it gave way with a loud creak.

CHAPTER 4

Inspecting the Lighthouse

He got back into his truck and drove through the gate. He stopped just past it to get out and secure it with the padlock again, before continuing down the well overgrown road. At some places the trees and vines seemed to close in around the road so that they would scrape against the side of the truck. Other places, the road seemed to open up into a clearing on one or both sides of the road. The going was pretty slow. From the looks of it, no vehicles of any kind had been down this road for decades. There were spaces where the asphalt was intact, but mostly it was broken up and much of the road was just dirt with plants and trees growing up. Several times along the way he had to stop and get the chainsaw out of the truck toolbox to cut down a tree that had grown up in the middle of the road and was too big for the truck to plow over or to cut up one that had fallen across the road. It took about an hour and a half to go the mile down the road, but finally he ended up at the end. From the map, the lighthouse would be to his right about five hundred to six hundred feet back up the road from where it ended. He hadn't seen it as he passed by, but that by itself wasn't unusual given the growth around the road on either side. He turned off the truck, put it in park, and got out. It seemed quietly peaceful here at the end of the road. A light breeze rustled through the treetops, and directly in front of the truck he could hear the ocean waves gently breaking on the shore. He walked closer to the bushes around the front of the truck and from one spot he could see the ocean. It didn't seem too far from where he stood, but the bushes made it completely impassable. He turned to his right and began walking back up the road, peering through the bushes to his left to try and get a glimpse of the lighthouse. At 105 feet, the lighthouse wasn't as tall as some of the other coastal lights in the area, but should be tall enough for him to see if he could get to just the right clearing. He walked back to a grassy area beside the road and walked through the grass over to the edge of the woods. He peered into the woods, searching for an area that wasn't as densely overgrown that he may be able to get through. By his general calculations, this should be about where the lighthouse should be. After looking for a few minutes, he found an area that he could get through and he walked a little ways into the woods. There was no sound out here other than the crickets, tree frogs, and other abundant wildlife and the lapping of the surf. No cars, air conditioners, or even other people. He was probably about a mile and a half from the Harbor Inn, and from what he figured, that was probably the nearest structure. This end of the island was completely uninhabited, and had been for almost the last century.

He continued on through the brush, being careful to watch out for snakes, gators, or any other dangerous wildlife that may be lurking nearby. He gazed off to his right, and from this vantage point, caught the first glimpse of the top of the lighthouse. The lantern house looked rusty, with apparently all of the glass either broken or missing. It was tilted to one side, where it looked like a lot of bricks had caved in and many were missing. He couldn't see any further down for the foliage. He began to make his way in that direction, having to weave in and out at several places to find a spot that was passable. After moving in and out around the trees and foliage, he stumbled across a rock wall about four feet high. There was a place a few feet to his right where several of the rocks had fallen out of the wall, leaving a three foot opening that was only two feet high. He stepped through the opening in the wall and found himself on the inside. He looked around and saw that the wall seemed to go completely around the clearing where the lighthouse stood in the center. The wall looked to be perfectly circular around the lighthouse. While there were no really large trees in the clearing, it was still difficult to move through the tall grass and weeds. In some ways it was harder to move through the tall grass than it had been in the woods. As he slowly approached the lighthouse, it was clear that the photo that he had received from the government had been taken quite a few years earlier. It had been evident in the photo that the place would need a lot of repair, but actually gazing upon it for the first time he saw exactly how hard the years had been on the old structure. As he had seen from the edge of the woods, the lantern house was rusty with all of the glass broken out. From this vantage point though, it appeared to be leaning almost to the point of falling off its foundation. Much of the east facing side had crumbled and there was a large hole left near the top that the lantern house was leaning into. Several more spots down the side of the tower were also missing their bricks which lay in a pile at the lighthouse base. The house itself was attached to the lighthouse tower. It was a two story brick house, but was in even worse shape than the tower. Most of the wall on the northwest side had fallen in leaving both the upper and lower floors exposed. The front entrance was completely overgrown with vines, but he was able to enter through a large opening where the wall had fallen in.

He entered what he thought used to be the front parlor. To his left, the upper floor had completely fallen in and he could see up through the roof to the blue sky. Vines had mostly taken over the interior of the house as well. From where he stood, it looked like most of the roof was missing. There were only a few rotting timbers still remaining of the roof supports. As he made his way into the entrance hall and into the kitchen, he was startled by a loud crash coming from the entrance to the dining room. His heart racing, he went over to check on the source of the crash. For the first time since he had arrived at the lighthouse, he was keenly aware of how really desolate this place was. He moved through the door leading into the dining room in time to see a rather large raccoon escape outside through an opening in the wall. He turned to his left to see a table and shelf with several pots and pans on it. Several large pots were also lying on the floor, probably the source of the crash he had heard earlier. A large dining room table, with chairs surrounding it was in the center of the room. While greatly weathered, the table still looked in decent condition given the number of years that it had been here. The chairs, however, were quite another story. Most were completely rotted and chewed up by various animals that may have been here over the years. None were still standing on all four legs. More vines and dirt were surrounding the table and chairs. He made his way out to the main foyer where the staircase leading to the upper floor used to be. Some steps still remained near the top, but all of the ones from the ground floor to about halfway up had caved in. There was a large hole in the floor right under where the staircase had been where most of the wood had rotted out. It appeared that he wouldn't be able to get to the second floor during this visit. Probably just as well, since most of the upper floorboards were probably not safe to hold any amount of weight. He made his way back outside through the back door, which broke completely off its hinges when he opened it. From this side of the house, he had a great view of the ocean. The cool breeze blew in from the sea, and he just had to stand there for a few moments taking it all in. As he was standing, completely mesmerized by the moment, some movement caught his eye at the edge of the woods to his left. He looked over that direction, and at first couldn't see anything in the shadows. He walked over toward the direction of the movement and was suddenly startled as two white tail deer came bounding out from the forest into the clearing. He stood completely still and they appeared not to notice him. After watching them for a few minutes, he turned and headed back toward the house. He could see that this side of the house had weathered the elements about the same as the other side. Neither was in very good shape. As he examined the house, he became aware that this was actually the front. What he had thought was the front door when he approached from the woods on the other side was actually the back. The front door from this side was at the top of four steps with two ornate columns on either side of the small landing at the top. Since it was difficult actually moving around in the tall grass, he decided to go back to the bed and breakfast that he had seen earlier and see if he could get a room. He needed to call and see if he could get someone to come out and clear the land before he could really do any work, but since today was Sunday, that would have to wait until tomorrow. He'd go into town and ask around to see if anyone knew of a good local company that did that kind of work. He looked at his watch and saw that it was 1:30 in the afternoon. Apparently he'd been out at the lighthouse longer than he had thought. No wonder he was getting a little hungry.

He walked around for a few more minutes, taking a few more pictures of the outside, before making his way through the woods back to his truck. Once he had walked through the rock wall, he tried to remember the way he had come in. There seemed to be vines and bushes growing up everywhere. He finally found where several of the smaller bushes had been trampled down and picked up his trail from earlier. Within a few minutes he was back at his truck and was making his way slowly down the narrow road. It was slightly faster this time since he'd already cleared away the bushes and trees while coming in. He was reminded by this that he'd also need to get a paving company to come out. He probably wouldn't pave it over completely with asphalt, but he did need it leveled and the chunks of old asphalt removed. After that, he'd get them to lay down a bed of gravel, which should make it much easier to get out here. He reached the gate, where he got out and unlocked it, then drove through, got back out to lock it, then proceeded back into town.

After a short drive back, Dan pulled into the road beside the Island Charm Bed and Breakfast. It was a narrow gravel road, really more like a small alleyway. Parking for the Island Charm was a gravel parking area just wide enough for cars to pull into that extended from the front to the back of the building. It was early afternoon, so most of the guests were out, but there were still some cars there. He pulled into a vacant space, got out, and proceeded to walk around to the front of the building. As he walked up the stairs, he noticed an older couple with a small dog sitting in the swing at the far end of the porch. They waved to him as he approached the door. They were probably vacationers staying at the house. He'd get to know them later. The front door was open, with only a screen door to keep out the insects. He opened the screen door and went inside. The lobby was spacious with a fireplace along the right wall. A large sitting area was through a door immediately to his right. To his left was a doorway leading to the dining room, and beside that was a long staircase leading to the upper floors. He walked straight back through the lobby past the fireplace. The lobby was dimly lit with no overhead lighting and only a few floor and table lamps. Sunlight streamed through a window near the back wall. Even though the day was reasonably cool, there was no fire in the fireplace. There appeared to be no check-in desk, but he did find the office at the back.

"Hello," he said, "anyone home?"

"Back here." came a woman's voice from the back. He looked around and saw an elderly woman, probably in her early sixties coming around the corner. She was smiling and seemed to have a charming demeanor.

"Welcome to the Island Charm," she said, "how can I help you?"

"I need to see if you have a couple of rooms available." Dan said, "If you have one with a couple of beds that would be nice. I have two friends coming later in the week."

"How long will you be staying?" she inquired.

"We'll probably need them for about three months." replied Dan.

"I have two rooms upstairs, facing the front," she said, "which should be just what you're looking for. The big room on the right has two beds and a sitting area. The other room's right across the hall. It's smaller, only one bed, but you can use the larger room for visiting, or you can come down to the parlor. The larger room rents for $1250 per week, but I can let you have it for $2700 per month for the 3 months. The small one goes for $1150 per month."

"Sounds like that'll work." replied Dan.

They took care of the check in, then she handed him the keys to both rooms. "My name's Barbara." the woman said as she handed him the keys.

"Dan Nelson." answered Dan.

She continued, "My husband Hank and I run the Island Charm. We have an apartment at the back, so we live here year-round. Just go down that hallway on the right and you'll come to it. During the day, one of us is usually around somewhere, but if you need anything pretty much after 9:00 you'll need to come and knock. One of our sons is usually here during the day as well. They help us maintain the place. Breakfast is served from 6:30 to 8:30 every morning in the dining room and dinner's at 5:30. We have a wine and cheese social every evening at 8:00. That's usually hosted by our daughter, Rachel. Since you're going to be here for three months, you may want to come down and meet your neighbors. We have ten rooms here and right now six rooms other than the two that you rented are occupied. Two are monthly renters like yourself, so they should be here the whole time that you're here. One room is a year round resident, Emma Peterson. She's lived on the island almost all her life, and basically wanted to retire here. The other three rooms are weekly renters. They just came in today and will probably only be here until next Saturday when a new group will come in. Most of the folks that stay here are pretty friendly, so come on down and meet them."

"Thanks," replied Dan, reaching out and taking the keys from her, "I'm from Cincinnati. I just bought the old lighthouse here on the island,

and me and a couple of friends are going to be fixing it up over the next few months. I'm planning on bringing my family down in June, after school's out for the summer. Hopefully by then we'll have it livable, but after going out and taking a look today, I'm not so sure."

Barbara was the first person since he had been down here that didn't get a funny look when he mentioned the lighthouse. Instead, she just seemed intrigued by the idea. "That sounds like quite a job!" she said. "I haven't been out there, but from the stories I hear it's been pretty much abandoned at the end of the island for the last century. I imagine it'll need quite a bit of work to make it livable."

"I was out there this afternoon," said Dan, "and you're right, it'll be quite a lot of work. It's not in great shape, and is even in worse condition than the pictures indicated. We'll do what we can, and hire contractors to do what we can't. It'll be close getting it ready for the family, but I think we'll make it. What do you know about some of the stories surrounding the lighthouse?"

"I'm afraid not much." she said. "Hank and I just moved here two years ago when we bought the Island Charm as our retirement investment. We both enjoy meeting new people, so we figured this would be just the right idea. Before that we lived in Georgia. We both had always wanted to retire to the coast, so this was our chance. Since moving here, we have been able to talk to some folks that have lived here awhile, and some do have stories to tell. Most of the stories that we've heard involve the two boys who disappeared about forty years ago. You may want to talk with Emma. She was the best friend of the one boys' mother. The mother also disappeared several years later as I understand it. Don't push her too hard, though. She took all of the disappearances pretty hard and hasn't really talked about them much lately. It was really difficult on her to lose her best friend. They'd pretty much grown up together here on the island."

"Thanks, I'll try and talk with her." Dan walked back toward the front and up the stairs. At the top of the stairs, he turned right and walked through a small sitting area to the room on the left. He put the key in the lock and opened the door.

The blinds were closed, which made the room dark. It took a

minute for his eyes to adjust, but he finally found the light switch. There was no overhead light, only three lamps, one on each nightstand on either side of the bed, and one on the desk in the far corner. He walked over to raise the wooden blinds and let some fresh light in. The room was large enough. The furniture was dark wood and was a matched set. A large four poster bed was against the right wall, with a nightstand on either side. A guest chair was in the far corner, with the dresser beside it against the outside wall. The desk was in the other corner against the outside wall, with a TV stand beside it. The 36 inch flat screen TV and the cell phone charging station on one nightstand were the only items in the room that didn't look like they belonged to that period. He went back out, and across the hall to check out the other room. This one would be Scotty and Greg's room.

He turned the key in the lock and went inside. This room had a mustier smell than the smaller one, like it had been closed up for longer. Like the smaller room, the shades were closed, so not a lot of light was able to get in. He walked past a small kitchen and dining area on his left into the sitting area where he opened the shades. He felt that he also needed to open the window for a while to air out the room, so he opened it up and a fresh cool breeze filled the room. He turned around to check out the room. It was big. A small kitchen was beside the entry door, and a dining table was between the kitchen and sitting area. The sitting area was spacious with a sofa, two end tables, a coffee table, and two chairs. This would be perfect for them to sit around during the evenings and discuss plans. A desk was against the wall between the sitting area and the bedroom. The bedroom was also spacious, even though it contained two double beds and a nightstand between them. He had just turned to walk across the room when there was a knock at the door. Opening it, he found an elderly gentleman with a medium build, gray hair, and a gray beard and moustache. He was wearing cotton pants and a plaid flannel work shirt.

"You Dan?" asked the man.

"Yes, Dan Nelson. And you are?"

"Hank Johnson," replied the man, "me and the wife run the inn here. Hope the rooms are to your liking?"

"Yes," answered Dan, "they're very nice. We should be comfortable while we're here."

"I hear you bought the old lighthouse."

"Yes. After it's fixed up, I'll be bringing my family down to live here on the island. It's something I've always wanted to do and this was the perfect opportunity."

Hank's face showed quite a bit of concern. "Don't do it." he said.

"Don't do what?" queried Dan.

"Move your family down here." answered Hank. "And you'd do best to go ahead and leave yourself. Barbara don't really believe a lot of the stories she hears, but I do. The island's been quiet since we've been here, and that's been about two years now. It's a real nice place to live. Vacationers come from all over because it's real peaceful. It's been peaceful here for at least the past twenty years, from what people tell me. But that's because the government sealed off the south end of the island where the lighthouse is. Nobody's been out there at least for the past twenty years, maybe more. After hearing the stories, I'm not sure that end of the island should be opened back up. Something's not right there. The lighthouse shouldn't be disturbed, or it may start again. You and your family won't be safe out there. You've heard of the fog?"

"Yes, I've heard about it all my life. We've been coming here since I was young."

Hank continued, "The fog's not like normal fog. It only appears on the south end of the island around the lighthouse. It never comes up this far. Oh, we have foggy days up here occasionally, but it's different. Up here it's just normal fog. I was down by Harbor Inn Lane one time about dusk. I had been down at Harbor Inn helping Joe Rogers fix up some of the rooms. I was coming back home. As I passed by the entrance to Lighthouse Road, something didn't seem quite right. I drove out to where the gate was, parked and got out. I went over to the gate and looked in. There was a thick fog inside the gate. A little bit was spilling over onto this side of the gate, but not much. It was a low fog that hugged the ground about six or seven feet up. I reached out and touched a wisp of fog, and it was cold. The way it was swirling around didn't look like any fog I'd ever seen either. I can't really describe it, but it felt funny. I'm not scared of much, but it sent shivers up my back. I got back in my truck and haven't stopped at that turnoff since. I just thought I should warn you."

"Well, I do appreciate the warning. I was out there this afternoon, and it definitely could use some cleaning up."

At this point Hank interrupted, "I don't think you understand. It's not safe. I'm not talking about cleaning up. I'm talking about leaving it alone! People aren't meant to be out there!"

"As I said, I do appreciate the concern, but since I'm here now, I plan to see for myself. It will need a lot of fixing up, but when we're done it should be fine. I'll be careful."

Hank seemed a bit frustrated, but he finally said, "Guess there's no talking you out of it then. Some folks just have to see for themselves. But do listen to this warning. Don't go into the fog. It'll come back, always does. Stay inside until it goes away. Whatever you do, don't go into the fog." Hank turns and walks slowly through the sitting area and begins to walk down the stairs. He stops, looks back at Dan and says, "Oh, I almost forgot. Welcome to the Island Charm!"

CHAPTER 5
March 16, 2016
We're Not Alone

Dan woke around 6:30 on Wednesday. He had found a company on the island that would clear out the woods near the lighthouse and they were scheduled to start today. He also had a crew coming in to work on the road out to the lighthouse, but they weren't scheduled until next week. There wasn't a paving company located on the island, so he had to get one from Wilmington. They were finishing up with some other projects and wouldn't have a crew available until Monday. He quickly got dressed and went downstairs. There were already some guests around the breakfast table. It smelled so good that he decided to stop and eat a little bit before going out to the lighthouse. He filled his plate with eggs, sausage, muffins, grits, and some biscuits and gravy which Barbara makes up special each morning. He sat down beside a gentleman in his forties named Steve and his wife Arlene. Steve was a relatively short, thin man with slightly balding hair and receding hairline. He had brown hair, but there were some hints of gray in it as well. He did look as though he exercised regularly, and appeared to be in good shape, so he shouldn't have too much trouble getting through the bushes and woods. His wife, Arlene was actually slightly taller than Steve, with strawberry red hair that hung down just above her shoulders. They were vacationing here from Iowa. Living in the Midwest, they hadn't gotten to the seashore much, but they had always wanted to save up and go. Since this was their first time to the coast, they wanted to make the most of it, so they rented their room for the month. Steve had been talking with Dan on Monday about the lighthouse. Even though he had never heard of it, he seemed very interested in a lot of the stories that surrounded it, and wanted to come out sometime during the month with Dan and actually take a look at it. "Morning Dan," said Steve in a very cheerful voice, "going out to the lighthouse this morning?"

"Yes, I'm headed out that way now. The guys are supposed to be out this morning to start clearing the land, so I'll need to go out and check on them. Not sure what your plans are for today, but you're welcome to ride out there with me. It's a bit rugged since the clearing's just starting, but it might be interesting. Arlene can come too if she wants."

"I think I'll just let you boys go out there." replied Arlene. "I was planning to take a walk uptown and look at some of the shops anyway."

"Guess I'll keep you company then." replied Steve. They talked some more as they finished up with breakfast, and then headed out.

When they got to the entrance of Lighthouse Road, the workers from the land clearing company were already there waiting. There were six men, two skid-steer loaders, one fitted on the front with a large trimmer, a tractor with a large cutting deck mounted on the rear, and a panel truck full of supplies like trimmers, push mowers, and a lot of other clearing and gardening supplies. There was also a white pickup truck with supplies loaded in the back, towing a trailer with a riding mower. When they stopped, a large man with red hair and a weathered face came over. He looked to be in his late forties or early fifties, with a healthy tan from working outside most of the time. "Morning," he said, "the name's Mike. I'm the foreman. Ready to get started? Me and the boys are really curious to see what's on the other side of that fence. We've been wondering for years now."

"Let's get going then." replied Dan. He walked over, unlocked the gate and swung it open. Within minutes all the trucks and machinery were headed down Lighthouse Road. Dan and Steve followed them in the truck, not bothering to close and lock the gate this time. The road wasn't quite as rough as Dan remembered it from the other day. The trucks, tractor, and skid-steer loaders going ahead of him were actually leveling the road a little bit. He had been out a couple of other times as well, so it was starting to get more packed down with fewer weeds.

They arrived at the end of the road, and all the vehicles stopped. The men from the clearing company were looking around wondering where the job was. It didn't appear that there was anything around at all. The road just ended with trees and brush on either side. You really couldn't see anything at all from the road. Mike pulled out a map of the area and walked back to the right with Dan. Steve walked back along the road, surveying the brush along the side as he went. Dan walked with Mike to the end of the road and showed him on the map the area to be cleared. Then they walked back down the road, past the stopped machinery, and found the trail that Dan had taken earlier. They made their way through the brush and trees until they came to the rock wall surrounding the lighthouse. The gate definitely wasn't large enough to get the big tractor through, but it looked as though it would be plenty wide for the riding mower. They made their way through the tall grass over to the edge of the woods and talked some more about what needed to be cleared. They turned around and walked back through the gate. Mike made notes and drawings on his map as they walked so that he could tell his crew exactly what needed to be done. They tried to walk around the lighthouse on the outside of the rock wall, but they got barely twenty feet before the brush became so dense that they had to turn back. They made their way back out to the road, where after a short briefing with Mike the crew began unloading the truck and got right to work. Both skid steer loaders went crashing into the woods, tearing down small trees and clearing the brush. They had quite a bit that needed clearing before they could even think about getting the lawn mower inside the wall. After the walk through, Mike estimated that they'd probably need an entire week to complete the work, even with all six of them working on it.

Once Mike and his crew started working, Dan walked down the road to find Steve. With all the noise from the machinery, it wasn't quite as peaceful as it had been on the previous days when he'd been out here. He finally found Steve about a tenth of a mile back up the road. He had found a small path into the woods that Dan hadn't noticed on previous trips. While it was on the same side of the road, this path didn't appear to lead to the lighthouse. It went back into the woods about three hundred feet then broke to the right away from the lighthouse. Neither one could figure exactly who or what made this path. Steve suggested maybe a deer path, or some other animal. While not showing signs of being used often, it was definitely a clear path through the woods that had been used much more recently than the twenty years that this area had been locked up. And as far as anyone knew, animals were the only ones that had been back here for just that long. Dan had seen some deer on an earlier visit. Still, there was something about the path that suggested something other than animals. After a few more minutes with the path not seeming to end, they decided to turn back. Along the way they talked about the history of the area, and Dan filled Steve in on the parts that he didn't know. He offered to let Steve borrow the Jack Carlson book when they got back so he could read for himself the accounts of the lighthouse. On the way back out to the road, Dan's phone rang. It was Greg. He was making pretty good time and said that he should probably be there in another couple of hours. That was good news. While he had made some new friends, including Steve, it would be nice having his old friends out on the island with him as well. Greg would be in today, and Scotty would arrive on Monday. After taking Greg's call, Dan and Steve decided to walk out to the lighthouse. Steve had been wanting to see it, and Dan wanted to take another look himself.

Dan and Steve both made their way through the woods to the gate. Once inside, Steve was really surprised at how run down the lighthouse looked from a distance. Actually, he really wasn't sure what he expected. After all, this part of the island had been fenced off for over two decades, and for the most part uninhabited for a lot longer than that. They made their way through the tall grass to the back door. As they approached the door, something didn't seem quite right. After studying the scene for a few moments, Dan realized that it was the back door. It had been completely overgrown with vines on Monday when he came out. So much so that he had to find another way in. Now the vines had been torn down from around the door and the door stood partially open. They went up the brick stairs and stood on the landing. Dan pushed the wooden door open the rest of the way. As he pushed, part of the wood on the top of the door broke off and fell in behind it. They walked into the back foyer. The staircase was in the center and they could look down the hallway and see the front entrance. They walked past the fallen in staircase. They both looked up through the opening where the staircase once was, even though it would take quite a bit of reconstruction before anyone could finally get up there. While he could bring a ladder out once the land was cleared enough and climb up through the opening, he wanted to get an engineer out to do a structural inspection before even attempting to walk across any of the upstairs floors. As they both made their way into the dining room, Dan immediately sensed that something was different. He brought out his flashlight and shined it around the room to illuminate the many areas that were in the shadows. As he shined his light on the shelf that was against the back wall he immediately saw what was different. The pots and pans that the raccoon had knocked over on Monday were all neatly stacked back on the shelves. Not one of them was still on the floor. This gave him an uneasy feeling knowing that someone else had been here in the house since he had been out on Monday. He was glad that Steve was here with him now, and that Greg would be coming in today. As they had been walking through the house, they had noticed footprints in the dust. There was so much dust that had accumulated over the years that every step that anyone made left a very discernible footprint. As they now looked over toward the entrance to the kitchen, they saw Dan's boot prints from Monday, but they could also make out another footprint made by a different sort of boot. It didn't have the same pattern as either Dan's or Steve's boots. It still looked like a hiking boot pattern though, and a slightly larger boot size than Dan's as well. He couldn't imagine who would have been out here, though. This was completely unexpected. When he was out on Monday, he had seen no other footprints except ones made by animals. Those were expected. Until now, the thought had never really crossed his mind that the lighthouse and the area around it were anything but completely deserted. Steve wondered if it could have something to do with the trail that they had found earlier. They hadn't walked up it enough to really see where it went. Maybe they'd check that out on another day. The clearing crew would be out here for at least another week, and they couldn't really start doing a lot around the lighthouse until that job was finished. After looking around the house for another half hour, they decided that it was time to go back to the Island Charm and wait for Greg. Dan called him when they got back and found that he was aboard the ferry on the way to the island. He gave him directions to the Island Charm, and then he and Steve went back inside. Steve suggested that maybe he should go down to the police station and report that someone had been in the house. Dan thought that might not be a bad idea. Since Greg was so close, they'd wait on him to arrive first, and then maybe take a walk into town. They may run into Arlene there as well, and possibly the four of them could have lunch.

While they waited, Dan and Steve sat out on the front porch and talked. "I still keep wondering about that trail you found." said Dan. "After all that I've read over the years, I really wasn't expecting anyone to be out there."

"I know," replied Steve, "maybe we should go back out tomorrow and follow it further in. We could see where it ends up."

"That might be an idea. I still want to go talk to the island police this afternoon, too." said Dan. "After all, the area is marked 'No Trespassing'. We need to find out who's been out there." He was interrupted by the horn from a white Jeep Patriot as it passed in front of the inn and turned down the alley to the side.

"There's Greg!" remarked Dan. Both he and Steve walked down the stairs and went over to meet Greg as he parked.

Greg was a tall man, 24 years old with a muscular build. He had sandy blonde hair like his father, and usually a mischievous smile as well. While Scotty had a full beard, Greg only had the moustache, but he always reminded Dan of Scotty anyway. After brief introductions, Dan and Steve both helped Greg carry his belongings up to his room. They went up the stairs and through the small lobby to the room on the right. Dan opened it with the key and they all went inside and put Greg's stuff down.

"It's a lot bigger than I thought it would be from looking at the outside." remarked Greg.

"It's one of the bigger rooms." said Dan. "I figured you and your dad could share a room. Mine's across the hall. It's a lot smaller."

"I like it." Greg replied. "It makes it more like home."

"How about let's go into town and get something to eat?" suggested Dan. "You must be getting hungry after the trip."

"Fine by me," said Greg, "I am getting pretty hungry about now." They locked up the room, then went down the large staircase and went outside. It was a sunny day, just the type of day that was perfect for a walk. Since the Island Charm was right at the edge of town, they didn't have far to walk before they were in the middle of downtown. Steve called Arlene, and she had seen a small diner earlier that looked like a good spot to eat. She gave him directions to it and they agreed to meet there in about thirty minutes. Dan wanted to go down to the police station first and file a report.

Upon entering the police station, they were met by the island's Chief of Police. Larger cities with much larger police forces and much more crime usually would have a regular uniformed officer at the desk. But on a small island like this, where the police force wasn't particularly large, the Chief would work almost every job in the department at one time or another. He was a big man with dark brown hair and a wide moustache. He looked like he could pretty much handle any situation that came his way single handedly. "I'm Chief Callahan, what can I help you with today?" asked the Chief. Dan explained to the Chief how he had purchased the old lighthouse and was going to fix it up and move out there with his family. Dan and Steve both recounted the story about how they had been out to the lighthouse earlier in the day and had found evidence that someone had been there since Monday. They also told him about the trail that they had found further up the road.

"That gates been locked for pretty much the past twenty years," replied Chief Callahan, "and we've never really had reason to go out there very often. The government did give the police department a key when they locked it up, probably the only key other than the one that you have. I'll send an officer out later today to have a look. I can't imagine who'd be out there though. When the government locked up the place twenty years ago, they built the fence to go from the ocean on one side to the ocean on the other side. It even went all the way around the tip of the island so that the whole area was fenced in. They were serious about keeping everyone out. The only way in was either through the gate, which was always locked or climbing over the fence, which would be extremely difficult with the barbed wire at the top. Still, if someone has been out there, we'll find them. Here's my business card. If you need me, day or night, feel free to give me a call."

Dan thanked him and gave him one of his business cards in return. A perplexed look came over the Chief's face as he seemed to intently study the card. It was almost a puzzled look which seemed strange on such a big man. Dan couldn't imagine what could be so interesting about his card. It was a standard business card; name, position, business address, phone number, and company logo in the top left corner. Maybe it was the fact that Dan's listed position was "CEO" that intrigued him?

"Thanks." he said with an odd tone to his voice. They said

goodbye and the three of them left the station.

A few minutes later they had met Arlene at the Sand Crab Diner and were feasting on the best of the island's fresh catch. Once some of the land had been cleared, Dan and Greg talked about buying a tent and camping out at the lighthouse. It was Greg's idea. "Nothing like seeing what goes on after dark to really get a feel for the place." he said. Arlene could sense that Steve wanted to be in on this little adventure as well, so she told him to go ahead. She'd made several friends at the Island Charm and they could sit and talk in the evening, or play some games. She had bought a couple of books at the island's only bookstore that she was anxious to start reading as well. They figured that Mike and his crew should have the area cleared enough in two to three days to be able to go out and set up a campsite near the lighthouse. Dan really liked camping. He'd been on numerous overnight camp outs with Danny. Usually Scotty and Greg would join them. Still, as much as he liked camping, and the outdoors, he couldn't help but think that it would be much more fun if they didn't know that someone was out there. Not knowing what to expect made him really uneasy. After discussing it some more, they all decided that even though the area should be cleared enough in two to three days, they should probably wait until Scotty arrived on Monday to go out. They'd give him the first night to settle in at the Island Charm and get to know everyone, then maybe try camping out either Tuesday or Wednesday night. If someone was out there, they figured that the more people that they had, the better.

After finishing their lunch, they all decided to go for a walk around town. It was a charming, friendly town. It seemed that everyone that they met greeted them and welcomed them. Most people that lived on the island simply thought that anyone that they didn't know was a tourist, since tourism was one of the primary industries on the island. Most of the tourists stayed at a rental or a condo out on Sea Spray Drive, or out at the Harbor Inn, which was the island's largest hotel. A few stayed in the town at one of the three bed and breakfasts that were there. Greg wanted to find the bookstore that Arlene had been to earlier, so they all walked the two blocks down to the "Little Book Nook".

The "Little Book Nook" was exactly what you'd expect from a small island bookstore. It was in a little corner shop right in the middle of downtown. The facade was painted white with green shutters. It had a green door with a small window near the top. A brown wooden sign with green letters said "OPEN". The four of them opened the door and walked inside. Upon entering, Arlene remarked that she liked it because it even smelled like a bookstore. They all agreed that she was right, even though no one could really say exactly what a bookstore smelled like. The books were all displayed on wooden shelves, which were arranged in several rows going toward the back. The entrance was on the right side of the front, so the right wall had bookshelves attached to it as it went straight back. To the left, there were three rows of shelves along the front next to the window facing Main Street. Another five shelves were arranged perpendicular to those and faced the window along the side street. Like many of these older bookstores, the counter was in the center of the store. Probably so folks with questions wouldn't have far to walk, but also probably so the clerk could keep a watch on the patrons as well. They all fanned out and went to the sections that most interested them. Steve had always been interested in woodworking, so he went to the woodworking section. Arlene was interested in home decoration, so she went over to that section. Greg liked both computers and photography, so he found his way over to those. Dan walked over to the desk at the center of the room. A small gray haired woman with large glasses sat behind the desk. She looked to be in her late sixties or early seventies and was reading a mystery novel.

"Hello." said Dan.

She looked up from her book and placed it on the counter as she got up, and said, "Why Hello. Can I help you?"

"Possibly," replied Dan, "I'm looking for anything you might have on the old lighthouse."

"Those are always popular." she said. "If you go to the shelf along the front window, there's a really good one by Jack Carlson. His son actually still lives on the island. It's one of our best sellers."

"Already have that one," remarked Dan, "and it is a good one. I was looking to see if you might have anything else, maybe about some other stories surrounding the lighthouse that may not be available anywhere else but here on the island."

"We do have some." she said. "They're along the back wall where we keep most of the 'Local' and 'Historical' books."

"Thanks." he said as he made his way to the back of the store. There was a lot of local history represented there. Most was not about the lighthouse at all. Some detailed how the island was founded, and the first settlers that came to the island. Most of the books on the lighthouse were ones that he already had read. They contained the accounts of the most famous stories surrounding the light. He did find two that he didn't have yet that gave the account of the Greg Baker / Tim Henderson disappearance from a couple of different perspectives. One was written by one of the people that lived on the island and had joined in the search. This one was aptly named "Searching: The Unexplained Disappearance of Greg and Tim". The other, which was especially interesting, was written by Abigail Henderson, Tim's mother, and was titled "Lost - A Mother's Story". Apparently, in the years following Tim's disappearance, she had begun to write her thoughts in a diary. This continued for the next six years until her own disappearance. When her car was found out on Lighthouse Road, the diary was found on the top step out at the lighthouse. Since there was a lot of interest in the old lighthouse, Tim's brother Alan decided to publish segments from the diary which pertained to the lighthouse and disappearance. It wasn't hard to find a publisher. Especially after Abigail's disappearance, interest in the lighthouse and the area was at an all-time high. He opened up the book and began to peruse through some of the pages.

In one of the entries he read, "I can hear Tim calling to me. He's still alive. I know it. When I close my eyes, he calls to me. He doesn't know where he is. I must find him. He's calling to me day and night." On another page, she writes, "I'm going out there tonight. He's calling to me from the lighthouse. I'll go to the lighthouse and find him tonight." This was one he had to have. The other was by one of the searchers, a man named Harvey Williams. According to the cover, he was good friends with the Henderson family and was called in for the search. Since he knew the family very well, it looked as though this one might have more detail than he'd found in the past, at least about this particular story. He took these over to the check-out where Greg was already buying several computer books and magazines. Steve and Arlene were waiting out front. The lady behind the counter remarked, "I see you found some. Hmm .. I didn't even know we had this one. I don't recall ever seeing it." She was referring to the one by Abigail Henderson, Tim's mother. The other one she said she had actually read and it was definitely a suspenseful one. After checking out, Dan joined the others out front and they made their way slowly back to the Island Charm. Dan was ready to settle in for the evening and do some reading.

CHAPTER 6
March 17, 2016
Police Investigation

It was around 6:10 in the evening when Officer Mark Collins arrived out at Lighthouse Road. Mike and the rest of the crew who were clearing the land had not yet left, so the gate at the entrance was still open. Chief Callahan had given him the key to the gate and had asked him to add Lighthouse Road and the old lighthouse into his patrol schedule. Since someone had obviously been out there, Chief Callahan wanted him to do a search around the lighthouse to see if there were any clues as to who might be there. As he pulled up to the lighthouse, Mike and the crew were just finishing up for the day and were getting ready to leave. He parked his patrol car in the clearing beside the road that had been recently cleared and got out. He walked over to where Mike was loading their equipment into the truck.

"Good evening." said Officer Collins, "How's it going?"

"Pretty slow." replied Mike. "There're so many weeds and vines that it's taking a bit longer than I'd hoped. Still, I think we should be done pretty much on time."

Mark Collins was acquainted with Mike, though the two were quite a bit apart in age. Mark was 24 and had joined the police force about three years ago. He had gone to school on the island with Mike's son, Josh. They had both been on the football team together and had been pretty close friends in high school, but had lost touch since college. Josh went to a school up north and never came back to the island to live after graduation, unlike Mark, who had always wanted to raise his family here. Mark had married a girl from the mainland, Amanda Taylor, about a year ago and they were expecting their first child in October. Amanda and her parents had moved to the island about three years ago, and they met while she was working as a waitress at the Sand Crab Diner. He'd frequently stop in there for dinner while on patrol, and they would usually chat. They began seeing each other soon after that and were married in April of 2015.

"Have you seen anything unusual while you've been working out here?" inquired Mark.

"None of my men have vanished yet, if that's what you're talking about." replied Mike.

"No, not quite that dramatic." said Mark. "Dan came by the station earlier today and said that someone had been in the lighthouse. He saw their footprints in the dust and said that they'd straightened up some things that were knocked over the other day. I was just wondering if you'd seen anyone, since you've been working out here all day."

"No, can't say as I have. It's been just me and my men, and a bunch of wildlife. We must have invaded thirty or forty rabbit dens already!"

"Ok, just checking. I'm going to walk out there and check it out."

"Want me to stay around and go out there with you?" inquired Mike. "I can send the boys home and you could drop me by my house on the way back into town." At first, he was going to say no, that he had it under control, but he could tell by Mike's expression that he was really curious at this point and wanted to help look around. And it actually would be nice to have some company out here.

"Sure," replied Mark, "that would be good. Two sets of eyes and ears are better than one."

Mike told the rest of the crew to take the truck and go ahead. He wanted to stay back with Officer Collins and check on a few things. After the truck had pulled out and had gone back up the road, they both headed out to the lighthouse. Since they'd only been working at clearing the place for one day, it was still pretty grown up. They made their way slowly through the woods to the gate. About twenty feet to their left, they could see a hole in the gate where several of the stones had fallen out. They walked through the gate into the tall grass. It was around 6:30 in the evening, so they didn't have too long. Sunset was at 7:30, so it would be completely dark out here in another hour and a half. Mark did have his large flashlight, but it still would be better if they were almost finished by the time it got dark. They walked over toward the lighthouse. Mark had seen photos in books, but gazing at it now he thought it really didn't look much like the pictures. It looked a lot more run down, but he thought there was more to it than that. Shadowed against the twilight sky it looked sinister and foreboding.

"Don't look like too much right now, does it?" asked Mike. "They got a lot to do before they can move in."

As they got closer, a shadow caught Mark's eye in one of the upstairs windows. "Did you see that?" asked Mark. "Something moved in that window!"

"I think you're seeing things." replied Mike. "Being out on this part of the island's got you a little jumpy!"

"No, it's not that." said Mark. "I did see something."

They approached the back of the house and climbed the stairs leading up to the back door. Everything was completely quiet except for the sound of a light breeze blowing through the rafters. Mark went in first as they both entered the house. As they walked into the large entrance hall their footsteps echoed in the empty room. As they got to the large hole in the floor where the staircase used to be, they both looked up into the dimly lit upstairs. It was dusk now, and inside the house it was even darker than it was outside. They both paused to listen. It was eerily quiet except for the light breeze. Strange how even on a small island like this, you get used to the sound of cars and people in the town, just the general hustle and bustle of daily living. Out here there's none of that, and it's a stark contrast. Every little sound seems magnified. A slight scuffling sound came from a room upstairs and to the right. Mark heard it first, and it definitely wasn't the wind.

"Did you hear that?" he asked Mike.

"Yeah," said Mike, "Shine the light up there." Mark shined his large "Police Issue" light up into the dark area above where the stairs should be. The light shone against the bare walls and exposed rafters, but no movement could be seen.

"Could've been the wind or an animal of some kind." suggested Mike.

"Could be … didn't sound too much like the wind, though." replied Mark. He changed position and moved the light to illuminate a different area of the upstairs, but there was still nothing. There was no sound now, except for the sound of their breathing, but both of them knew that they had definitely heard something, and both knew it wasn't the wind. From their position on the ground floor, though, they couldn't really see much of the upstairs. If there was only a way to get higher and see more of the room, that would help. Mark wondered if he could even hear the sound if it came again. All he could seem to hear now was his own heartbeat beating faster in his ears, and the sound of his own breathing. He hadn't really expected to find anything. The fact was he didn't WANT to find anything. He wanted this to just be a routine check on his rounds, except he knew that this was anything but a routine check.

He knew Chief Callahan wasn't happy about the current state of events; of Dan coming to the island to open up the old lighthouse. He'd seemed really edgy since Dan and his friends had stopped by earlier that day. That part of the island where the lighthouse stood had been fenced off for the entire time that he was Chief. And that time was relatively peaceful. He really didn't want to take any chances that the peace would be disturbed. There were too many stories about the area around the lighthouse. And something definitely had happened to the two boys and their mother out there. No one knew exactly what happened to them, and it was this mystery that always nagged at him. He honestly felt that that part of the island should be left alone. Criminals and drunks he could deal with. That was part of his job as Chief. He was a big man, strong and not afraid of much. But dealing with something that he couldn't understand, that no one understood, was not something he wanted to take on. So for the past sixteen years that he was Chief, he'd been content to leave that area alone. While it couldn't be explained, he had the feeling deep inside that if that area were disturbed something would happen again. But now Dan was here and he was forced to deal with the specter of what might happen. And the feeling of dread grew stronger.

Like many others, the Callahan family was among the original families that settled the island. Chief Callahan had grown up on the island. His family and the Henderson family had been best friends for generations. In 1974, when the disappearances had occurred, he was best friends with Tim Henderson and Greg Baker. The three of them were always together, and always on an adventure. In fact, the only reason that he wasn't with them the night of the disappearance is because he had come down with a bad cold and his mother wouldn't let him out of the house. He wanted to go anyway, and tried to fake that it wasn't too bad. He tried to convince her that going to Tim's house for the night wouldn't make it any worse. He could be sick there just as well, and be having more fun in the process. Still, she said she didn't want him going off spreading germs around, and that he needed his rest more than anything else, and he wouldn't get much of that with Greg and Tim around. He thought about sneaking out anyway, but knew the trouble he'd be in the next day. Really, he knew that he didn't feel like getting out of bed anyway, so in the end mom won out. Being left behind while his best friends were on a really great adventure, though, wasn't any fun at all. He did have a hard time getting to sleep that night, wondering what they were up to. Was it as scary as they had imagined it would be?

The next day, when his friends didn't come home and there was a full scale search going on, he was in total disbelief. Should he tell his parents what he knew? That they were really going out to the lighthouse for the night. That decision was made for him, though, when a couple of police officers stopped by his house to ask if he knew anything about where they might be. They just wanted to ask a few questions, but staring into the faces of the two officers made him feel like he was the criminal. He told them what he knew, that they were planning to spend the night at the old lighthouse. He got in just as much trouble as he thought he would, and was grounded for a couple weeks after that. Probably would have been longer, except that he could tell that his mom was more than a little relieved that he wasn't with them, especially after a couple of weeks of searching turned up nothing.

He finished out high school on the island, and then decided to go off to college to study criminal justice, then on to the police academy. He had always been interested in law enforcement, though not in a big city. He liked the island and planned to come back and join the police force here. The island's Police Chief then was Kevin Lawson. He had talked with him on a lot of occasions about joining the island's police force. "Not a lot of excitement goes on here." Chief Lawson would say. But that was fine. He wasn't becoming a police officer for the excitement. He liked the calm way of life on the island and saw this as a way to preserve that way of life. He had heard of many other communities being ruined by outsiders coming in, bringing crime, and a different way of life with them. He would be sure that didn't happen here. Chief Lawson promised him a job when he came back, which after a little over four years, he did. He married a girl that he met while off at college and settled in to the life of a small island police officer.

He was on duty at the front desk that day in 1994 when the Government Guys arrived. There were three of them and they all wore matching dark grey three piece suits. They flashed their government credentials and asked to speak with the Chief. He directed them to the Chief's office and went back to his duties at the front desk. The four of them were in the office for what he felt was a long time; about four hours. He was uneasy the entire time that they were there. He couldn't really place why. Their credentials all seemed to be in order. He had dealt with government officials before, even FBI and CIA. Still, while he couldn't place it, there was something about these guys that just didn't seem right.

After the three men had left, Chief Lawson informed him that a team from the Federal Government would be coming within the week to begin fencing off the south end of the island where the lighthouse was. The effort was to be led by the Coast Guard. He was to assist them in any way that he could. Within four months that area of the island was closed off to the rest of the world, where it would remain for the next twenty two years. They used heavy gauge fencing with barbed wire at the top. It was the type of fencing that usually surrounded prison yards. He remembered wondering at the time what could possibly be in there that was important enough to keep everyone out. But, remembering the disappearances of his friends and their mother, he also thought that it could also be to keep something in. Whatever it was, they were serious about that area not being disturbed.

Mark was definitely glad that Mike was along. Neither of them knew what was up there, but both knew they had heard something. While it was quiet now, they couldn't help but wonder what was up there. They continued on down the hallway that connected the back entrance with the front, and then continued out the front door and into the yard. They walked around the side of the house where they could get a view up into the upstairs windows where they had heard the sound. The sun had just set and it was full twilight now, so it was difficult to see into the upstairs windows from the angle that they were looking. There was a large tree in front of the window as well, which made it even harder to see in. If they got further back to try and get a better angle, the tree completely obstructed their view. Mark shined the light up into the window. He thought he saw a glimpse of movement, but couldn't tell if it was really something there or just shadows from his light. It was eerily quiet now. Not a sound, not even the wind. They heard a rustling sound from the woods behind them and turned in time to see a couple of white tailed deer come crashing into the clearing. They both breathed a sigh of relief, but their hearts were still racing. Mark couldn't quite place it, but being out here made him feel really uneasy. It was a feeling not totally unlike stalking a suspect, but it was different as well. The hair stood up on the back of his neck as he turned and looked toward the house again. In the fading light, the broken down lighthouse looked even more sinister than it had earlier. It was almost like it was warning them to stay away. Mark also couldn't shake an uneasy feeling that they were being watched. He didn't know if it was from something in the house or at the edge of the woods, but suddenly the darkness seemed to close in around them. As he shined his light back up into the upstairs window the beam illuminated a thin mist that was beginning to form. The stories that he had always heard about the fog came flooding back to him now.

"Ready to go?" he asked Mike.

"Yeah," said Mike, "it's almost dark now anyway."

As they went around the side of the house heading for the trail back to the road, a skittering sound caught their attention from the upstairs window facing the rear. Startled, Mark shined the light in that direction in time to see two squirrels jump out of the upstairs window into the tree near it and begin making their way down.

"Squirrels!" remarked Mike. "That must be what we heard."

Mark agreed. "That's a relief! I can't believe we were so jumpy about a couple of squirrels!"

But his voice had an uneasiness that conveyed that he still wasn't entirely sure that was all they had heard. The fog around the lighthouse was getting slightly thicker now, but was still thin enough for them to be able to see a good distance in front of them. They made their way through the tall grass to the gate, then through the woods and out to the road to the patrol car. If they had looked back as they were leaving, they would have seen a shadowy figure in the upstairs window of the house. A figure watching their every move as they left.

Back out on the main road their mood became much more relaxed. The events of the past few minutes seemed even more distant, and they were able to convince themselves that all they really had heard were only the squirrels. Mark dropped Mike off at his house, which was at the end of a dead end road right off of Sea Spray Drive, then proceeded back to the station to check in.

Upon entering the police station, Mark almost thought the Chief had left for the day. Except for the fact that the front door was still unlocked, he probably would have thought that was the case. It wasn't unusual to find the station quiet. It was a small island and they were a small police force. Counting Chief Callahan there were five officers on the force. Three regular officers to cover all three shifts and a floating officer that could cover any shift where needed. Mark was the second shift officer. He came on duty at 4:00 pm and worked until midnight. He liked this shift. On a normal night absolutely nothing happened. The tourists were at dinner, then either perusing the shops downtown or walking along the beach. On several occasions a tourist walking south along the beach would walk far enough to encounter the fence. It usually stirred up questions, since it looked so out of place there, being made of such heavy gauge steel and with the barbed wire at the top. It went out into the ocean about fifteen feet, and then extended around the southern tip of the island. The answer given was usually that the southern part of the island belonged to the government, and they didn't want anyone out there. If the person inquired further, Chief Callahan or any of the other officers would usually tell them a little of the history. Most of the full time residents of the island were quiet. Like any community though, it did have a few that liked to stir up trouble every now and then, but those were few and easy to deal with. After all, it was a small island where all of the residents pretty much knew each other.

Mark found the Chief back in his office. He knocked on the door and the Chief motioned for him to come in. The Chief looked totally lost in thought, and confused at the same time. He was staring at several business cards that he had laid out on his desk.

"What do you make of this, Collins?" he inquired. Mark walked over behind his desk and looked at the business cards. One was Dan's card that he had given the Chief yesterday. The other three had different names on them, but all four cards had a burgundy "P" with a white starburst exploding from the center of the top of the "P". It was the Perihelion Research Group logo. The names listed on the three cards were Bill Foreman, Harvey Rollins, and Stephen Nelson.

"I recognize Dan's card, but where did the other three come from?" asked Mark.

"These are the cards that the three government men gave to Chief Lawson twenty two years ago when they came to close off the south end of the island." replied the Chief. "It looks like our Dan Nelson is the current CEO of the same government contractor that fenced off that part of the island all those years ago."

"That is unusual, sir." replied Mark.

"We need to keep a close watch on Dan and his friends." said Chief Callahan. "We need to find out why he's really here. It doesn't make sense that he would just be here to fix up the lighthouse and move his family out there when it was his company that closed it off in the first place. He's here for something else, and we need to find out what."

"Should we question him, sir?" asked Mark.

"No. Let's not let him know that we suspect anything yet. Just keep a watch on him and his friends and try to find out what they're really doing out there. Track any shipments that he has sent out here as well. Anything that could give us a hint of what he's really doing. It can't just be a coincidence that he's here now."

"What about the name on that one card, Stephen Nelson? He has the same last name as Dan. Could that be a coincidence?" asked Mark.

"Don't think so," said the Chief. "It could be his father or brother. Just keep a close eye on him, and don't tip him off that we suspect anything."

CHAPTER 7
March 23, 2016
The Campout

Dan had been thoroughly engrossed in his reading, particularly the book by Abigail Henderson, Tim's mother. He had read it through twice already, and was now on his third reading. He hadn't known quite what to expect when he purchased it. He mostly expected the ranting of a distraught mother who had just lost her son, and those were certainly there. There was an underlying tone of despair throughout the entire book. But what surprised him the most was that it was clear after reading the first couple of chapters that she seemed to not think that her son was dead. She seemed to honestly believe him to still be alive and she was on a mission to find him. She believed the lighthouse held the key to where he was, and she would drive out there and spend hours at a time, sitting, walking through the woods, and searching. It was also clear that her son Alan, who had actually written up and published her diary entries, did not share in her optimism that Tim was alive. She had written several times about how he was always trying to convince her to accept the reality that Tim was dead and was not coming back. He had even written in his preface to the book about his unsuccessful attempts to convince her. He felt that she had totally lost touch with reality and that accepting Tim's death and dealing with it would have been a first step to getting on with her life. But he was never able to convince her, no matter how hard he tried. She wrote at one point that on a visit to the lighthouse, she actually heard Tim calling for her, but was unable to find him. She had been sitting on the steps of the house, writing in her diary when she noticed a fog starting to form just outside the wall around the lighthouse. She said that she had heard Tim calling to her from the fog, but was unable to see anything since the fog was too thick. She wrote that the fog was only outside the circular four foot wall surrounding the house. Inside the wall it was completely clear. She felt like she was in a large grey tube. This was one of two instances where she wrote that she heard Tim calling her. The other was in her last diary entry on the day that she herself disappeared. In the epilogue, Alan described the search for his mother, and it was a lot like the search for Tim and Greg, and the outcome was the same; no trace of her was ever found. Dan remembered that Ben had told him that Tim's brother Alan still lived on the island. After reading the book, he thought he'd like to find Alan and talk with him. He'd definitely be able to tell him a lot more about what had happened. And the more he found out, the more he wanted to know.

It was Wednesday morning now. Dan had only been out to the lighthouse a couple of times since last week, and that was mainly at Mike's request when some things came up that needed Dan's decision, and to give Scotty the tour when he arrived. The area was still too grown up to really be able to do much anyway, so he had decided just to stay away and let Mike and his crew do their job. He wanted to do some reading as well and this would be a good time to do that. He had his two new books about the lighthouse and he was anxious to get started. He also had called around and found a company that specialized in restoration of old homes and monuments. He had planned on doing most of the work himself with the help of Scotty and Greg, but after his initial inspections of the lighthouse, he decided that he'd probably need the help of professionals. The company he had chosen, Southeast Restoration Professionals, was scheduled to come out on Friday and give him an estimate of how long they felt it would take, and the cost for a job like this. He was planning to let them do most of the major structural work, while Scotty, Greg, and he would do most of the interior finishing.

Scotty had arrived on Monday, right on schedule, and he was as jovial as ever. He was looking forward to the next several months as a sort of vacation. He liked doing this kind of work, but didn't get to do much in his current position at Perihelion. When he arrived, one of the first things that he wanted to do was take a trip out to the lighthouse. His first words when he saw it were, "Whatever were you THINKING when you bought that thing?? It just needs a good demolition crew!!" Scotty was always plain spoken this way. He was halfway joking, but his remark did clearly convey his opinion of its current state of disrepair.

"It's not as bad as it looks." said Dan.

"Even if it's not as bad as it looks, it's still near impossible!" replied

Scotty.

While he didn't say as much, that was also what Dan was thinking. After seeing the lighthouse for the first time, he had thought then that it was going to take a lot more work than he had originally anticipated. That's why he had decided to get some restoration experts out to take a look.

Dan had filled Scotty in on the mysterious person that had been out at the lighthouse, and Scotty had been a bit curious. At first he had said that it was probably nothing to worry about, but upon reflection of the security that had been around the place for the past twenty years he reconsidered. It could be nothing to worry about, but they should still be careful.

"How do you suppose they're getting in?" he inquired, "After all, that fence is pretty formidable. Nobody's just going to climb over that one!" Dan admitted that he wasn't sure. There were several miles of fence line going around the southern tip of the island, much of it covered over by forest. There must be a break somewhere along the path.

"Maybe we should walk around the perimeter of the fence and check for breaks." suggested Greg.

"Possibly," said Dan, "but from what I've seen the woods are pretty grown up around the fence. It could be pretty difficult to follow it all the way around."

Steve came up with the best idea yet, "Why don't we follow that path we saw? Remember, it broke away from the lighthouse. It has to come out somewhere near the fence, eventually." Dan remembered the path, but in all of the excitement, he had completely forgotten to mention it to Scotty.

"There's a path?" inquired Scotty.

"Yes," replied Steve, "we found it the other day when we were looking around out at the lighthouse. It comes out at the road, but it still could be a way in for someone. Dan and I were going to go out the next day and follow it further in, but we decided to wait until you got here."

"That'd be a good start." remarked Scotty. They all agreed that they'd have a look at the path, possibly during the campout.

When Greg had mentioned the idea of a campout to his dad, he was completely in agreement. Greg knew his dad well enough to know that he'd be all for the idea. They both thought a lot alike, and they both liked the outdoors. They had all gone into Wilmington on Tuesday to pick up camping supplies. They needed tents, lanterns, cook stoves, sleeping bags, the works. They had found a store that had everything that they needed. It was one of the camping big-box stores. Steve went with them as well. Since he and Dan had met, they had both become really good friends. So good in fact, that they'd likely be lifelong friends from this point on. Arlene understood. She had made several good friends as well, and was enjoying spending time with them. This was the biggest adventure of a lifetime for Steve. He'd read through the books that Dan had given him about the lighthouse, and was definitely intrigued by the mystery surrounding it. He didn't want to miss out on anything. He was already talking about extending their stay past the month that they had already reserved. They all checked out with their load of camping supplies, piled all of the newly purchased items in the back of Dan's truck, and proceeded to head back toward Southport and the ferry that would take them back out to the island.

This Wednesday morning everyone was excited. The mood was happy and playful. It had been quite awhile since Dan, Scotty, and Greg had been on a campout. Planning for a campout made him miss Danny even more, since he was usually on these campouts as well. Dan knew that even if Danny was here he wouldn't take him on this one. There was too much unknown, and the thoughts of whom or what may be out there was slightly unsettling. Still, from the mood of everyone that morning, one would not suppose that there was any danger. It was the general excited mood that comes from the anticipation of any adventure. And in fact, all of them, including Dan, had gotten lost in the preparation for the campout and had generally forgotten that someone was out there. They packed all of their gear in the back of Dan's truck. From the look of all the stuff that they were bringing along, it looked as though they were planning to be gone for much more than one night.

After packing up the truck and getting everything ready to go, the four of them decided to go back in and have some of Barbara's breakfast. Arlene was there having a good breakfast conversation with some of her new friends, but she quickly made room for Steve. She knew that he really wanted to go with the guys on this campout, but she was also slightly nervous as well, and this was making her already start to miss him. She couldn't recall many times in the past that Steve had done anything which she would consider dangerous. While this was not the type of danger like rock climbing, sky diving or wrestling crocodiles, it was the unknown that made her uneasy. While she had been ok with him going along with them several days earlier, now that it was here she was having second thoughts. "Are you sure you really want to go?" she asked.

"Of course," he remarked, "This is the most adventure I've had in my entire life. I'm not going to miss this one!"

She knew he was right. They had a good life, but it was rather ordinary, especially the last several years. Since they had never had children, it had been just the two of them for the last twenty years. The first several years had been more interesting. They had enjoyed the outdoors and had gone camping, hiking, and vacationing, mostly around Iowa and the states bordering it. The last several years, however, had caught them settling in to a more routine existence. Steve got up and went to work each morning, came home and worked out in his wood shop in the evenings, then got up and did the same thing again the next day. Weekends were usually taken up working in his wood shop. He had turned the wood shop into a fairly profitable part time business, making tables, chairs, dressers, cabinets and almost anything else that could be made out of wood. Friday was always date night, where he and Arlene would go out to dinner and catch a movie, or some other form of entertainment. But even date night had become fairly routine lately. Their life really had been devoid of any adventure for the last several years.

"OK, but be careful!" she said with a worried tone.

"Don't worry, I'll be fine." he said. "These guys will be with me. Nothing's going to happen."

They finished up their breakfast, and then got up to leave. Dan assured Arlene that he'd watch out for Steve, and that seemed to make her feel somewhat better. As they made their way out to Dan's truck, they noticed one of the island's patrol cars sitting across the street from the Island Charm. The officer seemed to be looking their way.

"Wonder what he's doing?" remarked Scotty.

"Not sure," replied Dan, "but I wouldn't think he'd be too interested in us."

They all got in the truck and proceeded out to the lighthouse. They turned onto Lighthouse Road and Dan stopped the truck to get out and unlock the gate. Since Mike and his crew had finished clearing the land, he'd been locking the gate every time he came and went. He got back into the truck and pulled through the gate. Scotty got out to lock the gate behind them, then got back into the truck and they proceeded on down the dirt road. With all of the comings and goings of the past week, it was a lot smoother now than it had been the first time that Dan had travelled down it, so within minutes they had made the one mile trip. Dan pulled off the road and parked in the clearing that Mike had cleared just off the road. Since all the overgrown brush was gone now, the lighthouse and the fence surrounding it could clearly be seen through the trees from this vantage point. Still, it was about a tenth of a mile hike out to the lighthouse from here.

They quickly went to work unpacking the gear from the truck. Along with the camping gear, they had purchased two pull carts to carry all of the gear out to the lighthouse. They piled their tents, sleeping bags, cook stove, flashlights, lanterns, and several various other pieces of gear onto the carts. Steve and Dan pulled the carts, while Scotty and Greg carried the rest of the gear and the food. It was only 8:30 in the morning, but they all wanted to get an early start to have plenty of time to set everything up and then explore the area before it got dark. Since he had been here, Dan had really only explored the area immediately around the lighthouse. He didn't have any idea what was in the woods and the adjacent areas around it. Now they'd all finally have some time to explore it.

They reached the lighthouse and decided to set up camp on the side of the house facing the woods and the road where they had just come from. They picked a spot about twenty five feet from the back door of the house. It was far enough away that the house didn't obstruct their view to the sides. They began unpacking the carts and setting up the campsite. They had two large tents, one for Scotty and Greg, the other for Dan and Steve. Within an hour they had both tents set up. The cook stoves were set up between both tents and they had four folding chairs and two small tables set up beside the cook stoves as well. It was a cool day, even for late March. They were all glad they had worn their flannel shirts and heavy jeans. Along with the camping supplies, they had purchased two stun guns as well. Dan had a Ruger LC9 9mm handgun that he kept under the seat of his truck. He had a concealed carry permit as well, so he did bring the gun along, but they had purchased the stun guns because they really didn't want to use deadly force unless it was absolutely necessary. Since they had no idea what they might be dealing with, though, they did feel that having some protection was the wise thing to do.

After the campsite was set up, they decided to set out to explore the area. They walked around to the front of the house, and were struck by the view. Earlier when they had been out there, Mike and his crew were still in the process of clearing the area. Now, with the area cleared, they had a spectacular view of the ocean. The area around the lighthouse was quite picturesque. The circular rock wall that went around the lighthouse had two gates, a front gate which led out to the sound, and a back gate which faced the woods and the road where they had entered. They approached the front gate and Dan was really amazed at how much Mike and his crew had gotten done in only one week. The area leading down to the river was cleared enough to be able to walk all the way down to the beach. They walked down to the beach and for the first time saw the fence surrounding the lighthouse from this side. The fence went out into the water about fifteen feet and stretched to the right as far as they could see, and to the left until it wound around the southern tip of the island. It rose up about ten feet out of the water and had barbed wire at the top. Looking back toward the direction that they had come, that level of security really seemed quite unnecessary. The trees back up toward the lighthouse were relatively sparse where the clearing crew had thinned them out. They started walking up the beach to their right until they got to where the woods were much thicker. They walked inland away from the water just at the edge of the woods, examining them as they walked for any signs of a trail, or any area where the growth had been disturbed. They were past the lighthouse, almost around to the back gate before they saw any signs of thinning.

"Don't see anything in there," remarked Steve, "Maybe we should check out that trail."

"Good idea," answered Dan, "it might be a good idea to see where that leads. I figure it has to run into the fence at some point."

They made their way back out to the road and walked back up it until they spotted the entrance to the trail that Steve had found earlier. It was a bright sunny day, but as they started down the trail the trees and foliage made it much darker. They were back onto the trail about a hundred feet when Greg noticed some small tree limbs that were broken off near the ground, as well as some about shoulder high. They were still green, so they had been broken off recently, probably within the last couple of days. "What do you make of this?" he asked. "These haven't been broken for that long. And from the looks of some of them, they're too high to be an animal."

"Not sure." said Scotty. "It does look pretty recent, though."

They went further down the trail to where it broke off to the right. It didn't look like a trail that was used every day, but it did look clear enough to have been used fairly often. As they went further in, the canopy of trees became thicker and it became darker. There were several times that they startled a couple of deer and rabbits. After what seemed like an hour or more, the trail ran into the fence.

"What now?" asked Scotty, "The trail ends right here." And it did look as though the trail had come to an abrupt end at the fence.

"Not sure," said Dan, "There must be something we're not seeing here."

The woods had a thick canopy here and the light that was able to get through the trees was greatly subdued. Dan pulled out his flashlight and began to survey the fence. It was overgrown with vines and had bushes and foliage at its base. Greg was the first one to notice that there was more brush and foliage to the left of the trail than there was on the right. "Look there!" he said, "The trail doesn't end here, it continues along the fence to our right!"

They all looked that direction, and in fact the trail did continue along the fence to the right moving toward the road. Dan checked the GPS on his Smartphone to try and get an approximate position for them. It looked like they were about a half mile from the Harbor Inn which was located in the direction they were moving. They had gone slightly over one mile since they first started along the trail. About thirty feet further up the trail, it seemed to end again, this time with brush, vines, and trees in front of them and to their right, and the fence, overgrown with vines on their left. Upon further examination with the light, they discovered that a section of the fence had been cut out. It was a section about four feet wide and was leaning against the other sides of the fence to form a kind of door. They pushed on it, and were able to move it to the side enough to get through the fence.

"Who do you suppose did this?" inquired Greg.

"Not sure," said Scotty, "but from the rust and weathering along the edges where it was cut, it doesn't look too recent. It could have been done years ago."

"But whoever did it could still be using it to get in." said Dan.

"Why would anyone want to get in?" asked Steve. "There's really nothing there, except for the lighthouse. And in its current state, it's not much use to anyone."

"Not sure of that either," said Dan, "but I'll mark this position on the GPS app so we can get to it from the other side."

They all went back inside the fence and moved the section back into place so as not to tip off whoever may have cut it.

As they made their way back down the trail toward camp there were several times that all of them felt like they were being followed. On a couple of occasions Scotty stopped and held his hand in the air to signal to the rest of the group to stop and be quiet as well. Each time they listened but never heard anything. The last time, they stopped and listened intently for almost three minutes, but all they heard was a gentle breeze blowing through the trees. Still, they all were sure that they were being followed. The feeling was strong and they couldn't shake it. They continued back down the trail and finally came back out at the road, where they continued to make their way back to the campsite. Upon examining the campsite, they were relieved to discover that nothing had been disturbed. The thought had crossed each of their minds while they were gone that they might come back and find all or some of their supplies missing. It was almost 2:00 in the afternoon, so they decided to unpack their supplies, fire up the cook stoves, and have some lunch. They had brought with them a cooler filled with hot dogs and hamburgers, several bags of chips, and some two liter bottles of soda, along with the hot dog and hamburger buns and the condiments. They lit the cook stoves and placed the hamburgers and hotdogs on them, along with the buns. While they ate, each of them kept looking over toward the woods and toward the direction of the road. Even though they were back at camp now, they all felt that they weren't alone. They were being watched, but they didn't know from where and by whom or what. The feeling was very unsettling for all of them, but each of them did realize that the reason for this campout was to find whoever had been out here.

After lunch they decided to explore the area of the woods on the other side of the lighthouse toward the tip of the island. They walked out the front gate and headed toward the woods on the southern side of the island. These woods had just as dense growth as the woods on the northern side. They walked along the edge of the woods toward the sound, not finding any area that really looked disturbed. At one point they startled a deer, which bounded further into the woods. They approached the beach, where they again saw the fence, protruding up from the water about fifteen feet from shore. Looking south, it appeared that they could walk down the beach quite a ways in this direction. It was clear that they were the first ones to walk along this section of the beach in decades. Greg remarked how peaceful it was, with just the sound of the wind and the waves, along with the occasional boat off in the distance. They were able to walk all the way to the southern tip of the island. As they looked around at the island's tip, they felt a lot like caged animals in a zoo. The woods were on one side of them, and the fence, wrapping around the island's tip, caged them in on the other. It was a strange feeling. They had probably walked about a mile south along the beachfront, seeing nothing unusual along the way. As they continued along to where the beach curved around, making its way toward the other side of the island, that odd, uneasy feeling of being watched came back to them. Steve felt it first this time.

"Listen!" he said.

"I don't hear anything." replied Greg.

"Does anyone else feel like we're not the only ones out here?" asked Steve.

"I've been feeling it for the past few minutes." replied Scotty. "Someone's watching us. I've been looking around, but haven't been able to see anything. They have to be in the woods."

There was no conversation for the next few minutes, as they all listened for any sound to indicate where the watcher was.

"I'm not so sure I like this." said Dan. "Maybe we should head back to camp."

They moved slowly this time, stepping quietly, and listening for any sound. They stopped abruptly as a large twig snapped in the woods beside them. They approached the woods cautiously and Dan shined his light into the darkness. Even in the daylight, it was still hard to see anything in the thick canopy of the woods, even with a light. They moved a little further up the beach, hearing nothing now.

"It could have been a deer." said Greg, wanting to provide some sort of a logical explanation.

"It could have been." answered Dan. But somehow they all knew that it wasn't. It was just a feeling, but they all felt it. They weren't alone out here, and just knowing that fact stirred the uneasiness inside them.

"Maybe the campout isn't such a good idea." said Dan as they made their way back up the beach toward the campsite.

"No, we have to see this through." said Scotty. "I'm not going to let whoever this is run us off. This is your property now, Dan, and it's us who have the right to be here. If we're going to continue with our plans over the next few months, we need to find out now who's out here. I really don't want to be looking over my shoulder all the time while we fix this place up. We need to find out now what's going on."

It was about 5:30 when they reached the campsite. It was still a few hours before dark, so they spent the remaining daylight time that they had looking over the lighthouse and planning what needed done and where to start. Dan was really anxious to hear what the restoration company's engineer would have to say when they met with him on Friday. For now, they watched and waited, all the time surveying the area around them for any signs of movement. And the darkness approached.

CHAPTER 8

Uninvited Visitor

By the time dusk came, complete darkness was not too far behind it. They had bought six propane lanterns which they lit and set around the campsite for light. They had also built a campfire, which was now going strong as they put plenty of wood on it. Each of them had purchased a flashlight as well, not the small ones, but the bright LED ones which would completely illuminate the area. They definitely didn't want to be caught in complete darkness out here. After dark in late March, the temperature really dropped. Each of them was glad they had brought their heavier coats. They all gathered close to the fire, which gave off plenty of heat as long as you were close around it. The campsite was actually inviting, with the glow of the lanterns, and the crackle and flicker of the campfire, but beyond the glow of the fire and the lanterns, the night faded off into almost total darkness. One thing in their favor was a full moon. This provided some measure of light and allowed them to see a little of the woods and the area surrounding them. It was clear skies as well, which allowed for the maximum moonlight. Even if the moon didn't give off enough light for them to see clearly for very far into the woods, it should at least allow them to detect movement, and from the events this afternoon, having at least that advantage was welcome. Dan hadn't thought that he would be this uneasy. Earlier in the day, with the sun shining brightly, he had been fine, almost looking forward to a campout with the guys. Even when they'd heard the sounds and felt the presence from the woods, he was uneasy then, but it was a different sort of uneasiness. Here, now, with the darkness all around, he was thankful for the company of his friends. Still, he wondered if four people were enough. He reached down and felt for the Ruger handgun on his belt, mostly to reassure himself that it was still there if needed. Of course, he hoped he wouldn't have to use it, but knowing that it was there made him feel a little more comfortable. He didn't know about the others, but he wondered how he could ever get any sleep tonight. Right now he was wide awake, his senses on alert for the slightest sight or sound that seemed out of the ordinary.

"Being here makes you want to tell campfire stories doesn't it?" asked Scotty. "Remember the ones that we used to tell," he inquired of Dan, "when me, you, Danny, and Greg would go camping up on Caesar Creek Lake? One of our favorites was about the Creature with green eyes that roamed the woods in that area of the country. We had Danny and Greg scared to sleep at all on those nights!"

"I wasn't really scared," answered Greg, "I just stayed up to be with Danny. He was small and needed to know that someone else was awake with him after a story like that!"

"How about the one about the four guys that went camping near an old lighthouse, and were never heard from again?" asked Scotty.

"Don't even joke about that, dad!" replied Greg.

"You never know." answered Scotty.

Steve had been listening to their stories, but he was watching and listening for other sights and sounds as well. As interesting and fun as the campfire stories were, right now they were here, it was dark, and they had definitely heard something out here earlier in the day. He supposed he might not be quite this nervous if the events hadn't happened the way they did this afternoon, but right now Arlene's concerns didn't seem so out of place after all.

They sat around the fire and talked for several hours. Occasionally they would take turns swapping campfire stories, sometimes they'd just talk about things in general. Dan talked about fixing up the place and how nice it would be to bring his family out here. He thought about the kids and how they felt about the move. He thought Danny would be fine. He had been to the ocean a couple of times before, on camping trips with him, Scotty, and Greg. He seemed to like the seashore and seemed genuinely excited about the move. Amy, on the other hand had been quieter than usual since they had planned the move. She was 13 and her best friend Veronica lived on the same street that they lived on in Cincinnati. He knew that they'd miss each other terribly, since they were hardly ever apart. Veronica's dad,

Parker, was a Senior Engineer at Perihelion, and the two families knew each other very well. Dan had told Amy that he'd invite them out to the island once they got settled in, and maybe Veronica could spend a few weeks with them during the summer. That seemed to help a little, but he could tell that Amy still wasn't really thrilled about the move.

It was about 10:30 pm. Steve had gotten up to stretch his legs, while Greg pulled out some snacks and drinks for them. Steve walked around the side of the house and looked out at the moon shining off of the still water of the river. He was almost out of range of the glow of the lanterns, and the night seemed really peaceful. Even though the night seemed peaceful, he still felt an uneasiness. A cold breeze blew in from the water and a chill ran through him for a second as he zipped up his jacket further. As he turned to go back over to the campsite, a movement caught his eye over by the woods. He froze where he was and stared intently in that direction. He wasn't seeing anything, even in the moonlight. It was like one of those moments when you see something out of the corner of your eye, but when you look straight at it, what you thought you saw seems to disappear. He took a few steps in the direction of the woods, all the time never shifting his gaze from the spot where he saw the movement. As his eyes adjusted to the moonlit scene, he could almost make out the shape of a man standing just inside the edge of the woods. His heartbeat increased as he stared in the direction of the man. Was it really someone standing there, or just a shadow in the edge of the woods. He had to be sure, so he took a few more steps in that direction. The man didn't move. He seemed frozen in place just as Steve had been a few moments earlier.

"Hey! Did you get lost out there?" called a voice from the direction of the campsite. It was Dan. He had been so intently staring in the direction of the woods, blanking everything else out of his mind that the voice startled him and he looked away from the woods to the direction of the voice. He could see Dan, silhouetted against the glow of the fire, standing, looking in his direction. He didn't say a word, but raised his arm to motion for Dan to be quiet, and then he looked back in the direction of the woods. He pointed in the direction where he had seen the man, hoping that Dan would see him too. After looking toward the campsite and the fire, his eyes had to readjust to the moonlight shining on the edge of the woods. He wasn't making out the shape any more, and he wondered if it had been there at all. Dan came up beside him and joined him in the clearing.

"What is it?" he asked.

"I saw someone standing over by the edge of the woods." said Steve.

"Where?" asked Dan.

"He was over by those trees, near that big pine over there. But I'm not seeing him now."

"Could it have been a shadow in the moonlight?" asked Dan.

"It could have been," said Steve, "but I was sure that I saw some movement over there right before I saw the man."

"Stay here." said Dan as he walked back over to the campsite. He returned with two flashlights.

"Let's go check it out." he said. "Greg and Scotty can stay back at camp in case he comes around from another direction."

Dan had also brought one of the two-way radios that they had picked up at the camping store as well for times that they may have to separate. He keyed the mic and talked into the radio, "Scotty, can you hear me?"

"Loud and clear," said Scotty, "You two be careful out there."

"Don't worry, we will." said Dan. He and Steve then walked toward the river and went out the front gate.

They turned right and walked a little way around the wall, then started toward the woods. While the moonlight lit the way fairly well, Dan still used his flashlight to illuminate the area right in front of them where they were walking. As they approached the woods, they actually heard the loud crack of a branch breaking. They froze in their tracks. It could be a deer, or a raccoon, or any of a number of other animals that might be out there. They convinced themselves that was what it was, partly because they really didn't want to think about what else it could be. They were whispering now.

"Exactly where did you see him?" asked Dan.

"Over there by that big pine tree." said Steve.

They walked over toward that direction. That familiar feeling of being watched came back to them. They looked back toward the camp, and could see the outlines of Scotty and Greg, both standing now, no doubt looking in their direction. They turned their gaze back to the woods. Dan shined his light into the woods where Steve had seen the man. He surveyed the brush for any sign that someone had been there. It was difficult to tell with the area being so overgrown and it being so dark. He shined the light higher and deeper into the woods. The light met with two glowing eyes staring back at them. Their hearts were racing now, as they both gasped and froze where they were. As they looked into the eyes that were staring back at them, they realized it was only a deer, and he was probably just as scared as they were. He'd probably lived around here for years and this was the first flashlight that he'd seen. They also realized that if the deer were this close, that the man was gone, if there ever was a man. As they moved the light away from the deer, he went bounding deeper into the woods. They turned and began walking back toward camp.

Back at camp, they discussed what Steve might have seen.

"It could have been the deer that you saw." suggested Greg. "From that distance and in the shadows, if the deer were standing just right, it could have looked like a man."

"Possibly," agreed Steve, "but something about it just didn't look like an animal. The way it moved when I first saw it, definitely reminded me of a man."

"We'll probably never know," said Dan, "but if it was a man, he was watching us and he knows we're here."

"We probably won't get much sleep tonight!" replied Greg. And he was basically right. It was a little after midnight, and they were all still awake with the fire burning brightly. They were all tired, but with their senses on alert it was difficult to get to sleep. They talked and sometimes dozed off for a few minutes, but one of them was always awake. They had brought some blankets with them, which they wrapped up in while sitting around the fire, since the night was getting colder. Every once in awhile one of them would get up and walk over to the edge of the campsite and look over into the woods and out toward the river. It was a peaceful night, not much sound at all out here. A slight breeze blew in from the water, adding to the chill in the night air.

It was around 2:20 in the morning. Everyone had finally turned in about an hour earlier. The sleeping bags in the tents were so warm that even with the excitement of the day, and the uncertainty of who might be out here, none of them had much of a problem getting to sleep after all. The fire had died down to a few smoldering embers by now, so it wasn't giving off much warmth. The night was still and cold as they slept. Suddenly, though, Greg was wide awake. He wasn't sure exactly what had wakened him, but apparently whatever it was hadn't awoke his dad, who was still sound asleep in the sleeping bag beside him. He lay awake, listening to the night sounds. Everything seemed still and quiet, yet he still felt an uneasiness. He didn't know if he had reason to be uneasy or not. Perhaps this was one of those times where you're awakened by a dream and have no real reason to be anxious. We've all had those times, where we suddenly wake up in the middle of the night, not knowing if it was a sound that had awakened us, or simply a dream that we were having. But at this time, his senses were all on alert. He strained to listen for the faintest sound, not hearing anything. He sat up and looked around. Scotty was still sleeping peacefully. Since he was awake now, he slipped out of his sleeping bag and unzipped the door to the tent. Slipping on his coat, he walked outside and was struck by how dark it had become. The moon, which had illuminated the area earlier in the evening was now setting, and was so low on the horizon that it could barely be seen through the trees. He went back into his tent to get his flashlight, which he had placed beside his sleeping bag before going to sleep. He came back outside, switched it on, and then did a quick survey of the area around the campsite. Seeing nothing, he trained his light on the lighthouse. Illuminated by the beam of his light, the lighthouse looked like something out of a horror movie. His light cast shadows on the interior walls as it shone through cracks in the exterior. The moss and vines that were growing up around the walls gave it a really creepy look at this time of the morning. He walked over toward the house, still shining his light around the outside. It was an odd feeling being the only one awake in this lonely area of the island at this time of the morning. He almost wished someone else would wake up and join him. He walked around the side of the house and shined his light out toward the woods where Steve had thought he saw the man earlier. While the light did cast shadows, nothing appeared out of the ordinary there now. He walked a little way out toward the wall surrounding the lighthouse. As he stopped, near the wall, he felt a chill run through him, he thought partially caused by the chill in the night air, and partially caused by his imagination of what might be out here. He turned to walk back toward the house and the campsite. Since nothing seemed amiss, maybe he could lie back down and get some sleep before morning.

As he approached the house from the side, he moved his light up to one of the upstairs windows and froze in his tracks, his heart racing. There, staring back at him from the now glassless window was a face. It appeared to be an old man with a long white beard. While he couldn't see the man's face very well because of the beard, he could tell that he had a very disheveled appearance. His hair appeared not to have been combed, and his beard wasn't very neatly groomed. The man didn't move at all, but just continued to stare down at him. He couldn't find the strength to move from the spot where he was standing. Staring at the man, feeling really alone out here at this time of morning, he wished that he had woke up his dad to come with him. He felt all of the blood rush out of his face, and his body shook from the cold and with fear. While there was nothing particularly scary about the man's appearance, just the fact that he was here, where no one was expected to be, was unnerving. What was he doing here? Was he the one that was watching them earlier? To his relief, out of the corner of his eye he saw a light come on in Dan's tent. Hopefully Dan would come outside and over to where he was. He looked toward the campsite to see if Dan was coming out, and then looked back up at the window. The face was gone.

The fact that the face had disappeared from the window was almost worse than seeing it staring back at him, because this meant that he didn't know where the man was. The man could leave the house and surprise him from any direction. He looked back over toward the campsite, and this time he did see Dan, flashlight in hand, looking around the campsite. Dan must have awakened, pretty much the same as he had. He hadn't heard a sound, and presumably Dan hadn't either. He had purposely tried to be quiet so as not to wake the others. Dan shined his light in his direction, illuminating him in its beam.

At first, from a distance, he didn't immediately recognize Greg, and seeing someone standing over by the house had startled him. But within a few seconds he realized that it was Greg and he started walking that direction. As he approached Greg, and while still several dozen yards away from him, they both heard a crash from inside the house. Greg had seen the man, so he could figure that was the source of the crash, but Dan had just woken up, so he was completely taken by surprise. He picked up his pace and broke into a run toward Greg and the house. Scotty and Steve had heard the crash as well, and were now exiting their tents, flashlights in hand. Both had noticed that Greg and Dan were missing, but in the excitement, didn't really pause to figure what that meant. Assuming that the crash had come from the house, they both shined their lights in that direction, and immediately saw Dan and Greg.

"What was that crash?" asked Dan.

"Somebody's in the house!" replied Greg. "It's an old man. I saw him in the upstairs window looking down at me."

By this time Scotty and Steve had joined them and all of their lights were trained toward the house.

"Did you recognize him?" asked Scotty. "Was it someone you may have seen around town?"

"No," replied Greg, "I've never seen him before. I don't have any idea who he might be."

They decided to split up into pairs and go around opposite sides of the house. They didn't want whoever was in there to be able to slip out undetected. Greg and Scotty went around the back of the house, near the woods and the campsite. Dan and Steve went around front. While there were holes, some of them large enough for a man to get through, at various places around the house, the front door and the back door were the only entrances that they knew of. Now they all approached these doors, shining their lights as they went. They climbed the brick staircases to the porches on either side of the house, and looked inside. The flashlights cast harsh shadows on the interior, but no discernible movement could be detected. They all proceeded to go inside, each light shining toward the upstairs area where the staircase used to be. They all stopped and listened. Nothing could be heard. The air was completely still, and not even a breeze was blowing through the house now. Even if there was a sound, however, they might not be able to hear it, since all any of them could hear now was the sound of their own heartbeat, beating louder in their ears, drowning out all but the loudest sounds. They moved to try and get a better vantage point, to shine their lights into more of the upstairs area. No movement could be seen. Since the loud crash that all of them had heard earlier, not another sound had been heard from inside the house. Now they all heard what sounded like faint movement, not from upstairs, but from the area further behind where the staircase would have been. They walked down a short hallway and into a back room on the right. The room was filled with broken furniture, a table along the right wall, and a sink near the back. They saw a door straight back from where they entered. They approached it carefully, not knowing whether the man was inside. As Scotty carefully opened the door, the rest shined the lights inside. It was a small storage room, roughly half the size of the other room. There were no windows in this room, and all three walls were lined with built in shelves containing pottery jars, most were broken. Looking around this room, they determined that there would be nowhere in this room for anyone to hide. As they went back out into the other room, they heard movement from the other side of the wall to their right. There was an old cabinet leaning against this wall, along with other debris. It didn't appear to have a door anywhere, but as they studied it carefully, shining their lights, Steve noticed some door molding slightly visible behind the cabinet. The cabinet was definitely tall enough and wide enough to completely hide a door if there was one there. Dan moved some of the old wood and debris from around the cabinet so that they could get a better look. As they peered around the back of the cabinet, they saw what was definitely a door. They all began clearing the rest of the debris from around the cabinet, enough so that they could attempt to move it. It was heavy. Opening the cabinet doors revealed that it was a tool cabinet. Old tools from the 1800s and early 1900s were stored in it, most of them rusty but still in fairly good condition. Being in the cabinet had largely protected them from the elements. The top shelf contained glass jars and the skeleton of a dead rat. They removed the contents of the cabinet to make it easier to move, and then all four of them got beside it and began to move it away from the wall enough to be able to get the door open. The cabinet was hand crafted out of hardwood, so even with all four of them engaged in moving it, it was still remarkably hard to move. It took a few minutes, but it was finally away from the wall enough for the door to be opened.

The door itself didn't look as though it would be too hard to get open. There were several holes, some quite large, where the wood had rotted out. Even if it were locked, which it didn't turn out to be, a few pushes on the door would move it right out of the way. As they opened the door, the rotten wood tore loose from the rusty hinges, and it crashed onto the floor inside. They shined their lights into the room. This one was different than the others. This room was round. As they went inside and shined their lights up toward the ceiling, they realized that they were inside the base of the lighthouse. A wooden staircase, with many of the stairs either missing or in a state of disrepair, spiraled upward into darkness. Out of the corner of his eye, Scotty saw movement over behind a small makeshift wooden wall. He motioned for the others to shine their lights over in that direction. As they did, an explosion of wood and debris came falling down as a man darted out from behind the wall. He quickly exited through a small four-foot high door that they had previously not noticed over along the wall to the side directly opposite the door where they had entered. They all went through the door after him, pausing a few seconds after they got outside to listen and determine which way he went.

Hearing footsteps running along to their right, they immediately headed in that direction. They shined their lights in the direction of the footsteps and saw the man. He was fast and had gotten quite a bit ahead of them in the time that it had taken all four of them to get through the small door. They were now running as fast as they could, but still being careful since they weren't familiar with the terrain. They didn't want to fall into any holes or trip over any trees or bushes that they didn't know were here. Even moving as fast as they dared, they weren't closing the gap between them and the man very fast. He had run around the side of the house and was now headed for the back gate. He ran through the back gate and turned left toward the woods, moving parallel to the road. They all knew that he would know the woods much better than they did, and that if he reached them first, which it looked like he was definitely going to do, that they would surely lose him. They tried to run even faster as they rushed through the back gate and turned toward the woods themselves. They could still see him in the beam of their lights, but it looked like he was getting even further ahead. Since he knew the area better, he could go faster than they could in the darkness.

"What's that over to the right?!" yelled Scotty. They all slowed down just enough to turn and look over to the right. Up ahead and to their right, they all saw a light coming from the direction of the road. From the erratic up and down motion of the light, they surmised that it was a flashlight being carried by another unknown person who was also running. At first, they thought that he was coming toward them, but they quickly saw that he also was running toward the man that they were pursuing. "Looks like we've got more company!" exclaimed Steve. They all continued to pursue the man that they had seen in the lighthouse, who was getting closer and closer to the woods every second. They had lost more distance after being distracted by the light coming from the road, so they were now even further back. The appearance of the second man concerned Dan. The four of them felt like they could handle one man, but now the odds were doubled and if a conflict arose, it would be two against four. They wouldn't have near the advantage. He was also nearer to the fleeing man than they were, and would definitely reach him first.

As they continued the chase, getting nearer and nearer to the woods, the second man caught up to the first and appeared to tackle him. They both went down, their flashlights flying and landing a few feet away. As they approached, there didn't appear to be much of a scuffle. Both men were getting up, the second definitely holding onto the first. As the four of them approached the two men, who were now on their feet, and shined their lights on them, they immediately saw that the new man who had come from the direction of the road was wearing the uniform of the island's police force. The other man, the one that they had been pursuing, looked to be in his seventies, with a full white beard and moustache. He was slightly shorter and thinner than Scotty, though not by too much. He was dressed in jeans with a leather bomber jacket. They could see now that they were upon them, that the police officer seemed to know the old man. After about thirty seconds of trying to catch his breath, he finally said, "Bill, what on earth are you doing out here?!"

"You know him?!" inquired Dan.

"Yeah," said the police officer, "He's Bill Henderson. He's the father of Tim, one of the boys that disappeared out here in the seventies."

CHAPTER 9
March 24, 2016
More Questions Than Answers

As they looked at the scene in front of them, they were both relieved and bewildered. Dan hadn't known what to expect when he first discovered someone had been out at the lighthouse. He couldn't think of any reason for anyone to be there, which had led to all kinds of speculation. Since the area had been locked off for decades, he had figured it would be the perfect place for a wanted criminal to hide out. He figured that due to the remoteness of the place, that drug deals could happen there, without fear of anyone spotting them. But an old man in his seventies, and the father of one of the boys that had disappeared as well, was totally unexpected. He was relieved, though. Seeing the old man dispelled any fear of danger that he was thinking. Again the officer asked, "What are you doing out here, Bill?"

"Are you going to arrest me, Mark?" Bill asked. Obviously Bill knew the officer as well.

"It depends." said the officer. "These men have every right to press charges. After all, you were trespassing on their property."

The officer turned to Dan and offered him his hand. "I'm Officer Mark Collins." he said.

"Dan Nelson." replied Dan, "And these are my friends, Steve, Scotty, and Scotty's son Greg."

"Nice to meet you," replied Officer Collins, "though I wish it were under different circumstances."

"Again," asked Officer Collins, "What are you doing here, Bill?"

Bill hesitated for a moment. He didn't want them to think he was completely crazy. That might destroy any chance that he had of continuing what he came here to do. He didn't know these four men, so he didn't know how they felt about him being here.

"I'm looking for them, Mark." he finally said, "I think there's a chance that they're alive, and if there is, I want to find them." Dan knew immediately that he was talking about his wife and son.

"Bill, we've been over this before." replied Officer Collins. "It's been forty years. The police back then turned over every square inch of this island looking for them. They haven't been seen since then. I know you need to keep them alive in your memory, but they're just not here!"

"No, not in my memory!" said Bill. "They're here, and they're alive! Don't know quite how to explain it, but it's the fog. They're in the fog!"

He knew immediately that he had said too much. No chance of them not thinking him crazy now. But Dan was very interested in that last statement. "What do you mean, about the fog?" he asked.

Knowing that he had probably said more than he should have, Bill really didn't want to continue this line of questioning. He knew what he knew, but what he knew would be pretty hard for anyone who hadn't actually been there to believe. But he had opened the door, and now the questions would come.

After pondering the question for a minute, trying to decide exactly what to say, he finally replied, "The fog's different out here. It has a feel and texture not like anything I've ever encountered." Then turning to Dan, he said "Until you arrived I had been coming out here observing it. It's always a thick fog, never just a light mist. Even bright lights don't see very far into it. It's like it doesn't belong here. A professor friend of mine thinks it might be an 'alternate plane of existence' as he called it, and while I don't know much of what that is, I'm inclined to agree."

"Why do you think Tim and Abigail are in the fog?" inquired Dan.

"Because I've heard them." replied Bill, "It's definitely them."

"This is all very interesting," interrupted Officer Collins, "but if these boys are interested in pressing charges, we need to get back to the station and start the paperwork."

"I don't see any need to press charges," replied Dan, "no harm's been done."

"Well, if that's how you feel," said Officer Collins, "that'll make my job a lot easier tonight. If you want to come with me, Bill, I'll drop you off by your house and these boys can get back to their campout."

"Wait!" said Dan, "How would you like to finish out the night with us, Bill? You came out here to observe and I don't see any need to cut your night short. I'd actually like to hear more."

"Thanks, but I think I'll just go along with Mark here." replied Bill. "I'm actually getting pretty tired. Thanks for not pressing charges."

"OK," said Dan, "but if you decide you'd like to come by later, here's my card. We're staying over at the Island Charm."

In reality, Bill did want to speak with Dan. After all, Dan was the new owner of the lighthouse. If he had any hope of finding Tim and Abigail, he'd need to work with Dan to continue. But he needed a little time to think about exactly how he wanted to approach the subject. And being bombarded by questions out here in the early morning hours by four men that he didn't even know wasn't what he had in mind. He didn't want to come across as crazy. He knew he wasn't. He knew what he'd seen and heard out here. But to anyone else, his story would sound impossible, and possibly like he'd lost his mind. It just wouldn't fit with any normal person's perception of the world and what could be true and what couldn't. In the end, he'd decided to go along home and have time to think about what he'd say.

After Bill and Officer Collins had left, the four of them went back to the campsite. It was close to 3:30 in the morning by now. The last hour had been eventful. They were all tired, but after all of the excitement, none of them were really sleepy. Scotty went to the cooler and got a drink for himself and the others and they went back around to the fire, which had long since gone out. Greg brought over some more wood from the pile that they had put at the edge of the campsite earlier, and within minutes they had a warm roaring fire again.

"What do you think of Bill?" asked Greg.

"Quite a character!" said Scotty, "I think he actually BELIEVES his wife and son are in the fog!"

"You don't believe they could be?" asked Dan.

"Come on now!" remarked Scotty. "Don't tell me you actually believe his story could be true! That 'alternate plane of existence' works fine for Scotty Borland and the crew of the Perihelion, but this is the REAL world. Things like that just aren't possible!"

"You surprise me Scotty!" said Dan. "There was a time that you'd have believed anything like that was possible! You'd even go out and try to prove it!"

"I was younger back then, and more willing to accept the impossible." replied Scotty.

"Still," replied Dan, "there may be something to his story."

"He's a crazy old man who, sadly, lost his wife and son and has spent the last forty years thinking about them and holding on to the possibility that they may still be alive. He needs them to be alive, so his mind thinks up ways that it could be possible, however impossible those ways may seem to the rest of us." replied Scotty, "That's all it is."

Steve, who up until this point had just been listening and absorbing the conversation chimed in, "But what if that's not all it is? SOMETHING's been going on out here. I've read the Jack Carlson book that Dan loaned me. SOMETHING happened to those boys. Maybe his wife and son aren't actually alive in the fog, but apparently the fog is real, and apparently things happen when it comes in."

"Come back to earth guys!" Scotty replied, "Do you hear what you're saying?!"

"I know," said Steve, "And it is pretty unbelievable, and until this trip I wouldn't have even stopped to consider it myself, but being out here, you have to admit, does bring up questions."

"Questions, yes!" said Scotty, "There are a lot of questions, and I'll admit, I don't have the answers. But the things he's talking about, like his wife and son still being alive in the fog after forty years?! Well, that just can't happen."

"Maybe not," replied Dan, "but when I bought this lighthouse, it was partly because I wanted to find out what happened. I had grown up with these stories all my life since first visiting the lighthouse. I'm not simply going to dismiss him as a crazy old man. I'd actually like to talk to him and find out what he knows; or what he thinks."

"That's fair." said Steve. "What happened here is an interesting story. I'd actually like to know more myself."

When the sun came up, they all packed up their camping supplies and drove back into town. When they arrived back at the Island Charm, Barbara was just starting to serve breakfast. Arlene was there and jumped up when she saw Steve and gave him a big hug. "Well, how was it?" she inquired.

"You won't believe it!" Steve replied. "Let's sit down to breakfast and I'll tell you all about it." The aroma from the kitchen was just too inviting. They all sat down to breakfast, and Steve and the others told them the whole story from the night before. It seemed to make Arlene even more worried, though. Just knowing that there really was someone out there made her want to keep Steve home and safe. This time it was just a harmless old man, but what about next time. Still, she could tell by the excitement in Steve's voice that he'd go the next time as well. Nothing would stop him from going, and she probably shouldn't even want to try. He'd found new friends and was having the adventure of a lifetime. Barbara had been listening intently to the conversation while serving breakfast.

"What do you suppose Bill was really doing out there?" she inquired of anyone willing to answer.

"Not sure just yet," replied Dan, "but from what I know right now,

I'd say he really was looking for his wife and son. I want to talk with him some more, though."

Hank, Barbara's husband, had been sitting over in the corner of the room seeming to be reading his morning newspaper, but he had mostly been listening to the conversation. He got up and walked over to where everyone was having breakfast, sat down, and began spooning himself some grits and eggs into a plate.

"I'd leave it alone if I were you." he said, "I've been here for around two years now. It's a nice place to live, quiet and peaceful. Since we moved here, I've become pretty good friends with Bill. He's not crazy, I can tell you that, but he does have an obsession. Since talking with that professor from over at Wilmington, he's become obsessed with finding his wife and son. However impossible it may be, that professor's convinced him that they may still be alive. But I've told him the same thing that I'm telling you; leave it alone. I've told him that whatever he's hearing in the fog, it's not Abigail and Tim. It can't be! This time you were lucky, it was just Bill out there. Next time, who knows? I haven't been able to convince Bill to stay away, and from the looks of it I won't be able to convince you either, but I wish I could. I don't know what's out there, but something is. Don't know why the fog comes up either, or why the fog out there feels different than any fog I've ever seen. All I know is that it IS there, and it's not normal. I believe that Bill has heard something in the fog. I'll let him tell you about it, he's the one that's actually been into the fog. I'm sure he'll tell you. But be careful! Bill's so obsessed with finding Tim and Abigail that he's losing a sense of reality. He's taking chances, and he's not being as cautious as he ought to be. I've told him before, 'Leave it alone! It's not Tim and Abigail!' But he won't listen."

"What do you think causes the fog?" asked Dan.

"Don't know," replied Hank, "but like I said, it's not like any fog I've ever seen. It seems to wrap around you and pull you into it. Whatever Bill tells you about it, just believe me, it's not safe. If you're out there and it comes up, don't go into it! You might not make it back out."

After breakfast, Dan, Scotty, Greg and Steve went up to their rooms to get some sleep since they hadn't slept much the night before.

Even though he was tired, it was still difficult for Dan to get to sleep. Too much had happened in the last twenty four hours and he was still pondering what Bill and Hank had said. He wondered what he had gotten into. It all seemed so amazing and impossible. Yet as Steve had pointed out, something had happened out there. Greg, Tim, and Abigail had disappeared without a trace. There were the stories by Colonel Forrest and his men. And there was the fog, and whatever was causing it. What secrets did the fog hold? He knew that he had to talk with Bill. He obviously knew more about the fog than possibly anyone else on the island. Scotty had simply dismissed him as a crazy old man, but after all, wouldn't losing both your son and then your wife within just a few years, and not knowing what had happened to either of them make you a little crazy? But Hank had said Bill wasn't crazy. He felt like Hank knew more than he was telling them as well. He seemed really insistent that they stay away from the lighthouse, and even though he was a big man, the tone of his voice seemed to indicate that this insistence was driven at least partly by fear. Still, he couldn't imagine Hank being afraid of much. As he continued to lay there and think more about the events of the previous night, he started thinking about Officer Collins as well. What was he doing out there at that time of the morning? He was so quick to join in the chase that he had to be watching them. But why? The only thing that he could think of was that since he had reported someone being out there to Chief Callahan, that maybe he sent Officer Collins to keep an eye on them to keep them safe. But why would he do that? While he still reasoned that it must be to protect them, something about the whole situation just didn't feel right. It bothered him more than he felt like it should, but he couldn't figure out why? Did the Chief know more than he was telling them as well? As he lay there somewhat longer, staring at the ceiling, he remembered the meeting at the police station when he had first met Chief Callahan. It had been a perfectly normal conversation up until he gave the Chief his business card. He thought back to the look on the Chief's face and the odd tone in his voice as he looked at the card. It was almost like he had seen the card before and it reminded him of something. Dan supposed that he could have seen a Perihelion business card before with all of the people that worked for the company. Still, even if he had, why the perplexed look and the change in his tone? The more that he tried to make sense of everything, and think of all of the details, then piece them all together, the more that he realized that he still didn't have enough of the pieces. He finally drifted off to sleep, still going over the day's events in his mind.

CHAPTER 10

Bill's Story

Dan was suddenly wide awake, staring at the ceiling. For a moment he couldn't think of where he was. Then he heard a knock at his door. That must have been what had awakened him. He looked over at the window. There was still some light shining through it, so it was still daylight out. He glanced at the alarm clock by the bed which read 4:38. Again, there was a knock at the door. He sat up and got out of bed. It's always difficult waking up when you're awakened suddenly. He slowly made his way to the door and opened it. To his surprise, there was Bill. He had expected to have to go looking for him, but Bill had found him instead.

"Come in." said Dan.

Bill stepped into the room as Dan switched on a light. The two men stared at each other for a minute, both trying to find the right words. Finally, Bill spoke up, "First of all, keep an open mind about what I'm going to tell you. I haven't told this to many people, probably because most would think I was crazy. I wouldn't have believed me either if I hadn't seen and heard it for myself. My son Alan thinks I've pretty much lost my mind. He's as much as said so. But I haven't."

"OK," said Dan, "let's sit over here on the sofa and talk. I've been wondering about what happened here on the island for years, I'll keep an open mind."

"Let's go over to the diner." Bill suggested, "I'm getting a little hungry and we can talk on the way."

Dan grabbed his jacket, locked up his room, and the two of them headed down the stairs and out into the brisk air. Bill began, "I wanted to have this conversation between just you and me. I'm sure the others are fine men, and I'll let you discuss with them what you want. But I'm more comfortable just talking one on one, especially about the events at the lighthouse."

Dan was definitely more than a little curious by this point.

"It's really amazing how fast things can change." continued Bill. "One day you have the life you've always dreamed of having, a loving wife, great kids; everything's going just how you planned it. Then in an instant that's all taken away. The worst part of it is not knowing what happened. Wherever Tim was, did he miss us? Was he hoping we'd find him? Or was he dead? If he was, exactly how did he die? Did he die instantly, or did he have time to think about dying? Was it painful? These thoughts kept going around and around in my head until I thought I really was going crazy. Day and night, I obsessed with these thoughts. Still, me and Abigail never talked about it. Our lives had been changed forever, just in the short time between Friday and Saturday night. Nothing about the last forty two years is how I had it planned. After Tim disappeared, me and Abigail just went through the day almost in a daze. We didn't talk much, and we'd sit and stare out the window for hours. Luckily Alan was in his first year of college at UNC Wilmington, so he was away from home most of the time. We weren't very good parents to him after Tim disappeared. I guess we sort of drove him away. He started going home with friends for the holidays and even started spending his summers away from home, so it was mostly just me and Abigail. We didn't talk about Tim at all. Gradually even the two of us began to drift apart. When Alan got married, we did go to the wedding, but had really only met his new bride a couple of times before that. He still lives here on the island, but I've probably only seen him two or three times in the last year. We just haven't been close.

"Several years after Tim's disappearance, Abigail began going out to the lighthouse. She said it brought her some comfort and helped her deal with the situation. I followed her once without her knowing, and found her just sitting on the lighthouse steps staring at the ocean and writing in her journal. She had started keeping a journal after Tim disappeared. I didn't let her know I was there, I just watched for awhile then went on back to the house. This was her alone place, her place for dealing with the loss. Apparently, she spent a lot of the time out there just writing in her journal. I guess just being out there, at the lighthouse, at the last place that Tim had been, helped her cope. Usually, after she'd been out at the lighthouse, she'd come home kind of sad and depressed. She wouldn't say much, she'd just come in and go into the sitting room. She did this same routine for a little over a year. I'd usually just stay around the house, or sometimes go over and visit with Joe Rogers over at the Harbor Inn. We'd mostly just talk, and sometimes I'd help him with some of the repairs that needed done around the Inn. It was good to have someone to talk to, since Abigail didn't talk much those days. She just couldn't move on. After Alan went off to college Tim was her life, and now that was taken away. I missed him too, but I was trying to get on with my life, trying to at least be some kind of a father to Alan. She couldn't seem to get her life back together.

"One night, though, was very different, and at the same time really strange. After she had been out at the lighthouse, instead of coming home and quietly going into her sitting room, she burst into the house really excited! This change caught me completely off guard. I could hardly get her to slow down as she was telling me her story. 'Tim's alive!' she had shouted. 'I heard him! He's not dead after all!' Well, you can imagine that I really didn't know what to do or say at that point. This was the last thing that I had expected to happen on that night. 'What do you mean … Alive!?' I had asked. 'Yes,' she had replied, 'I talked to him! Well, not talking to him really, but I heard his voice, and I'm sure he heard mine!' 'Where was he?' was all I could think to ask. Obviously she believed that she had heard Tim. But how was that possible? 'He was in the fog!' she had replied. Apparently, according to the story that she told me, she had been sitting on the steps of the lighthouse. As she was sitting, writing in her journal, a really thick fog came up, almost out of nowhere. She said that it circled the entire lighthouse, but didn't come inside the rock wall. She went over and touched the fog, and said it had an odd feel to it as it wrapped around her hand. She said that while she was standing there looking into the fog, she heard a voice. She said that it was far away at first but began coming closer. She said she had definitely recognized it as Tim's voice. But I knew that it couldn't be Tim. He'd been missing for almost five years by this time. Still, she remained insistent. She called to him and when he replied back to her, she said his voice sounded a lot closer. She said the fog was thick so he probably couldn't go very fast, and possibly got confused as to the direction. She said that at one point he had asked, 'Mom? Is that you?' At the time, I wasn't sure what to make of that one, but later I understood. Anyway, a little bit before she felt like he was close enough that he could just step out of the fog and be back with her again, the fog began to get thinner and thinner until it disappeared entirely. After the fog was gone she said that she couldn't hear him anymore. But she felt like she had heard him, and if it happened once then it could happen again."

By this time they had reached the diner. Dan opened the door and held it for Bill to go inside. They made their way to the cash register, where a server picked up two menus from a tray on the side of the table and motioned for them to follow. They followed her as she weaved between tables to finally seat them at a table for two along the back wall of the diner. Shortly after, their server came and took their order. Dan ordered a ham and cheese deli sandwich with chips, and Bill ordered the fish dinner with fries.

"So what do you think it was that she heard?" asked Dan.

"That's the part that I wouldn't have believed myself until about three years ago." replied Bill, "I think she actually heard Tim."

"Why do you think that?" asked Dan.

"This might be hard for you to believe," replied Bill, "and if I were in your place I honestly don't think I'd believe me either, but I've heard them, and talked to them. Not both at the same time, it was on different occasions, but I did talk with them, and they answered me. Greg Baker was there too, with Tim. I'm not really sure how that could be, I don't understand much about those things, but I know that I heard them and they heard me. That's why I believe what I do. I'll get into this in more detail later, but first let me continue. As I was saying, Abigail believed that she heard Tim. And she began going out there more often. At that time, I really didn't believe her. Of course, I didn't tell her that. She seemed so excited, and more alive with hope than I'd seen since the boys disappeared. But it couldn't have been Tim that she heard. That's what I thought at the time." They both paused for a moment as the server brought their food and refilled their drinks. Bill continued, "As I was saying, she began going out to the lighthouse more often. Most days, she didn't hear anything, and some days the fog didn't even appear. But she was still energized into believing the impossible."

A different look came over Bill's face now. He looked away and stared out the window for a moment before continuing, "One day, I woke up and had a strange feeling. I went into the kitchen and Abigail was making breakfast. All through breakfast and into the afternoon I kept feeling that something was wrong. Not sure how to really explain it, but it was a nagging feeling of dread. It was April 6, and it was a bright sunny day. There was no apparent reason for me to feel the way that I did. Later in the afternoon, Abigail began getting ready to go out to the lighthouse. I told her about the feeling that I was having, and asked her not to go out there that day. She assured me there was nothing to worry about and that she'd be back later. I really didn't want her to leave, especially that day, but there was no talking her out of it. I offered to go with her, but she told me that really wasn't necessary. I wish I'd insisted on going now. As the evening got later, that strange foreboding feeling got stronger. I wished she'd come home early, so that I could stop worrying. But as it got later, and was past the time she normally would come home, I became even more concerned. I got in my truck and drove out there. As I drove down the dark, narrow road, the headlights of the truck cast shadows that made the place seem even more sinister. I finally spotted her car, parked along the road near the path out to the lighthouse. I pulled in behind it, reached under the seat for my big flashlight, and stepped out into the cool night air. Despite the fact that her car was there, and it would seem that she had to be out around the lighthouse somewhere, I had the sinking feeling that I was the only one out there. I began walking along the path toward the lighthouse, and then finally broke into a run. As I approached the lighthouse, I began calling for her. The more I called her name, and got no answer, the more frightened I became. This couldn't be happening! Not the same thing that had happened to Tim six years ago! I came across her journal on the lighthouse steps. I stayed out there all night, hoping that she'd step out of the shadows and I'd find that this was all a bad dream. But as the first light of morning reflected off the still waters of the Cape Fear River, I knew that she wasn't there. The island police conducted a search; they even called in the sheriff's department from the mainland. But just like in Tim's case, the search turned up nothing. Like Tim, we had a memorial service and set up a marker in the cemetery. Then I tried to get on with my life, but it would never be the same. Alan had his family, but we didn't talk much. The next thirty three years were the saddest and loneliest that I can remember. I do remember in 1994, when construction crews came and erected the fence around the entire lighthouse area. I used to go out there to think. Then, suddenly it was fenced in. They were serious about nobody going in there too. It was a substantial fence, with barbed wire wrapped around the top like a prison fence. I always remembered thinking that was a little much. It wasn't long, though, that I found a place to cut through the fence. It was pretty well hidden, about a half mile back through the woods behind the Harbor Inn. I used the piece that I cut out as sort of a gate. With the vines grown up around it, nobody would really notice, and I didn't think that too many people went out that way anyhow. I used that as a way to get in and out for years, and was still using it when you got here."

They paused for a moment, as their server came by to see if they needed anything.

"Do you know who put up the fence," asked Dan, "and why?"

"Not really sure," replied Bill, "I honestly didn't see a need for it. I'd always assumed that it was to protect folks, you know, tourists and the like. I figured they didn't want any more disappearances. But come to think of it, the timing was a bit odd. Abigail disappeared in 1980, and the fence wasn't put up until 1994. That's fourteen years! And in that time, I never heard of anything else happening that would have drawn attention to the place and make anybody want to keep people out. It was already getting so run down that I doubt they were too concerned about vandalism, either. But it wasn't because anybody was doing anything in there that they didn't want anyone else to know about either. After I cut the hole in the fence, I kept going out there for years. Never saw anybody. And no signs of anybody either. It just kept getting more and more overgrown. I did see the fog a few times. Never went in it at that time though. But I always wondered about it. It didn't really look and feel like any fog I'd ever seen. The first time that I was caught in it was when it came up quickly when I was still in the woods on the way to the lighthouse. And when I say quickly, I MEAN quickly! Probably was less than two minutes from the time there was no fog to fog so thick I couldn't see two feet in front of me! It was so thick that I had to just stop and wait until it went away. It was there for about forty five minutes then went away about as quick as it came. Anyway, I never saw anybody out there until you showed up."

"I may try to find out more about the fence and who actually put it there." said Dan. "It does seem rather odd for anyone to have been concerned enough to put it up so many years after the last disappearance. It makes me wonder if they put it up for another reason."

"Anyway," continued Bill, "I kept going out there for years. Despite what had happened there, it always seemed to me to be a peaceful place. I'd usually go out in the afternoon and come home just before dark. Sometimes I'd go first thing in the morning. And sometimes, I'd spend the night out there, in the upstairs room of the lighthouse. I even brought in some wood and fixed it up a little, especially the floor. I didn't want to fall through any rotting floorboards! Who'd find me out there?! On one or two occasions, when the fog came up, I walked a couple of feet into it. I didn't want to get too far that I couldn't see back out to the lighthouse. I discovered that the fog seemed to have a pattern. It seemed to appear on a semi-regular time period, usually during the time slightly before twilight, even though once when I was staying the night, it came up right around dawn. I began writing down these patterns, and got to where I could sometimes predict the fog, at least within one to three days. Not sure exactly why I did it. It was probably just to have something to do more than anything else. And I was beginning to be intrigued by it. I still had never heard anything, and still didn't believe that Tim and Abigail were in the fog, but it was a real mystery, and I wondered if it did have something to do with the disappearances.

"Then about three years ago, I was contacted by this college professor from UNC Wilmington, Dr. Paul Carson. He was a professor of physics, specializing in what he called Quantum Physics. Most of what he talked about didn't make much sense to me, but he said that he had always been interested in the lighthouse and in the mystery surrounding it. He wanted to go out there and study the area and especially the fog. He believed that this area may be sitting on an energy field that from time to time would open up a doorway into another dimension. He called this an 'alternate plane of existence'. His theories were really unusual, but he said that he believed that the physical world that we live in was only one of an infinite number of realities, each existing simultaneously in a finite space. Each reality would be the same yet different. He explained it this way: In one reality, Bob and Sue may have never gotten married. In another, they got married but never had kids. In yet another, they got married and had kids, who in turn might have gotten married and had kids of their own. So one reality may have some of the same people living in it, but also different ones as well. He said that to them we would be an alternate reality. He explained to me that if his theory was correct, then Tim and Abigail might not be dead after all, but living in another of the alternate realities. They both may not even be in the same reality. The important thing was that if they were in different realities, then it may be possible to get them back. One major unknown was how they may have changed the reality that they were currently in, since they weren't supposed to be a part of that reality. In the span of thirty nine years, Tim could have grown up, gotten married, and had kids of his own! He'd be more a part of that reality now than ours. And what about Abigail? What might she have been doing for the last thirty three years? It was all really difficult for me to comprehend.

Since I first met him, he's been out here maybe a dozen times, each time with a different set of experiments to prove his theory. I don't even pretend to understand everything that he's saying, but it did bring back the possibility that Tim and Abigail weren't dead, and if that was the case, then I had to find out."

Dan didn't know what to say. This was the most unusual conversation that he'd had since coming out here. What Bill was talking about was impossible, it had to be, yet in light of all that had happened here it made a certain odd sort of sense too. It seemed even more out of place coming from a 70 year old man.

"So what did he find out?" was all Dan could think of to say.

"Well, like I said," continued Bill, "most of what he talked about and did was beyond me. I do know that one time when the fog came up, we tied a rope to ourselves so we wouldn't lose our way, and then we went into the fog. We tied orange ribbons around several of the trees. We tied about six ribbons. When the fog went away, there was no trace of any of the ribbons. They didn't fall off; they just were no longer there. The trees seemed different too, some larger and some not even in the same place. The fog would last anywhere from about twenty minutes to an hour and a half. I don't believe we ever saw it last less than twenty minutes, so we were generally aware of how much time we had. And after going into it a couple of times, we could also sense a slight change in the fog right before it went away, so we knew when we had to get out of there. We never went very far into the fog, though, so there were definite limits to how much we could find out about the world inside it. One time I remember he brought out a little radio controlled vehicle. Looked a little like that one they sent to Mars. It had cameras and sensors on it and a monitor on the controller so he could see where he was driving it. It had really bright headlights to hopefully see a little further through the fog. He drove it into the fog and he lost the video signal as soon as it was all the way in. We stepped just inside the fog and he picked up the signal again. From just inside the fog, he was able to drive it quite a ways into the forest. It had sensors that collected data that he would take back and analyze once he brought it back and retrieved it. Each time he came back, he seemed really excited about his findings. The last time, though, he lost the vehicle. He drove it a little too far into the fog, and the fog started to go away a little sooner than on previous times. He wasn't able to get it back, and we couldn't find it once the fog left either. The vehicle had a GPS on it and it transmitted its position back to the controller so that he could always tell where it was. He was puzzled, though, that sometimes when it was in the fog the GPS didn't work, so he never was able to tell its exact location. He speculated that either the fog had a composition that blocked the GPS signal, which was less likely since on a couple of occasions the GPS had worked, or in that particular reality no GPS satellites were ever sent up. Anyway, since it transmitted video and data back to the remote, he still had all of the information from that last trip. Both of us watched the video from that trip, and during the last few seconds, as the fog was thinning, we both saw what appeared to be a person in the fog, and it wasn't us! Then we lost the video transmission. It went by so quick that we couldn't really get much detail, but it definitely looked like a person!"

"Is there any way that I could see that video?" asked Dan.

"Dr. Carson has it," replied Bill, "but I suppose we could ask. He's wanted to come back out here again, but I didn't know what to tell him since you and your friends arrived."

"Tell him to come on out. I'd like to talk to him, too," said Dan, "and ask him to bring the video."

"Ok", said Bill, "I'll see when he wants to come back out. He can fill you in on all the technical stuff. The part that really got me excited, though, was what happened a couple of times when I went into the fog without Dr. Carson. Remember that I said earlier that I had talked to Tim and Abigail?"

He continued, "The first time was a sunny afternoon during spring. It was April 12. That was one of the times that I had predicted that the fog would come. Actually, on this occasion, I had predicted it a day earlier, and I had come out then, too. But like I said before, my predictions are only accurate within a few days. And lately they're becoming less accurate. But anyway, on this day it was warm and sunny. I went out to the lighthouse to wait for the fog. It usually comes up around dusk. It was starting to get dark, and I was thinking that maybe today was another bust, when I noticed a slight haze at the edge of the woods. Then I realized that the haze was circling the lighthouse completely and was growing thicker by the second! This was it! I went over and tied a rope around a tree, then the other end around my waist. This was what me and Dr. Carson did to keep from getting disoriented and losing our way in the fog. I set my timer that I keep in my pocket for twenty minutes to remind me when to come back out. Usually I'll push it a little longer, especially now since I've gotten a feel for the fog and what it feels like right before it goes away. I had brought along a pretty good flashlight, so I went ahead and stepped into the fog. It was cold! It was at least twenty degrees colder than the clear air around the lighthouse. I kept walking, shining the light ahead all the while. It mostly illuminated trees and brush. At one point, I thought I heard voices over to my right. I couldn't make out what they were saying, but it was definitely a woman's voice. I was listening intently, trying to make out what she was saying when I was startled by my alarm. I figured at this point, I'd better start making my way back out. Just as I got to the clearing and had stepped out of the fog, I heard the voice again, closer this time. Definitely a woman's voice. 'Hello is anyone there?' the voice asked. I replied back, 'Yes, I'm over here! Who is this?' It was what happened next that almost made my heart stop. The voice asked, 'Bill? Bill, is that you?' It was then that I knew that it was Abigail! I'm just not sure how it could have been Abigail, though. She'd been gone now for around thirty years! But I knew that it was her! I recognized her voice. 'Over here,' I shouted, 'come over here!' 'I'm coming!' she had said. It was then that I noticed that the fog was getting much thinner. I started thinking that she might not make it out, so I ran in after her. This time, though, the temperature wasn't twenty degrees colder. In fact, it seemed the same as in the clearing. I called out to her some more as I raced through the thinning fog, but she never answered me again.

"The second time was a lot like the first only it was Tim and Greg that I heard. It was about eight months later, and I had gone out without Dr. Carson again. This time the fog came up on the second day that I was out. I had tied a longer rope to the tree and had gone into the fog a little further this time. I was about twenty five minutes in when I first heard voices. They sounded really far away, but I could make them out as Tim and Greg! They were shouting, 'Hello is anyone there?' I called back and Tim answered, 'Dad? Is that you? What are you doing here?' 'Where are you?' I called back. 'Over here,' Tim answered, 'It's hard to see where we're going in this fog!' At one point Greg called to me as well. I began walking toward the direction of their voices, even though I couldn't see very far in front of me. They were closer, but still a long way off when I felt the familiar thinning of the fog. It was always more of a feeling than actually being able to see the thinning at first. This time, I decided to stay in the fog and continue looking for them, but as the fog thinned their voices seemed to get further away. As I began to be able to see further, I started running in the direction of their voices, but the further I ran, the farther away their voices sounded, until finally the fog was completely gone. After this, I didn't hear them anymore. I realized then that I had actually been running out of the fog. Why it seemed like their voices were coming from that direction, I never knew. I packed up and went home, really disappointed at being so close to finding them. That's when I noticed a peculiar thing. My watch was exactly forty three minutes faster than all of the other clocks in the house, and that seemed to be pretty close to the time that I was in the fog. I mentioned this to Dr. Carson later, and he said that odd things can happen when you venture into an alternate reality. Time may stand still in one while moving ahead in the other. While I didn't fully understand what he was talking about, he did tell me a theory behind this."

"That's all fascinating!" exclaimed Dan. "Can you let me know the next time you think there may be a fog? I'd like to see it for myself."

"Maybe Dr. Carson can come too?" suggested Bill. "He can answer more of your questions than I can."

"Certainly!" replied Dan. "I'm sure that Scotty, Greg, and Steve will want to come as well."

By this time they had both finished their meal and decided to head back to the Island Charm. They talked more along the way and finally arrived at the front steps.

"You know, you really had us going when you followed us down to the tip of the island yesterday, Bill!" said Dan. "We kept hearing you in the woods, but never were able to see you. It made us a little nervous when nighttime came!"

"Follow you?!" asked Bill, "I didn't follow you! I came about four thirty and you were all away from the campsite. I was relieved that I could sneak into the lighthouse easily without being seen. I went in through the small door on the side of the lighthouse that I went out yesterday, and then climbed the wooden ladder that I had made to get to the second floor. I was trying to hide the ladder when you all came into the base of the lighthouse from the main house."

A puzzled look came over Dan's face. Since meeting Bill after discovering him out at the lighthouse, he had just assumed that it was Bill that had been following them earlier that afternoon. But if it wasn't Bill, then who?

CHAPTER 11
March 30, 2016
Dr. Carson's Experiment

Officer Mark Collins was perplexed. Over the past week he had been doing some investigating about the mystery surrounding the business card that Dan had given to Chief Callahan and the other three cards from twenty two years ago. At first it had seemed simple. Obviously Dan was the current CEO of Perihelion Research Group, which apparently was the company that authorized the fencing in of the southern part of the island, including the lighthouse. That automatically made a connection between Dan and the island's past. But in researching exactly what that connection might be, the story became even more bizarre. It seemed that Dan was not just the current CEO of the company, but was also the founder of the company, along with his partner Scott Duncan. He had discovered that the company was originally founded in 1992 as Nelson Internet Technology. The name was changed to Nelson Technology in 1995. But the next part is what Mark couldn't make any sense out of. The name wasn't changed to Perihelion Research Group until October 1999. This was five years after the three men had given their business cards to Chief Lawson. He had talked to the marketing company that had designed the Perihelion logo and discovered that it had been commissioned in April of 1999. And the logo wasn't just similar on all of the cards, it was exactly the same! A check of the public records validated that Perihelion had been incorporated in 1999. But if that was true, how could the men have had those cards back in 1994, five years earlier? He sat at his desk and pondered this question over and over, but no matter how much he thought about it, he just couldn't come up with an answer that made any sense. The only answer that worked was that Chief Callahan was mistaken about the year. It had to have been in 1999 instead of 1994 that the fence was put up. He decided to go in and ask the Chief about it.

As he stood at the door to the Chief's office, he could hear him on the phone with someone. He went back to the break room and poured himself a cup of coffee. He wasn't sure how to begin. He really didn't want to imply that the Chief was mistaken about anything. He sat and finished his coffee, thinking of exactly how he'd approach the subject. As he walked over to the Chief's office again, he paused for a couple of minutes to make sure he was off the phone. Upon hearing no sound from the office, he knocked on the door.

"Come in!" answered the Chief.

"Chief Callahan, sir," began Mark, "I've been looking into the business cards that you gave me, trying to find Dan's connection, and quite frankly I'm a bit confused about something."

"Well, what is it?" asked the Chief.

"First, are you absolutely sure that it was 1994 that the men came in to talk with Chief Lawson? Could it have been later, say as late as 1999?"

"Impossible!" replied Chief Callahan, "If it had been 1999, then I would have been Chief. Lawson retired about a year after the men showed up. No, it was definitely 1994."

"Then if it really was 1994, I can't make any sense out of these business cards." answered Mark. "According to my research, Perihelion wasn't founded until close to the end of 1999. The company that designed the logo didn't create it until April of that year. It seems impossible that the men had those cards in 1994!"

"Maybe whoever you talked to was mistaken about the year?" inquired the Chief. "After all, that was a long time ago."

"I thought of that," said Mark, "but I actually found the public records of when the company was founded. It was founded in 1992 by Dan as Nelson Internet Technology, but the name wasn't changed to Perihelion until 1999. All of the records that I've seen substantiate that. Even the records of the marketing agency, Creative Marketing and Consulting, agreed with the incorporation records as to the time frame."

Chief Callahan settled back in his chair, his face showing the lines of a man deep in thought. Both he and Mark were quiet for some time.

Finally the Chief spoke up, "It's clear then that the records have been altered."

"But why?" asked Mark.

"I don't know just yet," answered the Chief, "but I aim to find out. Seems like they went to a lot of trouble to fence in the lighthouse, and then alter records to make it seem impossible that their company had anything to do with it. Their mistake, though, was giving Lawson the cards. That tied Perihelion directly into the events surrounding the lighthouse."

"Wow!" exclaimed Mark, "I hadn't thought of that! It makes sense though. Still, to be able to alter public records, as well as company records is not an easy thing to do."

"I'm sure Dan knows some pretty wealthy friends, probably some with political connections." answered the Chief. "For the right amount of money, that kind of cover up would be pretty easy to do. Continue to keep a watch on Dan and his friends. This new information makes it even more important that we find out what they're up to out there."

As Mark left the Chief's office, he was more determined than ever to find out what was going on. It seemed that there was some sort of real conspiracy going on here. Unfortunately, any surveillance would have to be from a distance for now. While he'd like to put a wire tap on Dan's phone, he knew there wasn't a judge around that would grant that authorization. Even though it was intriguing, and all evidence was pointing to a conspiracy, they didn't have any evidence that any crime was being committed. And without that, they wouldn't be able to get the warrant for the wire tap. For now, he'd just have to keep his eyes and ears open and do some old-fashioned detective work.

After his conversation with Chief Callahan, this all made more sense. Obviously three men couldn't present their business cards with the Perihelion logo five years before Perihelion was even founded. So once you rule out what couldn't be the case, you're left with a conspiracy. Given this fact, he reasoned that Perihelion did in fact exist in 1994, even if it didn't exist officially with Articles of Incorporation. For some reason, someone wanted them to believe that Perihelion wasn't involved in closing off the south end of the island, so they went to great lengths to make it appear that the company wasn't even around at that time. Dan and his friends wouldn't know that he had figured this out and was watching them. This gave him the edge. He had figured out that they were up to more than they were letting on. He had to find out what that was, but he couldn't be so obvious that he'd tip them off that he knew something.

As he stepped out the front door of the police station, he spotted Dan and his friends walking on the opposite side of the street back toward the Island Charm. Steve and Arlene were with them as well. Dan spotted him as he came out the door and held up his hand to wave. He waved back, and then kept a sharp eye on them as they went down the street. He got into his patrol car that was parked in front of the station, cranked it up, and made a U-Turn back toward the direction of the Island Charm. He passed them, and then slowed down as he approached. Parked out front was a dark blue van with permanent government plates. He pulled to the side of the road to write down the license number of the van, and then proceeded on down the street. As he passed, he noticed Bill Henderson on the driver's side of the van apparently talking to the driver. That seemed rather odd, but he continued on down the street so as not to arouse suspicion. He made a left turn at the last street before getting out of town and went back and parked behind one of the shops. He got out and made his way down the back road toward the Island Charm. He wanted to find out what was going on, and what Bill's connection was. As he got to the Island Charm, he pulled out his notebook and pretended to write down the license numbers of the cars parked alongside. He was really watching the blue van as Dan and his friends came up and began a conversation with Bill and the driver. Unfortunately, he couldn't quite make out what they were saying, but this did confirm that the van being there had something to do with Dan and Perihelion. He saw Greg look his direction, say something to the others, and then Dan and Scotty both looked over his way. He pretended not to notice, finished up with the last car, and then made his way toward the back of the building.

As he approached the back of the building he saw Dan, Scotty, Greg, and Steve get into Dan's truck. A moment later he heard it crank up and back out of the parking space. Dan paused and waited up at the main road until the blue van had passed, then he pulled out onto the main road and settled in behind it. Mark then walked over to his patrol car, got in, and drove up toward the main road. He wasn't in any particular hurry. He knew where they were going, and he really didn't want to follow close enough for them to spot him anyway. He figured that Dan would lock the gate behind them this time to prevent any onlookers from just happening by and discovering what they were up to. He didn't want them to spot him as they locked up the gate either. He had a key, which was given to him by Chief Callahan that he could use to open the gate and follow them. As he slowly made his way down the road, he was intently wondering what they were up to. Why now? And did it have anything to do with the fog? After forty years, he couldn't imagine that it would have anything to do with the disappearance of the two boys and Tim's mother, but with Bill Henderson involved he couldn't entirely rule that out either.

As he turned onto Harbor Inn Lane and went the quarter of a mile to Lighthouse Road, his initial suspicions were confirmed. Dan had, in fact, locked the gate behind them. He pulled in and parked in front of the gate, got out and opened it, then got back into his patrol car and drove it through the gate. He stopped once more to get out and lock the gate behind him, and then he slowly proceeded on his way. He moved slowly so as not to overtake them. While he was law enforcement, and had every right to be there, he felt that he could learn more if Dan and his friends didn't know he was there. He continued on until he was maybe a tenth of a mile from the clearing near the lighthouse, then backed the patrol car off the road between several trees. He went around to the trunk and retrieved his binoculars, then proceeded up the dirt road toward the lighthouse on foot. He quietly moved into the woods just before the clearing when he detected motion up ahead. They'd be unloading the van in the clearing, so he needed to find another way in to have a good vantage point to see what was going on. He had to move slowly as he made his way through the woods. It was very difficult to move silently. At one point, he stepped on a twig that snapped, making a very loud crack. He froze where he was and looked over toward where Dan and his friends were taking several boxes and moving them inside the wall. To his relief, they hadn't seemed to hear the twig snap. He continued on until he found a good spot right at the edge of the woods. A fairly large overgrowth of bushes would conceal him from their sight while still allowing him to see fairly well what was going on.

He took the binoculars out of their case and looked through them in Dan's direction. He could see Dan and Scotty opening up one of the large boxes. Greg and Steve were unpacking another one while Bill and another man whom Mark didn't recognize were talking and motioning over toward the woods just outside the gate. After the first box was completely opened, Bill, Greg, and the other man began unpacking that box while Dan and Scotty walked back toward the van. As they unpacked the first box, Mark could see several metal poles, some coiled up cable, a metal box with some switches, indicators and dials that looked to be about four feet long by two feet high, and something that looked like a parabolic antenna. As the man he didn't recognize began assembling the parts taken from the first box, Bill and Greg began unpacking the second box which appeared to have more poles, more cable, and two more parabolic antennas, one being slightly larger than the other. The only thing missing from the second box was another metal box with dials and indicators, but Mark figured that the box was some kind of control panel and that everything plugged into it. As all this was taking place, Dan and Scotty returned, pulling a cart that looked to have two large tables and several chairs on it. They stopped near the others and began setting up the tables and chairs. He could see that the one man had assembled the poles into a tripod and had inserted the other poles to make a mast about ten feet high with the parabolic antenna at the top. He began assembling the others the same way until he had three ten foot high antenna supports with the antennas on top. He had attached the cable to the antennas, and then ran it down the side of the masts. At one point, Mark was startled when they began walking in his direction with one of the antenna towers, but they stopped maybe fifteen feet from his position. The growth of bushes seemed to do their job, as no one appeared to notice him. They walked back toward the box with the switches, dials, and indicators and plugged the wire from the antenna into the back of it. They kept one antenna near the box, and moved the other one in the opposite direction from where he was watching them. After all of this appeared to be assembled, they walked back toward the van. What now came out of the back of the van surprised him even more than anything previously. They had unloaded some kind of radio controlled flying drone and were now carrying it toward the box which had been set up. It looked larger than most of the ones that he had seen, maybe four feet in diameter. They set it on the ground in the clearing and the one man began working with it.

Apparently there were some parts in one of the boxes that fit onto the drone. The man took out two vertical antennas and mounted them to tripods. These antennas were about three feet long and when mounted on four foot tripods were only seven feet high. He placed one of them beside the control box, then took the other one and placed it outside the wall. He plugged the cables from both of them into the back of the box. They had taken the lid off of one of the boxes, but hadn't unpacked it. The man took about three cables and ran them from the control box and plugged them into something inside the box. He figured probably batteries were in the box. After checking all of the connections thoroughly, he sat down in a chair in front of the box while the rest gathered around to watch. Mark wished that he could get a better view of the monitors on the box. There appeared to be three monitors, one large one in the center and two smaller ones on either side. From what he could tell, the smaller ones appeared to be displaying data of some kind, while the larger one in the center seemed to be the color display for a video feed coming from somewhere. It didn't take him too long to realize that the video feed was coming from the drone. He heard the sound of its motors starting up, then watched as it lifted off and began to fly around the field. It went quite high, maybe a hundred feet or more before it finally was brought in for a landing near where it took off.

Mark looked at his watch and discovered that he had been there for a little over two hours. There wasn't much happening now. The flight of the drone had apparently just been a test flight. It hadn't moved since that initial flight. The monitors were still on and every once in a while the man would tweak a few of the dials. Mostly they were just sitting and talking. He wished that he had some audio surveillance equipment so that he could hear what they were saying. That type of equipment was expensive and since they were a small police department which usually didn't have a need for equipment of this nature, they didn't have any. After this, though, he would ask Chief Callahan about the possibility of borrowing some from one of the departments on the mainland.

As Mark sat and waited, he had a strange sensation that he was being watched. It wasn't from Dan or any of his friends. They were all accounted for as they were all sitting around the control box and talking. None of them were looking his way, so he was sure that none of them had spotted him. No, this sensation seemed to be coming from somewhere else.

He looked around to both sides and behind him, but couldn't make out anything through the growth of bushes. The sensation was there, though, that he wasn't alone. It was odd. He hadn't felt it before, but now he felt it even stronger. It was about 4:30 in the afternoon by now. The sun was still high in the sky, but casting shadows in the woods. He looked back over toward where Dan and his friends were and saw that they were all still there. He had almost dismissed the feeling as paranoia, when he heard a branch loudly snap over to his right. His heart was racing now as he looked over toward that direction. Could it be a deer or some other animal? Possibly, but the feeling of being watched came back even stronger now. As his eyes adjusted to the dimly lit woods, he thought he could make out the shape of a man. He unholstered his weapon as he slowly made his way toward that direction. Even though he was a trained police officer, these unexpected turn of events still made him edgy. It wasn't fear exactly, though that was one word that came close. It was more like an anxiety about the unknown. He continued to advance forward, but the man remained motionless, standing his ground. As he moved even closer, he realized that what he had thought was the shape of a man was just a large clump of vines and bushes. He let out a huge sigh of relief. His muscles, which had been tight earlier, began to loosen. He started to put his weapon back in its holster when he noticed movement up ahead at the edge of the woods.

He strained to make out any shape or outline as he looked toward where the movement had occurred. His eyes were more adjusted now as he surveyed the scene ahead of him as he slowly made his way toward the direction of the movement. Still, he wasn't detecting anything or anyone. His nerves were on edge and his senses on alert. If it was a person up ahead, he couldn't imagine who it might be. Dan and all of his friends were supposedly still huddled around the console. It was possible, he thought, that one of them could have noticed his movement and come over to investigate. But this movement was further back in the woods. If it was Dan or one of the others, they should be approaching from the edge of the woods. As he walked further into the woods, suddenly his gaze fell on a man, partially hidden behind a large oak tree. At about that same instant, the man bolted from behind the tree and began to run further back into the woods. Mark tried to give chase, but it was obvious the man knew these woods much better than he did. He kept stumbling over small bushes and fallen limbs as he tried to make his way through the woods. He realized that it was no use. The man was just too fast. He hadn't gotten a good enough look at him to determine his age, or if it was someone that he had seen around town. From his agility, though, he did appear to be young, maybe in his twenties or thirties even.

As the last faint sound of the man crashing through the woods faded, he became aware of a thin mist forming around him. He holstered his weapon and began making his way back in the direction from where he had come. He wanted to get back and see what Dan and his friends were up to now. He also wanted to verify that they were all there and that the person that he had seen wasn't one of them. As he made his way back, the fog became much thicker, so much so that he had to take his flashlight off of his belt to see where he was stepping. He was amazed at how fast it came up and just how fast it went from a thin mist to a full thick fog. Maybe two to three minutes at the most. The woods were much darker now as the fog blocked out most of the sun. He felt he was moving in the right direction, but he couldn't be completely sure. He could just be walking further into the woods. He wondered even more about the console that Dan and his friends had set up. Was it what was creating the fog? If so, then why exactly? As he continued on, a light caught his attention through the trees slightly ahead and to the right. It wasn't near the ground, and it appeared to be up some height. He began walking toward the light. It was dim, but still noticeable through the fog. It seemed to rotate, getting brighter and dimmer. As he approached the edge of the fog, he noticed that the light appeared to be where the lighthouse was. He came to the wall around the lighthouse and made his way to the right to the gate. This would be the front gate, facing the river. Dan and his friends were set up near the back gate, so he should be able to look around on this side without being seen. As he was making his way around the wall toward the gate, the fog was thinner and he could make out the outline of the lighthouse. It was standing tall, and the light did in fact seem to be coming from the lantern house. He arrived at the gate, and as he made his way through it, an amazing and impossible sight was before him.

CHAPTER 12

Unexplained Events

As he stepped through the gate he was completely out of the fog. It was like an invisible wall was keeping the fog out of the inside. But what was even more amazing, and what he just couldn't get his mind to understand because of the impossibility of it, was that the lighthouse that stood before him was completely restored, where just a few minutes earlier it had been in ruins. He just stood, totally fixed to his position, staring at the lighthouse. There were windows made of glass that wasn't broken, with curtains on them and light shimmering from inside. The beacon in the lantern house flickered as it slowly rotated. The lawn around the lighthouse was neatly manicured, and bushes were planted along the front on either side of the steps where weeds and vines had been climbing the steps and walls of the house earlier. As he walked toward the lighthouse, his mind kept going over and over how impossible this was. The lighthouse couldn't be in perfect condition, with lights and a revolving beacon. What he was seeing just couldn't be there. Yet it was! How was this possible? Then he remembered Dan and his friends, the man he didn't know, and the box with the monitors and antennas. Could Dan and his friends be creating this scene with some new technology? He'd have to research Perihelion a lot more. After this, he definitely needed to find out what they did. He pulled out his Smartphone and snapped a few pictures. He knew once he got back to the station that nobody would believe him, so he planned to take back proof.

As he approached the side of the lighthouse and began to walk around it, he walked slowly and carefully. Dan and his friends were on the other side, and he still would prefer not to be spotted. But as he rounded the corner and looked out toward the back gate, no one was there! Where could they have gone? They were there not ten minutes ago! It would take longer than that to pack up all the equipment that they had brought with them. He walked over to where they had been and couldn't find any trace that they had been there. There were no tracks in the grass where it had been pushed down by everyone walking around. No indentions in the soil from tables and chairs, or any other sign that anyone had been there. Yet he had seen them and watched them set everything up for over two hours! There had to be some sign that they had been there, but there wasn't. He took some more pictures of the lighthouse from this side, and then snapped a few of the fog. It was strange. From this vantage point it really did look like a wall of fog all the way around the lighthouse. He felt like he was encased in a large grey tube.

As he began to regain some of his composure he remembered that he had his police radio on his belt. He took it out, keyed it up and said, "Unit 2 to base. Chief, can you hear me?" There was no reply. He tried again, "Unit 2 to base, anyone there?" There was still no reply. He switched to each of the six channels on the radio, but got no response on any of them. This was interesting. There was always someone monitoring the channels. Even off duty, the Chief and all of the officers carried their radios with them. There was never a time that he could remember that he couldn't get anyone on the radio. Yet no matter how many times he tried, no one was answering. He wondered if there could be something wrong with his radio. Maybe they could hear him, but he couldn't hear them. He decided that just in case this was what was happening that he'd request assistance. "This is Unit 2. I'm out at the old lighthouse. Something's not right here. Request assistance. Unknown situation." He put out this call several times, but still got no reply. But if someone had heard him, he figured that they'd be out in about ten to fifteen minutes.

When he couldn't get anyone on the radio, he continued to walk around the perimeter of the wall. As far as he went, there was no break in the fog. And none of the fog spilled over inside the wall. He walked back toward the lighthouse. It looked as it probably looked eighty to a hundred years ago! He was still questioning what he was seeing. With his police officer training, his view was that everything had an explanation. But what he was seeing here went against all of this. As much as he tried to come up with one, there simply was no logical explanation for the scene before him.

He walked over to the lighthouse and looked through one of the windows. There was a large dining table in the center of the room. A china cabinet was against the back wall. The glow that he had seen flickering through the window was coming from an oil lamp in the center of the table. That didn't surprise him too much. As far as he knew, electricity had never been run out to the lighthouse. Then it occurred to him for the first time. If there was an oil lamp burning, then someone had to be here! He wasn't alone! While being alone out here, at least a mile from civilization did cause him to be slightly uneasy, the realization that someone else was here, in this scene which was completely impossible, caused him to be more so. The lighthouse, viewed in its current state just couldn't be here! The fact that someone was inside was even more amazing! Still, could it be possible that it was Dan and his friends that were inside? He didn't see anyone in the dining room, but he did see shadows while looking through the door into the next room. It was hard to tell if it was actual movement or just the flicker of another oil lamp. He needed to get a look in another window.

He walked around to the left, past the back door. This next window was slightly higher than the first one, and even straining he couldn't quite see inside. He went around to the side of the house and peered into the first window that he came to. There was another oil lamp on a desk in the corner, and a little girl, probably around eight or nine, sitting on the bed playing with a couple of dolls. He stared at this scene in disbelief. He had expected to possibly see Dan and his friends. But where did this little girl come from? As he continued to take in this scene, the girl looked over toward the window and their eyes met. For about a minute they were both frozen in each other's gaze. Then the girl began to scream! Her body shook with each piercing scream. At once, a woman came rushing into the room. She looked to be in her early thirties with long brown hair. She was wearing a long cotton dress with flower prints. The little girl couldn't speak. She just kept screaming and pointing at the window. The woman's eyes met his and she shouted, "William!! Someone's outside the window!" William came running into the room. He was a large man with a long black beard. He wore a black hat and a black suit. He looked over toward Mark, and then ran out of the room. Mark suddenly realized that William would soon be outside. He began to run straight toward the wall. He didn't run toward the back gate, since that would be visible from the back door, which was probably where William would be coming out. There was also a group of bushes probably half way to the woods that he could duck behind and maybe escape William. He got to the bushes and ducked behind them just as William came around the corner of the house. He was carrying what looked like a shotgun or rifle. He stood still, looking around and listening. Mark unholstered his weapon. This was a strange, unusual, and impossible situation that he found himself in. Since he couldn't really explain anything, he really had no desire to have to shoot William. He preferred to slip quietly back into the woods, but if it came down to either William or himself, he would have to do whatever is necessary to defend himself. He could understand William's perspective, though. After all, he had been peering into the windows of his house, into what was probably his little girl's room. But who were these people?! And what were they doing here? The lighthouse was in ruins after decades of decay. Yet here it was like new with a family that he didn't recognize living in it! And where had Dan and his friends gone? They seemed to have just disappeared! The more that happened, the more that he just couldn't make any sense of anything. Would anyone even believe him when he got back to the station, especially if the lighthouse was back in ruins again when they came out to look it over? If he wasn't here experiencing it, he didn't think even he'd believe him!

He could see William scanning the area around the woods behind him. He was relieved to see that apparently William didn't see him. He really wanted to avoid any conflict. He couldn't get into a conversation with William. He knew that William would want to know what he was doing there, and why he was looking into his daughter's bedroom window. If he was William, that's what he'd want to know. But he didn't know what he was doing here! He was looking into the window, but that was just to find out more about his current situation. Those people weren't even supposed to be here! The lighthouse wasn't even supposed to be here in its current original state! What would he say? There really wasn't anything to say. He had only questions, but no answers.

William began to walk toward the front of the house. That was a relief! At least he wasn't walking in Mark's direction, which meant that he hadn't been seen. As William turned to go around to the front of the house, Mark jumped up and ran for the woods. Just as he started, though, he heard a loud report, apparently William's shotgun being discharged. He froze in place and slowly turned around. The motion of him jumping up must have caught William's eye. William now was walking in his direction with the shotgun pointed at him. He still had his weapon down by his side, apparently concealed by the bushes.

"Who are you?! What are you doing here?!" shouted William.

"Officer Collins, Green Island Police Department." was all Mark could think of to say.

"The island don't have no police department!" shouted William, "It's just Sheriff Barnett and Deputy White. Come out from behind those bushes where I can see you!"

Mark slowly walked out from behind the bushes, still clutching his weapon in his right hand. Just as he came out from behind the bushes, the woman that he had seen in the house walked around the corner. "William, who is it?" she asked. As he turned around to tell her to go back into the house, he lowered his rifle, and Mark started to run toward the woods. What happened next happened so fast that it was just a blur. Out of the corner of his eye he saw William whirl back around and raise the rifle in his direction. As he did, Mark turned, raised his weapon and got off two shots. He saw William fall to the ground, still clutching the rifle. He ran for the woods as fast as he could. The wall was only four feet high as he leapt over it back into the fog, falling to the ground on the other side. His heart was racing as he slowly peered over the top of the wall. He could see William still lying motionless on the ground, with the woman now kneeling beside him. He had just shot a man! Since he started his career in law enforcement, he had never had to do that before! Part of him wanted to see if he could help, after all he hadn't wanted to shoot William. His hand had been forced. But part of him also wanted to stay in the safety of the fog. His mind still couldn't really get a handle on all that had just happened. And the woman would be afraid. She had just seen him shoot her husband. If he approached, she might just pick up the rifle and shoot him! Still, if William were still alive, he couldn't just let him die.

Just as he made the decision to go back and help, the decision was made for him. As he stood up, he could sense a noticeable change in the fog. And the scene in front of him was changing. The lighthouse still stood tall with the beacon shining, but he could also see holes appearing in it, and a pile of bricks, faint at first, then darker appearing at the lighthouse base. He stared in disbelief as William and the woman both faded from the scene entirely. Over a period of two to three minutes, the lighthouse was back in ruins, William and the woman were gone, and the fog had entirely disappeared! He stood dumbfounded, wondering what had just happened. Then he heard voices over to the right. He looked, and Dan and his friends were back at the edge of the gate! The control panel and antennas looked just as he had remembered them, even though they weren't there moments before! He walked the opposite direction along the edge of the wall, so as not to be seen. He wanted to get back over to the other side where his patrol car was parked and observe from there. No one was going to believe this! But he had proof! He had taken pictures. He pulled out his Smartphone as he walked and flipped through the photos. He had gotten some great pictures of the fog and the lighthouse. While it might not be able to be explained, at least they would have to believe him!

He crouched behind some bushes as he watched Dan and his friends. They were excitedly talking at this point. The man whom he didn't recognize was talking fast and pointing to the screens on the control panel. He seemed to be happy about what had just happened, though Mark still couldn't figure exactly what they were doing. He snapped a few more pictures of Dan and the others, along with the equipment they were using. The drone was back on the ground now, but seemed to be on the other side of the control panel from where he had seen it before. He'd take the photos that he'd taken back to Chief Callahan. Maybe he could make some sense out of them. He especially wanted to show him the lighthouse photos. While the Chief was typically good at coming up with rational explanations for almost anything that happened, he was really looking forward to his explanation for this one!

When he observed them beginning to pack everything up, he decided to make his way back to his patrol car. He still wasn't ready for them to know that he had been following and observing them. He felt that maintaining secrecy about this was still the best course to help him find out more information, so he wanted to be gone by the time they passed by so they wouldn't see his patrol car. If they knew he was following them, they'd be more careful, and purposely try to avoid him.

He made his way through the growth, trying to follow as best he could the path that he had made earlier when he arrived. It wasn't easy. The growth was pretty thick here, so he had to go slow. As he approached the road, he suddenly stopped, motionless, his heart racing again. Up ahead, standing at the edge of the woods where they met the road were two men. He couldn't quite make out their features, since they were standing in the shadows. It couldn't be Dan, or any of the others. He had left them back in the clearing and they were all there when he left. He didn't want to shout to the men, since Dan or the others might hear him. He drew his weapon and moved closer to the men. He had already shot someone today, and he really didn't want to shoot anyone else, but things were happening so quickly and he still couldn't come up with any explanation for any of it, so he felt like he should be cautious. As he slowly moved closer to the two men, neither of them moved at all. They both remained motionless, standing at the edge of the woods. Something about this whole scene made him extremely uneasy. He wanted to turn and go the other direction, but his patrol car was up ahead. If they didn't move, he'd have to confront the men, since they were standing right in the path he needed to follow to reach his patrol car. And confrontation, in a situation like this, where nothing seemed as it should be, was not what he wanted. He wanted to simply get to his patrol car and drive back to the normality of the police station. There, he'd have time to collect his thoughts while going over the photos that he'd taken on his phone. Alex, one of the other officers, should be on patrol now. Maybe he'd radio to him and they could meet somewhere and go over the events before talking to the Chief. He stopped, still keeping an eye on both men, his weapon still drawn, though not pointed at them. As he stood watching them, suddenly a bright flash emanated from the side of one of the men and flew toward him. It all happened so quickly that he didn't even have time to raise his weapon or even to dodge the approaching light. He could feel himself losing consciousness as the scene before him faded into bright, white light.

The next thing he remembered was waking up as the light faded. At first, he didn't know where he was. His mind was dazed and confused. He felt disoriented, the way one feels after waking from a dream. He felt like something had just happened, but as he regained his composure, like a dream, whatever it was drifted further and further from his consciousness.

He looked around and quickly determined that he was sitting in his patrol car. It wasn't yet completely dark, but he could tell that darkness was quickly approaching. The clock on the dash of his patrol car said 7:36. As he became more awake, he could see the left wing of the Harbor Inn straight ahead out the windshield of his car. What was he doing at the Harbor Inn? Had he been called here? He searched his memory, but couldn't quite remember. The last thing that he remembered clearly was coming out of the police station and waving to Dan and his friends as they walked back toward the Island Charm. He also vaguely remembered getting into his patrol car and making a U-Turn to go back in their direction. He thought that had been about 2:30 in the afternoon. After that, as much as he struggled, he just couldn't remember anything until right now. But that was five hours ago! What had he been doing for the last five hours, and what was he doing here at the Harbor Inn now?

He got out of his patrol car and made his way up the walkway toward the entrance to the Harbor Inn. If he had been called out to the inn, Joe Rogers would probably know why. As he walked toward the inn, he decided to check in with the station. He keyed the mic of his handheld radio and said, "Unit 2 to base." This time, he immediately got a response, "Unit 4 to Unit 2, Mark where've you been all afternoon? The last transmission logged was that you were going out of service at the Island Charm at around 2:45 this afternoon. When I came on my shift at 4:00, the Chief wanted me to keep an eye out for you. He said they hadn't been able to reach you on the radio since then. Did you turn it off?"

The way that he was feeling right now, he was relieved to hear Alex on the other end of the radio, but not at all comfortable with the questions. "Not sure," replied Mark, "Can you meet me at the Harbor Inn? I don't really want to discuss this over the radio."

"10-4," replied Alex, "Be there in about four minutes."

He waited on the walkway for Alex to show up. About three minutes later, he saw Alex's patrol car pull into the parking lot and drive over to where he was. Alex parked and got out. He was tall and muscular like the Chief. He was in his mid thirties with wavy brown hair and graying around the temples. He had been on the force longer than Mark, but since

Mark had joined, they'd become good friends.

"What's going on, buddy?" he inquired.

"Like I said, I'm really not sure." replied Mark. I was just going in to talk to Joe to see if he knows why I came out here. The last thing I remember is waving to Dan at around 2:30 this afternoon. After that, I woke up here around 7:35 in the evening. I must have driven here, possibly on a call, and then blacked out. I guess I've been here all afternoon. Maybe Joe knows why I may have gotten a call to come out here."

"No," Alex replied, "you haven't been here all afternoon. You had to have been somewhere else. When I drove through this lot at around 5:30, your car wasn't here. I'd have checked on you if it was. You mean you really can't remember anything?"

"No, I've tried. I sort of remember getting out of my car at the Island Charm, but even that's fuzzy."

They walked up the walkway and into the lobby of the Harbor Inn. They were greeted by the desk clerk as they came through the doors.

"Good evening Stephanie. Is Joe still around?" asked Alex.

"He came through here about fifteen minutes ago. Not sure if he was leaving after that or not." replied Stephanie.

"We'll go check his shop," said Alex, "that's usually where he is."

They walked down the right corridor to where Joe's shop was set up about half way down. They knocked on the door, and as expected, Joe opened it.

"What have I done this time Officers?" asked Joe in a joking fashion, "It must have been something really bad if you're both here to arrest me!" He stopped suddenly, however, when he noticed the serious looks on both officers' faces. "Anything wrong?" he asked.

"That's what we're hoping you can help us with." replied Mark. "Did I get a call to come out here earlier this afternoon?"

"Not that I can recall," replied Joe, "it's actually been pretty quiet here today. I can't imagine what you'd have been called out here for. But if you were, you should know better than anyone."

"I know," said Mark, "I can't really discuss it right now, but something strange is going on. Keep an eye out and let us know if you see anything odd, ok?"

"What exactly am I looking for?" asked Joe.

"Anything odd," replied Mark, "particularly if it pertains to Dan Nelson or the lighthouse."

A serious look came over Joe's face at the mention of the lighthouse. While he had discussed it some over the years with Bill Henderson, he had to wonder why the police were inquiring about it now. Could it be starting again? He hoped not, but he had to wonder.

CHAPTER 13
April 8, 2016
The Visitor Returns

Dan awoke around 7:00 am. He lay in bed for a few minutes just thinking about all that had happened. He had been here for almost a month now, and was in the middle of an adventure that he couldn't have even dreamed of a few months earlier. Scotty and Greg were in a room across the hall, he had met new friends, Steve and Arlene, and his family would be coming to the island in only a couple of months. During the past week, work had really gotten started on the lighthouse. He had gotten a paving company to come out and lay down gravel on Lighthouse Road. He decided that for now he'd see how just having a gravel road would work. He could always get them out to pave it later, if it seemed necessary. He wanted mostly to concentrate on the lighthouse. Southeast Restoration Professionals had started their work on Monday and already it was looking better. They had cleaned up all of the rubble around the lighthouse and surrounded it with steel scaffolding. Looking at the lighthouse now, it looked like it was inside a large cage. Dan, Scotty, Greg and Steve had started work on the inside. It was slow work, and they really hadn't gotten much more done than cleaning out the junk from inside and getting it ready for the new construction. Some of the building supplies were supposed to arrive today, so that would give them something to work with over the weekend.

None of them had seen the fog again since the end of March. Dr. Carson had taken all of his gadgets and the data they had captured and went back to Wilmington to analyze what he had. When he left after they had experienced the fog, he was really excited about what he was able to observe, and his first look at the data that his equipment captured had really amazed him. They had flown the drone into the fog. With its auto-avoidance technology, it had been able to go quite deep into the fog. He even flew it straight up, and at about 200 feet up the fog began to thin and the drone flew out of it. He flew it up another 300 feet, and the view looking straight down resembled a small hurricane, with the lighthouse in the exact center of the eye. He flew it back down into the eye rather than taking it back down into the fog and landed a few feet from where everyone was gathered. He was able to get other readings as well, though it may take some conversation with some of his colleagues to be able to interpret exactly what they meant.

Actually seeing the fog had changed things, though, at least in Dan's mind. Before this, the fog had been just a story, an interesting account by people he didn't really know. Now that he had seen it, and walked a little ways into it, it had become real. Now it went from being other people's accounts to his own personal experience. And that changed the way he viewed the accounts that he read as well. He had to really consider them all the more now that he was here and knew that the fog was real. And while he knew that the fog was real, he didn't know WHAT it was. That bothered him. For the first time since he had been here, he found himself wondering if he and his family would be safe here. After all, the two boys Tim and Greg had disappeared forever at the lighthouse, and no one really knew exactly what had happened that night. Could whatever happened that night happen again? He was also more concerned about the 1925 account from the Jack Carlson book where William MacGregor, the lighthouse keeper at that time was actually shot by a man impersonating a police officer. Presumably he had come out of the fog, since he was never seen again. William did recover, but he moved away with his family soon after that. According to his account, the man had been looking into his daughter Becky's window. What if something like that happened while he and his family were living there?

His thoughts were interrupted by a knock at his door and Scotty's voice asking, "Aren't you ready yet?" He had apparently been lying there lost in thought for longer than he realized. He got out of bed and went to let him in.

"What have you been doing?" asked Scotty, "It's a quarter till 8:00 already."

"Just thinking," replied Dan to the question. "Scotty, do you think we're doing the right thing?"

"What do you mean?" inquired Scotty with a puzzled look. He wasn't used to Dan asking these kinds of questions.

"Coming to the island," said Dan, "Restoring the lighthouse. It's been locked up for the last twenty two years. We don't really know what's happening out there, but after seeing the fog for ourselves, we know that something is. And we can't explain what it is. Dr. Carson's Alternate Reality Theory sounds as good as any, but every time I think of that it just sounds so unbelievable, so impossible. But actually seeing the fog has me wondering."

"Yep," said Scotty, "I'll admit that fog wasn't like anything I'd ever seen or felt. And I've been in fog plenty of times. I've never seen any fog come up that quick. And it must have been at least twenty degrees colder in the fog! Are we doing the right thing? ... Hard to tell. I'm having a hard time with the Alternate Reality Theory myself. Since seeing the fog, I've been trying to come up with other explanations that make more sense, but so far nothing."

Dan went on, "But do you think we're safe? I've talked to several folks since I've been here who've warned me not to go into the fog. But is the danger just IN the fog, or are we in danger just being out there? Remember William MacGregor? He didn't go into the fog, but he was shot by an intruder who probably came out of the fog. And we don't know anything about what actually happened to the two boys that night. We figure that they probably ventured into the fog, but do we really know for sure?"

Scotty paused for about a minute, appearing to be pondering what Dan had just said. Finally he spoke up, "I know it seems a little scary right now. And I can't honestly say that I'm not at least a little concerned. Since seeing the fog, I'll admit I've been looking over my shoulder more than usual while we've been out there. But we've come this far, and I am really curious about what is going on. After all we've seen, do you really think you could just pack up and leave and never know?"

"You do have a point, Scotty," said Dan, "I guess we've come too far not to see it through. Let me get dressed and I'll meet you and Greg downstairs for breakfast."

He went to the closet to find his clothes as Scotty closed the door behind him to go downstairs. Barbara would have a really good breakfast on the table by now. He was glad that he had talked to Scotty about his concerns. When something was bothering him, Scotty always had just the right thing to say to make him feel better. There was something else, though, that he hadn't mentioned to Scotty yet, but he wondered if he should. He didn't mention it just now, but it was definitely a part of what prompted the questions that he had just asked Scotty. Several times over the past week, he felt like he was being followed. And not just out at the lighthouse, but around town as well. He knew the feeling was unfounded, but he felt it nonetheless; like he was being watched. Once, after dark, he had looked out his room window and saw a man standing under the street lamp, looking up at his room. He quickly ran downstairs, but when he reached the street the man was gone. He looked up and down the street, but there was no sign of him.

The first time that he felt like he was being followed was about a week ago. It was the day after their encounter with the fog. It was about 10:30 at night, and he had run out of drinks in his room, so he had walked down to the local convenience store to pick up something, along with a snack as well. It was only a little over one tenth of a mile to the convenience store, and the town seemed safe, so he hadn't thought much about going out alone, even that late at night. He arrived at the convenience store, picked up what he had come for, and started back home. As soon as he had left the lighted area around the convenience store, a very uneasy feeling came over him. The night wasn't completely dark, since there was a half moon that night. He looked around as he walked. He didn't see anyone, but he still had an uneasy feeling like he was being followed. Nothing had happened that should have made him feel that way, and he hadn't felt it on the way to the convenience store. Now, however, the feeling was strong. He stopped and listened. He could only hear the wind rustling through the trees. He began walking, a little faster this time. He couldn't wait to get back to the Island Charm. He thought back to the day of their camping trip. He remembered how they had felt like they were being followed when they walked down to the tip of the island, and how relieved they were to discover it was only Bill Henderson. But he also remembered his conversation with Bill the next day. Bill had said that it wasn't him that had followed them. At the time, he had almost dismissed that revelation. But now, alone at 10:50 at night, those thoughts came back to him. If it wasn't Bill, then who was it? It could be that police officer, he thought. Officer Collins has seemed to be interested in what they were doing since they got here. And he had seen Officer Collins watching them at the Island Charm right before they went with Dr. Carson out to the lighthouse. He tried to convince himself that it was Officer Collins that was following him now, but he didn't really believe that. After all, why would Officer Collins have a reason to be following him when he went to pick up some groceries at 10:30 at night? That explanation didn't make sense, but he really couldn't think of any reason for anyone to be following him. He also remembered the man standing under the streetlight. That definitely wasn't Officer Collins that night. Once, he thought that he had heard a rustling in the bushes as he walked, but he quickly dismissed that as only the wind. He started walking faster, almost in a run. He finally made it back to the Island Charm and raced up the stairs to his room. He locked the door behind him, then with all of the lights still off, went over to the window and peered out. The night was quiet and no one was in sight. He breathed a huge sigh of relief that he was back in his room, but that uneasy, almost paranoid feeling continued. He hadn't gotten much sleep that night. He tried, but he just lay there thinking. Was it the wind and the darkness that had been playing tricks with his mind, or had someone really been following him?

He went downstairs to breakfast and everyone was already there waiting for him. Just as he thought, Barbara had cooked up a really hearty breakfast. Eggs, sausage, biscuits, gravy, the whole works. He grabbed a plate and fixed himself a large helping before they went out to the lighthouse for the day's activities. He was glad that they had met Steve as well. Steve enjoyed woodworking and would be a big help in renovating the interior. And four can definitely get more done than three. They finished up breakfast, and then the four of them walked out to Dan's truck and headed out to the lighthouse. At the edge of town, they passed Officer Collins in his patrol car parked on the side of the road, seemingly watching them. "We've been seeing him a lot lately!" remarked Dan as they passed.

When they arrived at the lighthouse, the crew from Southeast Restoration Professionals was already at work. There was a crew of five of them. Three were working outside this morning, while two were working on the inside of the lighthouse tower. Chris, the project manager, was inside surveying what needed to be done to rebuild the spiral staircase. Most of the old wooden one was already gone, so there was no way to get to the top right now. Nothing was really salvageable of the old staircase; they'd just have to build a new one from the ground up. Brandon, the project engineer was with him, writing notes and specifications into his notebook as they talked and measured. Scotty, Greg, and Steve went straight into the kitchen to finish clearing everything out. Dan came into where Chris and Brandon were discussing the staircase.

"Good morning Mr. Nelson!" remarked Chris.

"Good morning, Chris," replied Dan, "How are things looking today?"

"Tom, Eric, and Walt are making good progress on the outside. We're going to use the original bricks where we can. I'm having a load of bricks delivered early next week to replace the ones that are too broken to be able to use. We use a company that makes them by hand, the way bricks used to be made so the look will fit in with the old ones."

"Do what you think is best," replied Dan, "you're the expert."

Chris motioned for Dan to follow him into the next room, then outside.

"Come out here a minute," he said in a low tone so the others wouldn't hear, "there's something I need to mention."

They walked outside, then around the corner of the house.

"Is anyone else supposed to be out here?" Chris asked.

"No," replied Dan, "just you, your crew, and me, Scotty, Greg, and Steve. Occasionally Steve's wife Arlene might come out with us, but no one else. You, the island police and I have the only key. Why?"

"Because there was someone else out here this morning." said Chris with a concerned look. "When we pulled up, the sun was just coming up. As we unpacked our tools, Walt noticed motion over near the lighthouse. I looked over that direction just in time to see someone come out from inside the lighthouse and start walking toward the woods over there. I called out to him, but he started walking faster. He never said anything; he just disappeared over into the woods. Then when I came out a minute ago, about fifteen minutes before you arrived, I saw him standing over next to the edge of the woods near our trucks. He seemed to be watching us, but he went back into the woods when he saw me looking his direction. Who do you figure it could be?"

"Was he wearing a police uniform?" asked Dan. He was thinking at first that it could be Officer Collins.

"No," said Chris, "he was just wearing tan pants and a dark shirt, maybe black or dark blue. He looked to have either blonde or light brown hair."

"Hmm," replied Dan, "no one else is supposed to be out here, but there is a way they could get in. There's a path through the woods that leads to the fence that surrounds this area. The path goes over toward the Harbor Inn. There's a hole in the fence that's covered by weeds and bushes about a half mile from the Inn. We found it a couple weeks ago, and it's definitely big enough for someone to get through. I'd keep an eye out, though. I've had several occasions where I've felt like I was being followed. It could be the same guy. Until we know who he is and what he wants, don't take any chances."

"We'll be careful." said Chris.

They went back inside and continued to discuss the renovation. Dan would talk to the others about the mysterious stranger later. He felt like he shouldn't keep it a secret any longer, and the others could help him keep watch. He did wonder who it might be, and why they were taking such an interest in him and the lighthouse. He couldn't help thinking that everything that was happening now was somehow connected to the mystery surrounding the lighthouse and the fog. But he just didn't have all the pieces yet to be able to put it all together. There was a lot that he still didn't know, but hoped to find out. He also wondered why Officer Collins seemed to be taking such an interest in him. After discussing the renovation with Chris, Dan went back into the kitchen to help the others.

Around 12:30, they heard a car pull up out by the clearing. Dan went outside just in time to see a blue Chevy pull up next to his truck. It was Arlene. She had decided that everyone would probably be hungry by now, so she brought lunch from the Sand Crab Diner. She motioned for them to come over, and they all headed that way. As they walked, Dan was alert and looking around to see if anyone else was watching. He didn't particularly feel like they were being watched right now, but after what Chris had told him, he knew that someone else could be out here somewhere.

"Looking for something?" inquired Scotty, apparently noticing Dan cautiously looking around.

"Not sure," replied Dan, "I'll tell you about it at lunch."

At lunch, Dan told them all what he and Chris had discussed that morning. He wasn't sure how much he should mention in front of Arlene. She worried about Steve, and didn't want him to be in any danger. But he did emphasize the fact that they really didn't know if the man presented any danger or not. Still, he could tell by the look on her face that she was concerned. He probably should have let Steve discuss it with her in private.

"Do you have ANY idea who it might be?" she inquired.

"I'm afraid not." he said. "To be perfectly honest, I wasn't really prepared for any of this. My plan was to come to the island, renovate the lighthouse, and move my family out here in June or July. I had read the accounts of the fog, and the mysteries surrounding the lighthouse, but those were all accounts in the history books. When I arrived here, it never really occurred to me that the fog was still appearing even now. I never expected to encounter Bill or Dr. Carson. I expected to research the history surrounding the lighthouse, maybe even get an idea of what may have happened. But everything that happened would have happened in the PAST. When we all went out there with Dr. Carson last week, I didn't actually expect anything to happen. But it did! The fog came up, we walked into it, and at that point all of the stories that I had read over the years became REAL! It wasn't something that happened in 1974, or 1935, or way back in the 1800s. It was something that's still happening NOW! And whatever is still happening, we have to deal with it, and if I expect to live here, I have to accept it and learn more about it. I know that I'll need to find out a lot more about what's happening before I move my family out here. I'm still planning on them joining me in June, but we'll probably get a rental house out on Sea Spray Drive until I know more. From the looks of things, the lighthouse won't be ready to move into until sometime later in the summer or early fall anyway. Maybe by then we'll know what's going on."

They all agreed. Neither Scotty nor Greg had expected all that had been happening either. Even Scotty hadn't really thought there was anything to the fog stories. Not until he actually saw it himself. Now he was as puzzled as anyone else trying to explain it. Greg even remembered a few nights ago, when he had gone to get a magazine out of his Jeep, that he felt like there was someone else there. He had thought he saw movement out of the corner of his eye as he came around the corner of the building, and sensed that there was someone there, but when he stopped and listened, all he could hear was his own heartbeat. He continued to his Jeep, picked up the magazine, and went back upstairs without giving it another thought. Not until now, that is. Now he wondered if maybe there was someone watching him that night. Still, like the others, he couldn't imagine who or even why.

After lunch, Arlene went back to work with them to help work on the interior renovation. There were days that she did come out to help. With the five of them plus the five men from Southeast Restoration they felt pretty safe working out there during the day. They were cautious going out there after dark, though, and never went out alone. Even during the day, Dan preferred that no one go out alone. They worked the rest of the day without incident, with the mysterious stranger not being seen again.

At the end of the day, they packed up to head back to the Island Charm. Steve rode with Arlene this time, and the other three piled into Dan's truck. Restoring a lighthouse was definitely hard work. They were all pretty tired, and wanted nothing more than to go back, sit down, have some of Barbara's dinner, and then just relax the rest of the evening. As they were driving slowly down the mile long gravel road which led to the main road, they were more alert than usual, with everyone but the driver peering into the woods for any sign of movement which might indicate the presence of the man that had been seen earlier in the day. At one point Greg cried, "Stop the truck! There's something at the edge of that clearing over to the left!" Dan stopped the truck and they all got out. Steve and Arlene, curious as to why Dan had stopped, got out and joined them.

"Over there!" said Greg, trying hard to make out the figure standing at the edge of the woods. They approached cautiously. Whoever or whatever it was was still quite a ways off and they couldn't make out any detail. Suddenly, with a blur of motion, the object darted across the clearing, and they could see that it was only a deer. Relieved, they all went back to their vehicles and continued on down the road, glad when they finally got back out on the main road to head back to the Island Charm, and to Barbara's dinner. If they had stayed and watched, they would have seen what startled the deer. They, nor the deer, were alone out there. About a minute after the deer had bolted across the field, two shadowy figures emerged from the woods and walked along the edge of the clearing, disappearing into the woods on the opposite side.

They arrived back at the Island Charm, parked alongside the building in their usual spots, and then went in for dinner. The dinner conversation was lighter and not nearly as serious. They were laughing, and genuinely having a good time. While the renovations were going well, it still was a relief to get back home for the evening and just be able to relax. After dinner, they all went into the parlor and watched a DVD that Arlene had picked up from the library earlier. It was a murder-mystery, which was her and Steve's favorite genre of movie. Since they had been here, they had gotten the others interested in them as well, and they all had fun spending the evening trying to be the first to figure out who was the murderer. While there was no murder involved, Greg mentioned that the current situation that they found themselves in would make a good suspense movie. They all agreed, even encouraging him to be the one to write it.

Around 10:30, after the movie was over, they all decided to turn in for the night. Scotty had been the first to guess the murderer in tonight's suspense thriller. It wasn't who any of the others guessed, either. They all thought that it was the ex-wife returning for revenge. Nobody had suspected the son. He just seemed to be too nice. But that was what made Scotty suspicious from the start. In the end, he was proven to be right.

They climbed the stairs and went to their rooms. Out of habit, Dan went to the window and looked out. The night was quiet with no one in sight. He had almost expected to see a man standing under the streetlight, as he had earlier. Instead, he was relieved that no one was there and that everything was quiet. Everything seemed just as it should be. If he could have seen out the side of the building near where the cars were parked, however, he would have seen that everything wasn't as quiet as it seemed. A single man walked between the cars and back toward the rear of the building, a man who had been watching them through the parlor window that evening. But inside, everything was quiet and peaceful, and they all settled in for a good night's sleep.

CHAPTER 14
April 11, 2016
An Unexplained Object

It was Monday morning, and the sun shone in through the window as Dan woke around 7:00. The weekend hadn't been as productive as he'd hoped. Saturday, rain which was forecast for later in the evening, actually moved in around 2:30 in the afternoon and became a steady rain all day on Sunday. Since they were working inside, they stayed for most of the rest of Saturday, but stayed back at the Island Charm on Sunday, since the rain was falling harder. The weekend was pretty much a washout for Chris and his crew as well, who had to end the day early on Saturday. They'd start back this morning, and from what Dan could tell after getting up and looking out the window, it was going to be a great day for outdoor work, even if it was a little wet from all the rain.

Right on time, he heard Scotty's knock at his door. Scotty was actually a little surprised that Dan was already up and dressed when he came by. He usually had to go on downstairs to breakfast first, with Dan coming down a little later. This morning, however, with Dan anxious to get started back after the rainy weekend, they both went down together. Greg had already gone down and was fixing his breakfast plate when they arrived. They sat down to breakfast, and soon Steve and Arlene joined them. They had gotten a load of building supplies on Friday afternoon which they'd hoped to use over the weekend, but since they weren't able to do much during the weekend, having the supplies already delivered should make for a fairly productive week. Southeast Restorations had even gotten in a couple loads of brick, with more scheduled to arrive today. They all sat down to breakfast, and within a short time they were finished and ready to start the day out at the lighthouse.

Steve and Arlene decided to drive separately so she could come back to the Island Charm and get lunch for the group. The rest climbed into Dan's truck and they headed off to the lighthouse. When they arrived at the gate, it was already unlocked and open, indicating that Southeast Restorations was already out and hard at work. Lately, they'd been leaving the gate open during the day so that delivery folks could get out to the lighthouse. Since work had begun, there had been quite a few deliveries made, with a lot more to come before the work was finished. They drove down the mile long gravel road, which was a lot smoother now that it was being driven on daily. When they got to the clearing where everyone parked, Southeast Restoration's trucks were there and they could see a couple of men up on the scaffolding. A lift truck was out by the lighthouse as well, to lift the concrete mix and pallets of brick onto the scaffolding, as well as to lift down pallets of broken brick which they were removing. Everyone gathered up their tools and walked out to the lighthouse.

When they got near the lighthouse, Chris, who had apparently been watching for them to arrive, came out with a worried look.

"Someone's been out here again!" he said.

"How do you know?" asked Scotty.

"Come over here, I'll show you." Chris answered.

He took them over to the side of the house, and they all saw deep footprints in the damp soil. With all of the rain that they'd had over the weekend, the ground was soft. It hadn't completely dried out, even this morning, and every step that they took made an indention in the grass. They followed the tracks in the soil over to the back steps, where they ended, appearing that whoever it was had climbed the steps and went into the house. There was mud on the steps as well, where the person had climbed them. When they walked up the steps and into the foyer, they could see muddy tracks leading into the den. It looked like whoever had been in the house had moved around quite a bit since there were tracks going everywhere. They walked over to the front door where the tracks seemed to exit and more indentions were found in the soil at the bottom of the stairs which appeared to continue on out the front gate and into the woods.

"These weren't made by us," Chris said, "they were here this morning when we arrived. None of us had even gone into the house until you got here. We haven't seen anyone else around this morning, though, so we're not sure when the tracks were made."

"Wonder if it's the same person we've been seeing, the one that's followed me on a couple of occasions?" asked Dan.

"I'd bet it is," said Scotty, "Who else would it be? I guess it could be that police officer that's taken an interest in us, though."

"I don't think so." replied Dan. "I think it's the person that I saw that one night standing under the streetlight. That definitely wasn't Officer Collins."

"Do you think we should go back and talk to Chief Callahan?" asked Greg.

"No," replied Dan, "not just yet. Officer Collins seemed to start appearing wherever we were after our first report. He may just be following up on the report, but he seems to be keeping an eye on us for some reason. Until we know why, or exactly what the mysterious stranger's role is in all of this, I'd prefer to keep it between us. We'll be careful and keep a watch out."

After studying the tracks for a few more minutes, they all looked around, scanning for any movement or anything out of the ordinary at the edge of the woods. After seeing nothing, Chris went back to work inside the lighthouse tower, while the others continued clearing out the den. Arlene and Steve were measuring in the kitchen for new cabinets. They were planning on going into Wilmington later in the week to pick some out. It was while clearing debris out of the den, that a glimmer caught Greg's attention. He bent down to pick up the object, which was a shiny silver color that glimmered in any available light. He was startled when he first touched it, because it seemed to vibrate and become warm to the touch. He wasn't sure whether to pick it up or not.

"Dad, come look at this!" he called to Scotty.

Scotty came over and just stared at the object for a few seconds, noticing its shine even in the dim light. He bent down and picked it up, but dropped it with a start when it seemed to come alive in his hand. "What IS that thing?!" he exclaimed. At this, Dan also came over, and Steve and Arlene peered out from the kitchen door. Dan reached down and picked it up as well, but he held onto it even when it started to vibrate. He noticed that it wasn't exactly vibrating, but appeared to be sending minute pulses through the nerves in his hand. This was accompanied by a slight warm sensation that permeated the area around where he was grasping it.

"I'm not sure what this is," he remarked, "or what it could even be for!"

By now, Steve and Arlene had come out from the kitchen and were staring at it as well. It was unusual. It really didn't have many features. It looked like an elongated teardrop about eight inches long. It was about a half inch in diameter on the narrow end and about two inches in diameter on the wide end. Both ends were rounded. It was shiny like polished chrome, but not nearly as heavy. In fact, if it weren't for the feel of it, which definitely felt like metal, they would almost think it was plastic, since it was about the weight that they would expect plastic to be. Dan turned it over and over in his hand, inspecting every facet of it. It was still vibrating and was still warm, though he thought that it might not be vibrating quite as much now. It appeared to be molded into one piece, since he couldn't detect any visible doors, latches, or screws. He couldn't even spot any seam where it was initially put together. The entire object was completely smooth.

"Where do you think it came from?" Greg asked the group.

"I don't have a clue!" Dan and Scotty both remarked in unison. Dan continued, "I'm not sure where it could have come from, or even how long it could have been here. It looks new, but who knows? It kind of looks like some sort of decoration, but what I'm really stumped about is those vibrations and what's causing them. There must be something inside, but how it was assembled is a mystery to me."

"So what are we going to do with it?" asked Scotty, "After all it must have gotten here somehow."

Steve chimed in, "Do you think this may have been what the man that Chris saw, and the man that made those tracks, was looking for?"

"Could be." said Dan. "I'll probably go call Dr. Carson. They may have some equipment at the college that can analyze it."

Dan wandered over to where his truck was parked and put the object on the passenger seat. He got out his Smartphone and took several pictures of it. After taking a few pictures, he selected the text message icon and sent the pictures to Dr. Carson's phone. He then pulled up his contacts and scrolled down to where he had added him. He hit Dr. Carson's name and the phone began dialing. After a few seconds there was an answer, "Hello, Dr. Paul Carson."

"Dr. Carson? Dan Nelson." replied Dan, "We've found something kind of unusual down at the lighthouse. I just texted some photos to you."

"OK, let me take a look." Dr. Carson replied. After a short pause, he came back on the line. "How heavy is it?" he asked.

"It's not very heavy," replied Dan, "It almost feels like it's made of plastic, judging by the weight, but it feels like metal. It also vibrates and gets warm when someone picks it up."

"Is there anywhere where it looks like it could open up?"

"No, it's completely smooth."

After a few more questions, Dr. Carson decided that he needed to see it in person, and told Dan he'd be there in about an hour. Apparently they had found something extremely interesting, he thought, since Dr. Carson wanted to come right out and see it.

About an hour and a half later, Dr. Carson pulled in beside Dan's truck. This time he was driving a plain white Ford Focus, registered to the college.

"Good afternoon!" he greeted Dan.

"Afternoon," replied Dan. "Thanks for coming out so quickly. Here's the object that we found."

Dan presented it to Dr. Carson, who, like the others, quickly recoiled at the vibration.

"Interesting!" he remarked as he gained back his composure, "I know you mentioned that it vibrated, but I still wasn't completely prepared for it. It almost feels like a low level electric shock."

"That's what I thought too when I first touched it!" replied Dan.

Dr. Carson turned the object over and over in his hands, thoroughly examining every facet of its exterior. It was extremely shiny just like Dan had said and everything around reflected in it like a mirror, albeit more like one of those carnival mirrors that distort the image. He ran his fingers over it, trying to find some hint as to where it was put together, but it really was completely smooth all the way around. There didn't appear to be any imperfections at all. One thing that he noticed immediately was that despite being handled by Dan, the others, and himself, he didn't see any fingerprints. Usually any smooth shiny object would be covered with fingerprints by now, but this was still completely shiny and smooth. He actually pressed his finger against the surface and pulled it off, examining the spot where his finger was, but there was still no fingerprint.

"So, you found this inside the lighthouse?" he inquired.

"Yes," replied Dan, "in a corner of the den slightly hidden under some debris beside a cabinet."

"Any idea how it might have gotten there, or how long it's been there?" Dr. Carson asked.

"Hard to tell," Dan responded, "It could have been there since before we even got here, or it may be more recent. We've been in the house pretty much daily, but this was the first time that we'd cleaned out that corner of the den."

"I'd like to take it back to the college with me, if you don't mind." Dr. Carson responded, "We've got equipment there that can tell us a lot more about it. Right now, I'd say it doesn't look like any metal I've ever seen, but we won't know the composition for sure until we can analyze it."

"Fine," said Dan, "do what you need to. I'm curious as to what it is and what it's used for, so I'd be interested in anything that you could find out about it."

"So am I." replied Dr. Carson.

The two of them talked for another several minutes, and then Dr. Carson asked to see the location where it was found. They walked across to the lighthouse, with Dr. Carson still holding onto the object. Dan took him through the back door into the foyer, and then they both walked into the den. He showed him the cabinet in the back corner where they had found it laying on the floor. Dr. Carson gave the object back to Dan, then knelt down and examined the area closely. The cabinet had been moved out from the wall about a foot, so he shined his light behind it, but there were just dust and spider webs. He got back to his feet, appearing to be satisfied. He took a few pictures of the area with the camera on his Smartphone, and then they both slowly headed toward the door.

When they got back to the truck, Dan handed the object back to Dr. Carson. It immediately began to vibrate in his hand.

"This is going to take some getting used to!" he remarked, referring to the low heat and vibration which occurred every time it was touched. He walked over to his car and got a small cloth out of the trunk which he used to wrap it up, then got into his car and placed it on the seat beside him. "I'll let you know what I find out." he told Dan, and then he backed out and proceeded down the gravel road. As he slowly drove out toward Harbor Inn Lane, he puzzled over and over about the object. He had never seen or felt anything like it, and while he didn't say this to Dan, he believed that it probably came out of the fog; something from an alternate reality, and maybe finding out more about it would help solve some of the puzzles about that reality. He figured that Dan probably suspected the same thing, anyway. In all of his years as a scientist and teacher, he had never seen anything quite like this.

As he continued slowly driving, lost in thought about all that had happened within the last couple of weeks at the lighthouse, his thoughts were interrupted by a person standing in the middle of the road. He saw him up ahead and slowed down. The man wasn't making any gestures for him to stop; he was just standing there, staring in his direction as he approached. He looked to be in his middle to late thirties with sandy brown hair. He was wearing tan pants and a blue button down shirt. A man standing in the middle of the road, way out here struck Paul as rather odd, since this was one of the last things that he would be expecting after leaving Dan and his friends back at the lighthouse. He stopped the car several feet from the man, all the while wondering what he was doing out here. He wasn't anyone that Dan had introduced him to, or anyone that he had met before. Paul hesitantly rolled down the car window as the man walked around the car and approached the driver side door. The man wasn't smiling, or frowning for that matter. He simply had a rather blank expression on his face. Just the manner in which he walked as he approached gave Paul an uneasy feeling. Part of him wondered if he should just drive away after the man got beside the car where he wouldn't run him over. Instead, Paul found himself saying, in a slightly hesitant, uneasy voice, "Good afternoon! What can I do for you?" The man seemed to study Paul, but seemed to also be examining the interior of the car. This made Paul even more nervous and his desire to flee the situation grew stronger. Finally, the man spoke up, "I need the beacon."

"Beacon?" Paul asked in a slightly shaky voice. At this point, the man was really starting to scare him. He figured the beacon the man was asking for was the thing that they had found that was now lying on the seat beside him. The fact that the man still wasn't smiling or showing any emotion at all was really causing him concern. Who was he? And why did he call the object a beacon? None of them knew what it was.

Again the man spoke up, "Where's the beacon? Give it to me." The man wasn't shouting or speaking loudly. He had a slight monotone, matter of fact tone to his voice that made the hair stand up on Paul's neck.

"I'm not sure what you're talking about..." Paul began, but never quite got a chance to finish the sentence. Before he knew what was happening, or even had a chance to push the car's accelerator to get out of there, the man raised his hand and the last thing that Paul saw was a bright flash of light.

Paul awoke a little while later feeling extremely disoriented. Really, he didn't feel like any time had passed at all. One minute he was driving along, and then the disoriented feeling came on. It was like the feeling you get when you doze off for a second then wake up. You really don't feel like you've been asleep, but you feel a strange sensation when you wake up. The last thing that he remembered was driving down Lighthouse Road, and then he must have blacked out for a moment. At least he was stopped in the middle of the road and hadn't run off and hit a tree. He was definitely thankful for that. He had never blacked out like this before, though, especially while driving a car and this concerned him. He looked at the clock on the car's dashboard and determined that about eleven minutes had passed. He didn't feel like he'd been asleep that long. He tried to remember anything that had happened the last few minutes, but all he seemed to be able to remember was driving down the road, then waking up now with a strange sort of feeling. Alarmed, he glanced over at the seat beside him where the object lay, still wrapped in the cloth. He felt a rush of relief that the object was still there. He was regaining more of his composure now, so he decided to continue on down the road. He got to the end of Lighthouse Road, then made the right turn onto Harbor Inn Lane and continued on out to the ferry station. All the while he never could quite shake the feeling that something was wrong, but he couldn't quite put his finger on it. Throughout the ferry ride and along the route back to Wilmington, he went over and over in his mind what could have happened back on Lighthouse Road.

After Dr. Carson had left, Dan went back to help the others with the renovation. When he got back to the lighthouse, everyone else was already hard at work.

"Did he have any ideas about what it was?" Scotty asked Dan when he entered the room.

"Not really," answered Dan, "He took it with him back to the college so it could be analyzed there. Strangest thing I've ever seen, though."

"It really was a very unique object." replied Scotty. "It didn't look like anything that really fit in around here. Everything here is old and rusty, and that thing, well, it was just too shiny!"

"I know," said Dan, "And really weird the way it vibrated like that. You're right, though, it really didn't seem to fit in with all the other stuff we've been finding. I think it was dropped here fairly recently."

"Agreed." said Scotty.

The restoration effort was actually going well. Chris and his group from Southeast Restorations had already made a lot of progress on the outside. They had gotten most of the broken brick removed from the tower and put into a pile by the edge of the wall. Now, they were in the process of sandblasting the exterior of the tower in preparation for adding the new brick. Dan thought that it had been a good choice hiring them. Chris was easy to work with and the whole team seemed to know exactly what they were doing. It was obvious that this wasn't the first job of this type that they had done. The progress on the interior, however, was a lot slower. Being inexperienced at this type of work, Dan and his friends weren't progressing very fast. Still, progress was being made, and they were having fun. Chris offered to bring in a couple of interior restoration engineers from his company to help out with the inside and Dan thought that was a good idea. Chris said that he felt that it would make things go a lot faster indoors having someone who had done this kind of restoration before. They wouldn't be able to start until next Monday, but they would definitely be a welcome addition.

Arlene had gone back to the Island Charm and had picked up some boxed lunches that Barbara had made for them. They all were sitting around eating them when Dan's phone rang. It was Dr. Carson with some disturbing news, "The object is gone!" he said.

"What do you mean gone?!" inquired Dan, not fully believing what he was hearing.

"I mean gone! When I got back here to the college and took it into the lab to unwrap it, it was gone! All that was in the cloth was a smooth river rock about the same size."

"Could that have been it?" asked Dan. "We didn't know exactly what it was. Could it have turned into a rock-like object during transport?"

"Not likely. I mean what I have here is a real rock. I don't see how it could have changed so dramatically in such a short time."

"But it was with you the whole time. Did you stop off anywhere between here and there?" asked Dan.

"Well ... not exactly. Something strange did happen along the way though. At the time, I looked over to make sure the object was still there and it appeared to still be there wrapped in the cloth. I didn't unwrap it then, though, so it may have already been gone."

"What happened?" asked Dan.

"I had just started out and was about half a mile down Lighthouse Road when I apparently blacked out. No warning, it just happened. It felt like I'd only dozed off for a few seconds, but according to the clock in the car, about eleven minutes had gone by. Nothing like this has ever happened to me before, so it was kind of unnerving."

"Do you remember anything odd right before you blacked out?" asked Dan.

"No, I don't remember anything. I was driving along Lighthouse Road one minute, then the next it felt like I was waking up. I don't remember seeing or hearing anything unusual. Everything was quiet and peaceful. When I woke up, it took me a few minutes to gain back my composure, and then I looked over to make sure the object was still there, before continuing on. Funny thing was I don't even think I was tired, so I really can't explain what happened. The only thing that I can figure is that the object was swapped for the rock sometime in the eleven minutes when I was out, though I'm still not sure who could have done it."

"That is unfortunate," said Dan, "still, I'm glad you're ok. At least you weren't going very fast when you blacked out."

Dan hung up the phone and Scotty observed a strange look on Dan's face. He didn't have to say anything; Dan knew what he was thinking.

"The object's gone." said Dan to the others. "We're not sure what happened exactly. It was strange. Dr. Carson said he blacked out on

Lighthouse Road on the way out. It wasn't long, and he'd never blacked out like that before. He said it only felt like a few seconds, but the clock in his car indicated that it had been about eleven minutes. When he got back to the college, the object wasn't still in the cloth. Instead, it was a rock about the same size."

"Sounds like it got switched along the way." remarked Scotty.

"Yes, that's what it sounds like. And the only time that it could have happened seems to be when he blacked out. But he doesn't remember seeing or hearing anything odd either before or after. And who would be out here that could have switched it? This whole thing's really strange."

While they were all still in conversation about the object and what might have happened to it, they heard a vehicle coming down Lighthouse Road.

"Wonder who this could be?" inquired Scotty.

The question was answered a few minutes later when a black Dodge Journey came into view and parked beside Dan's truck. All eyes were on the vehicle, since neither Dan nor any of the others were expecting anyone else out here today. But to Dan's surprise, a woman got out of the driver's side, followed by a young boy from the passenger side and two young girls from the back.

"Kate!" Dan exclaimed, now running toward the vehicle. "It's great to see you Kate!" They embraced and kissed, obviously glad to see each other. Then Dan turned to Danny, "How's my man?"

"I'm great dad! Glad to see you."

He walked over to where Amy and Veronica stood and gave them both huge hugs.

"This is a great surprise!" he said, "but what are you doing here now? I thought you weren't coming for another couple of months."

Kate answered, "Well, the kids are on Spring Break this week, and we all have been missing you, so we decided to fly down for the week and surprise you!"

"Great surprise!" he said, motioning for them to follow him over to where the rest of his friends were. They obviously knew Scotty and Greg, but he introduced them to Steve and Arlene as well. Steve had heard so much about them the last several weeks, that he was finally glad that he got to meet them.

After the introductions, Dan was ready to take them on a tour of the lighthouse. As they started to leave, Scotty motioned for Dan to come over.

"Why don't you take the rest of the week off?" he suggested, "We've got things under control here, and I'm sure you have a lot of catching up to do with the family. Take them on a tour of the island as well. They're here for the week, might as well do some sightseeing."

"Thanks," Dan replied, "I'll do that. Give me a call if anything comes up, though. You know what I mean." Scotty nodded, fully aware of what Dan meant.

Dan walked back over to where his family waited and motioned for them to follow him toward the lighthouse. All of them had been staring at it for quite some time since they'd gotten here. Kate was silent. Dan studied her face to see if he could tell what she was thinking. The lighthouse wasn't quite as far along in the restoration as he would have liked for their first viewing. It was still extremely rough looking both inside and out. Still, Kate didn't seem to really disapprove. "It's got possibilities." was what she said, and in fact that was the closest to the truth that he'd heard. "Possibilities" was really a good description of the state that it was in at this moment. He cautioned them to be careful as they approached the back entrance, as the crew from Southeast Restorations was working overhead. They stepped into the back foyer and came at once out of the fresh ocean air into a damp musty atmosphere. It was the scent of an old abandoned structure that was just now coming back to life.

"Are we REALLY going to live here?!" asked Danny excitedly. He could tell immediately that he had his son's approval. For him, it would be every bit the adventure that it was for his dad. It was Amy and her mom that he'd have a harder time selling on the idea.

"I hope not!" remarked Amy with a look of disgust. She couldn't imagine living in such a dark, depressing place, miles away from anything to do, and anyone to do it with. It was different this trip. She had her best friend Veronica with her. Veronica could make things fun wherever they were. But when she was gone, what would there be to do? It would be just her, Mom, Dad, and Danny. And from what she could tell during the drive in, there weren't any neighbors for miles. And what was with that huge gate that they drove through on the way in? She remembered looking at that gate and wondering what it was built to keep out ... or IN. It just looked so out of place from the rest of the island.

"We won't be living here at first." replied Dan. "There's still a lot of work that has to be done on it. We'll probably rent a cottage for a few months while the renovations continue here. And believe me, it'll look a lot different when we finally do move in than it does now!"

That was a relief to both Amy and Kate. While Danny would probably move in right now, for the girls the idea of renting a cottage that was ready to move into was a lot more appealing.

"It looks a lot more run down than it did in the pictures." remarked Kate. Dan had known that she'd mention this. He had, in fact, noticed the same thing the first time that he had come out to take a look. He wasn't sure when the pictures that he had seen before buying it were taken, but it was obvious that they had been taken decades before, possibly even before it was fenced in.

"Yeah, I noticed that too when I first saw it. I think those photos were taken quite a bit earlier. Still, it just means it'll take a little more work to get it back in shape."

Amy made a face at her dad's use of the word "little". In her opinion, it would take a LOT more work, and that was assuming that it could even BE gotten back in shape, which looking at it now, she wasn't so sure. They continued their tour, with Dan excitedly sharing with them his plans for each room. As they walked out the front entrance onto the porch, the view of the Cape Fear River was spectacular, with the sun reflecting off the water. Kate remarked that the view almost made the place worth it. They all just stood for a moment, taking it all in.

As they stood, just admiring the view from the front steps, a shadowy figure was watching them just out of sight at the edge of the woods. It was the same shadowy figure that Dan had sensed on several occasions before. But here, now, with the joy of having his family here with him, he didn't notice. The figure stayed quiet and still, but all the time was watching them. Dan's family was here now, and the man knew what that meant. Things were falling into place, just as he knew they would. In a few days, everything about Dan's world would change forever, in ways that he couldn't even begin to imagine. The man knew this. But for now, he watched and waited.

CHAPTER 15

A Pleasant Surprise

After a good tour of the lighthouse and the grounds surrounding it, they all went back into town. Danny had been disappointed that they couldn't climb to the top just yet, but Dan assured him that next time he saw it, they should have the stairs installed and they'd be able to. Kate and the kids were staying for the week in a suite out at the Harbor Inn. She hadn't had any trouble finding it. It was one of the highest rated resorts on the island and the only one not out along Sea Spray Drive. Even though it wasn't ocean front, it had a lot of amenities that she and the kids would enjoy, like an indoor pool, tennis courts, bicycle rental, mini golf, horseback riding, and carriage tours of the island. She and Amy had already talked about taking the moonlight carriage ride along the beach. While the hotel itself was secluded back in the woods, it was only a mile from Sea Spray Drive, and they did offer an hour and a half carriage ride that went down to the beach, then along the beachfront. The kids all wanted to do the mini golf, and all of them liked relaxing by the pool. They'd probably rent bicycles for the week as well so that they could tour the island on their own. This was the perfect time of year for it, not too hot or cold. After dropping off the rented Dodge Journey in the Harbor Inn parking lot, they all continued to the Island Charm in Dan's truck. He wanted to introduce them to Hank and Barbara and show them where he had been staying for the past month.

When they arrived at the Island Charm, Kate remembered passing it on their way in and thought that she remembered that was where Dan was staying. Dan parked in his usual spot to the side of the building and they all got out and walked around to the front. Climbing the steps, Amy thought to herself that she'd much rather live here than all the way out at that run down lighthouse. At least this was in town and close to everything, like shopping. As they walked through the front door, Dan noticed Barbara in the sitting room on the right engaged in what must be a good book.

Barbara looked up as they entered, peering over her wire-rimmed reading glasses.

"I didn't expect anyone back this early!" she remarked, "You guys don't usually get back till late in the evening."

Dan replied, "Yes, that's usually true, but today my family surprised me and showed up here, so I decided to take the day off from working and show them around the island. This is my wife Kate, my kids Danny and Amy, and Amy's best friend Veronica."

"Well, nice to meet you all!" said Barbara, "I hope you'll all come for dinner tonight. Hank's grilling out. We're having hamburgers and hotdogs."

"Sounds good to me!" Danny replied excitedly.

"We'll be here." Dan replied.

Barbara remarked to Dan, "I hope you're not planning on crowding everyone into your room!"

Kate spoke up, "No, we're staying out at the Harbor Inn. We rented a suite so everyone would have enough room."

"That's a relief!" said Barbara, "I was wondering how you'd all fit!"

Just then, Hank, who had been in the next room rewiring a broken electrical outlet, appeared in the doorway. Dan repeated the introductions and Hank told them that he hoped they enjoyed their stay, but there was something in his mood that made Dan feel that he wasn't as glad to meet them as was his wife. He motioned for Dan to follow him into the next room while Barbara and Kate got better acquainted. The kids went outside to sit in the front porch swing that they had seen when they first came in. When Dan and Hank got into the next room, Hank was quiet at first, seeming to ponder what he was going to say. Finally he said, "Are you sure you know what you're doing, bringing your family here? You know how I feel about the lighthouse, and well, I've gotten to like you during the time that you've been here. I'd really hate for something to happen."

"Nothing's going to happen." replied Dan, "They probably won't even be out at the lighthouse that much. They'll be touring the island and doing activities out at the inn." But his voice didn't sound convinced of that. Hank's question had reminded him of the events that had happened lately. In all of the excitement of seeing Kate and the kids, he hadn't really thought about there being any danger to them by being here. But Hank's question had reminded him of actually seeing the fog out at the lighthouse, and the mysterious stranger lurking around out there. And the stranger wasn't confined just to the woods around the lighthouse. Dan remembered seeing him under the streetlight that one night, and being followed while walking back from the convenience store on another occasion. While he felt that he, along with Scotty, Greg, and Steve could handle most anything, he knew that he didn't want to put his family in danger. But he was glad to see them, and he couldn't just send them home so soon after they arrived. But Hank was right to be concerned. Did he really know what he was doing in any of this?

"I'm planning on staying with them out at Harbor Inn for the week," he replied, "so I'll be there to keep an eye on them. We've got a lot of help from the restoration company out there now, so I should be able to spend most of my time with Kate and the kids this week anyway."

Since they arrived, he had been planning on taking some time off this week to spend with them, but after Hank's comment he knew that he'd want to spend even more time with them. He'd want to be with them so that he could make sure they were safe.

"That's a good idea to stay with them." Hank replied. "Don't take that lighthouse too lightly. I still think it was a bad idea to open back up that section of the island, but that was your choice. Just be careful! Like I said, I like you, and your family seems really nice too. Keep an eye on them and watch for anything out of the ordinary."

Just then the kids came rushing in the front door. "Dad, there's a man outside!" said Danny excitedly.

"Whoa, what do you mean, a man?" asked Dan.

"He was across the street, and he just seemed to be staring at us while we were on the swing." said Amy and Veronica almost in unison.

Dan bolted for the front door, leaving the rest of them to wonder why he would run out in such a hurry. He threw open the front door and rushed out onto the porch. He was already out of breath as he looked up and down the street. Unfortunately, the man seemed to be gone. As he stood on the porch, trying to catch his breath, Danny came up behind him.

"He was right over there," Danny said, pointing at a wood frame building across the street, "Right in front of that building."

"Stay here, and go back inside!" Dan instructed. "I'm going to walk over there and have a look."

Under protest, Danny went back inside. All of them had walked up to the front door by now and were watching as Dan ran across the street.

"Dad said to stay inside." Danny told the others.

They all watched as Dan disappeared around the side of the building across the street. Kate had a worried look on her face, as she wondered what was going on. Everything had gone from friendly and carefree to unusual and a little scary when the kids had mentioned the man. And Dan's reaction scared her even more. It was odd that there was a man across the street, seeming to stare at them. And why had Dan been in such a hurry to get outside. The way that he sprang into action seemed a little more than just being protective of his kids, though she knew he was. She wondered if he had seen the man before this. They all watched and waited for Dan to reappear around the building. It seemed like an eternity, but finally Dan reappeared around the other side of the building and strolled back across the street and up onto the porch.

"Did you find him?" asked Danny.

"No, not a trace of him." replied Dan.

Dan was out of breath with a worried look on his face. Barbara brought him a fresh glass of tea from the kitchen.

"Have you seen him before?" inquired Kate. She knew her

husband well enough to know that he wouldn't be this worried just because the kids had seen someone across the street. He'd be concerned, yes, and he'd want to know who it was. But she didn't think that he'd be quite this agitated. Even the look on his face as he drank down the tea worried her. All he said was, "We'll talk later tonight."

Dan was cautious and looked around the area carefully as they left the Island Charm and began to walk down the street. His nerves were still on edge, and though he tried to regain his happy, glad to see them composure, Kate saw through it. Something was definitely worrying him. Maybe tonight, she'd find out what that was.

Since Dan hadn't had a chance to eat his sandwich which Arlene had brought out to the lighthouse earlier, and his family hadn't yet eaten, he decided to take them down to the Sand Crab for some delicious local island cuisine. That was a place that he frequented a lot, since the first day that he had found it. The food was always good, and at a reasonable price. And the atmosphere was one that he knew his family would like. As they walked down the street toward the diner, he actually began to feel a lot better. The day was sunny and a cool breeze was blowing. It was a perfect early spring day. The excitement and anxiety of what had happened earlier seemed to fade away, as they walked through town among other tourists and locals. The kids were chatting among themselves, and even Kate seemed to relax a little as they held hands while strolling down the street.

As they were approaching the Sand Crab Diner, Dan spotted Bud, whom he'd met on the ferry the first day that he arrived. This was actually the first time that he had seen him since then. He held up his hand to wave and Bud waved back to him. Then Bud gestured for him to hold on for a minute. Bud walked over to where they were all about to enter the diner, and Dan introduced him to his family.

"How do you all like our island so far?" asked Bud. He was looking at the kids as he said it.

"We actually just got here," said Danny, "but I like it so far, even with the excitement!"

"Excitement?" inquired Bud.

"Well, we had an incident over at the Island Charm right before we walked down here." replied Dan. "It seems the kids were swinging on the front porch and noticed a man watching them from across the street. I tried to walk over and see who it was, but he was gone by the time I got there."

Bud's face took on a more serious look as he asked Dan, "Can I talk to you a minute privately?"

Bud told Kate and the kids that he hoped they enjoyed their stay, then they went on into the diner while Dan and Bud stayed outside for a minute to talk.

Bud began, "I don't want to worry you, but something happened the other night as I was coming back from visiting Joe Rogers at the Harbor Inn that I think you should know about, especially after what just happened."

Dan became more concerned as he said, "OK, go ahead."

"Like I said, I was driving back from helping Joe Rogers with some things out at the Harbor Inn. It was probably around 9:30 at night. As I was passing by the Island Charm, I noticed someone out in the alleyway by your truck. I thought it might be you, so I pulled in to say hello. As my truck lights shone on the man, I realized immediately that it wasn't you. In fact, it wasn't anyone that I had seen on the island before. Of course, tourists come and go, but this man was acting really odd. As I pulled around, he started to run around the back of the building. I continued on around and tried to follow him, but he circled around and went between two of the other buildings. I drove around front thinking he would come out there. I stopped and waited a few minutes, but he never came out. I called Chief Callahan at the police station, and he sent out Officer Ken Rowland to investigate. When he arrived, I got out of my truck and we both made a thorough search of the area. We didn't find anyone, though. Apparently he had slipped out the opposite way when I went around front.

"What did he look like?" inquired Dan.

"Probably mid to late thirties, light brown hair I think, fairly tall. He was wearing light colored pants and a dark shirt." answered Bud.

Now it was Dan's turn to look perplexed. "That sounds just like the man that I saw under the street light one night." he answered. "He was just standing there looking up at my room. He was probably the one that followed me back from the convenience store one evening as well, though that night I didn't really get a look at anyone, but I heard footsteps and rustling in the bushes."

Bud was concerned. "I'd be really careful." he told Dan. "Like I said, I'd never seen him around here before, and he was acting very peculiar. Keep a watchful eye on your family too. We don't usually have many problems around here, but things have been getting strange lately. Joe Rogers over at the Harbor Inn said that Officer Collins was by there the other day, and even he was not acting normal. He asked Joe if he had been called out to the hotel for anything, like he didn't know why he was there. But, before that nothing had seemed to be wrong at the hotel. Before he left he asked Joe to keep an eye out for anything unusual, particularly if it applied to you or the lighthouse."

So that was it. Officer Collins probably had been watching him just as he suspected from all the times that they had seen him. But why? It must be the fact that he bought the lighthouse, but he just didn't know why that would arouse such interest now. But as he had discovered since he'd been here, people get a strange look when you mention the lighthouse. And he had to admit, the fog they had seen was unnerving. It wasn't like regular fog. Maybe Officer Collins thought that Dan knew more than he really did, but thinking of all that had happened, there was a lot that he still didn't understand.

"I'll be careful." he told Bud. They talked for a few minutes, then Bud went back to unloading his truck and Dan proceeded back into the diner. He found his family over in one of the window booths looking out at the street. They had probably been watching him and Bud as they talked.

"He seems nice." said Kate. "Is anything wrong?"

"No, I met him on the ferry the first day that I came to the island. He just wanted to catch me up on a few things."

That wasn't really a lie. He just didn't want to get into the "things" that Bud wanted to catch him up on just yet. Especially not in front of the kids, and especially not right after what had just happened. He'd have to discuss it with Kate, and he knew she'd ask later.

As he sat down with them and opened his menu, Amy asked, "Dad, do you know where the 'Little Book Nook' is?"

"It's the next block over from here. Why?"

Amy replied, "Did you see the flyer on the door as you came in here? Amy Davenport Westfall is scheduled to be there this Thursday for a book signing for her new book! I've never gotten to meet her before, but I've always wanted to!"

"We'll have to make plans to go then." he told her. "I wonder why she's doing a book signing out here? Doesn't she usually do the big cities?"

Kate replied, "I think she usually does, but I guess sometimes even famous people like to make stops off the beaten path. I'd like to meet her myself, actually."

Dan thought that he wouldn't mind meeting her as well. His whole family, including Danny enjoyed her books. She had a distinctive style of writing that they all liked. Her books were usually in the mystery/intrigue genre and the setting was always sometime in the future. That way her characters could always use gadgets that hadn't been invented yet. One of their favorite characters from her books was Andrea Harris. She was a CIA operative that had adventures around the world. There were even a couple of those books that had been made into movies, "Paris Starlight" and "The Chicago Conspiracy". These were two of the four books in the Andrea Harris series. One of Amy and Dannys favorite gadgets that Andrea always carried with her was her UMPC, an acronym for Universal Multipurpose Personal Communicator. The UMPC really was a multipurpose device. She could use it to video conference back to headquarters from anywhere in the world, a use which reminded them quite a bit of the video phone apps on their smartphones, as well as perform a variety of other tasks. In addition to video conferencing remotely, the UMPC even had a device in it where headquarters could always track her location using satellites, and at the push of a button, she could summon help. She even had a tiny robotic flying camera that she could control with her UMPC. It was small enough to fit in the palm of her hand and had a range of about three miles. She used it to do discreet surveillance of an area. The video from the camera was streamed back to the UMPC so she could see what it saw from a first person view. It seemed that Amy Westfall enjoyed thinking up really cool technical gadgets for Andrea to use. Amy and Danny couldn't help but notice that many of the gadgets in her books were surprisingly similar to actual gadgets that came out after the start of the 21st century, even though some of these books had been written some time earlier. Even Danny had a small quadcopter with a camera on it that he could control from his Smartphone. It even streamed the video back to the phone. Its range was a lot more limited than Andreas, however. Instead of three miles, his had a range of about three hundred feet. In addition to the Andrea Harris series, there were other Amy Westfall books that were among their favorites as well, with titles like "Night Colors", "The Plutonium Factor", and "Sky Wanderer", which next to the Andrea Harris series was one of Danny's favorites. In it, a crime organization used remote aerial cameras, a lot like the one that Andrea used, to pull off a series of crimes worldwide.

"Why don't we go down to the bookstore after this and see if they have any of the books in yet?" suggested Kate.

"Let's go!" chimed both kids in unison. Dan agreed.

Danny and Amy could hardly wait to finish eating. After they were done, they all walked to the next block to the "Little Book Nook". They walked past the large display window facing the street and stopped to look at the display featured in it. Most of the display window on the front of the store was dedicated to the book launch. There was a life-size cardboard stand-up of Amy Westfall in the corner. A large sign hanging from the ceiling in the middle read, "Meet Amy Davenport Westfall - Here Thursday April 14 from 5:00 to 8:00 pm - Signing copies of her new book, 'Displaced in Time'". Like the rest of her books, it had a catchy title which made a person want to pick it up to see what it was about. There were three cardboard promotional cubes hanging from the ceiling. The two cubes on the outside were identical. Each featured a photo of the book cover on opposite sides with the other two sides displaying the phrase, "Where the past catches up with the future". This fit perfectly with Amy Westfall's style.

She always liked an air of mystery to accompany all of her book launches to build excitement. The middle cube featured a head shot of Amy on opposite sides and a photo of the moon reflecting off of the ocean at night on the other two sides. It was the book's cover that held Dan's attention. It featured a lighthouse which was partially covered with fog near the base and the middle. There were clouds on the top third of the cover with rays of sunshine, shining through, one of them illuminating the lighthouse. He wondered if Mrs. Westfall had researched the events surrounding the lighthouse on this island and based a novel on them. If so, that would certainly explain why the book launch was taking place here.

The four of them entered the store and walked over to the Amy Westfall section. While they had several copies of most of her other books, the new one was noticeably absent. They walked over to the counter in the center of the store to ask about it. The woman that had been there the first time that Dan had visited the store apparently wasn't working today. There was a younger man, probably in his early twenties, helping a customer look up a title. They waited patiently, and within a couple of minutes, he turned to them with a cheerful smile and said, "Good afternoon. How may I help you?"

"Do you have any copies of Amy Westfall's new book in stock yet?" inquired Dan.

"Sorry," he replied, "those don't go on sale until Thursday at the book launch. Will you be attending the launch?"

"Yes," answered Dan, "we'll all be here."

"If you'd like, I can take your reservation for one and you can pick it up then. That'll make sure that you get one."

Dan looked over at Danny and Amy. He could tell they were disappointed, especially Amy, but of course they understood. And there'd be plenty to do in the meantime.

"Better reserve a couple of copies." he replied. He could tell looking at their faces that one wouldn't be enough.

He finished filling out the reservation form, and paying for two books, then they walked back outside into the sunshine. They walked a little further down the street, past "Bud's General Store" and past the police station. This was one of the few times that he went by the police station that he didn't see Officer Collins looking his way. There was only the Chief's car parked around to the side, so Officer Collins must be out on patrol. Danny, Amy and Veronica wanted to go back to the Harbor Inn and rent some bicycles so they could go down and ride them along the beach. Both Dan and Kate thought that to be a great idea as well, so they suggested that they rent five bikes and all of them go for a ride together. Despite the events of the last few weeks, he really was glad to see them, and was glad that they were here now. But as they crossed the street and headed back toward the Island Charm to get his truck, a man stepped out from the alley beside "Bud's General Store" and intently watched them as they walked away. He watched them until they disappeared around the corner, then he slipped back into the shadows of the alley.

CHAPTER 16
April 13, 2016
The Arrival

Amy Westfall stared out at the clear blue water as the ferry churned up a spray that misted her face. It was another bright, sunny day as the ferry made its way from Southport to Green Island. It was about 3:00 in the afternoon on Wednesday. As the ferry left the port for the trip across the sound, she had gotten out of their SUV and walked between the other cars over to the railing. The wind coming off the water felt refreshing as it hit her face and blew through her long blonde hair. Still, she didn't show much emotion as she quietly stared off into the distance as the first glimpse of Green Island came into view. She was totally lost in thought. There had been many times over the past thirty years that she had thought of this trip, and about the decision that she would have to make. Even now, on the way to the island, she still wasn't completely sure what she was going to do. What she did know, was that whatever she decided, it would affect the lives of countless people that she loved and cared about, including her own.

She shivered slightly as her husband Derrick came up from behind and wrapped his arms around her. "You alright?" he asked, "You've been pretty quiet since we started out this morning."

"Yes, I'm fine." she answered softly.

He couldn't help sensing that something was bothering her, and had been for the past several months. This year would be their twentieth wedding anniversary, and over the years he had learned to read her moods pretty well. Still, there was a part of her past that she never would talk about, not even to him. He wished she would. Perhaps he could help her deal with it. All he really knew was that it had to do with Green Island and with something that happened there thirty years ago. He felt like she would talk about it when she was ready, but so far she'd never been ready.

Rebekah, their daugher, came over and leaned against the railing beside her mother. Since Amy looked much younger than her 43 years, and her and her daughter shared the same blonde hair, people often would think they were sisters. Rebekah too could sense that something was bothering her mother, but like her dad, she realized there was really nothing she could do except just be there for her. She was 16 and a junior in high school. Except for when she was younger, she had never attended a regular school. She and her brother, Andrew, had been home schooled for most of their lives since their parents' schedule kept them on the road a lot with book tours and speaking engagements. Andrew was older than Rebekah, and a sophomore at UNC Charlotte. His spring break wasn't for another week, so he wasn't able to be with them on this trip.

Her husband Derrick had been her manager ever since she began writing about a year after they were married. Actually, she had started her first book while she was still a senior in college, but it hadn't been published until after her marriage. Derrick had studied Business Administration in college and had gone on to get his Masters Degree in Marketing. He had some friends in the publishing industry, so he showed some of them a copy of the book. One of them, Grant Petersen of Petersen Brothers Publishing, was extremely interested and met with them to sign her first publishing contract. The title of the book was "The Aurora Factor" and it was an immediate success. It went to the top of the New York Times Best Seller List in only four weeks, and her publisher was already pressing her for her next book. That book, which was the first installment in the Andrea Harris series, would establish the course of her career.

Her life even before her marriage to Derrick had been one that most people could only dream about. She was the daughter of billionnaire investor and hotel magnate Martin Davenport, who was the founder of Davenport Global Hotels, one of the largest and most exclusive hotel groups in the world. She was the youngest in her family, with a brother, who was four years older and a sister a little under a year older. They lived in a large lakefront mansion on Lake Norman just north of Charlotte. They attended the best private schools and were given every opportunity for success. She had known that she wanted to be a writer from about the time that she was 15. She had majored in Creative Writing with a minor in Marketing from East Carolina University. She had started what was to be her first book while in her senior year at East Carolina, and moved back home to continue it after graduation. She met her husband, Derrick Westfall at her sister's wedding in 1993. Derrick's sister and her new brother-in-law's sister were best friends. After dating for three years, they were married in what was to become the wedding event of the year. As the daughter of one of the wealthiest men in America, no expense was spared. Her wedding was the cover story that month in Society Bride magazine. Their first child, Andrew, was born a year later, and their second child Rebekah came along after another three years. Derrick had a position with a prestigious advertising agency in Charlotte, a position that he had held for a few years before meeting Amy, but after the book sales took off, he decided to resign and be her full time manager. Their home was also located in a lakefront community, just a little further north of Charlotte from where she grew up.

After her father, Martin Davenport, retired a couple of years ago, her brother Martin Davenport, Jr. became CEO of Davenport Global Hotels, and her sister took over as President. While Amy was on the board of directors, since she did own a quarter of the shares in the company, she preferred to continue her writing career, so her day to day involvement in the hotel business was minimal. Still, DGH was a family company. Martin Davenport had been a shrewd investor, and was able to fund the company startup with his own money without requiring other investors or taking the company public. He preferred it this way, and had done well with it. He had confidence that his son and daughter would continue the Davenport Hotel tradition and take the company to the next level.

Several blasts of the ferry's whistle indicated that they were approaching the dock on Green Island and that everyone should return to their vehicles. Derrick put his arm around his wife's shoulder and together with Rebekah they walked back to their SUV. He wanted her to know that he was here for her and she had his love and support in whatever she was going through.

They had a good life together with their two children, Andrew and Rebekah, and everything had seemed fine until about a year and a half ago when Amy began writing this latest novel. Everything seemed normal at first, but as time went on she seemed more withdrawn from the family. She spent more and more of her time isolated in her study completely engrossed in her writing. Even when she wasn't writing, she seemed more distant, like there was something bothering her. Derrick knew that something had happened many years ago on Green Island that she would never talk to him about, but over time he had thought that she had gotten past it. Her personality was usually bright and cheerful, and that's the way that it had been for most of the past twenty years of their marriage. It wasn't until about three months ago that he realized that what was bothering her was somehow connected to what had happened on Green Island.

They had been in a meeting with her publisher discussing the launch of the new novel. Her publisher, Carter Allen, wanted to have the launch in early June in New York where most of her book launches had taken place, but she had insisted that the book launch had to be this week, specifically April 14 on Green Island. The mention of Green Island caught Derrick completely off guard, since this was the first time that she had mentioned it in years. She had said that they could still have a gala event in New York in June, but the actual launch HAD to be on Green Island. That part she was adamant about and couldn't be talked out of. So Carter began working out the details for an April 14 launch on Green Island at the island's only book store, the "Little Book Nook".

Seeing how troubled his wife seemed, Derrick really wasn't sure that they should go back to Green Island at all. While she never talked about what had happened there, he could tell that whatever it was really bothered her. He had tried to talk with her on several occasions about cancelling the book launch and having it in New York like they always did. She wouldn't have any part of it.

The ferry docked and all of the cars began driving off. As they drove off the ferry and continued down the road toward town, she didn't say a word, she only stared out the window, seemingly lost in thought. As they made the left turn onto Main Street and began driving toward the Harbor Inn where they were staying, they passed by the "Little Book Nook" on the right. In hopes of making some light conversation, Derrick said in a half way cheerful voice, "There's where the book launch will be. Looks like they're expecting you from the sign in the window."

"Yes, they are." was all she said, with little emotion in her voice.

Derrick had to continue, "Amy, we don't have to do this if you don't want to."

She turned to him, "Yes we do." she said in a matter of fact tone. "I don't expect you to fully understand, and I wish I could tell you more, but I can't. Not right now. Just trust me when I say that this is something that I HAVE to do."

"OK," he replied, "but remember, if you need to talk, I'm here for you."

"I know you are," she replied, "and thank you."

They continued past the downtown area and proceeded past the Island Charm, past all of the hotels and condos on Sea Spray Drive. Amy didn't say a word as they made the drive out to the Harbor Inn. She simply stared out the window, remembering taking this same drive thirty years ago. It appeared to her that time had stood still for the island. To her it still looked the same as it had all those years ago. Each sight, sound and smell brought back memories long forgotten. It was almost as if she had returned back to that time again, that time all those years ago. They turned onto Harbor Inn Lane and as they passed Lighthouse Road, Derrick noticed her look over toward that direction. It was a quick glance, but he noticed it all the same. As he looked over at her, he couldn't quite read the look on her face. The closest that he could come was that it was a look of uncertainty, not really fear, but one of apprehension and anxiety. He didn't think she wanted him to notice, and definitely not ask any questions, so he didn't. But the thought did cross his mind again, "What happened here all those years ago? And why was it so important to her that she be here NOW? And why couldn't she talk about it, especially with him? She had seemed so preoccupied since they started planning this trip. And she had gotten even more so since they had arrived. He remembered the look on her face this morning, when he had tried to lighten the mood by telling her, "Relax, we're going to a book signing, not a funeral!" That look, and her present mood were actually starting to worry him.

They continued the drive down Harbor Inn Lane, passing through the rock columns with the sailboat emblems on them and the sculpted seagulls on top. As they passed through the rock columns, the Harbor Inn was directly in front of them. A circular drive went past the fountain in the center and led them to the front entrance. Derrick got out, went around to the other side of the SUV, and opened Amy's door. She stepped out of the SUV and walked with him and Rebekah into the lobby.

As the three of them walked through the front lobby doors, a flood of memories came back to her, momentarily taking her breath away. As Derrick went over to the front desk to check in, Amy strolled around the lobby, taking in the sights, sounds, and smells. The front desk clerk looked up as Derrick walked up to the desk.

"Checking in?" she asked.

"Yes," replied Derrick, "The reservation should be under Amy Westfall."

"Oh, Mr. Westfall," she said, slightly embarrassed, "I'm sorry, I didn't recognize you."

"That's OK," he responded, "Amy's the one most people recognize anyway."

"We have our best suite, the 'Blue Heron Suite', ready for you to check in." she continued, as she proceeded to print out the paperwork and encode the room keys. She handed Derrick the papers that had just printed out for his signature, then handed him the key cards.

"Where is Mrs. Westfall?" the clerk asked, "I've been dying to meet her ever since I heard she was coming."

"She's a little tired from the trip. I think she wants to go up and rest for a little while. She should be down later. I'll ask her to stop by."

When Derrick turned around, he saw Rebekah gazing at the fish in the large tank that separated the lobby area from the sitting area toward the back. It was a large salt-water tank with some of the most unique and colorful fish that he had seen. It was about ten feet wide and went almost up to the ceiling. The lobby and sitting area were both covered with light paneling. Pictures on the walls were of seashore themes with ships, lighthouses, whales, underwater expeditions, and storms among others. To the back of the sitting area was a fireplace and surrounding the fireplace were doors on each side leading out to a large covered patio with tables and chairs. The patio doubled as outdoor seating for the Mariners Cove restaurant which was located just to the right of the sitting area. Amy was nowhere to be seen, however.

Derrick said to Rebekah, "Why don't you go find your mother while I unload the SUV?" He held up the room keys so that he could see what room number was printed on the paper cover. "Looks like we're in Suite 214."

"OK, see you in a few minutes." she replied.

Derrick got a luggage cart and went out to the SUV to unload. As he was unloading, a man stepped out of the woods at the edge of the property and seemed to be intently watching him. The man strolled across the lawn and disappeared around the corner of the building completely unnoticed by Derrick or anyone else standing around.

Inside, Rebekah was having some difficulty finding her mom. She had originally thought that she was probably just around one of the corners looking at the decor, but after walking around each area and part of the way down each hallway, she still couldn't find her. There was a door leading out to the patio and gardens, so she thought that maybe her mom had gone out there. She opened the door and stepped outside. While it was a sunny day, the trees around the patio provided ample shade. There were only a few places where the sun was able to peer through. She noticed several paths connecting to the patio, and thought that maybe her mom had gone down one. She picked one and began walking down it. A little ways down the path she heard the sound of rushing water. As she went a little further down the path, it came to a small stream with a landscaped waterfall falling over river rock. It wasn't big, with the actual waterfall only falling about four feet. As she was standing, totally mesmerized by the tranquility of the scene before her, her Smartphone rang. It was her dad.

"Are you and mom coming up?" he asked.

"I'm still looking for her. She must have gone outside, but I haven't been able to find her yet. I'm on one of the garden paths by a small waterfall."

"I'll be right down." he replied.

A minute or two later, her dad joined her by the patio. Neither of them could figure where Amy might have gone, but they weren't too worried either. She must be on one of the paths that wound around the property. Still, she had been preoccupied lately with something. As they continued on around the path, they noticed Amy walking slowly back toward the inn.

"It all looks the same." Amy said when they caught up with her.

"Yes," Derrick replied, "These islands don't change much over the years."

"No, this is different," she said, not looking at them, but staring blankly off into the distance, "it looks and feels just like it did thirty years ago. Everywhere I go just brings back so many memories. Everything I see and feel and smell brings me right back to that time. It even reminds me of things that I had long forgotten."

"Let's go back inside." Derrick suggested, "It's been a long day."

As the three of them walked back toward the inn, they weren't as alone as it seemed. None of them noticed the man at the edge of the garden watching their every move. He didn't move; he didn't want to attract any attention. But he was watching and thinking. Everyone that needed to be here was here now. It was almost time.

CHAPTER 17
April 14, 2016
The Island Mist Charter

Thursday morning was overcast, with a forecast of a chance of rain. In fact, it had been raining overnight and still continued this morning. It was around 7:30 in the morning and Dan had actually been awake for about an hour listening to the rain outside the window. They had planned a sightseeing boat tour of the island and the surrounding area today, so he hoped that the rain would stop. He'd call the charter company when he got up and see what the weather forecast was and if they were still planning on going out. It was actually fairly peaceful in their suite at the Harbor Inn this time of the morning. Kate was curled up beside him, the sound of her breathing blending with the sound of the rain.

Monday night after they had gotten back to the hotel and the kids were asleep, he and Kate had talked about what had been happening on the island since he got here. They had discussed the stranger that he had seen on several occasions. While he didn't see the man that was watching the kids on the porch the afternoon that they had gotten here, he suspected that it was the same man that he had seen at the edge of the woods out at the lighthouse, the same one that he had seen under the streetlight, and probably even the same one that Bud had seen near his truck. He told her about Dr. Carson, Bill Henderson, and about actually seeing and walking into the fog. She had listened intently, and was definitely concerned. They had lain awake for awhile after going to bed discussing the situation. Kate thought that he should tell the police about the stranger. He told her why he didn't think that was a good idea, that it seemed that Officer Collins started watching him after his first report, but she just thought he was being a little too paranoid. She couldn't think of any reason why the police would take any particular interest in him, and actually neither could he other than the lighthouse. It bothered her that nobody seemed to know who the man was or what he wanted, just like it did Dan. The fog bothered her too. When Dan had bought the lighthouse, he told her about the stories that he had heard over the years. She had even read Jack Carlson's book. But like him, she hadn't really believed that any of the stories still held any real significance. They were something that had happened a long time ago. But now that Dan had walked into the fog she was worried. Like Dan she realized that it wasn't just something that happened years ago, and that meant that what happened then could still happen now.

After Kate had drifted off to sleep, he was still going over the events of the past month in his mind. It had been such a short period of time, yet so much had happened. Most of it he didn't understand, but hoped that he eventually would. He thought of his family, and how he really didn't want to bring them out here in June if he didn't understand the strange happenings any better than he did now. He'd seen the fog himself and walked into it. It wasn't just a story that he'd read in a book anymore, it was real. He couldn't deny that. The two boys, Greg and Tim, had disappeared forever forty two years ago, and since coming to the island he'd met Tim's father who was actually convinced that Tim was still alive. He'd met Dr. Carson with all of his scientific equipment and his "Alternate Plane of Existence" theory. He still couldn't quite get his mind around that one, but he had to admit, he really didn't have any explanations that would explain it any better. Then there was the police officer, Mark Collins, who had seemed to take an unusual interest in them since they had arrived. And there was the stranger who had been following him and watching him on several occasions, both at the lighthouse and around town. He wished that he knew who he was and why he was following him. But so far the stranger had just been too elusive. Here one minute, gone the next. Despite what Scotty had said, that they'd have to see this through, and that he was curious as to what was going on, Dan still had the unsettling feeling that maybe Ben, Hank and Bud were right. Maybe he should have left it alone. Maybe they should just pack up and leave now. Maybe the lighthouse and its secrets shouldn't be disturbed. For the first time since he had arrived, he found himself actually considering locking up the gate leading to the lighthouse and locking up all of the secrets within it forever. He'd just go back home and continue his life as usual.

A knock on his bedroom door brought him back to the moment. The door opened just a crack. "Mom, Dad?" It was Danny. He had just woken up and was wondering why no one else was awake. It was already

8:00. The sightseeing charter wasn't until 10:30, but Danny had heard the rain and was already wondering about the trip. Danny opened the door and came into the bedroom.

"Are we going to be able to go on the boat today?" Danny asked.

"Not sure just yet, let me call the charter company."

They were trying to whisper so as not to disturb Kate, but apparently she had been partly awake already.

"Dad's going to call the boat company to see if we can still go." Danny told her. He climbed into bed beside his mom. He felt a little uneasy this morning, like he had had a dream, but couldn't quite remember what it was about. But it had seemed to be an unsettling dream, not entirely pleasant, but not a nightmare either. A few minutes later, Dan came back into the room.

"The charter company says the rain should move out this morning around 9:30, so as of right now the trip is still on." said Dan.

"Alright!" exclaimed Danny.

Danny ran back into the bedroom to get his sister and Veronica up. They were harder to wake up than he had been. They had gotten back fairly late last night from another of Hank's cookouts at the Island Charm and had stayed up for awhile after that, so the girls wanted to sleep in. Still, with a little coaxing from Danny, they were up and getting ready to go downstairs and get some breakfast at the Mariners Cove restaurant.

The Mariners Cove restaurant was a rustic establishment which fit in well with the decor of the rest of the inn. It was paneled with a darker paneling than the lobby of the inn which gave it a more weathered appearance. The hostess station had one red and one green nautical light at each end. A small fishing net with several starfish and an assortment of shells was draped across the front. There were various nautical lights along the walls, with more nets, shells, life preservers, buoys, and other nautical paraphernalia. An old ships telegraph and wheel were on display behind the hostess station, and over in the corner beside the entrance was a six foot lighthouse complete with a revolving beacon. Each table had a dock light suspended above it. The whole family really loved the atmosphere.

As the hostess led them to their table, which was over along the windows facing the rear of the hotel and overlooking the outside sitting area and the gardens, they all looked around to see if maybe Mrs. Westfall was dining here this morning. Since this was the highest rated hotel on the island, they suspected this was where she was staying. They felt sure they would know her if they saw her from the photos on the back cover of her books. The restaurant was fairly full with the breakfast crowd, but Mrs. Westfall was nowhere to be seen. Dan suspected that either she was already up and had gone out, or possibly was having room service delivered. When they didn't see her anywhere, Dan explained to the kids that people that were famous frequently dined in their room to avoid people constantly interrupting them while they were trying to enjoy their breakfast or dinner. It was probably just as they would have done if they'd seen her. Dan thought that it was probably best to save the meeting for the book signing, anyway.

The breakfasts at the Mariners Cove were unlike any that you could get anywhere else. While they did offer the standard fare such as eggs and sausage and muffins, they also offered seafood themed dishes like crab and lobster omelets, fish and eggs, and a really delicious shrimp stir fry. The shrimp stir fry was Kate's favorite, while Dan and the kids preferred the omelets.

After breakfast, they all went back up to their room, picked up their cameras and other items for the day and went down to the hotel van, which they had reserved the night before for the trip out to the marina. They all climbed in and were on their way in no time. It was beginning to look more and more like the trip would be on. The rain had stopped and the sun was starting to shine through some breaks in the clouds. The charter company, Forrest Point Charters, was out by the ferry dock, so they had to go through town to get there. Hank was out front of the Island Charm fixing a section of the railing that had broken off. As Dan had observed, running a bed and breakfast seemed to be a never ending repair job. He looked up and waved to them as they passed by, and they waved back. The driver made the turn off of Main Street at Bud's General Store then proceeded out to the docks. Everyone was excited. Even Dan was looking forward to the trip. He had talked to the captain when he made the reservation for the charter and determined that the trip took them around the south end of the island to get a view of the lighthouse. In the month that he'd been here, he'd never actually seen it from that vantage point, so this was going to be a treat. He had spotted the charter boat as it sailed past on several occasions, though. He'd call Scotty as they were passing by and have them come out and wave.

When they arrived at Forrest Point Charters, they parked and walked down the walkway leading to the main building. As they walked along by the harbor, they spotted the luxury yacht that they would be sailing on, the "Island Mist", docked at the dock nearest to the building. There were people already on board and others boarding. It looked as if several families would be on the tour with them. They went inside and found the check in desk, Dan made the arrangements and payment, and then they were off to board the yacht. As soon as they boarded, Amy and Veronica went off on their own while Danny stayed with his parents. The girls were young teenagers and needed their independence.

Right on time at 10:30 the yacht backed away from the dock and began the tour around the island. By now, most of the early morning clouds had burned away and the sun was shining brightly on the deck. It was the middle of April, so it was going to be a warm day, but the temperatures down here hadn't really gotten too hot yet, so it should still be pleasant. It looked to be a perfect day for a four hour lunch cruise around the island and sound. The cruise would start out going around the east side of the island past all of the houses, hotels, and condos along Sea Spray Drive. It would then make a right turn and go around the south end of the island and sail past the lighthouse which was on the river side. From there it would turn and sail inland toward Southport, then head south down the coast before turning back up toward Green Island. The trip would end off with another view of the lighthouse as they passed by it again, sailing along the river side of the island before docking back at Neptune Landing.

Dan, Kate, and Danny found a table on the upper deck where they had a good view off both the port and starboard sides. Amy and Veronica had found a window table one level down inside the air conditioned cabin.

As they passed by the resort areas on Sea Spray Drive, Dan was surprised at how many condos, hotels, and rentals there really were out there. A lot of it was hidden from the road, so that just by driving down Sea Spray Drive you really didn't notice all of the buildings and houses. Seeing it from this perspective really showed how large of a resort area this part of the island had become. As they continued down the coast, Dan got his first glimpse of the fence surrounding the south side of the island. He knew that it looked out of place when looking out from the lighthouse, but looking from this angle just off the islands coast, you could really tell just how massive the fence was. With no obstructions, he could see it as it continued on down the coast line and disappeared around the tip. The "Island Mist" sailed around the southern tip and turned north on the Cape Fear River side of the island. Dan had walked over to the railing and had his camera ready. As they had passed by the southern tip, he had given Scotty a call to let him know that they were almost there. As they sailed north, most of the island was woods and forest, but he did see the clearing where the lighthouse was located finally come into view. Other than the lantern house leaning into the large gap near the top of the tower, the lighthouse didn't look quite as run down from this distance. The scaffolding erected by Southeast Restoration Professionals was highly visible from this angle. Scotty, Greg, Steve, and Arlene had walked out onto the front porch and were all waving to them as they went past. Dan snapped a few photos of them as they passed by, a few with the telephoto lens.

As he saw the lighthouse for the first time from the boat, an image of the cover of Amy Westfall's new book popped back into his mind. On the cover was a lighthouse, and while the image of the lighthouse on the cover was different than Forrest Point Light, it was still shrouded in fog. He couldn't help but notice the similarities. This new book MUST be based on Forrest Point Light! As the image of the cover came back into his mind, his mind focused on a detail that he had previously not really given much attention to: the title – "Displaced in Time". The particular word that stood out for him now as they sailed passed the lighthouse was "TIME". He wondered how he had missed it earlier.

He immediately pulled his Smartphone out of its case on his belt and dialed Dr. Carson's cell phone number.

"Hello." said a familiar voice on the other end of the line.

"Dr. Carson, it's Dan Nelson. We're on an island sightseeing tour, and as we passed by the lighthouse and I saw it from a different angle, a thought came to me! When the fog rolls in, instead of it being an alternate reality as you were proposing, could it be a different TIME?"

"In my opinion, it would be highly unlikely." replied Dr. Carson.

"Why exactly?" inquired Dan.

"Well, for one thing, I've never really believed that time travel was possible. My field of research is 'Alternate Reality Theory'. This theory states that there can be any infinite number of realities, but all of the realities take place on the exact SAME time line. So if it's 12:00 noon on a certain day in one reality, then it's also 12:00 noon on the SAME day in all of the others. So while different things happen in the different realities depending on the choices made in those realities, they all happen along the same time line. 'Temporal Displacement Theory', which is the theory of traveling to different places along the same time line brings with it too many paradoxes that in my mind just can't be resolved. Let's say a person can travel back to an earlier time that's still within his lifetime. He's still only ONE person, but there would actually be two of him of different ages occupying the same space at one instant in time. In all of my research, that would create a paradox that just wouldn't be possible. Then there's the age old question that's been asked many times before, 'What happens if a person goes back in time and kills his grandfather and his father is never born?' Or what if he inadvertently kills himself? There're just too many of these types of paradoxes which would create impossible situations. None of these paradoxes exist in 'Alternate Reality Theory', since all realities exist at the same time. This makes a certain logical sense and maintains a universal order. There's no possibility of a person going back and encountering himself."

"What did you call it?" inquired Dan.

"Call what?"

"The theory that you mentioned: the study of time travel."

"Temporal Displacement Theory." replied Dr. Carson.

"And 'Temporal' is another word for time? Right?" asked Dan.

"Yes, temporal means time."

"Thanks, you've been a big help!" said Dan excitedly as he hung up the phone. Temporal means time - Temporal Displacement Theory. And the title of Amy Westfall's book, "Displaced in Time". While he wasn't exactly sure what the connection was, it sure sounded like the same thing to him. He could understand Dr. Carson's position, and his reasons why time travel wasn't possible actually made sense. Still, even with all of Dr. Carson's reasons why the fog couldn't be a 'Temporal Displacement', in his untrained, unscientific mind, he still felt like that's exactly what it was.

The "Island Mist" turned inland and sailed toward Southport. Once they reached Southport, they turned south and sailed down the coast. The crew began serving lunch right after they turned inland and headed across the sound. The choices for lunch were a cheeseburger, club sandwich, or chicken sandwich with chips and a drink. Dan went back to the table and sat down with Kate and Danny just as the server was coming to take their order. He decided on the chicken sandwich while Kate and Danny took the club.

"Who were you talking to on the phone?" asked Kate.

"I called Scotty and told him to look for us as we passed by the lighthouse." he replied. "You saw them out front waving to us?"

"No, after that." she said.

"Oh, I called Dr. Carson. Remember I mentioned him yesterday."

"Yes, but what made you think to call him now?"

"Just something that occurred to me as we passed the lighthouse. I'll check back with him on it later."

They sat, ate lunch, and enjoyed the rest of the cruise. After lunch Dan took Danny over to the ships wheelhouse where they stood and watched the captain steer the ship. After a few minutes of watching, the captain actually noticed them and opened the door to invite them in.

"Welcome to the Island Mist's wheelhouse." he said, "My name's Captain Jimmy Shipley."

"That's a funny name for a man who drives a ship!" Danny replied.

"Danny!" scolded Dan, "That's not polite!"

"It's OK," Captain Shipley answered, "He's not the first person that I've gotten that from! When your last name's Shipley and you steer a ship you have to have a good sense of humor!"

He did look like he'd have a good sense of humor. He was an older gentleman, probably in his early sixties with grey hair and a wide grey moustache that turned up on the ends. He was a large man, but not really fat. He was friendly and genuinely seemed to enjoy being ship's captain and meeting the passengers.

He went on, "Let me show you around. As you've probably guessed, this big round thing here is the ships wheel. It's used to steer the ship. This lever to the right of the wheel is the throttle. The further I push it forward, the faster we go. Pulling it down to the middle is full stop, and pulling it back toward me is reverse. The gauge here tells us how fast we're going. And this round dial under this dome that looks like a big compass is one of the most important instruments on the ship. It actually is a compass and it tells us our heading. When you're driving a car, you just stay on the right road to get where you're going, but a ship can go in any direction when it's out in the middle of a lake or ocean. If you get lost and can't see land, you just steer to the proper heading and you can get back on course. Of course, we've gotten a little more high tech these days. We mostly use the GPS, which is pretty much like the one that you have in your car except with a bigger monitor. The monitor on the other side is our weather radar. It alerts us to approaching storms so that we can steer around them."

He showed them a few other things such as the ships log and radio, then asked Danny if he'd like to steer the ship.

"Boy, would I!" exclaimed Danny.

Captain Shipley let him take the wheel while Dan snapped several pictures. He even removed his Captains Cap and placed it on Danny's head.

"Now I'm a real ship's captain!" said Danny excitedly.

"You sure are!" answered Dan.

Captain Shipley even talked Danny through making the turn back toward the island. He showed him how to calculate the correct heading using the GPS, then how to use the ships compass during the turn to arrive at the correct heading to get them back to the island. Dan thanked him for his time, since he knew that this was something that Danny would be talking about for quite awhile. As they opened the door to go back outside, Captain Shipley gave Danny a sticker that said "Honorary Island Mist Captain".

As they were headed back into port, they passed by the lighthouse once again. This time, they didn't see Scotty and the rest out front. They were probably back inside by now. He saw Chris up on the scaffolding, but Chris didn't see him. They continued around the north end of the island until Neptune Landing came into view. Within a few minutes, they were docked and found themselves disembarking from the vessel. It had been a really fun day for them all, and an enlightening day for Dan. It was close to 3:00 by the time that they got on the road back to the Harbor Inn. They'd have a couple of hours to rest before the book signing this evening.

CHAPTER 18

The Book Signing

There was already a small crowd gathered around the front of the "Little Book Nook" by the time that Amy, Derrick, and Rebekah arrived a little after 4:00. Derrick pulled into the alley that went between the book store and the gift shop next door. Apparently no one in the crowd had noticed Amy arrive. They parked around back and knocked on the back door as they had been instructed to do earlier by the event coordinator, Mrs. Mitchell. The door opened up and they were greeted by a middle aged woman in her fifties.

"Welcome Amy! I'm Audrey Mitchell, the owner of the 'Little Book Nook'. Let me show you inside! We're extremely honored that you would have the book launch here on the island. If there's anything that you need during your stay here, just let me know."

"Thank you," replied Amy, "We've never had a launch in a small town before, and this island just seemed perfect for the occasion."

Audrey showed them around the book store, which was actually fairly small. She had rented some tables and chairs to set around out front and on the side for guests of the book launch to use, since if they have even a moderately large crowd there won't be room for everyone inside. Already they had forty six book reservations, but felt like more than that would attend. They had contacted the ferry company and they were extending their hours this evening to try to accommodate guests coming over from the mainland. There were balloons and decorations both inside and out. Audrey had asked her staff to move most of the bookshelves over toward the back of the store to accommodate more guests in the store and to have room for the line. Already, looking out the front windows she could tell that there was a fairly large crowd forming. She escorted Amy over to a long table set up by the counter. The table had a box of pens on the side, otherwise it was empty. There were several copies of the book laid out on the sales counter in two piles, those that had already been reserved, which contained a piece of paper with the last name of the person who had reserved them, and those that were for sale to the guests who hadn't preordered. Another long table was set up against the side wall just as you come in the front door. That table had a large sheet cake in the center, with mints, crackers and cheese, and other snacks including a large punch bowl on the end. This was the first book launch that this small town bookstore had seen, and they were determined to do it right!

Earlier in the day, a corporate jet bearing the green and white cursive "D" logo of Davenport Global Hotels had landed in Wilmington and taxied to the Corporate Aviation Terminal. A young woman in her mid forties with medium length dark hair and silver and black glasses had descended the pull out stairway. She was accompanied by a gentleman around the same age wearing a dark grey business suit and green tie. They both got into a waiting limo, which also featured the Davenport logo. The limo pulled away from the airport and exited onto NC 74 for the trip down to Southport, which from here should take about forty five minutes. The woman pulled her Smartphone out of her purse and pressed a speed dial number.

Back at the Harbor Inn, Amy's phone rang. From the display, she knew immediately who it was. She walked out onto the balcony to take the call. She talked for a little over thirty minutes as Derrick and Rebekah watched from inside. During the conversation Amy's face displayed the full range of emotion, from laughing, smiling, crying, frowning. It was an extremely emotional call.

"Who's that on the phone?" asked Rebekah.

"From the way she went outside and closed the door, I'm pretty sure it's her sister."

"What's going on Dad?" asked Rebekah, "I've never seen mom like this before."

"I only wish I knew!" responded Derrick, "But she just won't talk to me about it."

After talking for a few more minutes, Amy opened the door to come back in while finishing the conversation. The last thing that Derrick and Rebekah heard her say before hanging up the phone was, "Thanks for coming. We've always agreed that when this day finally came that we needed to be together. See you in a little while."

The crowd outside the bookstore had gotten larger by the time a long black limo pulled up out front around twenty till five. Assuming it was Amy arriving for the event, the crowd quickly shifted their attention to the limo. The driver got out and walked over to the passenger door of the limo, motioning for the crowd to get back and give them some room. Many were surprised, when instead of Amy a tall woman with glasses and dark hair along with a gentleman in a suit and tie got out of the limo and was escorted by the driver to the front door of the bookstore. All but the most loyal Amy Westfall fans, who recognized the woman as Amy's sister and her husband Rick, were left wondering who the mysterious guests were. Audrey came to the door, unlocked it to let them in, and then locked it back again. There was still another twenty minutes until the doors would be opened for the book signing. Once they were inside, the driver came back out to the limo and pulled away from the curb to park in the parking lot on the next block.

Dan and his family, along with Steve and Arlene were in the crowd outside the bookstore, which by this time was growing larger by the minute. Dan had been talking with Steve earlier about attending the book launch, and while neither Steve nor Arlene had read any of Amy Westfall's books, they both agreed that it would be a fun evening. Steve had even come over earlier in the day to reserve a copy of the book.

"Was that Amy Westfall in the limo?" asked Arlene.

"No, that was her sister. She attends most of the book launch events. Amy must already be inside by this time." replied Kate.

Once inside, and after brief introductions, Amy and her sister went into the back storage area for a private conversation, while Rick stayed in the store area and stood with his niece and brother-in-law. There was a lot of excitement in the little book store as the store employees made some last minute adjustments to the decorations and refreshments. After a few minutes, Amy and her sister came back out and Amy took her position at the signing table. A couple of the store employes had gone out the back entrance and were now out front trying to get the crowd to form a line across the front and down the side of the building. They'd be staying outside to try to keep an orderly line going into the store. This was the first time that any of these emplyees had ever even seen a crowd trying to get into the store, let alone have to worry about crowd control.

At slightly after 5:00, the doors were unlocked and the first guests in line filtered into the store. The line crossed in front of the checkout counter and the guests would either buy a book or present their claim slip if they had preordered. From there, they would proceed to the signing table to meet Amy. For those who had forgotten their claim slip, and a few inevitably would, they'd simply have to give their name and an employee could look up the claim number on the computer. For a small book store, the event was planned very well. The store was getting fairly crowded now as many of the ones who had already had their book signed were standing around talking. The store had opened the emergency exit door, which opens out onto the side street, for guests to exit the store after getting their refreshments and either leave or find a table outside to enjoy the rest of the evening.

It was around 5:30 by the time that Dan's group finally got inside the store. As the line wound in front of the signing table, Amy looked up and seemed to meet Dan's gaze. She smiled, and then went back to signing the books that were already being presented to her. As the line went around the side of the counter, Dan presented his claim ticket for the two books that he had ordered. He and Kate had decided to let the kids hand her the books to be signed, so after he had gotten them, Dan gave one to each of them.

When they finally reached the table, Amy was the first to present her book to be signed. She announced, "Hi Mrs. Westfall, my name's Amy too! I'm your biggest fan!"

"Are you now?" asked Mrs. Westfall with a smile as she reached out to take the book from Amy. She opened it and wrote inside the front cover, "To Amy, My biggest fan." She then signed it, "AD Wfl". This was a shorthand signature that she had adopted for book signings. During the first several signings early in her career, she had written out her full name, but she quickly discovered that after signing several hundred books, her hand could get very tired. She handed the book back to Amy who responded with "Thanks Mrs. Westfall!"

Danny walked up next and gave his book to Mrs. Westfall saying, "Nice to meet you Mrs. Westfall. I can't wait to read this one! My favorite so far is the Andrea Harris series. I even have a camera drone like Andreas, but mine doesn't go as far."

"Wow, that's pretty amazing, Danny! I'd like to see that sometime. I don't even have one of those!"

She signed his book, and then handed it back to him. Dan walked up next, and even though he didn't have a book to sign, introduced himself to her and mentioned that he was the new owner of Forrest Point Light on the island. "I couldn't help but notice the book cover." he said, "Is this latest book based on the lighthouse on this island?"

"Actually it is." she replied.

"I'd like to talk to you sometime about it, if you're available." he said, "Are you staying on the island after the book signing event?"

"Yes, Derrick, Rebekah, and I will be staying for a few days. We'll be here at least through Sunday, possibly a little longer."

"Great." he said, "Are you staying at the Harbor Inn?"

"Yes we are. Find me before you leave and I'll give you the room number."

Since the line for the signing was quite long and still extending out the door, Dan went ahead and moved along for now. Since she'd be on the island for a few days, he could catch up with her either tomorrow or the day after. Kate walked by and greeted her next, and then Steve and Arlene stepped up and had their book signed. Dan and Kate looked around to see where the kids had gone and saw that they were already over at the refreshment table. They walked over and also cut themselves a couple pieces of cake and picked up some cheese and crackers. Dan glanced over toward where Mrs. Westfall was signing the books and saw her glance his way momentarily before returning to greeting guests.

After getting their refreshments, they all went outside and pushed a couple of the tables together so that they'd all have room to sit and chat. Dan opened to the front cover of Amy's book and read the liner notes. It was very intriguing. It looked to be about a fictional disappearance around the lighthouse, but while no one really knew what happened to Greg and Tim, this book actually told the story from the perspective of the kids that disappeared. And it introduced a very interesting theory about what actually had happened. Dan felt that he'd probably at least want to start reading it tonight. Out of all the books that he had read on the lighthouse, all of the rest had been actual reported accounts. This was the first time that anyone had taken the events that have been occurring around the lighthouse for years and actually created a fictional story with a possible scenario of what might be happening. He'd like to find out anyone that she might have interviewed for her research as well.

The book signing was scheduled until 8:00, but due to the crowd, it actually went on a little longer. Dan's group was enjoying the evening, so they stayed around for the full time. Since he had known that parking would be at a premium for the event, he had parked his truck down at the Island Charm and they had walked down to the bookstore.

After most of the crowd had already gone, they decided to begin walking back to the Island Charm. As they were just beginning to cross the street, they heard a door open and a voice from the bookstore call to them, "Dan! Wait! Mrs. Westfall would like you to stay around for a few extra minutes, if you're not in a hurry." It was Audrey, the owner. They had met her earlier in the evening as she was mingling with the guests. Since she was a long-time resident of the island, she was very interested in what Dan and his friends were doing out at the lighthouse. Like everyone else who had been on the island for a lot of years, she'd heard all of the stories. She had even lived on the island when Greg and Tim had disappeared. They turned around and came back to the store. Audrey let them in the side door and they walked over to where Mrs. Westfall, her husband, and sister and brother-in-law were standing.

Amy Westfall turned to Dan as they walked up, "Thanks for staying behind for a few minutes." She turned to her husband, and said, "Can you excuse us for a minute?"

"Sure," he said, "take your time, we'll be here."

They walked over and sat at a table in the corner of the room. All of them felt honored that Mrs. Westfall was actually taking time out for them. She was the most famous person that they had ever met, yet here they were having coffee and donuts here at the same table with her!

Mrs. Westfall began, "I've done quite a bit of research on the lighthouse over the years. No doubt there's something going on out there. I know you haven't had a chance to read the book yet, but I wanted to get your opinion of what you think is happening out at the lighthouse, especially since you're the new owner and have been out there."

"Well, I'm afraid I don't know much more than you do about what's going on. It's still pretty much a mystery to me as well." replied Dan, "What made you want to write a book about the events happening out at the lighthouse, anyway?"

She paused a moment before answering, "It's always interested me, even when I was younger. There's just a certain mystery about it that I haven't seen anywhere else. Our family lived in Charlotte when I was growing up, so it wasn't a long drive down here. We vacationed at the beach usually at least a couple of times a year, and it was mentioned in several publications that I read. I've even talked with some scientists and college professors who specialize in unusual happenings."

"Have you talked to Dr. Paul Carson from Wilmington?" Dan inquired, "He has some interesting theories on the subject."

"No, for the book I mostly consulted with Dr. Robert Fitzpatrick from the University of Virginia. His specialty is Temporal Displacement Theory, which is the study of movement backward and forward across time and the various paradoxes that could be encountered. "

"I know what it is," answered Dan, "I've actually spoken with Dr.

Carson about it. He has his doubts that it's even possible. How about you? I know that you set your story around the lighthouse, but do you actually believe that temporal displacement is possible?"

"Actually, yes," she said, "I really do."

They sat and talked for a few more minutes, until they could tell that the bookstore folks were pretty much ready to close up for the night. They all walked outside to leave. They stood around and talked for a little while longer until the Davenport Global Hotels limo pulled up to the corner.

Rick Ellison, Amy Westfall's brother-in-law looked at the kids and asked, "Have any of you ever gotten to ride in a limo?"

"No!" all three chimed in unison.

And they actually hadn't. While Dan was the CEO of one of the largest technology and research corporations in the country, he never had really been a limo person. He preferred SUVs and trucks, and he really preferred driving himself rather than having a driver. So Perihelion didn't have limos.

Rick continued, "Well, if it's OK with your parents, how would you like to ride back to the hotel with us?"

"Wow, would we!" exclaimed Danny. Amy and Veronica agreed. Neither of them had gotten to ride in a limo either, so they were all really excited. The driver opened the door and all of them piled into the back. Dan gave Amy one of the room keys so that if they got back to the hotel before them, which they probably would, that they could go on up to the room. Amy Westfall even decided to ride back to the hotel with them in the limo, which made the kids even happier.

As she got into the limo, Amy Westfall slipped Dan one of her business cards. "Come by when you're ready and we can talk about it some more." she told Dan.

As the limo pulled away from the curb for the trip back to the hotel, Dan and Steve both shook Derrick's hand as they parted ways.

Derrick and Rebekah went to get the SUV, while the rest of them walked back to the Island Charm. Dan looked at the business card that Amy Westfall had given him. It was a standard business card with her name and contact information. He turned it over and looked at the back, where she had written in pen, "Harbor Inn Suite 214". Since she had obviously done a lot of research on the lighthouse, he definitely wanted to talk with her again before she left.

When they were about half way back to the Island Charm, Dan began to feel that familiar feeling of being watched. He looked around, but didn't see anyone or anything out of the ordinary. He didn't want to say anything to alarm the others, but he did pick up the pace slightly. All he wanted was to get back to his truck and back to the safety of the Harbor Inn. In a way he was glad that the kids were able to ride back in the limo rather than walk back with them. At least they were safe with the Ellisons in their limo and they wouldn't have far to walk to get to the hotel. They'd be dropped off at the front entrance.

They made it back to the Island Charm without any incident and went up onto the porch to chat with Steve and Arlene before wishing them goodnight. While there was no incident, Kate had noticed Dan start to walk a lot faster half way through their walk back. After they both got into Dan's truck and he cranked it up, she turned to Dan and asked, "Did you hear something back there?"

"What do you mean?" asked Dan.

"You know what I mean. We were walking at a normal, comfortable pace, and then suddenly you started speeding up. I'm not sure if Steve and Arlene noticed, but I did." she replied.

"It was more of a feeling than actually hearing something." he replied. "I've felt it before, and so have the others. It's a feeling of being watched and followed."

Dan put the truck in gear and backed out of the parking space. They pulled out onto Main Street to begin the drive back to the Harbor Inn.

"Are you sure about moving us out here?" Kate finally asked after a few moments of silence, "After all, someone was watching the kids on Monday when we first got here. And now you think someone was following us from the bookstore. You told me Monday night that you didn't know who he is. Maybe there are too many things that you still don't know about the lighthouse's history. And maybe some of those things could be dangerous."

"I've thought of that," he replied, "and I do think there's a lot that I still don't know and understand. I'd still like to find out more, but I agree, that until I do know more that it probably won't be a good idea for you and the kids to come out here to stay. It's only April. Maybe all of these mysteries will be cleared up and you can still move out here in June. If they're not, we can discuss then what we want to do."

As they pulled into the parking lot of the Harbor Inn, the limo was still parked in front of the main entrance. Rick Ellison was apparently enjoying giving the kids a tour of the limos amenities. He saw Danny sitting in the driver's seat, with Rick Ellison standing beside him, and the girls still in the back. He pulled the truck into the nearest available space and he and Kate walked over to the limo.

"Hi, Dad!" remarked Danny, "Mr. Ellison's teaching me how the limo works! This car has everything!"

"Glad you're having a good time." said Dan. "Are you and the girls about ready to come up?"

"I guess." said Danny, climbing out of the driver's seat.

Rick Ellison walked in with them while the driver parked the limo. Rick was friendly and outgoing and actually enjoyed the kids. And he was a pleasure to talk with, not at all like you'd expect the lead attorney for one of the largest hotel chains in the world to be. And while most people probably thought that he had gotten that position by marrying the owner's daughter, which with Davenport Global Hotels being a family company he probably did, he nonetheless was the best candidate that Martin Davenport could have found for the job.

After everyone else had gone back upstairs to their room, Rick went looking for his wife. He didn't think she would have gone upstairs just yet with her sister being here. They had only had a short time to talk after they arrived at the book signing, so they'd probably be catching up now. He looked around in the lobby, the lounge, and outside on the patio. He finally saw them from a distance walking slowly through the garden. They had had plenty of discussions like this over the past thirty years. But now the time had finally come. Whatever decision they made, they'd have to agree that it was the right one. And they both knew that there would be no second chances.

CHAPTER 19
April 15, 2016
The Disappearance

They all awoke on Friday morning to a beautiful spring day. The sun was shining in through the hotel room windows, and in the trees outside the birds were singing. It was just the type of day that made Green Island such a popular vacation spot. They didn't have any particular plans for today. Kate and the kids wanted to go down to the beach later. Danny wanted to build a sand castle and the girls wanted to look for seashells.

Dan did need to go out to the lighthouse and discuss some things with Chris, but that shouldn't take too long, then he could come back and join them. Some bids that Chris had requested had arrived by courier yesterday while they were out on the boat tour, and Dan needed to take them out and talk them over with Chris. Chris had also requested some blueprints to be drawn up by Bobby, Southeast Restoration Professionals' lead architect. He had hoped that those would arrive with the bids, but they hadn't shown up yet. Dan asked Kate to give him a call if they came in while he was out at the lighthouse.

They got up and went down to the Mariners Cove for their usual breakfast. They halfway expected to see Amy Westfall and her sister, along with their families having breakfast down there this morning, but they were nowhere to be seen. They were probably either having breakfast in their rooms, or were sleeping in after a busy day yesterday. They all got their usual breakfast and took their time, just enjoying the view of the gardens out the window beside their table. The temperature was already in the mid sixties, with an expected high around seventy four, so it was looking like it was going to be the perfect day.

"Dad, can me and Veronica take our bikes and ride along the beach this morning after breakfast?" asked Amy.

"I don't see why not," answered Dan, "Just be careful."

After breakfast, the girls got their bikes and rode out of the parking lot and down Harbor Inn Lane where it ran into Sea Spray Drive. They went about a quarter of a mile down Sea Spray Drive to where there was a public access beach entrance. Since they had been here, they had taken their bikes and ridden them down the beach several times, but this was the first time that their parents weren't with them. Amy had known what her dad had meant when he said, "Be careful". He meant for them to watch out for the man that they had seen the first day out front of the Island Charm. He didn't mention the man specifically, and he hadn't really brought it up since that first day, but she had been able to tell that her dad was concerned about him. He just wanted them to have a fun week's vacation here, so he didn't want to worry them too much. But during the week, they had been careful, and Amy had been keeping an eye out for the man, but since that first day he hadn't shown back up again.

There weren't a lot of people out along the beach this morning. Since it was mid April, the ocean water was still a little cool to go swimming, even though there were a handful of people that were braving it. Mostly it was folks fishing in the surf, joggers, and people just taking a morning walk. They also passed a couple more people riding their bikes along the seashore as well. Both girls were enjoying the ride, which was pleasant with the morning salt air coming in off the Atlantic Ocean and the sound of the surf singing to them as they rode. Nothing about this morning seemed like it could have any danger at all. In fact, nothing about the island seemed particularly dangerous to them and other than the strange man watching them the first day that they arrived it really was an island paradise.

Dan, Kate, and Danny went for a swim in the indoor pool. The water was nice and warm, which really relaxed them this morning. Dan had brought down one of the copies of Amy Westfall's new book. He swam a few laps in the pool, and then climbed out to sit in one of the lounge chairs to continue reading. He had started it the night before after the kids had gone to bed, and it was fascinating; one of her best novels ever. He was particularly interested in it because it took place on the island and was about his lighthouse. It was interesting to see in print one person's view of what could be happening. In it, there was a disappearance similar to Tim and Greg, though under different circumstances. But where all of the stories about Tim and Greg focused on the disappearance, this story was told from the vantage point of the kids involved. From that perspective, it was even more interesting, and put a completely different twist on the story than any that he had read so far. That was why Amy Davenport Westfall was such a popular author. For her genre of book, she definitely had a vivid imagination, and could immerse the reader into things that were definitely impossible and yet be totally believable.

His reading was interrupted by a call on his cell phone. It was Scotty. He was ready to go out to the lighthouse and meet with Chris on the new estimates. Dan kissed Kate goodbye and went up to the room to get the estimates before meeting Scotty in the lobby.

"Has anything arrived for me today?" he asked Patrick, the front desk clerk.

"Nothing yet," replied Patrick, "Are you expecting something?"

"Yes, I had some blueprints drawn up for the restoration and I need to take those out to the lighthouse today and discuss them with the project manager."

"I'll let you know if they arrive." replied Patrick.

"Thanks."

Dan and Scotty then walked out the front entrance and got into Scotty's car to drive out to the lighthouse.

"Having a good week?" asked Scotty.

"The best!" replied Dan. "You should get Belinda to come down for a vacation while you're here. Both of you really deserve a vacation. The boat tour's really nice, and you could take some time off from the restoration. The crew from Southeast Restoration Professionals seems to have everything under control now, even for a lot of the interior work. They're doing most of the heavy lifting anyway, and we'll mostly jump back in for the detail work."

"I'll give her a call." he said. "That sounds like a great idea! Since Greg's already here, we could have a family vacation. She'll love it!"

They pulled up into the clearing where the Southeast Restoration van was parked along with Chris's pickup. There was also another truck that belonged to a subcontractor that was working on the spiral staircase up to the lantern house, as well as Greg's Jeep. Dan and Scotty got out and walked out to the lighthouse. Greg and Steve had already been working for awhile in the foyer with the Southeast Restoration crew, and they came out to meet them. With all of the work that had been done over the past few weeks, it was definitely coming along. Since everything had been cleaned out, it looked remarkably better than the first time that Dan had seen it. He almost couldn't believe that he'd been out here for a month already. It really didn't seem that long.

Dan and Scotty met Chris as he came down the stairs from the foyer. There were some tables and chairs set up under a couple of pop up canopy tents right outside the rear entrance to the house. Chris motioned for Dan to spread out the estimates on one of the tables.

"Looks like things have been going pretty well out here this week." said Dan.

"It's going good," said Chris, "We're right on schedule and if the bids look good from the subcontractors, we should have quite a bit done within the next couple of months."

"Any more problems out here?" asked Scotty.

"We haven't seen anyone or seen any sign of anyone being out here since we talked on Monday." replied Chris. "It's actually been a quiet week."

"That's what we want." remarked Dan.

They spread out the bids on the table and sat down to discuss them. Dan informed him that Kate would call if the blueprints arrived. He was actually expecting them to arrive today.

Kate and Danny had finished up with the pool and were going down to the miniature golf course to play a round. As they came into the lobby, Patrick saw them and called for Kate, "Mrs. Nelson, a package just arrived for Mr. Nelson. Let me get it for you."

"Oh good, that must be the blueprints!" replied Kate as she walked over to the front desk.

Patrick went into the back room and produced the package, which was a cardboard tube about four feet long with plastic caps on each end. He handed it to Kate who walked over to where Danny was standing.

"We need to run these out to your father," she told him, "Then we can go play a round."

"OK," he said, slightly disappointed. Still, another trip out to the lighthouse wouldn't be too bad.

As they went out the front door with the blueprints, Amy and Veronica were just getting back from their bike ride along the beach. Kate motioned for them to come over.

"Amy how would you and Veronica like to ride out to the lighthouse and take this to your father?" she asked, "He's expecting it today."

"That'd be great!" they both said. "We haven't gotten to ride down Lighthouse Road yet, at least not by ourselves."

They tied the tube with the blueprints onto the rack on Amy's bike, and then the two girls took off across the parking lot while Kate and Danny went back inside to continue with their original plan. As they rode around the circle on the way out of the parking lot, they spotted Amy Westfall sitting on a bench in front of the fountain. They waved to her and she waved back.

Amy and Veronica were excited to get to ride out to the lighthouse by themselves. The five of them had ridden out there earlier in the week, and had actually walked around and looked it over. They thought about riding their bikes out to the lighthouse again after that, but had never asked because their dad had told them not to go out there by themselves unless he was with them. But since he was out there now, it should be OK, and after all, it was their mom who had sent them. It was about three quarters of a mile from the Harbor Inn to Lighthouse Road, then another mile out to the lighthouse. It took about seven minutes for them to reach Lighthouse Road, and from there they figured they'd get to the lighthouse in another ten or fifteen.

They turned and began the ride down Lighthouse Road. The road was paved until it got to the gate, but after the gate, it was gravel. Still, it was packed down pretty well, so the ride wasn't too difficult. While the sun was out and it was a nice spring day, because of the trees on either side of the road and the position of the sun at 1:30 in the afternoon, many parts were still shaded. The air was crisp and clear out here. As they continued down the road, however, they began to notice the sun's rays shining through light wisps of fog. It was so light that they really didn't pay too much attention to it at first; they just enjoyed how pretty the sun's rays looked shining through it. They were about a half mile down the road now and were making pretty good time. Just a few more minutes and they'd be out at the lighthouse. But as they continued further down the road, the light wisps of fog quickly became thicker.

"Where did this fog come from?" asked Veronica, "It was sunny and clear when we left the hotel."

"I don't know," replied Amy, "but it's not too bad yet. I think we're more than half way to the lighthouse, let's just keep going."

The more they kept going, though, the thicker the fog became. It had come up fast. Neither of them had ever seen fog come up quite so fast before, especially on an otherwise clear, sunny day. They had to slow down some, since even though they turned the bike headlights on, they still couldn't see very far in front of them. This fog wasn't like any fog they had seen, either. They could almost feel it against their skin. And it swirled in little miniature wisps that almost seemed alive.

"I think we must be almost there." said Amy hesitantly, a slight quiver in her voice. She was remembering her dad talking about the fog out at the lighthouse, and remembering the story of Tim and Greg that he had told them.

"I hope so," replied Veronica, sounding slightly anxious, "This is getting creepy."

They kept going but still weren't coming to the clearing where the cars were parked. And Veronica was right, it was creepy. It was a little after 1:30 in the afternoon, but because of the thickness of the fog, it had gotten fairly dark. Amy wished that they would hurry up and get to the clearing soon so that they could find her dad. She was also starting to get a little scared, with just the two of them out here all alone in the fog. She could tell that Veronica was also a little frightened as well. Her dad had warned them not to go into the fog. But they hadn't gone into the fog; the fog had simply formed around them. There was no way to avoid it. Now all they could do was try to get out of it as soon as they could. Amy thought that maybe she had misjudged how far they had to go. It seemed like it was taking forever to go the rest of the distance. Had the fog not come up, she was sure that they would have been there by now.

Finally, the vehicles parked in the clearing came into view in the bike's headlights. Amy and Veronica were both relieved. They'd find Amy's dad, give him the blueprints, then wait for the fog to clear before heading back to the hotel. They saw Mr. Duncan's car parked beside a van from the restoration company, so Amy knew that her dad was here. They leaned their bikes up against a tree in front of the parked cars, untied the tube containing the blueprints, and then walked toward the lighthouse.

As they approached the lighthouse, the fog seemed to get a little thinner, but it was still thick. Finally, they reached the wall and walked through the gate. Inside the gate, the fog was gone, but things still didn't feel right. Amy called for her dad, but didn't get an answer. They both looked around the clearing inside the wall. The fog went all the way around the outside of the wall, but none of it was coming inside.

"Dad, Mr. Duncan! Where are you?" yelled Amy.

"Where is everyone?" asked Veronica quietly.

"I don't know." responded Amy hesitantly, "Their cars are right out there, but no one seems to be here."

They walked over toward the lighthouse. Suddenly Veronica froze in her tracks, a frightened look on her face. "Amy?!" she said in a low slightly quivering voice, "Look at the lighthouse. It's not the same. What's happening here?"

Amy looked over at the lighthouse. Veronica was right, it was different. There was no scaffolding around it where the workers were doing the repairs. And even though it was old and run down, it didn't seem quite AS old and run down. The lantern house which had been leaning the last time they saw it, looking almost like it was ready to topple, was straight, with all of the bricks still around it intact. They heard the wind blowing through the trees, but that was the only sound that they did hear. No voices or any other indication that anyone was out here. The workers couldn't have made this much progress on the lighthouse in just a few days, could they?

They walked around to the front of the lighthouse, but no one was there. Though from Mr. Duncan's car, and all of the trucks parked over in the clearing, there should be a lot of people here, including her dad, Amy felt like they were all alone. The thought of being all alone at the end of a mile long road, with the thick fog surrounding the lighthouse made her even more fearful. She just couldn't understand what was going on.

"Dad, Mr. Duncan! Where are you?! Are you here?!" Her voice began to sound even shakier as they ran around the side of the house. They ran up the steps and ran into the foyer.

"Dad, where are you?!" screamed Amy now becoming even more frightened. Veronica had been running along behind her trying to keep up.

"What's happening?!" she cried.

They both stopped, just inside the dimly lit foyer. Dan had taken them on a tour of it Monday just after they had arrived. They looked over at the staircase, leading up to the second floor. They both turned to look at each other. Monday there had been no staircase there, only a large hole in the floor where the staircase had been. Now there it was, a staircase leading to the second floor. But it didn't look like a NEW staircase that had just been built. It looked old, like the rest of the house, with some of the stairs cracked and some of the molding missing. They quietly walked into the dining room. There was a dining table in the middle of the room, complete with four chairs pushed under it. They walked back outside and continued to look around. Dan had told Amy a little bit about the lighthouse when they were discussing moving out here. She knew there was a mystery surrounding it. She knew about the two boys who had disappeared back in 1974. And she knew a little about the fog. At least they were out of the fog now. They should be safe. They'd wait for the fog to clear, and then make their way back to the Harbor Inn. They both sat down on the steps of the lighthouse and stared at the fog surrounding them. They sat and waited.

It was about 1:30 in the afternoon. Dan walked over to where the fog had formed just outside the wall. He reached his hand in and touched it. The wisps of fog swirled around his fingers. The others had come over as well. For as long as they had been working at the lighthouse for the last month, this was the first time that the team from Southeast Restoration Services had seen the fog. Wayne, the project manager for the interior restoration had lived along the coast all of his life and was very familiar with the stories about the fog. He had even read most of the books about the lighthouse. But this was the first time that he had actually seen the fog for himself. He even stepped a little ways into it and shivered as the temperature seemed to drop at least twenty degrees. At one point, Dan thought he heard voices, but quickly dismissed that idea as just the wind in the trees. They didn't have any scientific measuring equipment this time, and Dr. Carson wasn't here. This was only the second time that he had seen the fog since they had been out here. He walked back over to the lighthouse and went in to get some rope and a flashlight. He tied one end of the rope to a tree which was just inside the wall, and tied the other end around his waist. Then he turned on his light and walked into the fog. As he walked over to where Scotty's car and all of the trucks were parked, he got quite a surprise. As he shined his light around in the fog, he discovered that Scotty's car and the other trucks were no longer in the clearing. In fact, there was no clearing! Just grass, bushes, and trees where the clearing had been just moments before. Suddenly, he heard someone come up behind him in the fog. He turned quickly, to see that Scotty also had tied a rope around his waist and had ventured into the fog.

"We have to be careful," he told Scotty, "the fog could go away at any time, and when it does we need to be back out of it."

"This is the strangest thing I've ever seen!" remarked Scotty. "Did you see how fast it came up, and with no warning either? Just like the first time we saw it last month."

"According to Dr. Carson, we're walking around in an 'alternate reality' right now." said Dan.

"Yeah, not sure I really believe that stuff, though." replied Scotty.

"Not sure I do either," said Dan, "but right now I'm just not sure what to believe."

They explored the woods just inside the fog for a few more minutes, with the others watching from inside the wall, and then they came back out of the fog and into the clear air around the lighthouse.

"What's in there?" asked Chris.

"Just more trees and bushes," replied Scotty, "we're just not sure WHAT trees and bushes."

They all watched the fog, went over to the edge, and walked into it. All of them were curious about it. They didn't dare go too far, not without something tied to them. They just stepped into the edge, just enough to feel the difference in the air, but not far enough that they would lose sight of the lighthouse. It had been about thirty minutes since the fog had come up. It was around 2:00 in the afternoon now, and it seemed that the fog was getting thinner. They could detect a distinct change. And now, through the quickly thinning fog, they could begin to see their vehicles, Scotty's car, and the trucks belonging to Southeast Restoration Professionals. But those cars and trucks hadn't been there just a few minutes before when they had walked into the fog! Dan and Scotty were sure of that.

After the fog had completely lifted, Chris and the others from the restoration company went back to work on the lighthouse. Greg and Steve went back in to work with them. After the fog came and went though, they all had an uneasy feeling. It was hard to get back to work. All any of them could think about was the fog. And Dan felt an unusual feeling, like something wasn't as it should be, even though everything seemed exactly the way that it had been before the fog came up. He hadn't felt it the first time that they had seen the fog, however, and it gave him a really uneasy feeling.

Dan and Scotty went back out to the clearing and got into Scotty's car to drive back to the Harbor Inn. Kate hadn't called yet, so he wondered if the blueprints were going to arrive today. He figured that if they didn't, they could always come back out and discuss them tomorrow. The girls should be back from their bike ride by now, so maybe they could go and get some lunch, and then decide what they wanted to do for the rest of the day.

He found Kate and Danny at the miniature golf course.

"Who's winning?" he asked.

"I am!" retorted Danny, "Mom's pretty good, but I'm better."

"Are the girls back yet?" asked Dan.

"They got back about forty five minutes ago." replied Kate, "Didn't you see them? They rode out to the lighthouse to take you the blueprints. The blueprints arrived just as they were getting back from their ride along the beach."

Dan's face went completely white, a growing panic building inside him. All he could think about was the fog, and the girls getting caught in it. Kate had never seen this particular look on his face before, and it did frighten her. He raced back through the lobby, and bolted out the front doors, leaving Kate and Danny staring after him, wondering why he was acting so strange. Scotty was just backing out of his parking space to go back out to the lighthouse. He saw Dan running toward his car, his arms waving wildly.

"Scotty, wait! We need to go back out to the lighthouse!"

He was completely out of breath as he opened the passenger door and got into the car.

"Hurry!" he said to Scotty, "We need to get back out to the lighthouse! It's Amy and Veronica; I think something might have happened!"

Scotty sped down Harbor Inn Lane and turned onto Lighthouse Road. They made the trip in record time. As they pulled into the clearing to park, Dan noticed something that he had previously missed as they left a few minutes ago: leaning against a tree at the edge of the clearing were two bikes. He threw the car door open and went running through the woods toward the lighthouse.

"Amy, Veronica! Are you here!" he screamed.

Greg and Steve, along with Chris and the others came out from the lighthouse to see what all the commotion was about.

"Greg, have you seen Amy and Veronica?" he asked, almost completely out of breath.

"No, I don't think they've been out here today." he replied.

"They're here!" yelled Dan, "Their bikes are back in the clearing! They have to be here!"

By now Scotty had made his way outside. Dan had run around the front of the lighthouse, calling for Amy and Veronica. He was completely overtaken by fear.

"What's going on, Dad?" asked Greg.

"I don't quite know," answered Scotty, "and I'm not sure I really want to know. Amy's and Veronica's bikes are over in the clearing in front of the cars. And Dan's hysterical with panic. I hope I'm wrong, but I think something may have happened to Amy and Veronica in the fog."

But in his mind, Scotty had a feeling that he wasn't wrong. They had seen the fog, and had walked into it. And it had come up within just a few minutes, probably around the time that Amy and Veronica were on their way out here. He had the sinking feeling that the girls were gone, maybe forever.

CHAPTER 20

The Search

By 6:00 in the evening, Green Island was a flurry of activity. Chief Callahan had been notified of the missing persons, Amy and Veronica, and his officers were conducting a full scale search of the area surrounding the Harbor Inn and the lighthouse. Since their bikes were found in the clearing at the lighthouse, the search was concentrated around that area. Detectives had been called in from Wilmington, as well as Coast Guard Search and Rescue. Volunteers who lived on the island had joined in the search as well, including Bud, Bill, Bill's son Alan, and Hank. Of course, Scotty, Greg, and Steve were part of the search party as well.

Commander Vernon Bates from the U.S. Coast Guard was coordinating the search and rescue effort, which included officers from the island police department as well as all of the volunteers. He had set up a command center in the clearing near the lighthouse, where he and his strategists had divided a map into grids. Searchers were assigned to certain grids, and were in the process of going one grid at a time to perform the search. Several portable generators provided power for the radios and laptop computers that they were using to coordinate the search. He also had a search and rescue helicopter flying over the island to try and spot them from the air. He wanted to get as much area as he could covered while it was still light. By 8:00, the searchers had covered quite a few grids, still with no sign of the girls. All of the searchers were given radios and had been asked to report in when they either cleared a grid or had something to report. Each time a grid was cleared, a mark was made for that grid on the map. It was just after sunset now. Soon it would be completely dark. The moon was waxing gibbous, slightly larger than a half moon, so that would give off some light, but in the dense cover of the woods, it wouldn't be enough. They probably would have to call off the search until tomorrow at first light. Lighthouse Road had been sealed off with a police barricade and no one except for the searchers and families of the girls were allowed to go down the road.

Dan was trying to comfort Kate, but he himself was almost as distraught and emotional as she was. They had taken Danny over to the Island Charm where he was going to spend the night with Hank and Barbara. Dan felt like Kate blamed him, and he wasn't so sure that he didn't blame himself as well. After all, there were plenty of warnings that he had chosen to ignore. He recalled all of the warnings and turned them over and over in his mind.

On the way to the island, Ben had told him, "If I was you, I'd turn right back around and go back where you came from."

He had encountered Bud on the ferry to the island who had warned him when he found out that he had bought the lighthouse, "Not sure that's such a good idea. You do know the history of the lighthouse right?"

And then there was Hank, who while he had only been on the island for a couple of years tried to convince Dan on several occasions that moving out to the lighthouse was a bad idea. Dan recalled him saying when they first met, "Don't move your family down here. And you'd do best to go ahead and leave yourself. Something's not right there. The lighthouse shouldn't be disturbed, or it may start again. You and your family won't be safe out there."

And most recently, after Kate and the kids had arrived, "I've gotten to like you during the time that you've been here. I'd really hate for something to happen."

But he had chosen to ignore all of these warnings. And now something HAD happened, and he couldn't help but feel that it was his fault. Why had he come out here? Why didn't he take the warnings seriously, especially after he had seen the fog for himself? He kept asking himself why? He could hear the warnings so clearly now, but at the time he had just chosen to brush them off. Why had he stubbornly insisted on staying to find out what was happening?

Even Scotty had the nagging feeling that he had given Dan the wrong advice. When Dan had asked if they were doing the right thing, Scotty had replied, "Do you really think you could just pack up and leave and never know?" Now he was thinking that's exactly what they should have done. But they were all too intrigued by the lighthouse, the fog, and the mystery of it all. This had started out to be such an adventure, that they had all been blinded to the danger that was out there. People had DISAPPEARED out there, without a trace, and were never found! And now, people that they loved had disappeared as well. The warning signs were definitely there, they had all just chosen not to see them.

After her initial outbursts where she had screamed at Dan, hitting him and blaming him for what had happened to Amy and Veronica, Kate had not said another word. She just sat and stared blankly out the sliding glass door of their hotel room off to the trees in the distance. She sat motionless, with just that blank stare. Dan had tried to get her to eat or drink something, but she didn't even acknowledge that he was there. While she had initially blamed Dan, she also thought that she was partially at fault as well; after all, she had sent the girls out there. She had talked with Dan about the things that had been going on here. She should have known better than to send the girls out there alone! There was a counselor that had been brought in by the police department to help them deal with the situation. The counselor tried to stay positive, at this point not even mentioning the posibility that the girls may never be found, but even the counselor couldn't get a response from Kate.

Earlier, Dan had called Parker, Veronica's dad, back in Cincinnati. This was the hardest call that he had ever had to make. How do you tell someone that their only child, whom they had entrusted to your care, is missing? Parker had seemed to remain calm and take the news well, but Dan knew how HE felt, and figured that Parker must be feeling most of the same emotions. But he also wasn't sure that Parker fully understood what they were dealing with here. Parker had replied, "They should turn up soon. After all, it's not a very big island. Where could they go?" Under normal circumstances, he could agree. But this was Green Island. And this was Forrest Point Light. He asked Parker to let him know their flight schedule and he'd have someone come to meet them at the airport, then he hung up the phone and went back over to Kate. She was still just staring out the window, with the sandwich that he had brought her from the Mariners

Cove still untouched.

Slightly after 8:00, a news van and motor home from Channel 10 Action News in Wilmington, along with SkyStar 10, the station's satellite uplink truck rolled down Main Street on their way out to the lighthouse. This was big national news, and the station's producer, Jack Williams, was sending SkyStar 10 to provide a live feed to the RBS network. Channel 10 was an affiliate of the Reliant Broadcasting Service, RBS, and the network producer was waiting to get a live national feed on the air. The trucks turned down Harbor Inn Lane and were stopped at the police barricade at Lighthouse Road. They wanted to set up the live broadcast actually out at the lighthouse, but Commander Bates wasn't allowing the news media out there. Officer Collins, who was stationed at the entrance to Lighthouse Road, directed them on down the road to the Harbor Inn. They proceeded down the road where they drove through the gates of the Harbor Inn, went around the circular drive, and then turned right into the parking lot. They decided to set up for the broadcast in the northeast parking lot, which had a good view of the front of the hotel as well as the gardens around to the right side.

Jack Williams had sent one of the station's most popular reporters, Holly Harper, to cover this story on location, while Megan Barnett and Wes Walters reported from the anchor desk. The station had designed a banner to be displayed along the top of the screen and also a title box to be displayed at the upper left corner of the screen for live news reports. The stations production staff had dug up some old photos of Forrest Point Lighthouse and had used these along with a foggy background and photos of Amy and Veronica to design the banner and title box. They had even given a catchy name to this news coverage, "Foggy Point Light 2016 – The Search for Amy and Veronica". They also had given this broadcast its own bumper music which played along with the banner display every time a news update came on. Since it was to air nationally, everything about the production had to be professionally orchestrated.

It took about thirty minutes to get everything set up in the Harbor Inn parking lot. Holly's cameraman, T.J. McNeil, got some test shots that he fed back to the studio to adjust the lighting since it was nighttime. The satellite technicians rotated the big dish antenna atop the satellite truck to intercept the network satellite and performed some tests of the feed. The live broadcast was set to begin at 9:00 pm. At 8:55 everyone was in position in the studio as well as on location. The producer in the studio gave the signal – 3, 2, 1 – Action. At exactly 9:00 pm eastern time, the entire nation was watching the events unfold at Green Island, and the entire nation became acquainted with Amy Nelson and Veronica Norwood.

Megan Barnett began the broadcast by introducing some background on the story:

"Good Evening, this is Megan Barnett, Channel 10 Action news with continuing coverage of 'Foggy Point Light 2016 – The Search for Amy and Veronica'. Around 2:00 pm this afternoon, Amy and Veronica began what should have been an uneventful bike ride to take Amy's dad some blueprints out at the lighthouse on Green Island, but sometime after they arrived at the lighthouse, something went terribly wrong and neither girl has been seen or heard from since. Their mother and brother watched as their bikes disappeared around the bend of Harbor Inn Lane. This was the last time that anyone saw the girls alive. Their bikes were found propped against a tree out by the lighthouse, which indicated that they had made it that far, but so far search efforts by the Coast Guard, Green Island Police Department, and numerous citizen volunteers have turned up empty. For more information on this breaking story, we take you now to Holly Harper, Channel 10 News Correspondent, on location at Green Island."

The red light on T.J.'s camera came on indicating that they were on the air and signaling Holly to begin her report.

"This is Holly Harper, Channel 10 Action News on location at the Harbor Inn on Green Island, where about seven hours ago, Amy Nelson and Veronica Norwood, two teenage girls vacationing here from Cincinnati, began their fateful trip out to the lighthouse. Behind me you can see the Harbor Inn where the family was staying for the week, and where the trip out to the lighthouse began. We're still trying to get an interview with the girls' parents, but so far they are declining to speak to the news media. What we do know is that around 2:00 pm this afternoon, Amy and Veronica rode their bikes down Lighthouse Road to take some blueprints to Amy's dad out at the lighthouse. They seemed to have arrived at their destination, since their bikes were found leaning against a tree, but what happened after that is still a mystery. We've learned from reliable sources that the fog that comes up out there periodically, and is the subject of several books on the lighthouse, did form this afternoon around the time that the girls disappeared. We are still investigating what connection, if any, the fog may have to the disappearance. Amy Nelson's dad, Dan Nelson, one of the owners of Perihelion Research Group, which is one of the leading technology and government contracting companies in the country, was in the process of restoring the lighthouse and was going to move his family out here in June. We're not clear just what his family was doing here now, but possibly they were just on vacation for spring break. One moment, there seems to be something happening over at the entrance drive. There's a patrol car with lights flashing coming through the entrance. T.J., are you getting this? Let's move over that direction and see if we can get a look."

Earlier in the day, Parker and Ellen Norwood had called with their itinerary. After the trip over to the island aboard the ferry, they were met at the dock by Officer Clark Seabrook of the island police, who provided them with a police escort out to the Harbor Inn. As they drove through the entrance to the hotel, Officer Seabrook had to hit his siren one time to clear the crowd from the entrance. Jay, one of the production assistants inside the broadcast van who had been monitoring the police frequency stepped outside and informed Holly that the couple coming through the gate was Parker and Ellen Norwood, Veronica Norwood's parents. As they drove over to the hotel entrance, Holly and TJ followed them, with the camera rolling. As they parked, Officer Seabrook go t out of his patrol car first, and motioned for the news media to back away and give them some room. As Parker and Ellen exited their rental car, Holly shouted to them, "Mr. and Mrs. Norwood, how does it feel to have your only daughter missing? What are you going to do if she's never found?"

"How do you think we feel?!" snapped Parker, as he and his wife were whisked inside by Officer Seabrook and a couple of security guards who were watching the entrance. They had been instructed that only registered guests and friends and family of the Nelsons and the Norwoods were to be allowed inside. As the Norwoods disappeared inside the hotel, T.J.'s camera was still focused on the doorway that they just went through, watching as they met with police and hotel staff inside.

Holly continued, "We've just witnessed the arrival of Parker and Ellen Norwood, the parents of Veronica, one of the girls who has been missing, now going on about eight hours. We can only imagine how they must feel, knowing that they may never see their daughter again. But as tragic as this story is, it's not the first time that there have been disappearances around the lighthouse. For some Foggy Point Light history, let's go to Wes Walters in the studio."

The red light on T.J.'s camera went out and the broadcast returned to the studio, where Wes Walters reported some of the history of the lighthouse, including the story of Greg and Tim back in 1974 and the story of Colonel Forrest, whose name had been given to the lighthouse after his encounter. The production staff had even dug up some photos from the 1974 search as well as family photos of Greg and Tim that they showed on screen as Wes was narrating his report. After Wes's report on the lighthouse's history, he returned the broadcast back to Holly Harper live at the Harbor Inn on Green Island.

At around 10:30 pm, Holly got news that the search was being suspended until morning. It was just too dark to really continue. Holly speculated, "As dark as it is now, I wonder how the girls are feeling? We can only wonder where they might be. Hopefully tomorrow we'll get good news. Until then, our prayers are with them tonight. We'll resume the live broadcast at 6:00 tomorrow morning. Until then, this is Holly Harper, Channel 10 Action News, live at the Harbor Inn on Green Island. We'll go now back to Megan Barnett and Wes Walters."

Holly handed the microphone to one of the broadcast assistants and walked over toward the edge of the parking lot. Earlier in the evening, during one of the broadcast segments, she had seen a man standing over at the edge of the parking lot, away from everyone else. He seemed to be intently concentrating on the broadcast. She wanted to find out if he might still be there and if he had any information. T.J. looked over toward her direction, wondering what she was doing. After a few minutes of searching and not finding anyone, she returned over to where T.J. and the others were still standing around, discussing the night's events.

"What were you doing?" inquired T.J.

"I saw someone over at the edge of the parking lot earlier when we were live. I just wanted to see if they were still around." replied Holly, "It looks like they've already gone."

She told T.J. goodnight, then walked over to the station's motor home, which would be her home for the rest of the evening. This afternoon, she had only had a short time to prepare for the broadcast. Now, she switched on her computer and began to research Green Island and the lighthouse. She wanted to find out as much as she could that she could incorporate into the news coverage tomorrow. Depending on how the search went, and most searches actually go pretty slow, she may have a lot of time to fill. As she was about to turn in for the night, she got a call on her Smartphone. It was her producer, Jack Williams. He wanted to let her know that he had arranged for her and T.J. to broadcast a segment from the search and rescue helicopter tomorrow. They'd need to be over at the docks near the ferry station where there was a helipad at around 7:00 am.

The Norwood's' suite had been available for them when they arrived and they had gotten settled in there. This had been a day that they would like to forget. It had started out normal enough, but after they had received Dan's call, everything changed. They quickly booked a flight to Wilmington and rented a car to go out to Green Island. They both hoped that things would turn out alright, that by the time that they got to the island, the girls would have been found and Veronica would be there to greet them. They'd stay for the weekend and enjoy the island together. But that wasn't to be what would happen. When they got to the Harbor Inn there were crowds of people still gathered around, and a TV news crew doing a live broadcast. They had even been chased down by one of the reporters as they exited their car and went into the hotel.

After checking into their room, Parker and Ellen met with Dan down in the lobby so as not to disturb Kate. Dan had finally gotten her to lie down in the bed and, exhausted from the stress of the day, she had finally drifted off to sleep. Down in the lobby, Dan tried to catch Parker and Ellen up on some of the events from the day. He did leave out some details, since at this point, he really didn't want to let them know just how many warning signs that he had ignored. They discussed how the search was going and not fully understanding the situation with the lighthouse, Parker felt sure that tomorrow the girls would be found.

But the next day they weren't found. Holly and T.J. did go up in the search and rescue helicopter, and they circled the island for about an hour, with T.J. getting some really good aerial shots of the island, and of the lighthouse. But at the end of the day, they seemed no closer to finding Amy and Veronica than they were yesterday. There just weren't any leads to go on. Other than the bikes propped up against the tree, there was absolutely no evidence that either of them had been out there. The searchers were getting more and more frustrated. The girls had to be somewhere, right? They couldn't just disappear without a trace, could they? But that was exactly what had happened to Greg and Tim forty two years ago, and it was beginning to look like that's what may have happened again.

Sunday wasn't any better. The search just wasn't going anywhere. After two days, the news media was running out of material. Nothing new was happening, and they still weren't allowed out to the lighthouse. Dan and Parker had joined in the search on Sunday, because both of them were tired of just sitting around doing nothing. Ellen stayed with Kate, both of them feeling totally helpless. With each day that went by, that sinking, hopeless feeling grew stronger. Kate still hadn't said a word since the disappearance. During the day, she simply sat and stared out the sliding glass door, and at night she slept, though not very well. At least Barbara had said that Danny could stay with her as long as they needed. That was a relief. Dan wondered what Danny must be thinking about the whole situation. He had gone over to see him a couple of times. He seemed to be handling it pretty well, but he had been watching the news coverage. Once, Danny had asked him, "Is Amy ever coming home?" He had to look away. All he could think of to say was, "I hope so, buddy. I hope so."

Saturday afternoon, they did have a glimmer of hope. A couple of searchers in quadrant seven found a small cabin that looked like it had been occupied recently. More searchers, including Dan, Parker, Scotty, and Greg went out there and did a thorough search of the area around the cabin, but that search came up empty as well. Still, Dan wondered about the cabin. Was someone living there, and could it be the mysterious man who had been following him? The detectives came out to take a look, but couldn't find any evidence that would connect the cabin with the girls.

As Sunday came and went, with the search being no closer to finding the girls than when it first started, Dan was beginning to wonder how long the police and Coast Guard would continue the search. It had already been over two days, with absolutely no leads whatsoever. They had searched every quadrant at least twice and had come up with nothing. With each passing day, the knot in Dan's stomach grew tighter, as his hope was dwindling. He didn't want to give up, but there simply wasn't anything left to hold on to. Still, he had to hold onto some hope. He just couldn't bring himself to accept the possibility that he'd never see Amy again, that she'd be gone forever.

That night, folks from all over the island and some from the mainland gathered in the hotel gardens for a candlelight vigil and prayer service. Holly Harper was there, and it was broadcast live on Channel 10. Dan went down for it even though he couldn't persuade Kate to go. He was really moved by the turnout, with everyone being given a white candle. The service was led by Reverend Walt Anderson of the First Baptist Church on the island. There must have been more than a hundred people gathered in the garden that night, with the glow of a hundred candles lighting up the night, renewing his hope.

CHAPTER 21
April 18, 2016
Always Consider the Impossible

Monday morning Dan and Parker went back out to the lighthouse to talk with Commander Bates. He informed them that the Coast Guard was bringing in divers later that day to search the waters around the tip of the island. This wasn't the news that either of them wanted to hear, because that meant that they were giving up any hope of finding the girls alive.

"Are you sure we need to bring in divers this soon?" asked Dan.

"Mr. Nelson, I want to find the girls alive as much as you do. But we've been over most of the grids at least twice if not three times already." replied the commander, "It's time that we expanded the search, whatever that may mean."

Dan knew that he was right. They had been searching for two and a half days already. While he couldn't quite bring himself to consider what the divers might find, he knew that it was something that he had to face sooner or later. Over the past couple of days he had also been considering the fact that, like Greg and Tim, they may never be found. He remembered the talk that he had had with Bill Henderson the day after the campout at the lighthouse.

He finally understood the emotions that Bill was feeling when he told Dan, "It's really amazing how fast things can change. One day you have the life you've always dreamed of having, a loving wife, great kids; everything's going just how you planned it. Then in an instant that's all taken away. The worst part of it is not knowing what happened. Wherever Tim was, did he miss us? Was he hoping we'd find him? Or was he dead? If he was, exactly how did he die? Did he die instantly, or did he have time to think about dying? Was it painful?"

Dan was having these same thoughts now about Amy and

Veronica. He wished that somehow, he knew what had happened. He really didn't know if he could face never knowing what happened to them if they were never found. He knew that Kate must be feeling this same way too, she just wouldn't talk about it.

Steve and Greg, who were still a part of the search, had seen Dan and Parker arrive and walked over to where they were.

"How are you holding up?" Steve asked.

"Pretty good," Dan replied, but then he was silent for a moment before replying with a slight quiver to his voice, "Actually not too good. I just feel so helpless. She's always depended on me to be there for her and to protect her, and now there's nothing that I can do."

"We're doing what we can." said Steve, "Don't give up hope."

But he felt like he already was giving up hope. After two and a half days, he wasn't sure that he had too much more hope left. Steve and Greg went back to the search, which was limited to a ground search now. Commander Bates had stopped running the helicopter yesterday. Even the TV station, while still maintaining a news crew on the island, had stopped the round the clock broadcasts. There just wasn't anything new to fill up the time. Progress on the search was mentioned every newscast, though, even if it was just to say that there was no new information. He and Parker decided to go back to the hotel. How long would it be, thought Dan, before they would call off the search altogether. He just couldn't bring himself to think about that right now.

They pulled up in front of the hotel, parked, and went inside. When Dan got up to his suite, and went inside, Kate was gone. Arlene was there instead.

"Scotty came by the room earlier." she said, "He finally got her to take a walk. I think they're out in the garden. Is there any news yet?"

"No, nothing yet." Dan said, "They're bringing in divers this afternoon to search the water around the island." She noticed a tear run down Dan's cheek as he said this.

"Don't give up hope, Dan" she replied, "Until they actually find them, there's always hope."

Dan nodded in agreement, knowing she was right, but still finding it hard to find that glimmer of hope right now. "I think I'll go down and find Kate and Scotty." he said.

He went downstairs and found them sitting in the garden. They both had a plate with sandwiches and chips that they had gotten from the Mariners Cove and Kate had already eaten half of hers.

"Why don't you go in and get something to eat and come join us." said Scotty.

"Thanks, I'll do that." replied Dan.

Dan was glad that Kate was at least eating something. The last few days had been hard on her. At least Scotty had been able to get through to her. She had always liked Scotty. The three of them had met while in college and had developed a special friendship even then. She actually had dated Scotty first, before she met Dan, and Scotty had been the one to introduce them. After graduation, the two families had maintained their special friendship. They would go on vacations together, and even go to dinner and movies around town. Scotty and Belinda were definitely their closest friends.

In a few minutes, Dan joined them in the garden with a fish sandwich and chips. Kate actually smiled at Dan as he sat down. This was the first time that he had seen her smile in several days, even if it was only a halfway, forced smile. While she didn't say much during the meal, she did talk a little and that was an improvement. She asked Dan how the search was going. While he really didn't want to answer that question truthfully, he knew that she had a right to know.

"They're still searching." he replied, "Hopefully they'll come up with something soon."

He purposely left out the part about them bringing in the Coast Guard divers. Partly because he couldn't quite bring himself to say it again, and partly because he didn't feel like she was ready to hear that just yet. He could tell that she was noticeably disappointed that they hadn't found them yet, but then how could she not be.

"There's not much news on the TV anymore. They've stopped the live broadcasts." she said.

"That's because there's not much for them to report, but that doesn't mean that there are no new developments and there isn't any progress." replied Scotty. "They're still not letting the news people actually out to the lighthouse, so there are only so many new developments that they can have while camped out in the hotel parking lot."

This explanation seemed to satisfy her, at least for the moment. After lunch, Scotty decided to go back out to the lighthouse and see if there was any new information. He'd call Dan if he found out anything. Dan and Kate decided to drive out and take a walk along the beach. He thought that the fresh air would do her good after staying up in the hotel room for the last few days. He asked Scotty to go and bring his truck around to the side entrance before he went back out to the lighthouse. Holly Harper and the rest of the news crew were still camped out around front, and the last thing he wanted for Kate after finally getting her out of the room was for some reporter to ask her how it felt to possibly never see her daughter again.

Scotty drove the truck around to the side entrance and Dan helped Kate into the passenger side. He thanked Scotty for being there for them, then got into the truck and proceeded out the front entrance onto Harbor Inn Lane and out to the beach. He found a parking spot near the boardwalk that led to the public beach access. They walked across the boardwalk and breathed in the cool salt air. The walk was refreshing, and much needed. The sound of the surf as they walked was peaceful and calming. They held hands as they walked slowly down the beach, not talking much, but just being there for each other. And right now, that seemed to be enough.

After a good walk on the beach, which did seem to refresh them both, they decided to drive over to the Sand Crab Diner for dinner. They both enjoyed the food there, and Dan felt like they needed to get out a little after the stress of the last two and a half days. The others could handle the search; they just needed to get away from it all for awhile. Kate actually talked more during dinner than she had since the disappearance. During their walk down the beach, she had told Dan that she really didn't blame him anymore. She realized that there had been no way to know that anything would happen. While he should have been more cautious given all of the warnings, she understood that sometimes people may not realize the danger until it's too late. She knew Dan better than anyone, and knew that he would never put his family in danger if he realized the danger was that great. Even she hadn't realized the danger when she sent the girls out to the lighthouse that day.

After dinner, Kate wanted to stop by the Island Charm and see Danny. While Dan had gone by for several short visits during the weekend, she hadn't seen Danny since Friday. When they parked and walked up the steps of the Island Charm, Danny greeted them at the door and gave them both a big hug. He was in the sitting room playing a game of checkers with Barbara.

"Who's winning?" asked Kate.

"He beats me every time!" remarked Barbara, "How are you two holding up? I can't even imagine what it would be like!"

"We're doing about as well as can be expected," said Dan, "which isn't all that well really. It's just difficult waiting and knowing there's nothing we can do."

"Why don't you both come into the sitting area and have a cup of tea?" suggested Barbara.

"That sounds wonderful!" answered Kate.

The four of them went into the sitting room, and visited for about two hours. It was good having this time together, and Barbara was such a good hostess. Dan played a game of checkers with Danny while Kate and Barbara chatted over on the sofa. During the visit, Danny didn't really ask about Amy. Mostly because he felt that his dad would tell him if there was any news to tell, but also because he was afraid of getting bad news. He and his sister were as close as any brother and sister could be. He had really been missing her the last few days. Unlike the adults, however, he was still too young to realize that she might not be coming back. For him, it was just a matter of WHEN she would be back, not IF.

After visiting with Barbara over at the Island Charm, it was around 7:00 in the evening when they got back to the Harbor Inn. Seeing the news crew still there, Dan pulled up to the door to let Kate out so she wouldn't have to walk through the parking lot, and then went to park the truck. She was waiting in the lobby for him when he came through the front entrance and they both took the elevator up to the second floor together. After they got back to their room, Dan noticed the red light blinking on the phone, indicating a message. He walked over to the phone, lifted the receiver, and pressed the message button. He hoped that it was good news. He didn't think that he could handle any more bad news at the moment. While he had hoped for good news, he still was relieved that it was just Ellen Norwood. She was having a difficult time dealing with Veronica's disappearance and asked if Kate could come down to her room for a little while to talk. Parker had gone out for a walk, and she needed someone to talk to. Kate agreed, thinking that visiting with Ellen might do her good as well. After two days of just sitting and staring out the window, today had been a refreshing change. She was still worried, but she discovered that talking with others actually did help her to try and cope with the situation a lot better.

After Kate had left to go down to the Norwood's room, Dan sat on the edge of the bed and put his face down into his hands. He was mentally and physically exhausted, and not knowing what the next few hours or days would bring seemed only to drain what little strength he had left. As he walked over to the window to look out, he noticed a corner of Amy Westfall's book sticking out from under a newspaper that had been put on the table. He picked up the book and went out on the balcony to sit for awhile. He stared at the cover, with the lighthouse and the fog. The fog seemed to jump right out at him. He was remembering the fog that had come up out at the lighthouse on Friday afternoon. He had read through the first several chapters the first night that they had gotten the book and was fascinated with what he read. The story was similar to what happened in 1974 with the disappearance of Greg and Tim, but in Amy Westfall's story, it was two girls who had disappeared, Stephanie and Jessica. The circumstances were also similar, but still quite different. He stared at the title, and pondered it in his mind over and over: "Displaced in Time". He stared out at the gardens, totally lost in thought. He looked back down at the book, then opened to the front cover and read the inscription. Apparently when he was reading on Thursday night, he was reading Amy's book, where Mrs. Westfall had written, "To Amy, My biggest fan." He didn't recall reading this inscription before, but now it stood out in his mind as he read it, "To Danny, Always consider the impossible. AD Wfl". It was an odd inscription. As he sat on the balcony studying the inscription, he actually started thinking the impossible. He tried to put it all together in his mind. The cover of the book with the lighthouse surrounded by the fog: the title, "Displaced in Time": the inscription, "Always consider the impossible". And what he was actually considering at this moment was definitely beyond impossible. He could barely force himself to even consider that it could be possible, but was it?

He pulled out his wallet and took out the business card that Amy Westfall had given him the night of the book signing. He turned it over and read the back, "Harbor Inn Suite 214". Mrs. Westfall had told him to come by when he was ready, and he definitely needed to talk with her now.

He opened the door to his suite and walked out into the hallway and down to Suite 214. He paused for a minute, trying to think of exactly what he would say. The inscription had read, "Always consider the impossible", and right now what he was wondering and what he wanted to ask her was beyond what any reasonable, sane person would even let himself consider. In fact, what he wanted to ask was just so crazy that he had almost talked himself out of it before even knocking on the door. He turned and started to walk back down the hallway toward his room, but those thoughts kept coming back to him. "Always consider the impossible." He turned that phrase over and over in his mind. After all, this wasn't a normal place. This was Green Island, and this was Forrest Point Lighthouse. Maybe what was impossible anywhere else might actually be possible here. He was about half way back to his room before he turned around and walked back. After a couple more minutes of trying to decide exactly what he was going to say, he reached out and actually found himself knocking on the door to Suite 214. He heard the latch click from inside the room and the door opened.

"Come in, Dan." Amy said, "Derrick and Rebekah are down at the pool.”

As he entered the room, which was dimly lit by two lamps over by the sofa, and one in the kitchen area, Amy walked over to the window and stared out at the trees surrounding the inn. Dan looked around the room, trying to think of exactly how to begin. It was difficult at this moment to find just the right words.

Finally he said, “Mrs. Westfall … I’ve read a few chapters of your new book, and well … there’re a few questions that come to mind.”

“Like what?” she asked.

“Well, like … how did you get the idea for the book exactly? What made you want to write about this lighthouse, on this particular island?”

She was silent for a few moments, pondering the question that he had just asked. This time it was Amy who was looking for just the right words to say.

“It was actually based on another true story surrounding the lighthouse and the fog … but it was one that you hadn’t read … one that you couldn’t have read in any of your books about the island.” she replied.

“Mrs. Westfall … the other night you told me I could stop by and … and, well, I’ve been looking at the cover of your book, and the title, and just today, I noticed the inscription inside Danny’s book, ‘Always consider the impossible’ … and it made me actually start to consider the impossible.”

He paused again, trying to think of just how to ask what he wanted to ask, without sounding like he had totally lost touch with reality. He continued, “This is probably going to sound absurd, and forgive me if I’m too presumptuous, but … I was wondering … are you …”

Dan paused again to collect his thoughts. This was more difficult than he had imagined when he came down here. Part of it was that the logical, down to earth voice inside him was telling him that what he was thinking just couldn’t be possible. But the other voice inside was urging him to ask the question, however crazy he might sound.

He continued, "Mrs. Westfall … I was wondering if … This may sound crazy, but … are you …"

"Yes." she said in a soft voice.

"Yes … What?" asked Dan, a slight quiver to his voice now.

"Yes is the answer to the question that you're trying to ask me." she continued, turning to face him this time, "You want to know if I'm your daughter … and the answer to that question is 'Yes'."

Dan was speechless. They both stood staring at each other in awkward silence, each trying to think of what to say next. While this possibility had occurred to Dan, however impossible it seemed, and he had come over to Amy's room intending to find out for sure, deep down he didn't really think he expected it to be true. In his rational mind it just couldn't be.

"But how?" he asked, so overcome with emotion that he could barely speak.

"I don't know how," she replied, "I only know that it did happen." She walked over to where Dan was standing, still in total shock and disbelief. She gave him a gentle hug. She had waited thirty years for this day to come. After a couple more minutes of just enjoying the reunion, she suggested that they go for a walk. They stepped into the hallway and walked down to the elevator, took it down to the lobby, then walked out into the garden. It was a little before 8:00 and the sun was almost below the horizon.

As they both walked through the garden in the fading light of day, she began, "For you, it's only been three days. For me, it's been thirty years. I don't know how it happened, I don't even know how it could have happened, but somehow on that day when the fog came up unexpectedly, Veronica and I found ourselves back in the year 1986!"

Dan continued to listen intently, as he reached out and took her hand. It really was Amy! He could tell that now. The shape of her face, her smile, even her eyes, they were all Amy's!

Amy continued, "That Friday afternoon, Veronica and I were

riding our bikes out to the lighthouse to bring you the blueprints that you were expecting. As we were on the way, the thick fog that we had heard you mention came up. By then we were most of the way out to the lighthouse, so we decided to continue, but the farther that we went, the thicker the fog became. Finally, we made it out to the lighthouse, but we couldn't find you or anyone else. There was simply no one out there. And the lighthouse looked different as well, not quite as old and run down as it does now. And while we didn't know what it meant at the time, and couldn't quite put our finger on it, the air smelled different as well. But since you had told us not to go into the fog, we waited at the lighthouse, where it was clear, until the fog lifted. But after the fog lifted, everything was different. The cars weren't in the clearing any longer, in fact, where the clearing used to be was grown up with grass, weeds, and bushes. And we couldn't find our bikes anywhere either. For that matter, we couldn't even find the tree where we had leaned our bikes! By this time we were really getting scared. It was quiet out there, over a mile from anything else. We walked the mile and three fourths back to the Harbor Inn. It looked ALMOST the same, but there were differences there as well. The first thing that we noticed was that all the cars in the parking lot seemed old. Not old and run down, they all looked shiny and new, but they weren't like the cars that we were used to. Walking into the lobby, there were subtle differences there also, like the large fish tank in the lobby was missing. In its place were a table and several chairs. We took the elevator up to our room and that's when we noticed the most striking difference: There were no card readers on the hotel room doors! It looked like they had key locks on them instead. And the wallpaper in the hallway was different.

"We went back downstairs and showed the lady at the front desk our room key, and she didn't seem to know what it was! She asked if it was a credit card. I asked which room you were registered in, and she said that there was no Dan Nelson registered at the hotel. We didn't know what to do at that point. We went over and sat on the sofa in the lobby to think. By now Veronica was really scared. She was crying, and I was close to tears myself. I even tried to call you on my Smartphone, but it didn't have a signal. We went back to talk with the front desk clerk and told the lady that we had lost our parents and our Smartphones didn't work. She asked us what a Smartphone was and I showed her mine. She appeared to have never seen one before. She just thought that it was some kind of toy. She called the police station and had an officer come out to help us find our parents.

"When the officer arrived, we told him we had gotten separated from you and mom and we were staying at the Harbor Inn, but that you didn't seem to be registered there any longer. He took down our names and information, such as our current address, city where we were born, and birth date. We gave him this information, and he looked at us like we were trying to play a trick on him. He asked us again what our REAL birth dates were. We hadn't yet figured out that we were back in 1986, so we didn't understand why he was acting so strange when we told him our birth dates. I was born in 2003 and Veronica was born in 2002. Thinking about it afterward, what else could he have thought other than we couldn't be telling the truth? He made some calls, and about thirty minutes later, the minister in town, Reverend David Taylor, came and picked us up and took us to his house for the rest of the night. He and Mrs. Taylor fed us a good meal for supper, and we sat and talked during the evening. We told him the story of what had happened. Not sure he really believed us, especially not the part about 2016, but he was nice and we liked him, even if we couldn't quite figure out what exactly had happened to you and mom. Those first few hours and days were really scary. The first hint that we weren't in 2016 anymore was when we spotted a calendar on the wall in their kitchen. It was turned to April, and the year at the top was 1986. We asked Reverend Taylor about it. He seemed to wonder why we seemed to not know what year it was, but he was nice about it.

"The next day, two men came over from the mainland to talk with us. We quickly learned to say 1986 anytime we were asked what year it was. They couldn't quite understand 2016, and we actually couldn't either. I won't go into all of the details of the next few months, but those weren't the best months for us. Nobody could figure out where we came from. Obviously, since we wouldn't be born for another sixteen years, there were no birth certificates to be found. At first, they were thinking that we weren't giving them our real names. Especially since to them we were obviously giving them fake birth dates. For the next three months we lived at some sort of facility near Wilmington. They made us take a lot of tests, and all of these psychologists came in to talk to us. They gave us lie detector tests, and even used hypnosis. They still appeared to have a hard time figuring us out, though, especially since we were passing all of the lie detector tests, even when we told them the year was 2016! We told the story of how we got there numerous times, to various people, but I don't think anyone ever really believed us. Probably because that wasn't something that their minds could even comprehend as being possible. After they had gotten about all of the information that they thought they could get from us, and were satisfied that we really didn't know how we got there, we were sent to a group home for girls in Charlotte, where we lived for the next five months until we were adopted by Martin and Elise Davenport. The girls' home didn't tell them anything about the circumstances around which we were found, and our claims to be from the year 2016. Thinking about it now, I don't even think that the girls' home knew anything about it."

Dan asked, "So Veronica grew up as your sister? Martin Davenport adopted both of you?"

"Yes, Veronica Davenport Ellison. She married Rick Ellison in 1993, and they have a daughter, Lisa, who's 21, and a senior in college."

"Parker will be glad to hear about Veronica." he said.

"Anyway," she continued, "after we were adopted by Martin and Elise Davenport, things definitely got better. Martin Davenport was a partner with three other men in a hotel management company, DMRL Hotels. DMRL was the first letter of the last names of the four partners. They owned six hotels in North Carolina and were doing pretty well. While they had a nice house in Charlotte, it wasn't exactly what we were used to. You own one of the largest research and development companies in the country, and Parker is the chief engineer for that company. The houses that we were used to were quite a bit larger and more elaborate.

"Anyway, even with the smaller house, things were still quite a bit better than they were at the group home. At least we were finally a family, and I still had Veronica. Not a day went by, though, that we didn't wonder what really did happen, and where you and mom were. Possibly because we were still getting adjusted to our new situation or possibly because it was just difficult to comprehend how it could even be possible for us to go back in time in the first place, it didn't dawn on us until about a month later what being adopted by the Davenports really meant. It occurred to me one night right after we had gone to bed. We had just turned out the lights, and I was lying in bed just staring at the ceiling, pondering what everything meant and how we could have gotten here when I remembered attending the book signing on the island. I remembered looking into Amy Westfall's face and telling her that I was her biggest fan, and I remembered the look on her face as I said it! I sat straight up in bed and said, 'Veronica! I just figured it out! Do you know what this means?! I'm actually Amy Davenport Westfall, famous novelist! And you're Veronica Davenport Ellison, President of Davenport Global Hotels!' And at that point we knew a lot about what our futures would be like. I suppose that I'm the first author in history that read all of her books before she even wrote them!

"One problem that we quickly discovered, though, was that there didn't seem to be any Davenport Global Hotels, and it didn't look like Martin was moving toward that direction either. He seemed perfectly content where he was. Veronica and I talked about it and decided one day that maybe he needed our help. After all, we were from the future, we were from the year 2016, and that meant that we knew things about the future that no one else could possibly know, things that could make us very wealthy. We got an investment magazine and looked for small or startup companies that we knew would be big. Our disadvantage was that we were teenage girls, and that meant that we hadn't exactly been following the stock market and investments before this. We could recognize names of companies, however, some which had even become household names in 2016. Once we made a list, the hardest part was convincing our new dad to invest in the companies that we had picked out. Still, he wanted to encourage us in our newfound interest, so he gave each of us five hundred dollars apiece to invest however we wanted to. After we had turned the thousand dollars that he had given us into sixty thousand within ten months, he started to take notice. He began to feel like we had a talent for investing and maybe he should listen to us. Using our tips, he made over a hundred and fifty million within a period of two years, and used this as seed money to start Davenport Global Hotels. We also went on to turn our new sixty thousand dollar profit into over twenty million in the coming years."

Dan and Amy walked together and talked for another hour and a half. As they walked back toward the hotel from the gardens and waterfall,

Amy spotted Derrick and Rebekah sitting out on the patio having a snack. She took Dan's arm and held him back for a moment.

"Just a moment," she said, "there's something that I need to tell you. Derrick and Rebekah don't know. Actually you're the first one that I've ever told. I'll have to tell them now, but I need to find the right way to bring it up. I'll probably do it later tonight, maybe with Veronica and Rick there as well."

"Ok," Dan said, "I won't say anything. See you tomorrow?"

"Yes, tomorrow." she replied, "And one more thing that I need to ask of you. Veronica and I have discussed this quite a bit over the last thirty years. We'll talk more tomorrow, but we felt that it would be better if no one but our families know about this. You can tell mom and Danny. You can even tell Scotty and Greg, since they're like family. But we felt that limiting this knowledge to our immediate families is the only way to be able to continue living our lives normally. I really don't want my picture on the supermarket tabloids next to lizard boy and the cow with three heads."

"I agree," said Dan, "I won't mention this to anyone but Kate, Danny, Greg, and Scotty. And we may need to find a good way to break the news to them as well, especially your mom. It'll be a lot for her to accept. Maybe tomorrow we can come up with a good way to tell her."

"Thanks," she said giving him a smile, "Goodnight dad."

CHAPTER 22
April 19, 2016
The Past Catches Up with the Future

The next day, Dan awoke around 7:00 am and just lay there beside Kate staring at the ceiling. He remembered the events from the previous night, and they had all seemed so real at the time, but with the morning light streaming through the blinds, he had to wonder if it had all been a dream. It had to have been a dream, he thought, thinking clearer and more rational this morning. Walking through the gardens with a grown up Amy, while she revealed to him the most fascinating and impossible story that he could ever imagine. Yes it had to have been a dream, because things like that just aren't possible. The realization of this made his heart sink, because that meant that Amy was still missing. He'd have to go back to the reality of the search today, and the reality that he might never see Amy again. He got out of bed and walked over to look out the window. Today was overcast and it looked like there may be a chance for rain. Kate was still sleeping soundly, and after the ordeal of the last few days, he decided to let her sleep.

He got dressed and decided to go downstairs and get some coffee. As he was going down, he continued to ponder last night. While his logical thinking told him that last night must have been a dream, the part of him that wanted it to be true still considered the possibility that last night was real, and that he really had been strolling through the hotel gardens with his daughter. When he got down to the Mariners Cove he saw Parker sitting at a table over by the window looking extremely lonely and depressed. He knew that if it turned out that Veronica Ellison was really Veronica Norwood, that Parker would be as relieved as he had felt last night. But he really didn't want to say anything to Parker just yet, at least not until he could meet with Amy again today and be sure that last night wasn't just a dream.

He walked over to where Parker was sitting and asked, "Need

some company?"

"That would be nice." said Parker, "I just came down here to think. The last few days have been difficult. Veronica is our only child. Ellen's talk with Kate last night seemed to help some, but what really can help? How do you get through something like this?"

"I know," replied Dan, "It hasn't been easy for us either. But there's still hope that they might still be found. We can go out to the lighthouse and talk with Commander Bates if you'd like. Maybe he can give us an update."

Parker thought that might be a good idea. At least it would be better than just sitting around thinking about the situation. It had been almost four days now, and with each day that went by, Parker was losing more and more hope. He had watched rescues and searches on TV before, and he knew that the more time that passes, the less the chances for finding them alive, if they even find them at all.

Dan walked over to the counter and purchased a coffee to go, and then he and Parker left and went out to his truck. They looked over toward where the news media were camped out, and it looked like they were in the process of packing up to leave. As they drove out the entrance, Dan did notice that the motor home that Holly Harper had been using for the past several days had apparently already left. They continued out Harbor Inn Lane until they reached the police roadblock at Lighthouse Road. Officer Collins recognized Dan's truck and removed the barricade so that he could get through.

The entire situation with Dan puzzled Officer Collins. He had been following Dan ever since they had discovered the connection between his business card and Perihelion, the company that fenced in the island all those years ago. He and Chief Callahan had both suspected something when Dan came to the island with the stated intention of restoring the lighthouse. But if he was here for another reason other than he was letting on, then how did he let this happen? Unless an accident had happened with whatever they were trying to do out there that he didn't anticipate. Unexpected accidents can and do happen. Officer Collins was still suspicious of Dan, even with the events of the last few days, but he still wasn't any closer to discovering what Dan was really doing on the island.

Dan and Parker continued on down Lighthouse Road until they arrived at the search command center. There was still a lot of activity going on there. Four days had passed since the girls disappeared, and while Commander Bates was still cautiously optimistic, some of the rest of the searchers didn't share that optimism, especially the ones that had been on the island for awhile and had either helped in the search for Greg and Tim or followed that search on radio or TV when it happened. Still, Commander Bates had witnessed miracles in his years with the Coast Guard, even when he had thought all hope was lost. He was hoping for a miracle this time as well. When they arrived at the command center, Commander Bates informed them that the divers had come in and were currently searching the waters around the islands tip, but they hadn't come up with anything yet. While the news that divers were currently searching the waters wasn't exactly what Parker had wanted to hear, he had known that they were coming, and he was at least relieved that they hadn't found anything. Commander Bates did inform them that they still had searchers on the ground combing the island as well, so they hadn't completely given up. He did caution them, however, not to get their hopes up too much at this point, since the chance of finding them alive does go down drastically after the first twenty four to forty eight hours. Still, to give them some hope, he told them that the fact that they hadn't found anything yet still leaves open the possibility that they'll eventually be found alive.

They got back to the Harbor Inn around 10:30 and Parker went up to his room to check on Ellen. He'd have to tell her that they still didn't have any news and he wasn't looking forward to that. Each day she kept hoping that this would be the day that the girls would be found. After Parker went back up to their room, Dan saw Kate and Danny coming out of the restaurant. He spotted his dad and went running over to him.

"Dad, Mom says that I can come back over and stay with you and her! Mrs. Barbara brought me back over a little while ago."

"That's great," replied Dan, "We've been missing you a lot these last few days."

"I've been missing you too. Mom says there's still no news on

Amy."

"No, not yet," answered Dan, "but Parker and I just got back from talking with Commander Bates out at the lighthouse and he says they're still searching so they could turn up any time." While he said it for Danny and Kate's sake, he still wasn't sure that he believed it himself. Still, the more that he thought about last night, the more that he was trying to convince himself that it really had happened. In the light of day, however, it just seemed so unlikely.

"Danny and I are going horseback riding over at the stables." said Kate, "Want to come along?"

"I'd like to," replied Dan, "but Scotty's coming over this morning. I have a few things that I want to discuss with him. I may join you in a little while, though." While Scotty really was coming over, secretly he hoped to meet Amy again and find out for sure about last night, so he wanted to stay near the hotel.

"OK, see you in a little while."

One of the things that Kate had always enjoyed back home was horseback riding. It was something that they all enjoyed. Perihelion even had its own stables on the campus that employees could use. The four of them each had their own horse that was kept at the company stables, and most weekends they could be found riding around the campus. There were plenty of places to ride. To maintain privacy, the main Perihelion campus was at the center of five hundred acres of woods, and those woods made perfect riding trails.

While this morning, Kate didn't really feel like doing much, back home she would frequently go riding when something was bothering her and she just wanted to think. Now, she thought the fresh air would help clear her mind and help her to relax. It was definitely better than just sitting in the room and thinking.

After Kate and Danny had left to walk over to the stables, Dan went back out to the patio to think. Scotty was coming over in about an hour, so he had time to himself to recount the events of the last few days in his mind. He wanted to talk to Amy Westfall to find out if last night had really happened or whether it was all just a dream, but he couldn't quite bring himself to go back up there. Right now, he was clinging to the hope that last night was real, and he was afraid that a meeting with Mrs. Westfall would dash that hope and verify that it actually had been a dream after all. He wasn't sure that he was ready to find that out just yet. He walked down the garden path in the direction of the waterfall. Just the peacefulness of the morning seemed to calm his nerves.

As he approached the waterfall, he was startled by a familiar woman's voice calling to him as she came up from behind, "Good morning dad." He turned to see Amy Westfall walking up the path toward him. A smile came to his face, as he realized at that moment that last night really had happened after all! His worst fear, that it had only been a dream, quickly faded away. He had known when they talked last night and went for the walk in the garden that she really was Amy, his daughter. But today, along the garden path, seeing her walking toward him wearing jeans and a t-shirt, she looked more like the thirteen year old Amy that he remembered than Amy Westfall, successful writer.

"I've been looking for you all morning." she said, "I started to go up to your room, but since I didn't think that you'd told mom yet, I decided to wait and try to find you."

"I went out with Parker earlier to the lighthouse." he replied, "We just got back a few minutes ago. I would have looked for you earlier, but I wanted to be sure that our talk last night had been real. When I first woke up this morning, it felt so much like a dream that I had almost convinced myself that it really was, until I saw you walking down the path just now. It just all seems so impossible."

"I know," she replied, "Thirty years ago, it seemed impossible for me too, so I know how you feel. But I've had thirty years to realize that not only was it possible, but it actually happened! I've had plenty of time to get used to the idea, and to accept it, but you've had less than a day! Why don't we go for a walk? We've got a lot of catching up to do."

"You're right." he said, reaching out and taking her hand as they walked, the way he had done the previous night.

As they walked along the path, he continued, "There is one question that I have, though, that I've been thinking about since last night. Since you came here to the island, and you knew what was going to happen, why didn't you stop her? You knew exactly what time they were leaving for the lighthouse. You could have delayed your younger self just enough so that she and Veronica wouldn't have been trapped in the fog."

A serious, slightly sad look came over her face. She lowered her head, not really looking at Dan, but trying to find just the right words to say to explain why.

"I'm sorry," she replied almost in a whisper, "I know you wanted your little girl back, and I hope you'll forgive me for not making the decision that could have given you that. Believe me, this was the hardest decision that I've ever had to make. Even last Wednesday on the trip to the island, I still wasn't sure exactly what I was going to decide. When Veronica got here, we talked it over and made the decision together."

"No, it's not that," Dan replied, "There's nothing to forgive really, I was just wondering why that wasn't the decision that you made. You must have had your reasons."

They stopped and sat down on a park bench beside the path.

Amy began, "Thirty years ago, when Veronica and I somehow found ourselves back in 1986, we actually thought of that. Not at first, maybe, but after we'd had a chance to think about it and start to accept what had happened. We did some research, and even watched movies and TV shows dealing with time travel. All of them were purely fiction, but they did give us some ideas of what might be possible. With everything that we saw on TV and in the movies, and everything that we read on the subject, we finally determined that if we showed up at the Harbor Inn on April 15, 2016, at around 1:00 in the afternoon, that it might just be possible to delay ourselves just long enough that we wouldn't get caught in the fog. And if we didn't go down Lighthouse Road at that particular time and get caught in the fog, that everything would revert back to the way that it would have been. We'd leave to come home on Sunday just like we'd planned, we'd go back to our friends in our home town, and our lives would continue the way they were originally supposed to. Our disappearance would simply never have happened. Even after we were adopted by the Davenports, this was still our plan. While we did have a good life with them, I still wanted to come back to you and mom, and Veronica still wanted to come back to her parents. And this remained our plan; for awhile.

"But thirty years is a long time, and before we knew it, our lives were involved more in that time than in this one. Six years after we went back, Veronica met Rick Ellison and they were married a year later. Two years after that, their daughter Lisa was born. I married Derrick Westfall in 1996 and Andrew was born a year later. Rebekah was born in another three years. My first novel came out a year after the wedding right around the time that Andrew was born. Over the years, Veronica and I raised our families together, went on vacations together, and made many happy memories, all in that time period. And as our lives touched other lives, we changed the course of history for some. Without us living in that time period, but knowing things about the future, Martin Davenport might never have had the cash to start Davenport Global Hotels. He may still be in business with his partners, making a good living operating several smaller hotels, but not realizing the full potential of what could have been.

"On the trip out to the island last Wednesday, I was contemplating what decision I should make, and for a time even then I was considering stopping myself from going out there. Veronica and I had been thinking about this day ever since we went back to 1986. Over the years, we thought about it a lot. And as April 15, 2016 drew closer, so did the realization that we had only one chance in a lifetime. Whatever we decided on that day, and at that time, would be forever. Our lives had finally caught up with the day of our disappearance, and there would be no second chances. Like I said, it really was the hardest decision that I've ever had to make, and it was a decision that couldn't be delayed in order to have more time to think about it. Thirty years ago, we thought that if our lives didn't turn out the way that we wanted, we had an automatic do-over, on April 15, 2016. This actually gave us the strength to keep going. But our lives had turned out even better than we could have hoped. I was a successful novelist, and Veronica was president of one of the largest hotel chains in the world. We both had the best lives that we could have ever imagined ... lives that most people only dream of. Did we really want to give that up? But what actually made the decision for me was looking over at Derrick and Rebekah on the ferry while we were on the way to the island. I really couldn't imagine being married to anyone else. He's the most wonderful, charming, thoughtful man in the world, and I couldn't bear the thought of him being married to anyone else. And where would Andrew and Rebekah be? They wouldn't have even had the opportunity to be born. When Veronica arrived last Thursday night at the Little Book Nook, we talked it over in the back room before the book signing, and she had come to the same decision as I had. After getting back to the hotel later that night we both discussed it some more. We had to be sure that it was the decision that we both wanted, and not a decision that we would regret.

"I really do hope you understand. We just couldn't give up the lives that we had lived for the past thirty years. Those lives were too much a part of who we are. But that doesn't mean that you can't be a part of our lives now, and I want to be a part of your lives again as well. It won't be the same, and I'm sorry that you missed me growing up, and your grandkids growing up. You've met Rebekah, and I want you to meet Andrew as well."

"I'd like that too, and I'm sure that your mom will want to as well. I'm not sure exactly how to tell her, though. I've heard the stories about the lighthouse for years, I've talked with some of the island residents about the disappearance of Greg and Tim, and I've even talked with Dr. Carson about his 'Alternate Reality Theories'. In addition, I've actually seen and walked into the fog. But your mom hasn't been here with me for the past month, so she hasn't been exposed to any of this. It'll definitely come as quite a surprise when she meets you!"

Amy continued, "Veronica and I never told anyone about this when we were growing up. Even Martin and Elise Davenport don't know. When we were moved to the girls' home in Charlotte, the lady that had taken care of us at the facility advised us not to tell anyone the story of how we had arrived from thirty years in the future. They wanted us to have a normal life, so they didn't even tell the staff of the girls' home. They created us new identities, complete with new birth certificates, and social security cards. Looking back, I'm not sure they really believed our story, even after interviewing us for several months. Derrick and Rick didn't even know until last night. The four of us got together down at the Mariners Cove and sat out on the patio until way into the early morning hours. Veronica and I told them pretty much the same story that I told you. They were harder to convince than you were, but then you already had it mostly figured out when you came to my room last night. At first they thought we were joking around, but they quickly determined that we were serious. Both Derrick and Rick knew that something had happened here on Green Island thirty years ago that neither of us would ever talk about, but when we finally told them the full story, neither of them were prepared to believe what actually happened. When you're trying to get someone to believe something that they've always KNOWN was impossible, you have to explain it in just the right way. Rebekah on the other hand, accepted the story a lot easier than Derrick, but I could tell that she also had her doubts. It was a lot to accept."

"Why didn't you try to contact us earlier?" asked Dan, "Why did you wait thirty years?"

"We had our reasons for that too. Before I was born to you and mom, how could I have really come to you and told you that I was the daughter that would be born to you both in a few years? Would you have believed me, when I really wouldn't have had any proof? You wouldn't have been ready to accept it then, and would have simply dismissed me as crazy. And after I was born, you had me with you. I was your daughter then. If I showed up at your door as my older self, how could you possibly believe that I was also your daughter at that time? No, the timing had to be right, and it had to be now. You just wouldn't have believed or accepted it before now."

"You're probably right," remarked Dan, "I probably wouldn't have accepted it then, but I do now and we need to find a way to gently break the news to your mom too. I'm not too worried about Danny. He's 10. He's not too old to have stopped believing in the impossible."

"Veronica and I have talked about that too. I think mom would be more willing to believe it if I were there too. And Veronica's parents will be hard to convince as well. This'll be the last thing that they expect, since unlike you, they haven't been exposed to the mysteries of the island. And for someone who's just hit with this news, unexpectedly out of the blue, it's a lot to ask them to believe. Why don't we all have dinner in town tonight at Grant's Steak House? We could all go; you and mom, Parker and Ellen,

Veronica and Rick, and me and Derrick. We could have dinner, and then go for a walk afterward. During dinner, hopefully they'll notice some things about us that are familiar. That'll make it easier when we break the news to them later in the evening. It should be easier with us all together. How about we meet out front at around 6:30? We can pick you up in the limo."

"Sounds like a good plan. I'll get everyone together. Maybe Danny can stay with Scotty and Greg for the evening. He'd enjoy that. I'm meeting Scotty a little later, so I can ask him then."

That evening, they met downstairs in the hotel lobby at around 6:30 dressed in their finest evening wear, ready for a night on the town. Parker had been a little hard to convince to come. He originally said that neither he nor Ellen was really in the mood for a fancy dinner. But when Dan kept insisting that there was something important that they needed to talk about, he finally convinced Ellen that maybe it was a good idea and would get their minds off things for awhile. Even Kate was a little surprised when the Davenport Global Hotels limo pulled up out front to take them to the restaurant. She only wished that the circumstances were different and she could enjoy it more. She didn't realize that Dan even knew the Ellisons and the Westfalls all that well, let alone well enough to be taken to dinner in the company limo. The driver got out and opened the door for the guests and they all got into the limo, which was plenty spacious for everyone. Parker and Ellen sat with Rick and Veronica, and Dan and Kate sat with Derrick and Amy.

Grant's Steak House was one of the most exclusive places on the island. Every night there was always a crowd, and tonight was no exception. Every eye in the crowd turned when the long black stretch limo pulled up in front of the restaurant. Most of them wanted to see who would get out. When the driver, Larry, got out and opened the limo door, some people in the crowd recognized Amy at once, but they didn't know who any of the others were. Larry held back the few autograph hounds that were encroaching on them as they made their way to the front entrance. Inside, they were whisked past the waiting crowd into a private dining area at the back of the restaurant. This was the first time that Parker and Ellen ever remembered bypassing all of the other waiting patrons and going straight in to the dining area at any restaurant. It helped to have important friends.

Back in the private dining area, everyone was busy studying the menus to decide what they wanted. The waiter came over to take their drink orders and to make recommendations for the evening. The night started out slowly, with Parker and Ellen not being particularly talkative. At first they felt a little guilty for enjoying dinner at an exclusive steak house, while Veronica was still missing. After awhile, though, they did seem to start enjoying the evening, and several times Dan noticed Parker appear to be studying Veronica. As the night went on, Parker found himself having several conversations with her and he couldn't help but notice how much she reminded him of his daughter. Her mannerisms, her voice, the way she pronounced certain words, it was uncanny how much she was like his Veronica. She even wore the same style of plastic framed glasses that his daughter always liked! This also made him a little sad as well, as he thought of the search currently going on. He couldn't help but wonder if he'd see his daughter again. But having this conversation with Veronica Ellison was somehow helping in a strange sort of way that he didn't quite understand just yet.

"Veronica is such a pretty name." Parker told her, "Our daughter's name is Veronica too."

"What's she like?" asked Veronica with a slight smile.

"She's funny, and smart, and pretty. She's extremely organized and likes to be in charge. She just got elected as class president this year. I could see her running her own company one day." Parker had to pause at this last statement, a tear running down his cheek as he thought of how this may never happen now.

After taking a few moments to get back his composure, he continued, "Actually, she's a lot like you. I've been noticing all evening how much you remind me of her."

Ellen, who hadn't really had a lot to say all evening, looked at her husband and then over at Veronica when he said this. She had been thinking the same thing all evening, but in her current state of depression hadn't given it a lot of thought until Parker actually said it. But now, she let herself actually notice the similarities between Veronica Ellison and their Veronica. It was really strange, but ever since the ride over in the limo, both of them had felt a sort of connection with Veronica Ellison that neither really understood.

Kate, also, had been talking quite a bit with Amy Westfall. Since Amy was her favorite author, she was really enjoying the dinner and the opportunity to get to talk with her. Dan was glad that they were getting along so well. Still, when Parker said how much Veronica reminded him of his daughter, Kate actually thought for the first time what had been in the back of her mind all evening too; Amy Westfall also reminded her a lot of her Amy. And it was quite a coincidence that both sisters were also named Amy and Veronica.

After dinner, the limo pulled up in front of the restaurant to pick them up, then headed out to Sea Spray Drive. Rick had planned the evening to end with a pleasant walk along the beach. After the limo parked, they all got out and walked across the boardwalk which provided public beach access. They walked along the beach and talked as they went. Even Ellen was starting to talk more and seemed to be actually enjoying the evening as her and Veronica got to know each other better.

As they continued on down the beach, suddenly Kate stopped in her tracks and looked over at Dan with a bewildered, confused, almost slightly scared look. The others stopped as well, all looking at Kate, wondering why she had stopped.

"Dan?" she said in a low, tentative voice, "What's happening here?"

"What do you mean?" asked Dan, at this point, like the others, not realizing why Kate had stopped either. He knew that she had been walking beside Amy, but what he didn't know was that as Amy's hair blew in the breeze, Kate had noticed something that she had previously missed at the restaurant.

Kate continued, "Remember, our Amy has a small birth mark shaped like a heart behind her right ear? Just now I noticed that Amy Westfall has that same birth mark, in exactly the same place! What's going on here, Dan?"

"Let's go over to those benches and sit down." suggested Dan, so they all walked over to the boardwalk and sat on the benches, listening to the waves against the surf.

They all sat in silence, with Dan wanting to explain, but just not finding the right words to start. After several seconds of awkward silence, Amy took over.

"There is an explanation for this, and it's not an easy one to believe. But what dad's trying to say is that I am Amy, I am your daughter."

"That can't be," replied Kate, "Amy's only 13!"

"It can be, and it is. It's the fog," replied Dan, "somehow when they were caught in the fog four days ago, they were sent back in time, specifically to the year 1986."

During the next few minutes, they all sat in total disbelief as Amy told the story that she had told to Dan last night, about how they went back, and how they came to be here today.

Parker listened both in disbelief and renewed hope as Amy brought their remarkable story to life for them. Parker actually was the first to ask, though both he and Ellen had come to the realization as Amy was telling her story, "So Veronica ... she's ..."

Veronica spoke up, "Yes dad. I'm your Veronica ... I'm your daughter."

CHAPTER 23
April 27, 2016
Final Goodbyes

The past week had been eventful and extremely tiring as well. It had taken quite a bit of getting used to, but Parker and Ellen were finally accepting the fact that Veronica Ellison was in fact their daughter. It hadn't taken quite as long for Kate. After the initial shock of noticing the birth mark, she had almost instinctively known that Amy Westfall was her Amy. No one, including Dan, knew how it had happened, but everyone seemed to accept the fact that it had. They all spent the next several days getting to know each other again and catching up on the last thirty years of their children's lives.

For Dan, this did answer a lot of questions. What happened to Tim Henderson and Greg Baker back in 1974, and Tim's mother Abigail six years later was probably the same thing that happened to the girls. They were in a different time instead of an alternate reality. Still, none of them had shown back up yet, which made him wonder exactly where they were? Were they sent further back in time so that it took longer to get back, or were they sent so far back that they lived out their entire lives in that time period, never living long enough to return back to this one? Or, possibly, could they have gone into the future? Was travelling into the future even possible, since it hadn't happened yet? Those were all questions that were yet unanswered. He wondered if they ever would be.

The fog, itself was difficult to research. Due to the unpredictability of when it would appear, and its relatively short duration, it was impossible to go exploring very far into it without risking being trapped in that time period. He may need to go back to the university and talk with an expert on temporal displacement. Of course, even for the experts in the field it was still just theory. None of them had actually gone backward or forward in time. In fact, at this point, Dan probably knew more than some of the experts, since he could actually talk with someone who had gone back in time. This turned it into fact and not just theory. Of course, to honor Amy and Veronica's wishes that no one except family know what happened, he couldn't tell any of the experts the full story behind why he was so interested. He did understand why Amy and Veronica preferred that no one else know. It really was the only way for them to live normal lives. After everything that had happened, though, he thought that he knew enough to ask intelligent questions without letting on that it had actually happened to someone that he knew, and he had proof. He didn't think that the experts would really expect it to have actually happened anyway, so it shouldn't be too hard. One of the main things that he'd like to find out was what actually caused the time displacement, but he doubted that even any of the experts could tell him that. That's the one thing that Amy and Veronica couldn't tell him either. They knew what it was like to go back in time, and they knew that a person could actually see and talk to their other self in that time period, since Amy had actually talked to the 13 year old Amy at the book signing. They even knew that a person could influence future events by interacting in that time period. What they or no one else knew, though, was what could possibly cause it, and what were some hypothetical explanations for why it was occurring around the lighthouse? Was it a natural phenomenon or was it man made? These were all questions that he still had, but they'd have to wait until later. At this point, he really didn't know if he'd ever find out. But he had Amy back, and for him that was all that mattered now.

Early Thursday afternoon, Dan was called out to the command center at the lighthouse by Commander Bates. He regretted to inform Dan that the search was being called off. He apologized, but said there was really nothing more that they could do. They had already been over the island multiple times, and the divers hadn't come up with anything in the waters surrounding the lighthouse either. Of course, by this time Dan had known that the search wouldn't find anything, at least not Amy or Veronica. Still, he thanked Commander Bates and went on back to the hotel.

A prayer service for the two girls was organized on Friday night and held at the First Baptist Church on the island. Reverend Anderson officiated at that service, which appeared to be the largest turnout at the church that the island had seen since the memorial service for Greg and Tim, and even Abigail. It almost seemed like the entire population of the island was gathered at the church that night. Everyone that he had met since he had arrived was there, including Hank and Barbara from the Island Charm and all of their kids. Even Officer Mark Collins was there with his wife, along with the entire island police force and their families. There were also a lot of people that Dan didn't know. Some he recognized, some he didn't. He couldn't help but wonder if somewhere in this crowd was the mysterious stranger that had been watching them.

The prayer service was very touching. At the front, right under the pulpit was a small table with framed photos of Amy and Veronica. Candles burned on two stands on either side of the photos. The service was so moving that Kate and Ellen, even though they knew that their daughters were alive, still couldn't help but cry. It even brought a tear to Dan's eye as well as he realized that he would never again see the bright eyed thirteen year old that was his little girl. He'd never have the opportunity to give her away at her wedding, or see his first grandchild born. While he still loved the grown up Amy, he would always secretly wish that she'd have made the other decision, the one that would have brought his thirteen year old back to him. In a way, even though the rest of the people were there for a prayer service, not a memorial, in his mind, he really was saying goodbye to his little girl today. The service ended with Reverend Anderson saying a prayer that wherever the girls were that God would keep them in his care. Dan knew that prayer had already been answered.

On Saturday morning, everyone got up and drove to the airport in Wilmington to fly back to Cincinnati for a prayer service that evening at Dan and Kate's home church. Rick and Veronica Ellison had offered to fly everyone to Cincinnati and back aboard the Davenport Global Hotels corporate jet. This would avoid the long lines at the airport and get them there sooner. By 10:00 am they were in the air headed across North Carolina for the three and a half hour flight to Cincinnati. The flight gave them even more time to get acquainted. When they arrived at the airport in Cincinnati, Belinda was there to greet them and to pick up Scotty and Greg. Rick and Veronica were going to stay with Parker and Ellen, and the Westfall's would stay with Dan, Kate, and Danny. The service was at 5:00 pm, so there were still a few hours left for them to visit, and then get ready.

When they arrived at the Nelson's residence, Amy was again simply overcome with memories. They all came flooding back in waves, as she first saw the house as they drove up the long circular drive, and then walked through the front door to scenes and smells that she had last witnessed thirty years ago! The house and everything in it seemed to her to have been frozen in time. It really did bring her back to her childhood, and she somehow actually felt thirteen again. She went up to her room, which was completely unchanged since the last time that she saw it all those years ago, and the thirty years that had passed seemed to vanish away. She was back in this time period, and the memories that it stirred up were memories of being a child again. Even though it had been decades since she had been here, it seemed like only yesterday.

Dan and Kate, as well as Parker and Ellen arrived at the church early for the prayer service. They met with their pastor, Reverend Adam Walters, who would be officiating at the service to go over the last minute details. Amy and Veronica, along with their families were there at the church early as well, but they had all gone to the sanctuary to find a seat prior to the service. On the way to Cincinnati, the jet had landed in Charlotte to pick up Derrick and Amy's son Andrew, and Rick and Veronica's daughter Lisa, before continuing the trip. Dan and Kate had already met Rebekah, but this was the first time that they had gotten to meet their grandson. Rick and Veronica's daughter, Lisa, also finally got to meet her biological grandparents. The thing that seemed the most unusual for all of them was that their grandparents were only a few years older than their parents. They basically seemed right around the same age.

There was standing room only at the service. Dan and Kate had many friends in the area, most of whom had been watching the search unfold over the last week. It appeared that most of the teachers and a lot of the students from Cameron Road Middle School were there as well. Amy's homeroom teacher as well as several of her and Veronica's closest friends from school spoke at the service. Attending the service felt really strange for Amy and Veronica. Not only was it an odd feeling to hear family and friends talk about you at a prayer service, but it also felt strange that all of the people that spoke about them, including their best friends, who were all still twelve and thirteen, looked and sounded exactly like they did all those years ago. And none of them would ever know the truth about what really had happened.

The service from start to finish lasted a little over an hour, and ended with a prayer by Reverend Walters. After the service, the Nelsons and the Norwoods both went to the church fellowship hall where guests filed past to offer their support. There were so many people in the fellowship hall that for the most part, Rick and Veronica blended in with the crowd unnoticed, but a few had recognized Amy Westfall and went up to speak to her. She told them that she had met the Nelsons while on the island for a book signing, and had become friends after their daughter had disappeared. No one that talked with her seemed to even suspect anything, probably because their minds just wouldn't be capable of even considering what really happened.

That night, after the prayer service, Parker and Ellen began packing for the trip to Charlotte. They had a lot of catching up to do, and Veronica had invited them to spend a couple weeks with them at their home in Charlotte. Kate and Danny would be staying back in Cincinnati, since Danny had already missed a week of school already and really needed to get back. The principal of the school understood the situation, and offered for them to take as long as they needed, but Dan and Kate both wanted him to go back as soon as possible, since neither of them wanted to take a chance that he'd have to repeat this grade. Dan, however, was going back to Green Island. He had considered packing up and leaving, even after finding out what really happened to Amy. It was actually Amy that had convinced him to continue with the restoration. It would seem odd to the island's residents that he would choose to continue after what had happened, but he actually did want to, and after discovering that the fog was really some sort of a time portal, both he and Amy wanted to find out more. She knew what had happened, but she would like to find out more about it as well. Amy, Derrick, and Rebekah were going back to the island with Dan. Knowing how much that she wanted to stay and find out more, Derrick had arranged for them to rent a beachfront cottage out on Sea Spray Drive for the next month. Scotty and Greg were going back as well, since both of them also wanted to continue what they had started.

It was Wednesday morning, and it almost seemed like nothing had happened. Dan, Scotty, and Greg were at the breakfast table at the Island Charm eating a hearty breakfast of eggs, sausage, and muffins cooked up by Barbara. Steve and Arlene were there as well, with Steve planning on going back out to the lighthouse with them this morning as well. Dan had contacted Chris with Southeast Restoration Services and informed him that the restoration would be getting started back today, if he still wanted to continue with them out there after what had happened. The police had finished with their investigation and had taken down the tape and barricades. The case was officially labeled a "Missing Persons" case, but after all that had happened, and the circumstances around it, Chief Callahan suspected that there was more to it than that. He just didn't have anything else to go on to be able to call it anything else.

As they ate their breakfast, Hank was sitting in his chair over in the corner reading his morning paper. Hank was the one that seemed not at all happy that Dan was back and intending to continue the restoration on the lighthouse. Dan knew why. He had been against the lighthouse being restored and that end of the island opened back up since Dan had arrived. And Dan now had more insight as to why he felt the way that he did. There really was something going on at the lighthouse. The pieces were being unwrapped, one piece at a time. Little by little he was finding out more about what had been going on at the lighthouse for decades, even back to the time that Colonel Forrest first saw the lighthouse several years before it was even built. Hank's answer would be to lock the gate and forget about the lighthouse, and Dan knew that he probably had hoped that's what would happen now. He felt like it shouldn't be disturbed, and maybe it shouldn't. But that wasn't Dan's way of dealing with it. He'd have to be careful, no doubt about that. Now that he knew what was happening, he felt like he'd be equipped to be more cautious. He still wondered, however, about the mysterious stranger. What did he want, and why was he watching them. He hadn't seen him in the last week, but he had been away from the island for a large part of that, and when he was here, the search was underway. After Amy and Veronica had disappeared, he didn't even know if he would see the man again. He'd be more careful now, though, and watch out for the man, especially now that Amy was here with him. He'd lost her once, and he had no intention of losing her again.

Hank got up out of his chair and asked Dan to come out onto the front porch for a minute. Dan followed, expecting another lecture on why the lighthouse shouldn't be disturbed.

But Hank began, "I just don't understand you! How can you even think of continuing restoring that lighthouse after what just happened?! Most people would pack up and leave and never come back. They'd want no part of that place ever again! I'll admit, after the prayer service last Friday night, I thought everything would be over. I expected you to come back, pack up all of your belongings, and leave. That's what any normal person would have done. But now you're back here and you and all of your friends are going back out there to continue what you were doing like nothing has happened! Haven't you learned anything from your daughter's disappearance? The place is not meant to be disturbed! I'd think you of all people would realize that by now!"

"I know most people would just leave. And the last week and a half or so hasn't been easy. But I'm just not ready to leave yet. Maybe in an odd sort of way this is my way of dealing with Amy's disappearance." replied Dan.

"I still don't understand you." Hank continued, "What's keeping you here? My feelings about the lighthouse haven't changed. They're probably even stronger now after what's happened. And personally, I think that you should leave it alone. Now that we know that what happened years ago can happen again, I think it really should be left alone. But I know you're not going to, and that's the part that I really can't understand. Just be careful out there. I still have grown to like you since you've been here, and I really am truly sorry for what happened to your daughter."

"Thank you," replied Dan, "and I will be careful."

By this time, the rest of them had made their way to the front porch, ready to go back out to the lighthouse. Arlene came out to see Steve off. Secretly after what happened out there, she wished that he wouldn't go back. She really didn't feel like she could go on if something happened to him. But she also knew him well enough to know that she wouldn't be able to stop him. Dan and Steve got into Dan's truck to go out to the lighthouse and Scotty and Greg drove out in Greg's Jeep. When they got to the entrance to Lighthouse Road, they turned left and quickly saw several trucks and an SUV stopped in front of the gate. When the police had taken down the barricades, they apparently had locked the gate back to prevent unauthorized intruders. Dan got out and passed Amy, Derrick, and Rebekah in their SUV. All three of them were here to help out at the lighthouse, and Dan had to admit that it would be nice to have them here. He unlocked the gate and soon they were all headed down the road toward the lighthouse. When they got to the clearing in front of the lighthouse, the Southeast Restoration Professionals crew began unloading their trucks and taking materials and tools out to the site.

Dan took Amy, Derrick, and Rebekah on a tour of the lighthouse and the surrounding area. This was the first time that Amy had been back out here since she had arrived for the book signing. She thought now that it looked like she had expected it to look when they rode their bikes out to deliver the blueprints. The scaffolding was surrounding it, and it looked very old and run down.

As they walked around to the front, Dan thought he caught a glimpse of movement over by the woods. He stopped and stared intently in the direction of the movement.

"Dad, what's wrong?" asked Amy.

"Not sure it's anything," he replied, "I just thought I saw movement over there at the edge of the woods."

"Was it the man?" she asked.

"Not sure," he said, "I didn't really get a good look, I really just saw movement."

"What man?" asked Rebekah tentatively. Her mom hadn't told her about the man that they had seen the first day that they arrived at the island when she was thirteen. Amy had almost forgotten about him as well after all of the time that had passed for her, but her dad seeing something over by the woods brought back the memory of him.

Dan replied to her, "I really don't want to alarm you, but since I got here, I've seen a man several times that appeared to be watching me. He was also watching your mom, Veronica, and Danny the other week as well, when your mom was thirteen."

"Are you sure it's safe for us to be here?" asked Derrick.

"It should be," answered Dan, "as long as we stay together. He hasn't appeared to be dangerous so far, I just don't know who he is or why he's here."

They continued with their tour, and then went inside to get to work replacing the molding around the floor in the foyer. The interior crew from Southeast Restoration Services was in the process of building a new staircase to the second floor. They had already put in new flooring underneath where it had fallen in. No one had really been upstairs yet except for the structural engineer who came out the second week that Dan was on the island. He used a ladder to get to the second floor, and he determined that most of the flooring was solid, but there was still some that would need replaced. They were building the staircase first to allow easy access.

A little after noon, Arlene showed up with sandwiches, chips, and drink for everyone. They were all relieved to get a break and Arlene was relieved to see Steve. She had brought out lunch on other occasions as well, but today she especially wanted to because it gave her a good excuse to come out and see Steve, since it was their first day back out at the lighthouse after the girls' disappearance. She wasn't too thrilled about Steve being out here before, but now she found that she was worrying about him all day. She thought that if she could see him and spend a little time with him during the day, even if it was just over lunch, that it would help. During lunch, she asked Steve if there were any new people helping out. He thought that was an odd question, so he inquired why she was asking.

"Well, as I was on my way out here on Lighthouse Road just a few minutes ago, I saw a couple of men walking across the clearing not too far from here." she replied, "They were pretty far from the road, so I couldn't see who they were very clearly, but now it looks like everyone that I know is here."

"Were they walking in this direction?" inquired Dan.

"No, they were going the other way, back toward the direction of the Harbor Inn."

Dan was puzzled. Maybe he actually had seen someone at the edge of the woods after all. "They're not anyone from out here." Dan said, "We've got everyone accounted for. I doubt any of us would be walking across that clearing anyway." Still, he had to wonder. Now there were two men, not just one? He tried to think back. He didn't recall seeing two men before, just the one.

After lunch, Arlene actually decided to stay and help, especially since she had seen the two men. She figured that she would worry less if she was out here with Steve and could see that nothing was happening rather than staying back at the Island Charm and not knowing. And they all actually welcomed the help.

During the afternoon, she actually talked with Amy quite a bit. Even with all of the excitement of the last couple of weeks, she had managed to read a few chapters of Amy's new novel and couldn't help but notice the similarities between the girls in the book, Stephanie and Jessica, and Amy and Veronica. It was obvious from what she read that the book was written about the lighthouse, but there was just no way that Amy could have known that the girls would disappear. Still, the similarities were quite a coincidence.

"I've read the first few chapters in your new book." she told Amy.

"So, what do you think so far?" Amy inquired.

"It's very interesting." she said, "It is about THIS lighthouse, isn't it?"

"Yes, it is."

"What made you write a book around the disappearances at this particular lighthouse?" Arlene inquired.

This was the only time that anyone had asked her this question since her dad had asked on the Monday night after her disappearance. It did catch her slightly off guard and she chose her words carefully. While Arlene and Steve were friends of her dad and she knew she could probably trust them, she also realized that the more people that knew her secret only increased the chance of that secret being exposed.

"I had heard stories about the lighthouse from my dad when I was younger." she said, actually referring to Dan this time and not Martin Davenport. "He told me stories about the mysteries surrounding this lighthouse. He had visited it as a child with his parents and he brought us out here to the island as well. After that, I was always interested in finding out more." Of course, she did leave out the real reason that she was so interested in the lighthouse.

"It does seem to be a fascinating book," she told Amy, "I can't wait to read more."

After lunch, Dan got Scotty and the two of them took a walk down the road toward the clearing. He filled Scotty in on what Arlene had told him during lunch about seeing the two men. It took them a little over five minutes to get to the clearing. When they got there, they walked across it toward the direction of the woods farthest from the road. As they were a little over half way to the woods, Dan began to get that same familiar feeling of being watched. It was getting to be almost like a sixth sense to him now.

"I think there's someone watching us." he told Scotty.

"Where?" asked Scotty.

"I'm not sure. I just feel that we're not the only ones out here."

They both scanned the edges of the woods all around them. There was no movement, but they did observe that there would be plenty of places for someone to hide and observe. As they approached the woods on the left, they did hear movement. They both stopped to listen. It was a low rustling in the bushes, probably just from an animal foraging for food. They spent another half hour looking around at the edge of the woods, but never saw anyone. They decided to head back to the lighthouse and see what was going on back there.

After they finished up for the day, Dan followed Amy and her family back to the beachfront cottage that they had rented. Amy had invited him over for a cookout on the deck of the cottage. Derrick was cooking hamburgers and hot dogs. He always liked to be the outdoor chef when they would go on vacations and either rent a cottage or take the RV to a campground. As he cooked, they all sat around and talked and enjoyed the beautiful view of the ocean.

"So you really don't have the slightest idea who the man is that seems to be watching you, or what he might want?" Derrick asked Dan. He, like Dan was concerned for the safety of his family, and he didn't like the idea of not knowing.

"No, I wish I did. He's a mystery to me. And I found out this afternoon that there may actually be two men. Arlene saw them walking along the clearing out by the lighthouse."

"Not sure I like the sound of that." Derrick replied, "Could it possibly have something to do with Amy being back here?"

"It could." he said. "I can't help but think that it does have something to do with the fog. I saw him when I got to the island, though, even before Amy arrived, so if anything it may have something to do with me and of me buying the lighthouse. He seems to not want to talk to me, though, because every time I've tried to find him he's gone."

After discussing the man for a little longer, the conversation turned to more pleasant topics. Dan wanted to know more about how Amy and Derrick met, and what her life had been like for all of the years since she had disappeared. She had been one of their favorite authors, so he already knew a lot about her life that was shared in the press. They also talked about the lighthouse as well. Dan planned on continuing the renovation, but now he wasn't so sure that he was going to move his family into it. He still didn't know enough about what was going on with the fog and the mysterious stranger. He wasn't sure what he was going to do. He thought about turning it into a museum, but with the unpredictableness of the fog, he wasn't so sure that would be a good idea. He was seriously considering moving to North Carolina, though, so that he could be closer to Amy. After thirty years, they still had a lot of catching up to do, and with all of the lost time, he wanted to continue to be a part of her life now. To everyone but family, they would just be good friends that had met on Green Island amid a trying time for Dan and Kate. That should work. He couldn't imagine that anyone would ever guess the truth.

It was about 10:00 at night before Dan finally left. It had been a good evening. The more he visited and talked with Amy, the more that he could tell that she really was his daughter. He had seen her several times over the years, on TV talk shows and documentaries. He couldn't believe that he hadn't seen the resemblance then. But, he thought, why would he? At that time he had Amy with him, and he wasn't looking for her as an adult. Even if he had noticed some similarities, they couldn't have both been Amy. There would have been no reason for his mind even to consider that, which was the primary reason that she hadn't introduced herself to him earlier.

He pulled into the alleyway beside the Island Charm, got out of his truck and went inside. Barbara, along with some of the guests, was chatting in the sitting area. She said hello to him as he walked by and went up the stairs to his room. He had halfway expected to see Scotty and Greg downstairs, but wasn't too surprised when he didn't. They were probably both back up in their room. They had all had a busy day, with everything that had been going on with resuming the lighthouse renovations. He put the key in the lock to his room, opened the door, and switched on the light. As the light came on, he noticed a small piece of paper on the floor, like it had been slid under the door. It was folded, and on the outside was written his name. He opened it up to discover a note written inside:

Dan,

It's time that we met. I have an urgent issue that we need to discuss. If you want to find out what causes the fog, meet me at 10:00 am tomorrow morning at the boardwalk on Sea Spray Drive. Please come alone. The business that I need to discuss is only between you and me.

Dr. Philip O. Chandler

He stood staring at the note. It was signed, "Dr. Philip O.

Chandler". He didn't recognize the name. He tried to think back. Did he remember meeting him anywhere? But his mind still drew a blank. This was the mysterious stranger, it had to be! He'd finally find out what had been going on. Still, it was the "Come alone" part that worried him. It could be dangerous. He'd take one of the stun guns with him, just to be sure. Dan had to wonder, however, after all this time, why did he want to meet now? Still, he knew that he'd have to go. Philip said that he KNEW what caused the fog! And now he was ready to share that information with Dan. His mind would be wandering. He knew that he wouldn't be getting much sleep tonight.

CHAPTER 24
April 28, 2016
Dr. Philip Chandler

Dan had been right. He hadn't gotten much sleep last night. His mind was going back and forth all night, switching from excitement and anticipation one moment at the prospect of finally finding out the mystery surrounding the fog, to anxiety and trepidation that he was asked to come alone. This was the person who had been following him since he had arrived on the island, never making his presence known, but always lurking in the shadows just out of sight. And now he wanted to meet. Who wouldn't have at least a little anxiety at this invitation? Still, he had to find out. He wondered if he really had a choice. What would the man do if he declined the invitation, or if he did bring someone else along? Something inside told him that he really didn't have the option to turn down this invitation. He had said that they had urgent business to discuss. If he didn't meet him tomorrow, he'd find another way to get to him to have the discussion. He wondered what urgent business they needed to discuss. He supposed that it had something to do with the fact that he owned the lighthouse now. Most everything seemed to have something to do with it. Anything that the man wanted to do that pertained to the lighthouse would have to be discussed with him. Just like Bill Henderson wanting to continue going out to the lighthouse. Bill realized that if he wanted to continue, he would need to discuss it with Dan, and that's what he did. Still, after everything that happened, he could understand Bill wanting to continue going out to the lighthouse. He didn't know this new man, or what his involvement with the lighthouse might be.

It was only 7:00 in the morning, but since he was wide awake, he decided to go down and have some breakfast. Barbara's eggs and sausage and muffins seemed just what he needed to start this day. When he got downstairs, Steve and Arlene were already there and had finished about half of their breakfast already.

"Good morning Dan. You're up early!" remarked Steve.

"I know," said Dan trying to sound cheerful, but afraid that he was coming across as slightly worried instead. "I have some business this morning. I probably won't be out to the lighthouse until sometime this afternoon."

"That's fine. Scotty will probably be down around 8:00. I'll just ride out with him and Greg."

"Great! Can you tell Scotty that I had something come up this morning and I'll be joining everyone out at the lighthouse a little later?" he asked Steve.

"Sure thing!" said Steve.

Steve and Arlene finished their breakfast and went out for their morning walk that they always did around this time of day. They were early risers and their favorite time of the day was the mornings.

After Dan finished his breakfast, he still had a couple of hours before he needed to be out at the boardwalk, so he decided to ride out to the lighthouse. The Southeast Restoration Professionals team didn't usually get there until around 8:00, so he'd have a few minutes just to walk around out there before they arrived. When he got there, the morning sun was shining through the trees and into the clearing where the lighthouse stood. He got out of his truck and walked through the gate and over to the lighthouse. It was a peaceful morning. He was the only one out there and the only sound was the breeze and the sound of the waves as they hit the shore down by the river. He studied the edge of the woods for any movement, but today everything was still. Not even the animals made any sound or movement this morning. The stillness of the water, along with the quiet of the morning actually did seem to calm his nerves a little. He walked up the stairs and through the back entrance leading into the house. Inside, he looked around, his footsteps echoing throughout the house. This was the first time that he'd actually been out here alone since the first week that he was here, and the stillness of the morning actually caused him to reflect on that time. He studied the interior and noticed how much had been accomplished. Actually, quite a lot had been done in the month and a half that he'd been out here. A staircase leading upstairs was now in the entrance foyer, where only a large gaping hole in the floor had been when he had first seen it. He realized that he hadn't yet been upstairs since they had built the staircase. He walked over and climbed the steps. Each footstep echoed through the empty foyer. He'd have to be careful where he stepped upstairs, since all of the floorboards hadn't been replaced yet. The structural analysis had been done, and between the existing boards, and the newer boards that Bill Henderson had nailed down when he was coming out here, it was generally sound. There were still some weak spots in the flooring, though, and he needed to watch out for those. He paused, looking out the upstairs window toward the sound. The sun glistened off the water as it rippled up onto the shore, producing little dancing rays of light on the opposite wall as it shone through the window. It was the only movement that he saw, other than the trees swaying in the light breeze.

As he looked out the window, then around the upstairs room, he wondered what his plans should be for the lighthouse. Right now, he planned on continuing with the restoration, but he did think that his plans had changed about moving Kate and Danny out here. He'd been fortunate with Amy. She had shown back up and was now still a part of his life. But Greg and Tim had never been found. If Danny or Kate somehow disappeared into the fog, he had no assurance that they'd come back to him. He'd have to just wait and see. Maybe the meeting with Philip Chandler this morning would help him make the decision of what to do.

After a few minutes of just standing, enjoying the tranquility of the morning, Dan went back downstairs. He walked out the front door and across the front lawn, out the front gate, and down to the sound. He stood looking out across the sound, thinking of the last month. It had definitely been an adventure, and knowing what he knew now, he wasn't sure that he really would do the same thing again. His life had totally changed, just in the period of a few weeks. He thought back to the trip out to the island a little over a month ago. He knew now that he hadn't really expected there to be anything to the stories about the lighthouse. The disappearances of Tim and Greg and their mother must have had a logical explanation. While it was exciting to buy a lighthouse that had some mystery surrounding it, in the end that's all it was; just some stories in a few books. Now, his whole idea of what is real and what is not real, what is possible and what is impossible, what can happen and what can't happen, has been turned totally upside down. The world that he lives in, and his perception of that world has changed completely just in the month that he's been here.

He turns around and begins to walk back toward the lighthouse. It's almost time for him to head back out to Harbor Inn Lane and to the boardwalk on Sea Spray Drive. He gets to his truck, cranks it up, and heads back down Lighthouse Road. As he gets to the end of Lighthouse Road and turns right onto Harbor Inn Lane his heart is racing with anticipation. He finally gets to the end of Harbor Inn Lane and turns left onto Sea Spray Drive. He goes about a tenth of a mile, then parks in one of the spaces on the left side of the road across from the boardwalk. He turns off the truck and just sits there for a few minutes thinking. What was he about to find out? He couldn't even imagine. He looks around to see if he can see the man anywhere, but there doesn't appear to be many folks out here this time of the morning.

He gets out of his truck and walks across the road toward the boardwalk. He climbs the boardwalk's steps, and then walks across it in the direction of the beach. He gets to the end where the benches are and the steps go down to the sand. He looks up the beach and down the beach. There are a few folks out this morning, some are running, some are walking, and some are just sitting in chairs watching the surf come up. As he looks down the beach, there are some children playing in the surf and digging up sand with a plastic shovel and bucket to build a sand castle. At least there were other people out here and he didn't feel quite as alone as he had just a few minutes ago sitting back in his truck.

As he stood looking out toward the ocean, he heard footsteps on the boardwalk behind him. He quickly turned around and walking toward him only a few yards away is the man in the dark blue shirt and tan pants that he had seen on several occasions before this.

"Thanks for coming, Dan. Shall we sit here?" offered the man.

"Sure." was all Dan could think of to say. Seeing the man up close, and hearing his voice, he didn't seem at all dangerous. Still, he noticed a leather pouch attached to the man's belt. His first thought was that it was a holster for a gun. It was around the same shape, but it didn't look exactly like the shape of most of the holsters that he had seen either. Still, Dan wondered what it was, and if the man was some sort of detective or private investigator.

The man began, "My name is Dr. Philip Oliver Chandler. I've been waiting to talk with you for quite some time now."

"Then why have you waited until now? And why have you been watching us?" asked Dan.

"The time wasn't right before." continued Philip, "You wouldn't have been able to understand what I have to tell you. Until your daughter Amy disappeared in the fog and you accepted the fact that she had actually gone back to 1986, you wouldn't have been open minded enough to believe the story that I'm going to reveal to you. You had to have time to accept the fact that Amy Westfall was actually your daughter, or you would have just dismissed what I have to tell you as fiction. You'd have thought me to be crazy."

"How do you know about Amy?" asked Dan, taken by surprise that this man would know the truth, "We haven't told anyone except for family and a few close friends. How did you find out? Were you there the first night when Amy and I were walking in the garden?"

"I have been watching you, that's true, but that's not how I know. I've known the truth about who Amy Westfall really is long before you, even before you came to the island."

"How do you know then?" Dan asked again.

"Let me continue," Philip said, "I think it'll all be clear soon enough. Let's just say that I've been interested in you and Amy for quite some time now."

This last statement put another thought into Dan's mind, and he had to ask, "You've been watching me since I've been here on the island. Was it you who followed us to the tip of the island the day of the campout?"

"Yes, that was me." Philip answered.

"Then if you've been here all this time, and you knew about Amy, then why didn't YOU stop her from going out to the lighthouse that morning? I understand why Amy decided not to stop herself, but you could have. Why didn't you?"

Philip continued, "I had my reasons, and you'll understand them soon enough. That's all part of the story that I'm going to reveal to you. You see, Amy and Veronica aren't the only ones that have gone back in time. I also am not from THIS time. I came here from the year 2164."

"So you also got caught in the fog?" asked Dan, extremely interested at this point.

"Not exactly," Philip replied, "with me it didn't happen the way that it did with Amy and Veronica. Their time journey was accidental. I came to this time on purpose, and with a planned mission. But don't be alarmed. I mean no one here, including you any harm. There's just an urgent discussion that you and I need to have."

"OK," replied Dan, "You've got my attention. What do you want from me?"

"First, I need to give you some background of why I'm here, and the first thing that you need to know is that the fog isn't a natural phenomenon. It's completely man made. When I first introduced myself, I said that I was DR. Philip Chandler. I'm not a medical doctor; my doctorate is in Temporal Displacement. I was one of the lead scientists that developed the Vortex Accelerator, the device that makes time travel possible. So you see, unlike your scientists here, where temporal displacement is just a theory, in my time it's a reality."

Dan interrupted, "A couple weeks ago, we found something interesting in the lighthouse. It was smooth and silver. Is that the Vortex Accelerator?"

"No, that's a device called a Beacon." Philip reached down and pulled a device out of the pouch on his belt. Immediately Dan recognized it as the one that they had found.

"What does it do?" asked Dan.

"I'll explain that a little later," replied Philip, "there are several things that you need to understand first. One thing about the Vortex Accelerator is that it's not small. In fact, it's a massive machine. It completely surrounds the lighthouse outside of the circular wall. In 2164, things are not like they are now. The world as you know it has completely changed, and not for the better. This island is not open to tourists any longer; it's a top secret government installation. There is no more town, all the buildings along main street and the hotels out on Sea Spray Drive have been torn down to make room for the infrastructure to support the Vortex Accelerator. The island is a 'no fly' zone and any private boats are not allowed within five miles of the coast. The government is serious about keeping what goes on here a secret. The few planes and boats that have accidentally strayed into the five mile limit have been taken out by high powered laser cannons. There are no warnings. With all of the secrecy, the news media, especially the tabloids, have invented their own stories about what goes on here, including the numerous disappearances of boats and planes over the years. There have even been a few movies and documentaries made about the island. The movies are very interesting. I have to laugh when I watch them, just to see their interpretation. Knowing what really happens here, they're not even close. Even the documentaries have it all wrong. Most say that the island is an interplanetary base for aliens and flying saucers. Or it's sitting atop the ancient city of Atlantis. To me, the truth is just as fantastic.

CHAPTER 25

Revelations of the Future

"Let me start off with a little about the history to give you some background." continued Philip, "In the middle of the twenty first century, around the year 2055, scientists were studying the energy fields surrounding objects. The idea was that these energy fields persist, even after the physical objects or people no longer occupy that space. This study actually branched off of the data gathered by paranormal investigators or 'ghost hunters', but went much further into examining it more scientifically.

"The first real breakthrough came when a young scientist who had been studying the data collected by paranormal investigators over the years proposed that these 'ghosts' that people were seeing and hearing weren't actually spirits or any physical presence at all. They were simply created by the energy fields left behind by the people and objects that had occupied that space previously, sometimes many years before. That's why the manifestations would frequently do the same thing over and over. They were simply replaying a scene that had happened there at an earlier time. He explained that it was similar to watching a movie. In a movie, the cameras capture the actors on film and that film can be replayed many times, each time with the actors performing the same actions. The actors are not really in the movie theatre, yet we can see and hear them, nonetheless.

"The scientist's name was Edwin Langtree, and his theory became known as the 'Langtree Hypothesis'. Langtree's theory became widely accepted in the scientific community and created an entirely new branch of science, 'Energy Field Theory'. The problem with the way that traditional paranormal investigations had always been conducted was that the investigators were trying to communicate with the manifestations, like they actually had the capability to interact. Langtree concluded that trying to communicate with them would be as futile as trying to communicate with the actor on your television screen. The investigations needed to be conducted a different way, in a way that would try and discover the source of the manifestations, that is, what caused them to appear. The second problem was that the manifestations weren't consistent. On any given investigation, you might see and hear something or you might not. So scientists started going down a new path. They were now trying to discover the cause of the manifestations, and once they knew their source, they could work on getting the manifestations to appear when they wanted them to instead of just randomly. New scientific instruments were developed that could map the energy fields and discover important new information about them. Since these energy fields were derived from events that happened in the past, it was concluded that if they could control when they appear, then they would actually be able to see into the past.

"A new study was commissioned by the U.S. Government to create a 'viewer' that could see into the past, just like viewing a movie. The project was code named, 'Project Second Sight' and it was begun right here on the island out at the lighthouse. A series of emitters were constructed on poles completely surrounding the lighthouse. A three level control room structure was built off to the side and outside the lighthouse gate. By energizing the emitters, then viewing through a special plasma infused glass in the control room, the energy left behind from previous years would be supercharged enough to become visible. This could be done regularly, with the lighthouse appearing in different time periods each time. Sometimes it would be completely restored, with a functioning light, other times it would be in ruins as we see it today. A few times they even saw people wandering around in the scene, a man tending a garden along the north wall, a woman hanging clothes on a clothesline. None of the people in those scenes could see them or any of the control room structure and emitters since they were only "viewing" the past, they weren't actually there. One problem that they encountered was that they didn't know exactly when the scene that they were viewing happened. They would supercharge the emitters and view the scene, but they had no way to know the date or time that it occurred. That part was still random. It actually took quite a few more years of research before they could not only know what date and time they were viewing, but actually view a specific date and time of their choosing. The concept was proven out at the lighthouse, but the device was enormous and not moveable. They could only view the lighthouse and the area around the lighthouse at any given time in history, which didn't provide them with a lot of information. Another issue that they quickly discovered was that they could only view events in the past. They tried to view beyond the current date, but never were quite able to accomplish it. They just couldn't look into the future, possibly because the future hadn't happened yet, so there were no energy fields left behind to pick up. Still it was a breakthrough just to be able to see into the past, and was enough to get the extra funding to research how to make a device that would be portable. Unfortunately, that part took a lot longer than anyone expected. It took another ten years of research before they could miniaturize the device and make it portable enough to carry around and set up at different locations. And 'miniaturize' was still a relative term. The smallest that they were ever able to get it was about the size of a tractor trailer truck, even though conduit from the main generators in the truck could be routed indoors and hooked up to portable emitters to view events that happened inside structures. For transporting, the control room and generators fit inside one truck, and the emitters and poles would fit inside another. It could be taken to any remote location and set up. There were large emitters for viewing large areas such as outdoors, and smaller portable emitters for viewing indoors, such as a room in a house.

"Once they were finally able to construct a mobile version, it could then be used for practical applications. One of the main applications was for criminal investigations. You can imagine how helpful it would be for investigators to actually watch as items were stolen, or to see a murder actually taking place. Of course, it still wasn't perfect. Criminals sometimes wore masks, and murders sometimes took place at another location and the body was moved to the scene where it was found. Still, it helped solve many crimes that previously may have gone into the cold case files. Another of its primary uses in solving crimes was in establishing alibis for suspects. Now for the first time in history, the court system didn't have to rely on another person's corroboration to establish an alibi. Now an Ionic Field Generator, as the device that came out of Project Second Sight came to be called, could be used to prove that the suspect was in fact where he said he was when the crime was committed. If a suspect simply said that he was home alone, it could be proven that they actually were home alone. Testimony in a trial could now be validated by simply using an Ionic Field Generator. Trials became much more accurate and many more criminals were convicted by using the Ionic Field Generator in conjunction with testimony to give the jury a lot more valuable information. Evidence gathered using Ionic Field Generators became one hundred percent admissible in court. It was viewed as the 'Gold Standard' in evidence gathering.

"In addition to solving crimes, it was also used for historians to document history. Now historians could see back in time and actually watch the Declaration of Independence being signed, and watch as Thomas Edison tested the first light bulb. Mysteries that had never been solved were able to be discovered as well, such as was there really another shooter on the grassy knoll during the Kennedy assassination? It was a great device that opened up all kinds of new possibilities that hadn't previously been available. Now we could watch history unfold first hand. Videos were produced of major historic events and students were able to watch these videos of the ACTUAL historic event! It was a wonderful time of learning. Sometimes things that were thought to be true in history were actually disproved by the project. Project Second Sight was a tremendous success, and had already increased our knowledge of history exponentially.

"Soon after the first successful tests of the Ionic Field Generator, and during the time that another team was working to miniaturize the generator, a new project was begun out at the lighthouse. Not even most of the people who had worked on Project Second Sight knew what this one was all about. Government Officials, impressed with the success of Project Second Sight, and seeing the value of it, had started thinking on a whole new level. While they were impressed that Project Second Sight could let them see into the past, they were sometimes frustrated that they could only look, but not change the events. They decided that if they could see into the past, that they should be able to open a door to the past that they could travel through. If this were possible, then events in the past could not only be viewed, but altered as well! This project was code named 'Project Second Chance'. There was quite a bit of opposition in Congress to it and discussions went on for several years. Many Senators and Congressmen felt that we shouldn't tamper with events that happened in the past. They felt that it would be too dangerous, and was something that should be left alone. Others were convinced that it would be a tool that could be used to alter past events and make the future better. Unfortunately, the first group was right, but the second group won the argument and 'Project Second Chance' was granted funding.

"While the island was still open to tourists during 'Project Second Sight' and the only area that was secured was the area around the lighthouse, before the start of 'Project Second Chance' the entire island was shut down for tourists. The government bought up all of the homes and businesses and turned the entire island into a research facility. This is when it became a 'No-fly' zone and the area encompassing five miles around the island was off limits to private and commercial boating. Sophisticated missile batteries were installed around the island to defend against intrusion. These were later replaced with high-powered laser cannons. They simply weren't leaving open any chance that what they were doing here would be discovered. Sadly, the many planes and boats that accidentally strayed too close were eliminated during the years that the Vortex Accelerator was being developed and in the years that it was in operation.

"Originally, it was thought that time travel could be accomplished by modifying the original Ionic Field Generator design, but it was determined after about fourteen years of effort that the Field Generator design wouldn't work. It just couldn't generate the right kind of temporal field. It was initially thought that providing more power to the Ionic Field Generator would actually trigger the portal, but it was soon discovered that a whole new approach was needed. While the scientists working on the project thought that success was imminent on several occasions, they finally discovered that simply supercharging ionic particles wouldn't open up a doorway in time. Something else was needed. They went back to the drawing board and in two years time came up with an entirely new and revolutionary design, partially based on Einstein's Theory of Relativity. It was called the Vortex Accelerator, and it was such a massive undertaking that it took a full twenty-two years to complete. Part of the reason that it took so long was the power needed to operate it. As you can imagine, it takes an enormous amount of energy to open a hole in time. Four hydrogen fusion power plants were built here on the island to power the Vortex Accelerator. The combined power produced by these plants would be enough to power three quarters of the United States. Project Second Chance was officially begun in the year 2095, and fifty-seven years later, on November 7, 2152, the Vortex Accelerator was brought online at full power.

"During the first year of tests, the temporal field produced by the Vortex Accelerator wasn't stable enough for anyone to be able to safely walk through. As soon as the field would approach maximum temporal capacity, the frequency would start to fluctuate and the field would collapse. During that first year, we lost a couple of men when they walked into the field and it collapsed a few seconds later. We never really determined what exactly happened to them, as they were never found. It was determined after the loss of the men that we needed to be able to create a matrix that would stabilize the field. I was right out of college at the time, after completing my Doctorate in Temporal Engineering. It was a new science, and I was excited to be able to get in on the ground floor. Our team was one of the ones assigned to develop a way to stabilize the matrix. We worked pretty much around the clock for that year and finally made the breakthrough a little over a year later, which involved constructing something called a Temporal Dissipater and mounting it in the lantern house of the lighthouse. A stabilizer field was aimed at the Dissipater, which would create a dissipation field from the center where the lighthouse was located and eliminate the fluctuations that were occurring. The lantern house was just the right height off the ground to be able to do what we needed. During our research, we also discovered that one of the side effects produced by the temporal field was that it ionized the water droplets in the air around the accelerator, producing the thick fog that you've become familiar with. The dissipation field produced by the Temporal Dissipater kept the ionization outside the circular wall. That's why the area immediately around the lighthouse was always clear and the fog only formed outside the wall.

"The way that the Vortex Accelerator worked was that we would decide what date and time that we wanted to travel to. Once we had the date, we would calculate the exact frequency and enter the parameters into the matrix that would open a doorway into that date. We would energize the temporal field and within about thirty minutes it reached maximum temporal capacity and the scene inside the lighthouse wall would change. The area inside the wall including the lighthouse would be the date and time that we selected, and the area outside the wall including the Accelerator would still be the current date and time. If anyone happened to be walking around inside the wall during this time, they would see a thick fog appear outside the wall, just like you and your friends have seen, followed by the trees around the outside of the wall being replaced by the Vortex Accelerator and its glowing emitters. Once the field was stable, we could walk into that time period simply by walking through the lighthouse gate. We would wait at the lighthouse until the temporal field was brought down. Once the temporal field was brought down, the area surrounding the lighthouse outside the wall would then return back to the same time period as the area inside the lighthouse wall and the person or persons that had walked through the gate and were waiting at the lighthouse could then walk out the gate into that time period. They could go anywhere in the world and they would still be at that same time period in the past. Time would continue to advance for them in that time. If they stayed for a week, they would experience that whole week exactly how it originally took place. The only way to return to 2164 was to come back to the lighthouse and use the Beacon to let someone in the control room know that they were ready to come back. It worked somewhat like pushing a button on an old style elevator to light up a light to let the elevator operator know which floor to come and pick you up on, but the way the Beacon worked was to create a disturbance in the temporal field that could be picked up by our sensors. Once the control room operator determined the exact date and time from the Beacon, then he would set up the matrix and energize the Vortex Accelerator. Once the field was stable, whoever was inside the lighthouse wall could then walk through the gate back to 2164."

"That's really quite amazing," exclaimed Dan, "but there's still one thing that I don't fully understand. When we've seen the fog appear, the area around us has still been trees and forest. We've never seen the Vortex Accelerator as you describe it. When Amy and Veronica got caught in the fog and went through the doorway, they went back in time to 1986, not forward to 2164."

Philip replied, "That's one of the unfortunate side-effects of the Vortex Accelerator that we were never quite able to control. We didn't even discover that it was happening until about a year after we brought the Accelerator online. We discovered that every time that we open a hole in time it creates ripples, like ripples in a pond. Those ripples open up random holes at different dates and times. We have no way of knowing when one will open up, or even how many will be created. When they do open up and someone inadvertently walks into them, we have no way of knowing exactly where they are. We know that Greg and Tim walked into a ripple back in 1974, but even with our technology, we still don't know where they went. We just haven't found a way to track the ripples that are created. We've actually searched for Greg and Tim, but have never been able to find them. We're not exactly sure, but we assume that even if the Vortex Accelerator were shut down completely, that the ripples would continue since they've already been started. Possibly, though, like ripples in the water they would fade over time."

At this point Dan thought of another question, "When I was talking with Bill Henderson, he mentioned that he had heard Greg and Tim in the fog, but this was only a few years ago. You're saying now that they disappeared into a ripple in 1974, so how was it possible for him to hear them almost forty years after they disappeared?"

Philip continued, "That's another mystery of ripples that we don't fully understand. A single ripple seems to be able to span multiple time periods at the same time. While the area around the lighthouse was 1974, we don't know what time period the fog that they entered actually was. When they were in the fog, that same ripple could touch multiple periods in time. If one of those was the time period that Bill was in, then it could be possible to hear and talk to them. It's a difficult concept for even the scientists that worked on the project to fully understand."

"So Bill probably did hear them then?"

"That certainly could have been possible," replied Philip, "and there's no reason to believe that it didn't happen."

"You mentioned using the Beacon to signal that you're ready to go back. Is the Beacon that you showed me the same one that we found in the lighthouse?" asked Dan.

"Yes, it's the same one." replied Philip, "We had to get it back because we couldn't risk you accidentally activating it and giving away our location to the observers back in 2164. They don't know where in time we actually are and it has to stay that way. If they knew where we were, they would come to stop us, and they wouldn't hesitate to use deadly force. Nothing would be too extreme if it would protect the Accelerator. You'll understand more as I reveal more of the story. We accidentally lost the Beacon one day when we were inside the lighthouse, but had to leave quickly because the restoration team that you hired came in a little earlier than usual. Unfortunately, you found it before we did."

"How did you get it away from Dr. Carson without him knowing it?" asked Dan.

"In the hundred and fifty or so years since your time we've developed some highly sophisticated technology. We know a lot more about how the human brain actually works and processes information than you do during this time period. Your charts of the brain really don't show anything compared to ours. Our charts have over two hundred brain centers; yours have around ten to thirteen. We've developed a device called a Disruptor that produces a bright white light of a certain frequency that disrupts the Quadron Processors in the brain, effectively causing the person to black out for a period of about ten minutes."

"What's a Quadron Processor?" asked Dan.

"You haven't discovered them yet." said Philip, "They won't be discovered until around 2109. They're the part of the brain that sorts and retrieves information from the memory centers. If they're shut down, the brain is essentially shut down. We never actually shut them down, however, we just disrupt them. Once they're disrupted, the brain will black out for ten to fifteen minutes while the Sequencing Processors resequence the anterior neurotransmitter banks that link the various sections of the brain. It's actually completely harmless, since the brain has a natural ability to resequence itself after being disrupted. It's much safer than the Tasers that you use in this time period which can stop your heart. After being disrupted, we can use a Blocker to erase certain parts of the short term memory. Recent short term memory is always stored in the Alpha Bank. Events are stored there anywhere up to about thirty minutes. After that time the Quadron Processors will have shifted it to either the STIS 1 or 2 banks for Short Term Intermediate Storage or the PLT 1 or 2 banks for Pre Long Term Storage. The PLT banks are for items that a person has made a conscious effort to remember, therefore going into long term memory sooner. We really can only accurately erase from the Alpha Bank, since research is still continuing on being able to access the NeuroData Bank, which is basically the directory for all information stored in the brain.

"So in Dr. Carson's case, I just scrambled his brain with a Disrupter, and then used a Blocker to erase his memory of me. I erased about eleven minutes, which is the time where he first spotted me. He had no memory of either seeing me or of me taking the Beacon after that. I wrapped up a smooth rock to put in its place so that he wouldn't suspect anything until later.

"We also had to use the Disrupter on Officer Collins the day that you and your friends went out to the lighthouse with Dr. Carson and set up the experiments. He had followed you without you being aware of him and had taken pictures of your experiments. He also accidentally stumbled into the time period that you were analyzing and took pictures of the lighthouse there too, which at that time was intact and had a keeper and his family living in it. We couldn't have him showing those pictures to anyone and getting investigators out here at that point. What we were trying to do needed to be kept secret."

"This is all really quite fascinating," said Dan, "but you said earlier that there was an urgent discussion that we needed to have. What does any of this have to do with me?"

CHAPTER 26

An Urgent Request

"It has quite a lot to do with you actually." replied Philip, "You see, Project Second Sight and Project Second Chance are both Perihelion projects."

"So," Dan asked, "it was my company who built the Vortex Accelerator about a hundred fifty years from now?"

"Yes," replied Philip, "the fact that you purchased the lighthouse actually enabled the Vortex Accelerator to be built. The disappearance of Greg and Tim, and all of the strange sightings that have happened over the years, all were a direct result of your purchase of the lighthouse. We've always known that what happens in the past can affect the future, but in this case what happened here in this time period has affected both the past and the future. All of the stories that you've grown up hearing over the years have been a direct result of your decision to purchase this lighthouse earlier this year."

"Wow, this is going to take some getting used to. It all sounds so complicated." replied Dan.

"It is complicated," answered Philip, "and there's really no way to tell all of the damage that's been done by it over the years. Anytime anything is changed in the past, there can be multiple effects of that change, some not even known for years, some possibly never known. Several years ago in our time, a group of us working on the project started to question the ethical ramifications of the Vortex Accelerator. After quite a bit of discussion, our conclusion is that the Vortex Accelerator should have never been built. It's totally destroyed the world that I live in, and most people that live in that time never even have a clue that their lives could have been so much better if we hadn't tampered with time. Since what goes on at the island is kept so secret, they don't even know that we did."

"So you've actually been changing the past?" asked Dan.

"Yes," answered Philip, "Not at first, but eventually. When the Vortex Accelerator first came online there were no laws or mandates for its use. No one had been able to go back in time and change the past before, so there were no precedents. There should have been laws in place when we brought it online, but they weren't put in place until later. I don't think anyone really expected us to be successful. The first few years after it was in operation, President Graham made an executive order that it was only to be used to EXPLORE the past. As visitors to that time period, we were to take extra care that none of our actions affected anything or anyone. We were simply to be observers and have minimal interaction with the people in that time period. There were certain interactions that were permitted. We could dine out at a restaurant, or check into a hotel. These actions were considered low risk for changing the future and necessary for us to observe. We could even talk with people in that period, but we had to be extremely careful of what we said. We were not under any circumstance permitted to reveal our true identities, or to give anyone in the past advice based on our knowledge of the future.

"Gradually, however, things changed. A new President was elected, new Senators and Congressmen were elected, and their ideas were different. President Thomas McCain was much more liberal than President Graham and the Presidents that came before him. And the Congress that was elected with him was more liberal as well. Together they decided that if it was possible to make the future better by changing the past then we should do it. The problem was in the definition of BETTER; better for whom? And who would decide what was better? Of course that would be the President and certain members of Congress, and their advisors. They began authorizing excursions as they were called to make calculated modifications to the past. These modifications were small and experimental at first. But once they got started, the modifications grew in size. They took more risks, which exposed another problem that hadn't been considered, but should have been. Many of the modifications had unintended consequences that couldn't be foreseen. You see, we could only make the modifications based on what we THOUGHT it would accomplish. We couldn't actually see into the future to tell everything that a modification would change. And we couldn't always tell what changed, even after the modification was made.

Once a modification had been made, the future changed into the future that the modification created. No one had any memory of the future before the modification, so it was difficult to compare which was better. As time went on over the next ten years, excursions were made to correct some of these unintended consequences as well, which mostly made things worse by introducing more unintended consequences. The President and Congress began authorizing modifications that would promote their agenda, regardless of the harm that they might do. Over time, driven by power and greed, the modifications were mostly done to create the world that they envisioned, one where they had complete control. In the world that I come from, personal freedom has all but been destroyed. President Nicholas Cortelli, aided by his advisors, began authorizing excursions that would eliminate the democracy and make him ruler for life. Congress should have stopped him, and they could have when he first started. The Constitution gave them that power. But they did nothing, and eventually President Cortelli eliminated Congress, the Supreme Court, and the Constitution and created a monarchy controlled by the Cortelli family. Now there are no elections any longer, and people practically have no say in their own lives. Governors of the states are appointed by the Cortelli family and they in turn appoint members to the local offices in their states. The United States has been renamed simply America, but it's not the America that you know. It's a dark America created by a government who got their power by using the Vortex Accelerator to manipulate the past. And the boundaries of America have been enlarged as well to encompass Canada, Mexico, Central America, and the northern states of South America. It's not a good place to live, and it was all created by abusing a power that man was never meant to have.

"During the years leading up to the fall of the United States and the creation of the American Monarchy, the entire island was a restricted military installation. Everything was kept ultra secret, even to the senators and congressmen who weren't on the Time Management Committee, as it came to be known. The government obviously didn't want any private citizens knowing what was going on at the island. It was better for them that way. You can imagine what would happen if folks found out that the government and military now had the capability to go back in time and change the past, and that they were actually doing that. Even members of congress that weren't on the Time Management Committee still thought that we were only observing. With each excursion, the government and military got even bolder. The President established the top secret Department of Time Management through an executive order so that no one outside the Time Management Committee would find out what they were really doing. No one really knew whether the President was authorized to do this or not, but no one that knew about it questioned it. It was a power that they all wanted, and they didn't want to do anything that would jeopardize that. The Department of Time Management was what I consider the most dangerous department ever created by the government, and it was one of the key pieces used by President Cortelli to establish his family as the ruling family in America. Its director established departments of Planners, whose job was to study the past and make recommendations based on goals established by the government, or other management within the department. Once it was decided what to change, operatives called Emissaries carried out the plans. They would go back to the predetermined time and place, make the modification, then return. Some modifications were large and some were really small, such as possibly just delaying someone for a specified period of time or stealing something relatively insignificant. Sometimes, though, the plan was to have someone killed. Operatives called Assassins would carry out these assignments. Even though John Hinckley Jr. was convicted and went to prison for the crime, it was actually one of our assassins who carried out the assassination of President Reagan in March of 1981. This was one of the more high profile assassinations. Most were so low profile that they didn't even make the evening news.

"Remember earlier that I mentioned the unintended consequences? Almost every excursion had them, and some we probably never even found out about. Some were large and some were small. Some were good and some were bad. The point is that while we had the ability to change the past, thus altering the future, it didn't work like some of the movies and TV shows depicted. We didn't have the capability to see ahead of time everything that a modification would change. We couldn't even really tell if the modification would change what we wanted changed in the way that we wanted it changed. Some worked, some didn't. Some that seemed for the best turned out not to be. And some consequences didn't show up until years after the modification. One excursion rescued a ten year old boy from drowning after the rowboat that he 'borrowed' from a neighbor capsized. One would think that rescuing a child would be the best course of action to take. But nine years later that same boy killed twenty seven people at a shopping mall in Columbia, SC with a homemade bomb. There was no way that we could have known that would be the result prior to the modification. Of course, that same boy could have become the brilliant scientist that discovered the cure for cancer. The problem was that we just didn't know everything that would result from each modification.

"Then there were the issues created by the ripples. It's impossible even to tell how many ripples have opened up over the years, or what consequences they've had. The one that Greg and Tim walked into and the one that sent Amy and Veronica back were probably the most famous ones. We don't know how many more opened up and caused changes to the future that we don't even know about. And we can't even tell how significant the changes created by ripples were. Since they can open up at any time, it's simply impossible to track them. Once we discovered that the ripples existed, the project should have been shut down. They would cause too many unknown variables to be acceptable. But the government and military wouldn't hear of shutting it down. They said that the ripples actually were 'acceptable risks'. We did make some attempts at fixing the problem. We needed the area around the lighthouse to be off limits to tourists so that we could run some experiments. It was actually us who fenced in the lighthouse back in 1994 in order to be able to run experiments without taking the chance that someone would be there. Three of our operatives posed as government officials and orchestrated the fencing in of the area around the lighthouse. The one mistake that they made was giving Police Chief Lawson business cards. We didn't think to make up phony government cards, so they gave him their real Perihelion ones. The problem was that in 1994, Perihelion wasn't around and wouldn't be for another five years. Luckily it wasn't found out then and everything was fine until you showed up and gave Chief Callahan yours."

"That might be why Chief Callahan looked so perplexed when I gave him my business card! Were theirs the standard Perihelion ones with the burgundy 'P' and the white starburst?" asked Dan.

"Yes they were. That probably is why the Chief was wondering about you. It's probably the reason that he's had Officer Collins watching you since you've been here. I've been watching too and noticed that several times after you leave an area, Officer Collins follows you. He probably thinks that you had something to do with the fencing in of the lighthouse and that there's more to you being here now than just fixing it up."

"That originally was all I came here for!" remarked Dan, "But things have certainly changed!"

"Yes they have, and things are probably going to change a lot more. All of what I've just told you are reasons why changing the past is something that man shouldn't have the power to do. This power should be left up to God, who does know the future. A large group of us who were working on the project came to the conclusion that it was arrogant of man to think that he could improve on God's original plan. We began to meet secretly to try and find a way to destroy the Vortex Accelerator.

"At first, there just didn't seem to be any way. As you could imagine, the security around it in 2164 is really tight. And just the size of it would make it virtually impossible to destroy. There are security cameras covering every inch of the installation, which makes it extremely difficult to do anything in secret. We were even lucky to be able to get here to 2016 undetected."

"We?" asked Dan.

"I was going to tell you," replied Philip, "I'm not the only one who came back in time. I just felt you'd be more comfortable meeting one on one with me first. His name is Ryan Langtree, and he's the Great Great Grandson of Edwin Langtree, the originator of the Langtree Hypothesis. Ryan wrote a large part of the computer code that performs the calculations necessary to load the parameters into the Vortex Accelerator to enable it to open a door into a specific place in time. Since every excursion is tracked on the computer system that controls the Vortex Accelerator, he had to modify the program to erase all traces of where we came. They don't know that we're in 2016, but I can only assume that they're looking for us. If they've figured out that we came here to find a way to destroy the Vortex Accelerator, then finding us will be top priority. We can only hope that

Ryan did his job so well with the program that our trail is completely untraceable."

"You've come here to destroy the Vortex Accelerator? How?" asked Dan, "The Vortex Accelerator doesn't even exist in this time."

"We figured out that even if we destroyed the Vortex Accelerator in our time period, it would have still been online for ten years. Everything that had been modified in that ten year period would still have affected the future. We needed to alter the past so that the Vortex Accelerator is never built. That's why we're here, and that's why we need your help."

"What can I do?" asked Dan, "I don't even fully understand what's going on here."

"We need you to sell the lighthouse." said Philip, "As long as you own it, it will eventually be owned by Perihelion and Project Second Sight and Project Second Chance will be started here on the island."

"That might not be so easy." said Dan. "Where would I find a buyer? And how would we be sure that it wouldn't eventually find its way back to Perihelion anyway?"

"There's no way to really be sure, but we've been planning for that as well. Ryan has a plan that might work. He thinks that the best course of action is to establish the Green Island Lighthouse Preservation Society and get the lighthouse listed on the National Register of Historic Places."

"So let's go back a minute." said Dan, "If we're successful with getting the ownership transferred to a newly created Preservation Society, what's supposed to happen exactly?"

"If Ryan is correct, which I think there's a good chance that he is, then the entire time line going backward and forward will revert back to whatever reality would have existed if the Vortex Accelerator were never built. If Perihelion doesn't eventually own it, then it won't be available for their experimentation. Of course, that's not to say that Perihelion or some other company won't eventually develop a way to travel in time, but we've at least eliminated this one. It won't happen on this island. We just have to take one step at a time."

The first thing that Dan thought of when Philip said this was that he would get Amy back, the 13 year old Amy! He remembered what his life was like prior to coming to the island and it would be great to be able to get that life back again. But, what should he consider about Amy's wishes? She had the opportunity to stop herself from going out to the lighthouse and going back in time and she chose her current life. If he went along with Philip's plan, then she'd lose the life that she's known for the past thirty years. She'd lose her husband and her kids. And the life that she's had has been a good life, even better than most people could dream of. But who's to say that her life if she had never gone back to 1986 wouldn't end up being just as good? And he'd have the opportunity to finish seeing her grow up, and be a part of his grandkids' lives as they grew up as well. It was an extremely difficult decision, with a lot to consider.

"So, will you help us?" asked Philip.

"Probably," Dan said, "but I need time to think. I am wondering why you needed to involve me at all. Couldn't you have just gone back and prevented me from finding out about the lighthouse being for sale?"

"We actually thought of that. But you found out about it from an internet advertisement. We couldn't figure out a good way to remove the ad from the internet. If it had been as simple as stealing your morning paper so you wouldn't see a newspaper ad, then that would have been much easier. After giving it much thought, though, and discussing it with the group, we felt that involving you in the plan would be the best way to insure that the lighthouse is never owned by Perihelion. The only issue was involving you at the right time. You had to accept that time travel is possible before I approached you with this idea. And that's why Ryan and I came here to 2016, and why we've been observing to find just the right time to approach you."

"Come by the Island Charm tomorrow, how about around 1:00 in the afternoon? I want to discuss this with Scotty and Greg."

"That's fine," replied Philip, "Ryan and I will be there. But remember what I've told you. If you really believe that the power to travel through time and change events in the past is not something that man should be entrusted with, then please help us. And there's one more thing that you need to know as well. Remember when we first began talking, you asked me why I didn't stop Amy from going out to the lighthouse that day? Six years from now, Amy's daughter Rebekah will marry Eric Chandler and they'll have a son, who will have a son, until my father, Robert Chandler is born. So, you see, you and I are related, even if very distantly. If I'd stopped her from going back in time and marrying Derrick Westfall, then I wouldn't have been here to ask for your help and the Vortex Accelerator would probably have still been built. Ryan wouldn't have been here either. His family line is descendents of Rick and Veronica."

"This is really getting complicated!" remarked Dan, "We don't know how many things that have happened over the years happened because of the Vortex Accelerator and how many would have happened anyway."

"That's correct." answered Philip, "The past as we remember it will probably change significantly from what we remember now. The past and future are so intertwined that undoing every modification that the Vortex Accelerator enabled will create a completely different past. But think about what I said before, 'Do we really think that we can do better than God?' I can only think that the original past and future that God intended will be better than the one that we created."

They got up from the bench, shook hands, and walked back across the boardwalk and out to the street. Dan got into his truck and sat there for about thirty minutes just thinking about the conversation that he'd had over the past hour. It was unbelievable. What Philip had told him was something out of a science fiction movie, not something that could ever happen in real life. Yet neither could his daughter disappear into the fog and show back up a few days later as an adult with a family. The past month had been filled with impossibilities. And what Philip just revealed to him did seem to explain what has been happening. He didn't want the world that Philip had described to be the future for America, and after listening to Philip, he felt that man really didn't have the restraint and wisdom to be trusted with the power to alter the past.

It was about quarter till twelve when he finally cranked up his truck and headed back out to the lighthouse. When he got there he could tell that the others had been hard at work for several hours already. He parked his truck in the clearing and just sat, looking out at the lighthouse. It already didn't seem like his anymore. He had told Philip that he needed time to think, but what was there really to think about. He knew that he didn't want the future of America to be what Philip described, even if it was a future that was so far distant that he'd never see it.

He got out of his truck and walked over to where everyone was busy at work on the lighthouse. As he walked up the stairs and in through the back door, Amy saw him come in and walked over to give him a hug.

"Decide to sleep in today?" she asked playfully, "We've all been hard at work for a few hours now."

"No, I just had something that I had to do this morning." he replied with a serious look on his face. Seeing her here reminded him of how his decision would completely change her life. She obviously noticed his odd reaction to her statement.

"That's fine, I was just joking!" she said, "It really is good to be back. I've really missed you all these years and wondered what it would be like when we finally met back up again. I know you don't agree, but I'm glad now that I didn't stop myself from going out to the lighthouse. It's a different relationship, but you, I, mom and Danny are back together again, and I still have Derrick, Rebekah, and Andrew. I really wouldn't want to think of giving up the life that I've had with them. And now that we're back together again, I can't imagine how it could be much better. Derrick and I are even thinking of moving out here to the island to be near to you and mom. I can do my writing from almost anywhere, and it is beautiful out here with the ocean surrounding us. I think I'll enjoy island living!"

He liked the fact that Amy wanted to be near him and Kate, and if he hadn't just had the conversation with Philip he knew that he'd be thrilled at her news. But in light of what Philip had just revealed to him, he had to look away from her when she said this. How could he tell her that he was about to make a decision that would eliminate the last thirty years of her life? He knew that he should be honest with her, but he just couldn't bring himself to tell her, at least not yet.

"Is anything wrong?" she asked, "I thought you'd be thrilled that we're thinking of moving out here."

"I am happy about the news." he said, "I just have a lot on my mind right now. I'd love having you living near us."

Still, while he said the words, he just didn't have the enthusiasm that she thought he'd have. He seemed almost to be trying to avoid her now.

"I'm glad to hear that!" she replied, "Are you sure there's nothing bothering you? You seem so preoccupied this morning."

"I just need to talk to Scotty about something. Have you seen him out here?"

"I think he's upstairs working with Greg." she said.

"Thanks," he said, "I'll talk to you later. I really am thankful to have you back Amy, and of course I'm thrilled that you're thinking about moving out here to be closer to us."

He turned and walked up the steps into the upstairs hallway, with Amy watching him, still curious about his strange mood today. He found Scotty and Greg working in the last room on the left.

"Looking good." he said.

"It should be!" remarked Scotty, "We've been doing all the work this morning while you've been goofing off. What did you have come up? Doing some surf fishing down by the beach I bet!"

The look on Dan's face however showed him that Dan wasn't in a joking mood.

"What's up buddy?" he asked Dan, his mood getting more serious as well.

"Let's go get some lunch in town." Dan suggested, "Just you, me and Greg. There's something that I need to talk with you about."

With the look on Dan's face and the tone in his voice, neither of them questioned whether they should go with him now. They all walked out to Dan's truck, and in a few minutes, they were headed down Lighthouse Road toward town. On the drive into town, Dan began revealing some of the details about the morning meeting with Philip to them.

"So this is the man that's been following you?" asked Scotty.

"Yes, that's what he said." replied Dan.

"And you think that you can trust him?" asked Scotty, "Maybe he's just trying to get you to sell the lighthouse to him for some other reason."

"I don't think so," answered Dan, "and I don't think he wants me to sell it to him. He wants to meet tomorrow afternoon to discuss Ryan's plan. I think he just wants to get it away from Perihelion any way that he can. I'd like you and Greg to be at that meeting as well."

They continued the conversation for the rest of the drive to the Sand Crab Diner. After they got there, they were seated at their usual table. Dan could tell that Scotty was skeptical, but what else could he do? And why would anyone make up a totally unbelievable story like that just to get him to sell them the lighthouse? He actually did think that Philip was legitimate, however impossible his story seemed. He knew that he wouldn't have believed it at all if it hadn't been for Amy's story. Philip was right; he did have to have just the right timing. Before Amy had disappeared, Dan knew that he would have just dismissed Philip as a nut with a story like his. Now that he knew that time travel was possible, he was willing to accept a lot more.

"What are you going to tell Amy?" asked Scotty, "You do know that she made her choice not to stop herself from going to the lighthouse that morning. She wants the life that she's had for all those years, the life with Derrick and her kids. How are you going to explain to her what you're considering?"

"I don't know. A little while ago when she saw me come into the lighthouse, she told me that she and Derrick were thinking about moving to the island to be near to us. I'm not sure that I actually can tell her."

"You have to. It affects her too. Don't you think that she deserves a say in this?" Scotty asked.

"Why do I really have to?" asked Dan, feeling a little guilty that he was even considering not telling her. "If what we're doing is successful, she won't even remember anything about her previous life. Not telling her would just save her all of the anxiety about the decision."

He really thought that he should tell her, and discuss it with her. But what was there really to discuss? Hadn't he already made up his mind? He'd just be attempting to justify his decision to her, and after thirty years of her life with Derrick and building a family with him, he wasn't sure that she'd really understand, especially since she had just told him that she felt like she'd made the right decision. He still felt guilty, like he was taking the easy way out by not telling her, but he reasoned that it would be the easiest way for Amy as well.

CHAPTER 27
May 20, 2016
Executing the Plan

For Dan, the past month had gone by quickly. He'd had a lot to do in the short time since he had the conversation with Philip Chandler. Here, sitting on the porch of the Island Charm with Scotty, Greg and Steve waiting for Carter Hawthorne, legal counsel for the newly formed Green Island Lighthouse Preservation Society, they were all discussing the events of the past few weeks.

Their 1:00 meeting with Philip Chandler and Ryan Langtree the day after Dan had met Philip had been interesting. They both seemed like very likable men now that they weren't hiding in the shadows watching them. They were both in their late thirties with sandy brown hair, and since both had their doctorate degrees, they were also extremely intelligent. After brief introductions and some questions from both Scotty and Greg, Ryan began outlining his plan for eliminating the Vortex Accelerator. He used the word "eliminating" because they weren't destroying it exactly. You can't destroy something that never existed in the first place, and if Ryan's plan was successful, then it would in fact, have never existed.

His plan seemed too simple really, but his reasoning seemed sound. He had said that since Perihelion had been the contractor who had built the Vortex Accelerator around the lighthouse, then if Perihelion never owned the lighthouse, then the Vortex Accelerator would never be built. And since the Vortex Accelerator was used to change a large number of events in the past, events that also would shape the future, then if the Vortex Accelerator never existed then the world, both past and present, would revert back to the world as it would have been without it. Since it was Dan's purchase of the lighthouse, and also Dan's connection with Perihelion as its founder that enabled the Vortex Accelerator to be built, then if Dan didn't own the lighthouse, and it was owned by another entity not connected to Perihelion, then Perihelion would never have control of that property to be able to build it out there.

Philip and Ryan had both told him that they had tried to keep him from purchasing the lighthouse before now without him knowing about it, but they couldn't find a way that would work. They couldn't think of a way to prevent him from seeing the advertisement on the internet that day. They had thought of contacting him once he had decided to place a bid on it, but what would they say? At that point, how would he have reacted to two men showing up and saying they were from the future and it was a bad idea to purchase the lighthouse? He actually knew how he would have reacted.

Still, the thought of what they were about to do was a daunting prospect. As with all of the other modifications to the past that Philip and Ryan had told him about, there was no way to tell what the final result would be. Some things they could speculate about. The obvious was that if Perihelion didn't come into possession of the lighthouse, then the Vortex Accelerator would never be built, as Ryan had already stated. But just as important, if the Accelerator was never built, then Amy and Veronica wouldn't go back to 1986 and marry Derrick and Rick. And if that never happened, since Edwin Langtree was a descendant of Rick and Veronica, then the Langtree Hypothesis would never be formed. And since the Langtree Hypothesis was the basis for the government contracts that led to experimenting with time, hopefully it will all end there. Could someone else in the future come up with a similar hypothesis, and could a time machine be built somewhere else? Of course, that could happen, but that was a variable that they couldn't control at this time, so they just had to move ahead. And there really was no way to tell if what they were doing would make the future better, or worse. But since they already knew that the future which would happen about a hundred fifty years from now was much worse, they all agreed that they had to try.

There were other unknown factors as well that Ryan had hesitated to mention, but he felt that they all should at least be aware of all of the possibilities. Undoing all of the modifications that had been done was in affect the largest modification of all, and it would affect both the past and the future in ways that would be impossible for any of them to predict. Since hundreds of time modifications had been made over the ten years that the Accelerator had been in operation, the cumulative results of those modifications not occurring could directly or indirectly affect ANY of their lives. For example, if a modification either directly or indirectly had prevented Dan's father or grandfather from being killed in an accident before Dan was born, then without the modification they could still be killed, and Dan may never be born. Some of their friends may never be born either due to similar circumstances in their family history. Circumstances in any of their lives that had been affected in some way by a modification could drastically change their life, and there was no way to tell whether that change would be good or bad. And this theory could apply to anyone. There was just no way to tell what would happen, or how any of their lives could be altered. According to Ryan, modifications had been made as far back as 1934, so anything after that date could change significantly. And since the ripples went back even further than that, as evidenced by Colonel Forrest's encounter, then history could have been changed even earlier than 1934. There was really no way to tell how far back the ripples went, they could have gone on indefinitely. While this thought did give Dan and the others cause for concern, they all still felt that they had to try.

According to Ryan, the best action to take was for Dan to sell the lighthouse. Of course, that's easier said than done. And what's to prevent the person that he sells it to from someday selling it back to an individual that has some connection with Perihelion? It had to be done in a way that would preserve the lighthouse and also prevent it from falling back into the hands of Perihelion sometime in the future. They only had one chance to get this right.

After discussing the plan among themselves with Philip and Ryan giving their input, it was decided that the best course of action to take was to create a Lighthouse Preservation Society. That would be a legal entity that the lighthouse and all the property around it could be sold to. They'd need someone to be the CEO of the Society and to handle the day to day operation of restoring the lighthouse and getting it ready for public display. That person could then petition for protected status under the National Register of Historic Places. That should prevent any modifications to the lighthouse and surrounding area in the future. Of course, just to be safe, they'd hire an attorney and put some clauses in the contract that would prevent the lighthouse from ever being sold to Perihelion, anyone connected with Perihelion, or any future entities owned by Perihelion. They felt like this should cover all their bases. They'd need a generous benefactor to get the society started, since restoring a structure that's in as bad of shape as the lighthouse is a costly venture. Dan agreed to donate a few million to get it started. Officially the benefactor would be anonymous so as not to have any documented connection with Dan. Future funds could then be raised through donations from others and fundraising events.

The next order of business was to find someone to take on the role of CEO for the Preservation Society. They discussed several candidates, but finally decided that Steve would be the best choice. He was far enough disconnected from Perihelion that he'd be a relatively safe choice. Of course, they couldn't be sure that some events back in his family history hadn't been influenced in some way by the Accelerator and that possibly he wouldn't exist in a world without it. It seemed unlikely just knowing him, but we don't always know everything about our family histories, especially quite far back. His family had grown up in Iowa, though, so he was probably the safest choice that they had at this point.

Steve was hesitant at first. After all, his family and his life was all back in Iowa. He wasn't sure about moving to the island. It was a nice place to visit, but he hadn't really given much thought about living there. After talking it over with Arlene, however, he decided that maybe it was time for a change. It did sound appealing, actually running the Lighthouse Preservation Society. After it was restored and open to the public it would be a nice career change, just settling in to the day to day operation. The more he thought of it, he actually could see himself living with Arlene on the island. They picked out a house that they liked on the northern part slightly above the vacation area along Sea Spray Drive. Their new home did have a view of the ocean, and they both felt that they could make it home. Dan took care of the home purchase for them and they were able to move in without the encumbrance of a mortgage. He even instructed the Real Estate Division at Perihelion to purchase their old house back in Iowa and take care of selling it. They'd take care of moving most of their belongings after the lighthouse deal was finalized. Dan also gave them a generous moving allowance as well.

The last few weeks they had been busy putting this plan into motion. The first thing that Dan had done after their initial few meetings, was to discuss with Steve the possibility of him moving down to the island to become the CEO of the Green Island Lighthouse Preservation society. He didn't quite understand why Dan suddenly wanted to sell the lighthouse, but he figured that it had something to do with Amy's disappearance. While Dan did trust Steve, he still thought it best not to disclose everything about why he was selling the lighthouse. Once Steve agreed and they had discussed the plan, the next step was to incorporate the Lighthouse Preservation Society. They hired an attorney, Carter Hawthorne, to take care of the incorporation, and to manage any legal affairs of the Society. At first he was going to use one of Perihelion's corporate attorneys, but after discussion with the group it was decided that hiring an attorney that wasn't connected in any way with Perihelion would probably be the best choice.

Incorporation took place in the sitting room of the Island Charm around two weeks ago. Steve would be the President, Arlene would be the Treasurer, and they convinced Hank and Barbara to be directors. After all of their signatures were in place, Carter Hawthorne took the documents and filed for incorporation. The incorporation was finalized two days ago, so they were now ready to transfer the ownership of the lighthouse from Dan to the Green Island Lighthouse Preservation Society.

As they sat on the porch, still discussing the events of the past several weeks, Dan spotted Carter Hawthorne's dark blue Ford coming down Main Street. He passed in front of the Island Charm, giving them a wave as he passed by and turned left into the alley to park next to the building. He parked, got his briefcase out of the car and walked around to the front and up the steps.

"Good Morning Carter." said Dan.

"Good morning Dan." Carter replied, "Are you ready to do this?"

"I'm as ready as I'm going to be." answered Dan. "It will be a strange feeling, knowing that the lighthouse doesn't belong to me any more, but it's for the best. Kate and Danny are back home in Cincinnati, and I felt that it's time for me to get back there as well and get on with my life with them. Let's move inside to the sitting room and go over everything there."

Everyone moved from the porch to the sitting room and pulled out the chairs around the table. Carter opened his briefcase and spread out the documents to go over with them. As they all sat around the table as Carter explained each of the documents, Dan thought of Philip and Ryan. They had helped plan this, and it was basically Ryan's plan that they were executing now. Still, they had all agreed that it would be best if they weren't at this meeting, since no one else knew about them except for Scotty, Greg, and himself. He wondered where they were; knowing what was going on here. Dan understood why this had to be done, but a part of him still was hesitant. His entire life had been lived in a world based on modifications that had been done using the Vortex Accelerator. Just not knowing what may change made him a slight bit anxious. But Philip and Ryan had made a compelling argument about why this had to be done. Still, he thought, good things had come from the Accelerator. While he personally would rather have had the 13 year old Amy back, she was happy and had had a good life all those years, even if it was without him. Her and Derrick were good together and had built a wonderful life. The same was true with Veronica as well. And now they were all back together again even if it wasn't the same. And who knows if wherever Greg and Tim went, that they may have a good life as well?

As Carter went through each page, with Dan signing some of the documents, and Steve and Arlene signing some others, and all of them signing some, Dan still had some doubts if they were doing the right thing. Steve didn't know the real reason that they were selling the lighthouse to the Preservation Society. He simply thought that it was because after Amy's disappearance that Dan just wanted to get on with his life. He didn't know about Philip and Ryan.

As they reached the last page of the Ownership Transfer document, there was a line for Dan to sign as the seller, and a line for Steve to sign as Trustee for the Lighthouse Preservation Society. Steve would sign first, and then Dan would sign it. Then what? Even Ryan couldn't really tell them what to expect. Dan had thought that it would be easier than this. After all, as President of Perihelion, he'd had to sign hundreds of documents before. But this one was different. This was one that could actually change the world as he knew it, and not knowing whether it would change for the better or worse gave him more than a little cause for concern. Then there was Amy.

At first he had decided not to tell her, to just do this and if it worked the way that Ryan had said that it should, she'd never know. She'd just be 13 again and not even remember the past thirty years of her life. But he had decided to tell her. Three days ago, they had taken a walk along the beach and he had told her everything. He told her about the meeting with Philip where he had learned about the Vortex Accelerator and he told her about Ryan's plan for eliminating the Accelerator and returning everything back to how it would have been without it. He had tried to convince her that he really didn't have a choice. If it was within his power to prevent what would eventually happen to America, then he should do it. Amy, however, hadn't agreed. She had reacted just the way that he thought she would. She had reminded him that everyone has a choice, and this one was HIS to make, not Philip's or Ryan's. She wanted to go on with her life here and now; her life with Derrick, Rebekah, and Andrew. She did understand about the future, and how it had turned out, and even why Philip and Ryan felt that it had to be fixed. But she still couldn't bring herself to willingly give up the life that she'd lived for the past thirty years. After all, the future that Ryan and Philip spoke of was still almost a hundred and fifty years away. She had asked her dad not to go through with it. Couldn't there be another way? They'd had an argument that night and hadn't exactly parted on good terms. He hadn't been able to make her understand and he fully understood why she didn't. That talk with her along the beach that night, and their argument, and even thinking about some of the things that she had said, all made him question whether he really was doing the right thing. After his talk with Philip and Ryan he had thought that this was the only way, that he didn't really have a choice. But after talking with Amy, he understood that there were always choices, it was just a matter of looking at all the options and making the best one based on what you know at the time and what's most important to you. He knew what Philip and Ryan wanted to do, and he understood from their viewpoint why they wanted to do it. It was THEIR world that they were trying to save. Still, this was HIS choice. Should he make the choice based on what he was told would happen a hundred and fifty years from now, or should he make the choice based on what he felt was best for HIS family, right now?

His pen hovered over the paper, his hand shaking. Finally, he put the pen down on the table and looked away.

"Dan?" Scotty asked, "What's wrong? Aren't you going to sign it?"

"I don't know." replied Dan, "Is this really the right thing? Do we really know? Maybe it's best to leave things alone, to let things just take their course, and us to go on with our lives."

Carter and Steve were a bit confused at Dan's hesitation and his last statement. Did he know something that they didn't? All that would happen would be that the ownership would pass from Dan to the Lighthouse Preservation Society. They both had thought that this was what Dan had wanted. After all, he's the one that had approached them both with the idea.

"Take a few minutes." suggested Scotty, "Go for a walk outside. Come on, I'll go with you."

"We'll be back in a few minutes." Scotty told the others sitting around the table.

As they got up from the table to go outside, they met Amy at the door.

"Dad?" she asked hesitantly, "Are you going to do it?"

"I don't know yet. I'm not even sure that it's the right thing to do anymore. After our conversation the other day, what you said really got me thinking. You did have some good points, and I'm really glad that you're here now. I've missed you the last three days, and I'm sorry that we had that argument. Come walk with me and Scotty and let's talk about what we should do. You were right the other night; I should be thinking more of my family than what's going to happen a hundred fifty years from now."

The three of them walked out the door and into the early afternoon light. They turned down the sidewalk and walked toward town.

"I've been thinking a lot about this since we talked." Dan said to Amy, "I should have included you from the beginning. It's just that after talking with Philip, I really didn't think that I had a choice. But you made me realize that there's always a choice. Life is made up of choices, and we can't always let others make those choices for us."

"I was wrong too." Amy said, "When I came here to the island, I didn't know what choice that I would make. I had given it a lot of thought, and ultimately decided to go on with my life the way that it was. After thirty years, it was the life that I was more comfortable with. And most people in their forties probably wouldn't go willingly back to being 13 again. But you were right as well, and I don't believe that you were letting anyone make the choice for you. Knowing what Philip told you about the future, I believe that you are the one that made up your own mind that this would be the best choice to make. And this choice is much bigger than you, me, or even our families."

"So, are you saying that you think that I should sign the papers to transfer the lighthouse ownership?"

"I'm not saying that I like the idea," she said, "and if it were up to me I'd still choose to continue my life as it is. But I have been giving it a lot of thought over the past few days since we talked. We have to consider the future, even more than our own desires. I talked it over with Derrick as well, and both he and I support your decision. If you feel that this is the best choice, both for us, and for the future, then you have our support."

"Thanks," said Dan, "That means a lot, but I'm still not sure that it's the right choice. There are just too many unknowns. Even Philip and Ryan admit that."

"There are a lot of unknowns in life too," she reminded him, "but we still have to make the choices that we make based on the best knowledge that we have."

"You're right." Dan said, "That's all we can do."

They walked back to the Island Charm and back up the steps and into the sitting room. Having Amy's support definitely made it easier, but he still wasn't sure that this was the right choice. Still, she was right, he had to make the choice that he really felt was for the best. Nobody here knew what would happen, but they all believed that having the power to change the past and the future just isn't something that should be within anyone's ability to do. If they have the power to stop it, then they should.

It was a little before 2:00 in the afternoon when Dan sat back down at the table and picked up the pen.

"I'm ready now." he said.

As Carter slid the papers back to him for him to sign, Amy put her hands on his shoulders. She hadn't told him everything, but now she wondered if maybe she should have. Since her and her dad had talked the other night, she actually had become even more convinced that selling the lighthouse was the wrong thing to do. And it had nothing to do with her own personal desires to continue with her life. In fact, she had an uneasy feeling that she just couldn't explain. She knew that Ryan had it all planned out. They had a reasonable idea of what to expect, she'd simply go back to being 13 again and continue their lives as they would have if she hadn't gotten caught in the fog. But still, even now, she couldn't shake the feeling that there was something else, that there was something seriously wrong with this decision that no one was thinking of. She tried to dismiss it, however, as simply the anxiety of knowingly giving up the life that she'd known. That was a difficult decision that she'd contemplated over the past three days. And she really was trying not to let her personal feelings influence her dad's decision, which she felt was the reason that she hadn't mentioned this to him earlier. But now, as Dan picked up the pen, a new feeling swept over her that actually frightened her. She had the sinking feeling that this was the last time that she'd ever see her father. The thought did occur to her that maybe she should speak up now, but as Dan put the pen down on the paper and scratched out his signature, legally transferring ownership of the lighthouse to the Preservation Society, all that she quietly whispered was, "I love you Dad."

CHAPTER 28

The Lighthouse Dedication

Dan and Danny were sitting around the table in the sitting room of the Baker Family Bed and Breakfast waiting for his wife and daughter to finish getting ready.

"Go up and check on your mom and sister." Dan told Danny, "See if they're about ready. It's already almost 2:00. We need to be going out to the lighthouse soon."

Danny bounded out of the room, and started up the stairs. Just as he reached the top of the landing, he saw them coming out of their room.

"They're coming dad!" Danny shouted back down the stairs, as he turned and ran back down.

Dan got up from the table and met them in the foyer.

"Sorry it took us so long", said Dianne as she gave him a kiss, "but we have to look our best for the reception."

"You and Rebekah look gorgeous!" replied Dan, "Let's get going, they'll be closing some of the roads soon."

The four of them went out the door and over to Dan's truck which was parked alongside the bed and breakfast. They all got into the truck and Dan pulled out onto the main road. There was a lot more traffic today than there had been during the earlier part of the week, but this was a huge event for the island. Their lighthouse, which was one of the longest continuously operating lighthouses in the country, was celebrating its one hundred fiftieth anniversary today! As part of this celebration, a plaque would be unveiled at around 3:00 pm marking Green Island Light Station's inclusion in the National Register of Historic Places. Except for a few brief periods during World War II, it had remained lit for its entire one hundred fifty year existence.

The whole town was alive with celebration. There were banners hung from every street lamp, and banners across the road in the downtown area. There were games for the kids, street vendors selling various foods, even a small carnival at the edge of town. All of the hotels and bed and breakfasts on the island were filled up with tourists anxious to be a part of this big celebration. Some had come from hundreds of miles, each making the journey here for their own personal reasons. Some had connections to the island, while some were just curious. But everyone was having fun.

The island was special to Dan as well. He remembered vacations here with his family when he was about Danny's age. It had always been one of his favorite places. Usually when they vacationed here, they would stay out at the Harbor Inn, which was a very nice older inn. It wasn't oceanfront, but it had other features that made it attractive for a family with children. There were plenty of things to do. Dan and his younger brother Don, who was four years younger, liked to rent the bikes and go for rides out to the lighthouse. While it wasn't open to the public during those visits, since it was still manned by the Coast Guard, they enjoyed going out there nonetheless. They could still explore the adjacent woods, and there was even a trail which was open to the public that went beside the fence around the lighthouse out to the beach area on the river side. Sometimes, they'd even ride out to Sea Spray Drive where they would ride the bikes down the beach. There were things to do actually at the inn as well. They had an indoor pool, game room, tennis courts, and even carriage rides around the property. There was even a fishing pond where the boys enjoyed spending time just seeing what they could catch. While it was only about a mile from the seashore along Sea Spray Drive, and only a half mile from the ocean on the river side, it seemed very remote, nestled among the trees. If they had to pick one place, he thought that this was definitely his family's favorite vacation spot.

While he enjoyed all of the vacations that his family took here, it was the summer vacation of 1984 that he remembers the most. It was June and he had just turned 18. Instead of staying out at the Harbor Inn like they usually did, his parents decided to stay at a charming bed and breakfast called the Baker Family Bed and Breakfast. Upon arrival he immediately fell in love with the beautiful brown haired girl at the front desk. He watched every move that she made as she checked them in. She even glanced his way a couple of times and smiled. He just had to find a way to meet her. He later found out that her name was Dianne Baker, she was 17, and it was her father and mother that owned the bed and breakfast. For him, it really was love at first sight. On the second day that they were there, he actually got up the courage to ask her out on a date, partially due to the prodding of Don. Younger brothers are always fascinated about older brothers falling in love. To his surprise, she accepted, and their first date was at the Blue Harbor Seafood Shack. He remembered like it was yesterday that he had the fish special and she had the crab cakes. They talked during dinner, and he found out that she had noticed him as well when he first walked in. On their way in last weekend, he noticed that the name had changed to the Sand Crab Diner now. Their first date went so well that they were virtually inseperable for the rest of the trip. He was glad that she seemed to feel the same way about him as he felt about her. There was an instant attraction between them right from the start. She showed him around the island, and they would take long walks along the beach. Their first kiss was on the boardwalk leading out to the beach on the last night before he left to go back home. Before they left the island, Dan made sure to get her private phone number. After he got back home they would write letters to each other and talk on the phone at least two or three times a week.

After graduation from high school, they both decided to attend the same college so that they could be together. While Dan had originally planned on attending MIT, and had already been accepted, after meeting Dianne, who was looking at East Carolina University, he decided to apply there instead, even though it did mean that he'd have to start a year later. It was worth it to him for them to be together. He did his research, and discovered that they did have a good engineering program. During college, they would frequently discuss their plans for the future, which by their sophomore year started including plans for marriage. He proposed to her in the rose garden at the college during his senior year, and a year later, soon after her graduation, they were married in a lovely outdoor ceremony overlooking the ocean on Green Island out by the lighthouse. They had their honeymoon at another place that Dan and his family had enjoyed over the years, the Mountain Park Inn in Asheville. They had a spectacular honeymoon at the inn, going for drives in the surrounding mountains during the day, and taking romantic walks around the hotel property at night. It was during this visit that Dan met the young maintenance supervisor, Gerald Hensley, who went by Jerry. They had an issue with the sink in their room, and Jerry came to fix it himself. When he found out that they were on their honeymoon, Jerry showed them photos of his wedding which he and his fiancé also had chosen to have at the inn. Jerry was able to give them advice on what to do, what to see, and where to eat around the Asheville area. He even gave them gift certificates for dinner for two at the Mountain View Terrace Restaurant, which he said was a wedding gift.

After Dan's graduation, he had gotten a position with a small computer company in Greenville, so that he could continue to be near Dianne. After their honeymoon, they both moved back there, and she found a position with the same computer company as a marketing representative. In a few years, the internet would come along and they would decide to start their own company, Nelson Internet Technology, which they could both run together as a family business. Today, their company was one of the leading internet design, hosting, and social media marketing companies in North Carolina. Within a few years, their first child Dan Jr., who went by Danny, was born, and then two years later, their second child, Rebekah came along.

As they now drove down Henderson Road on their way to the lighthouse dedication ceremony, they would spot dark colored cars every so often at the edge of the woods or in a field.

"Those cars that we keep seeing along the edge of the woods are Secret Service." he told Danny and Rebekah, "They're making sure that everything is safe for the President, since he'll be coming along this way in about an hour."

That was the other big news of the day. The President of the United States was actually coming to speak at the lighthouse dedication ceremony. It wasn't often that an event like this could persuade the President to attend, but since he was on his reelection tour, and he was originally from Green Island, it wasn't altogether surprising.

As they turned onto Harbor Inn Lane, they immediately ran into traffic as they approached the inn. Since parking was limited out at the lighthouse area, parking for the event was either at the Harbor Inn parking lot or out at one of the public lots along Sea Spray Drive. They had shuttles which went back and forth every few minutes taking people from the parking lots out to the lighthouse. As they went through the gate of the Harbor Inn, an attendant directed them to a space at the far end of the lot. They parked and walked over to where one of the tents had been erected for guests to wait for the shuttles. They waited about ten minutes for a shuttle then they were off for the mile drive out to the Green Island Light Station.

When they arrived, there was already a big crowd out at the lighthouse. There was a stage set up facing the grandstand with the lighthouse behind the stage. A band played on the stage, providing entertainment while everyone waited. Dan had noticed the news van from Channel 10 in Wilmington parked over next to the woods when they arrived, and now he watched as the reporter interviewed one of the band members. He had watched Channel 10 often enough during visits to the island to immediately recognize her as Holly Harper. It actually made sense that they would send her to cover the President's visit, since she was one of the station's most popular reporters. Seating was mostly lawn seating, but Dan and his family actually had seats in the grandstand thanks to his brother-in-law, Greg, who was the President's Press Secretary. They found their reserved seats in the grandstand and sat and waited for the festivities to start.

A little after 3:00 in the afternoon, the island's Mayor, Wayne Harmon, got up on stage to welcome everybody to the event. He introduced a local historian, Jack Carlson, Jr., who recounted for the crowd the islands history, complete with a thorough history of the lighthouse. After Jack Carlson Jr., had finished with his part of the program, Mayor Harmon introduced the directors of the Green Island Lighthouse Preservation Society, Steve and Arlene Warren. Their presentation included the work that the Lighthouse Preservation Society had been doing to get the lighthouse ready for public tours, as well as future plans. Dan and his family came out to the lighthouse yesterday, and they met Steve and Arlene then and talked to them some about the lighthouse. Dan mentioned coming out to the island as a child, and his history with the island, including meeting his wife Dianne here. Steve had given them a tour of the lighthouse then, since today there wouldn't be any public tours. After the ceremony, the President and his family were scheduled for a private tour, which would probably take the rest of the afternoon with interviews by the press as well as photo opportunities.

Since seating was limited out at the lighthouse, there were only a limited number of tickets sold. Most of the rest of the island's guests and residents now lined Main Street in anticipation of the President's arrival. At about twenty minutes past three, the President's motorcade turned left onto Main Street after coming in from the ferry port. As the President passed by, folks waved and threw confetti in the air. The President rolled down the window on the limo as well so that he could wave back. After all, this was a campaign stop for his reelection. Since all of the festivities were going on, the President's arrival was accompanied by more excitement than usual. Since he grew up on the island, and his parents and brother still lived here, he would slip onto the island unannounced several times during the year, including the holidays. But today there was no just slipping onto the island. He was greeted with a full blown welcome for one of the most popular Presidents in recent history. Just after 3:30 in the afternoon, the motorcade arrived out at the lighthouse. Applause erupted from the crowd as the motorcade came into view and pulled into the parking lot. Members of the Secret Service got out and lined each side of the stage.

As the President got out of the limo, waving to the crowd, flanked on each side by Secret Service, the band on the bandstand played their rendition of "Hail to the Chief". The Mayor came back up on stage to do the formal introduction as the President waited in the wings beside the stage.

After a few remarks about the President and his years growing up here on the island, Mayor Harmon finally said, "Ladies and Gentlemen, please join me in welcoming to Green Island and the Green Island Light Station, the President of the United States, President Timothy Brian Henderson!"

The band again played a few more bars of "Hail to the Chief" as President Henderson climbed the stairs onto the stage, waving to the crowd as he did. They all loved him. Being from the island, he was definitely one of them. His dad, Bill and mother Abigail were seated on the front row closest to the stage along with his brother, Alan and his wife and kids. As President Henderson took the stage, the applause went on for so long that he finally had to raise his hands to quiet them. When the applause had died down, he began.

"Fellow islanders, guests, and friends, it is truly a pleasure to be here with you today. As a young man, growing up here on the island, I had many good times here around the island and the lighthouse. Some of my favorite memories are getting to climb up to the top and look out over the Cape Fear River at sunset, an activity that I hope to repeat today. My close friend Greg and I, who's now my Press Secretary, developed many close friendships with the men who served out at the light station over the years, many of whom are here with us today. I'd like to recognize these men now, some that I met while growing up, and some that have served since I left the island. Please stand if you've ever served at the Green Island Light Station." There was a huge round of applause as more than thirty men and several women stood. As the President asked them to be seated, he continued, "Now as the torch is passed to the Green Island Lighthouse Preservation Society, I know that under the capable supervision of Steve and Arlene Warren, whom I look forward to meeting in just a little while, the lighthouse will continue to burn bright for many, many decades to come, a shining beacon welcoming residents and tourists alike to the island paradise that we call Green Island. And now, let us all take the journey, a journey back in time, out to the lighthouse for the unveiling of the plaque, welcoming the Green Island Light Station onto the National Register of Historic Places and preserving its place in history forever."

As the President descended the stairs from the stage and began the walk out to the lighthouse, everyone in the crowd got up to follow. As the procession neared the lighthouse, they could all see a covered plaque mounted beside the door. President Henderson walked up the stairs and stood at the top of the landing as everyone else spread out to form a semicircle, all looking toward the President. After everyone had gotten in their place around the lighthouse, he made a few more remarks, and then pulled the covering from the bronze plaque, revealing the inscription, "THIS PROPERTY HAS BEEN PLACED ON THE NATIONAL

REGISTER OF HISTORIC PLACES BY THE UNITED STATES DEPARTMENT OF THE INTERIOR". More applause erupted from the crowd as the covering was removed and the shimmering bronze plaque glowed brilliantly in the late afternoon sun.

After the ceremony concluded, the President walked from the lighthouse over to a large banquet tent which had been set up for the Presidential Reception. Since the tent couldn't possibly hold everyone who attended the ceremony, it was reserved exclusively for those who received special invitations. Dan and his family were on that list, and Danny and Rebekah were both looking forward to meeting the President. Surprisingly, neither had ever met him before, despite the fact that their uncle Greg was his Press Secretary and also his closest friend, and their mom had even dated him in high school for awhile.

As they entered the banquet tent, the President and First Lady were over in the far corner talking with the Mayor and his wife. President Henderson looked over toward their direction and motioned for them to come over to where he was. As they walked up, he shook Dan's hand and gave Dianne a big hug.

"Nice to see you both." he remarked, "I'm glad you were able to attend. This must be Danny and Rebekah."

"Glad to meet you Mr. President." Danny and Rebekah both said in unison.

Since President Henderson had been President for the last four years, they had actually studied him in school this past year, so they knew all about his history growing up on the island. Danny thought that it was really neat to get to meet him in person. Now he'd have something to write about when the English teacher in the fall had them write their essay on "How I Spent My Summer" the way that she always did.

"My son Ron's around here someplace." he told Danny, "You might want to go find him. He's 17, so he's a little older than you, but you still might find you have a lot in common."

Danny went off to see if he could find Ron, while Rebekah stayed with her parents and visited with the President some more.

After the banquet was finished, Dan and his family along with Greg and his wife and kids were invited to tour the lighthouse with the President. It was twilight now as they walked out to the lighthouse, surrounded on each side by members of the Secret Service. The lighthouse beacon shone brightly as they all entered. They all walked through the doorway leading to the lighthouse tower and President Henderson started up the stairs, followed closely by Greg and their wives and kids. As they reached the top of the tower, they spread out around the railing and looked out over the island and out to the sound. Back toward the grandstand and banquet tent, workers were cleaning up from the afternoon festivities, and the Secret Service stood guard to keep anyone else from coming out to the lighthouse right now.

As the sun was setting, bringing to a close the day's celebration, a bright orange glow reflected off of the river as the water glistened in a rainbow of color. Rebekah thought that it was the most beautiful sight that she had ever seen. The Lighthouse Preservation Society directors, Steve and Arlene, gave them some additional history about the lighthouse as they gazed off into the distance. The island was peaceful now, most of the guests had left, and there was only the sound of the workers cleaning up as well as the waves softly breaking down by the water's edge.

Tim and Greg both looked out over the river, remembering the days of their childhood here on the island. A lot had changed in their lives since they would ride their bikes out here, but Green Island Light Station was the one thing that always stayed constant. It still looked almost the same as it had when they would come out here as children, then as teenagers, reminding them that no matter where life takes you, sometimes you really can come back home. They both had their families here with them, both of their parents were here, and everything seemed just as it should be. Soon they would descend the lighthouse stairs and go back to the pressures of being the most powerful leader of the free world, and the press secretary that keeps up his public image. They would be followed by Secret Service everywhere that they went, with their schedules being planned for them. But right now, they simply enjoyed the peacefulness of the moment, here at what they always used to consider the top of the world.

They walked back down the spiral staircase and Steve and Arlene gave them the tour of the rest of the house. Danny and Rebekah both wondered what it must have been like to be the lighthouse keeper all those years ago, living way out here in seclusion from the rest of the island. Green Island Light Station didn't need a keeper any longer, so no one actually lived here. Now it had an electric beacon which was automated. During the day, it would be open to the public for tours, and at night the beacon would still shine brightly warning ships of the dangers of the coastline.

When they all got back to the parking area, President Henderson asked Danny and Rebekah if they would like to ride back to the Harbor Inn with him in the Presidential Limo.

"Wow, would we!" remarked Danny.

As the kids got into the limo with the President and started down Lighthouse Road, Dan pulled in behind the motorcade. President Henderson and his family were staying at the Harbor Inn in Suite 214, the Blue Heron Suite, so that was where the motorcade was headed. They arrived at the front entrance, where the motorcade pulled around to let the President off. As Danny and Rebekah got out of the limo, they were beaming from ear to ear. It was the perfect end to an exciting day. What a story they would have to tell their friends when they got back home. This had been a great start to their summer vacation.

As they said their goodbyes to the President and First Lady and walked out to where their truck was parked, they all were thinking about what a wonderful day this had been. They all got into the truck and headed back to the bed and breakfast. On the trip back, Dan turned on the radio where a newscast from the mainland was wrapping up the news of the day with an excerpt from the President's speech earlier that afternoon:

"… the lighthouse will continue to burn bright for many, many decades to come, a shining beacon welcoming residents and tourists alike to the island paradise that we call Green Island."

ABOUT THE AUTHOR

Lighthouses have always held a special fascination for me. As anyone who's ever been in my house can attest, there are dozens of lighthouses in all sizes in every room. Some are small sculptures, while some are slightly larger and actually light up. Through the years, from the time that I was growing up in a small town in upstate South Carolina, I've had the opportunity to visit all of the North Carolina lighthouses and several of the South Carolina and Georgia ones as well. I've even climbed the spiral staircases in some to get a spectacular view from the top. And no trip to the top of a lighthouse would be complete without a thorough examination of the lantern house. All lighthouses seem to have stories surrounding them, and some even have a few mysteries as well. For these reasons, I felt a lighthouse would be the perfect setting for my first novel. By combining elements of the mystery around a one hundred fifty year old fictional lighthouse with the added mystery that surrounds the fog, I attempted to take the reader on an adventure that blurs the lines between possibility and impossibility. Bringing the story of Foggy Point Light to life over a period of time took several twists and turns that even I hadn't anticipated. I hope that you enjoyed taking this adventure with me as much as I enjoyed writing it.

- Jeff Burns

"…we assume that even if the Vortex Accelerator were shut down completely, that the ripples would continue …" *Dr. Philip O. Chandler*

The Complete Foggy Point Light Trilogy Availability

Volume 1 - "Foggy Point Light" – Jan 2016

Volume 2 - "Ripples: Return to Foggy Point Light"–Dec 2017

Volume 3 - "Project Vortex" – Early 2019

www.ingramcontent.com/pod-product-compliance
Lightning Source LLC
Chambersburg PA
CBHW060946120726
47910CB00002B/508